Also by F. Paul Wilson

HEALER (1976)*
WHEELS WITHIN WHEELS (1978)*
AN ENEMY OF THE STATE (1980)*
BLACK WIND (1988)
SOFT & OTHERS (1989)
DYDEETOWN WORLD (1989)
THE TERY (1990)
SIBS (1991)
THE SELECT (1993)
**DEEP AS THE MARROW (1997)

The *Adversary* Cycle:
THE KEEP (1981)
THE TOMB (1984)
THE TOUCH (1986)
REBORN (1990)
REPRISAL (1991)
NIGHTWORLD (1992)

editor: FREAK SHOW (1992)
DIAGNOSIS: TERMINAL (1996)
* [combined in THE LaNAGUE CHRONICLES (1992)]
** forthcoming

IMPLANT

F. PAUL WILSON

A TOM DOHERTY ASSOCIATES BOOK

NEW YORK

IMPLANT

Copyright © 1995 by F. Paul Wilson

Cover photo by Don Banks

A Forge Book
Published by Tom Doherty Associates, Inc.
175 Fifth Avenue
New York, NY 10010

Forge® is a registered trademark of Tom Doherty Associates, Inc.

ISBN: 0-812-54470-6
Library of Congress Card Catalog Number: 95-21886

First edition: October 1995
First mass market edition: September 1996

Printed in the United States of America

0 9 8 7 6 5 4 3 2

ACKNOWLEDGMENTS

The author wishes to acknowledge John L. Jackley's excellent book, *Hill Rat,* as a principal source as to what goes on behind the scenes on Capitol Hill.

I'd also like to thank the congressional staffers who took time to talk to me and show me how things get done—and don't get done—on the Hill. In deference to their wishes, they shall remain anonymous. You know who you are. Thanks.

The Joint Committee on Medical Ethics and Practice Guidelines does not exist, but all its members do. I simply changed their names.

THE WEEK OF SEPTEMBER

17

1
GINA

"STILL FLAT-LINED," SOMEONE SAID.

I know that, dammit, Gina Panzella thought as she stared helplessly at the monitor, willing the featureless thread of light to show systole, even a muscular twitch. It ignored her. Nothing but a little sixty-cycle interference marred its placid, unwavering course.

The sick sour smell of death filled the air and the three nurses who made up the Code Blue team were watching her expectantly, waiting for her to admit the obvious.

All right, she told herself. Call it off.

She sighed. "No use. He's not coming back."

The nurses nodded and began repacking their gear into the crash cart. Gina stepped back and took one final look at Mr. Nussbaum's pale, bloated, naked, lifeless, fifty-two-year-old body. His limbs were splayed, a ribbed plastic tube protruded from his slack mouth, wires strayed from plastic patches on his chest, clear IV tubes ran into both arms and under his right clavicle. He'd had a laparoscopic cholecystectomy yesterday, and he'd come through just fine. Tonight—

this morning actually, at 3:05 or thereabouts—he'd gone into cardiac arrest and a code had sounded.

None of the staff cardiologists had been in the hospital, and no way could one of them arrive in time, so Gina, as house doctor, had run the code. The team had already slipped the board under Nussbaum's back and started CPR by the time she arrived. Gina had intubated him, then under her direction the team worked on him for forty minutes. She threw everything they had at Mr. Nussbaum: intracardiac injections, repeated defibrillation, the works. Everything short of cracking his chest and squeezing the heart with her hands.

Nothing. The Nussbaum heart had decided to quit and nothing she tried could change its mind.

"Good code, Doc," said Judy Hooper, giving Gina's shoulder a squeeze. She was tall, thin, with a halo of bushy blond hair around her angular face; late thirties—maybe ten years older than Gina—and a veteran of more codes than Gina ever hoped to see.

"Not so good," Gina said, cocking her head toward Mr. Nussbaum. "He's going to the cooler instead of the CCU."

"You gave him every chance. Ten to one the post will show a major PE. Not much you can do about that."

Gina nodded. These obese patients, when they arrested like this, usually it was due to a pulmonary embolism—a big clot shooting to the lung from somewhere in the leg. All the drugs and electric shocks in the world couldn't clear a clogged pulmonary artery.

"Good working with you," Judy said, then went back to unhooking Mr. Nussbaum.

Yeah, Gina thought. Real good.

She hoped her skin never got as thick as Hooper's seemed to be. Then again, in Hooper's position a thick skin was probably essential for survival.

Gina felt her tense muscles begin to uncoil in the dimly lit silence and antiseptic tang of the hallway. She was halfway to the elevator when a young nurse approached her. She had short red hair, bad skin, and a considerable overbite. Her badge said *T. Graves, RN.*

"Dr. Panzella, would you mind very much taking a look at an IV in 307?"

"Where's the IV team?"

"Well . . ." She nervously rubbed her hands together. "I'm it on this shift, and I can't seem to . . ."

The nurse seemed terrified of her.

"Let's take a look."

"Oh, thank you!" She led Gina down the hall to her right. "I can't tell you how much I appreciate this."

"No biggee."

"Well, I asked Dr. Grady last night for help with another patient and he . . . he got upset."

If I know Grady, Gina thought, he probably damn near took your head off. A third-year resident at Georgetown, Grady was very bright but tended to be a little full of himself. Lynnbrook was a community hospital in the north-west section and dwelt in the shadow of Georgetown Medical Center. Not a teaching hospital like its renowned neighbor, but it served its purpose.

Gina knew how some house docs, especially those who considered themselves high-powered, got uppity when asked to start an IV. Gina got annoyed herself at times. After all, the hospital was paying an IV team to do its job and paying Gina to do hers. But sooner or later everyone, no matter how good they were, ran up against a wall trying to find a vein.

"She's in the window bed," Graves said. "One of Conway's patients. Had pneumonia. Been on IV antibiotics, now she's just on D-5-W. Didn't have many veins to start with and those are all used up. The last usable one infiltrated the end of last shift and I can't find another."

Gina found a frail old woman with thin, pinched features and short white hair. She sat up in bed, wide awake, staring at them. She had the top of the sheet bunched in her hands and was kneading it like dough.

"Please don't send me home tomorrow," she said.

"She's scheduled for discharge tomorrow?" Gina said.

Graves placed the chart in Gina's outstretched hand. "Tentatively."

The chart said "Harriet Thompson" on the front. Age seventy-eight. Dr. Conway was one of the local family practitioners—quiet, competent, with a loyal following. Gina had met him a few times and liked him. She flipped through the ream of color-coded paper. Mrs. Thompson's last chest X ray was clear. Dr. Conway's scrawled progress note from the morning read, "Try again for disch in AM."

Gina found the order sheet and wrote, "Hold IV until AM." She scribbled her name and handed it back to the nurse.

"There. That solves the IV problem."

Graves smiled. "Great." She picked up her basket of needles and tubing and hurried to the next patient on her list.

"Do you know Dr. Conway?" said Mrs. Thompson.

Gina turned. "A little."

"Tell him not to send me home tomorrow. I'm too weak."

"I can't tell him what to do. I'm just the house doctor here tonight."

"But all my strength is gone. I don't know what I'll do."

Gina patted her hand. "Tell you what, Mrs . . ." Her name had slipped away.

"Thompson. But you can call me Harriet."

"Okay, Harriet. If I see Dr. Conway I'll mention it."

"Thank you," she said, smiling for the first time. "You're very kind."

Gina hadn't expected to be able to deliver on that promise, but as she was running a brush through her glossy black, blunt-cut hair and debating whether to bother fishing out her lipstick, Dr. Bill Conway strode into the doctors' lounge.

"Cutting out early?" he said, smiling. "Starting your own practice?"

He was young, maybe two or three years older than Gina, and good-looking—he could have been another Baldwin brother. Gina found him immensely attractive, liked his attitude and liked his looks. But he was wearing a wedding ring. Very married.

"Grady's covering," she said. "No private practice yet. My day job is assisting Duncan Lathram a couple of times a week."

His eyebrows rose. "Whoa! I didn't know you moved in such rarefied circles. And since when did you become a surgeon?"

"Usually I hate surgery, but what Duncan does is fascinating. It's like art."

"*The Art of the Nose Job.* Good title for a book."

"Why not? If Donald Trump can write one, why not Duncan Lathram? Guaranteed big sales inside the beltway. Oh, by the way, the IV on one of your patients infiltrated last night and I put a hold on it till you came in."

"Thompson on Three North?"

"Right. Her veins are shot."

"Damn!"

Gina was a little surprised by the reaction. She hadn't seen any pressing reason for the IV.

"You could always go subclavian if—"

"No, it's not that. The PRO's been on my back about getting her out. According to their guidelines she doesn't need a hospital: Her pneumonia's cleared, ship her out."

"She said something about how weak she was feeling, and she was scared to go home."

He was nodding. "One of those wonderful situations where she looks good on paper—her chest X ray's clear, fever's down, white count back to normal, electrolytes balanced—but she's not ready to take care of herself. Can't get into a nursing home for a week, scared to death of having some stranger stay with her, and her daughter lives in San Diego and can't or won't come back and stay with Mom for a few days. So what do I do?"

"Tell the PRO to take over her case," Gina cracked.

"Yeah, right," Conway said. "When was the last time those paper shufflers treated a patient? If they had real practices they wouldn't have time to stick their noses in other people's charts." He sighed. "That IV was useless, but it gave me an excuse to keep her a few more days. But now, without a line running, they're really going to push for discharge. Want to guess how many hours before I get a call from the administration?"

"Sometime right after lunch, I'd say."

She knew what the hospital administrators would be worrying about: money. The PRO board couldn't kick Mrs. Thompson out, but it would rule that her condition no longer required hospital-level care. With that, Medicare would stop all further payment for services. The hospital would have to eat the extra days she was kept on, and Dr. Conway would not get paid after today. Gina was pretty sure Conway didn't give a damn about treating Mrs. Thompson a few more days at no charge. But she doubted the hospital would be so casual.

Once again Gina found herself wondering whether she wanted to go into private practice. Sometimes moonlighting as house physician for the rest of her life didn't look so bad.

"So what are you going to do?"

Conway shrugged. "Screw 'em. She stays till she's ready to go."

Gina gave him a thumbs-up and waved good-bye. But she wondered how long he'd be able to withstand that sort of pressure.

The sun was rising, the air was fresh and invigorating, and birds were chirping like a roomful of cardiac monitors in atrial fib. She hopped into her old red Pontiac Sunbird and headed for home. But not to bed. She had an important appointment coming up. Sleep was not in the cards.

Gina wasn't tired. As chief resident in the Tulane University internal medicine/public policy program, she'd been putting in more than a hundred hours a week until only a few months ago. Now with her three twelve-hour shifts a week as house doctor at Lynnbrook, plus doing physicals and assisting with surgery at Duncan Lathram's surgicenter three mornings, it all totaled out to only sixty hours a week.

Almost like a vacation. She hardly knew what to do with so much free time.

Well, yes, she did. Or at least she knew what she *wanted* to do. Senator Hugh Marsden was chairing the Joint Committee on Medical Ethics and Practice Guidelines. She wanted to be on his staff, to work as a legislative aide. And at 10 A.M. she had an interview in his office.

Everyone she knew thought she was crazy. She'd tried to make her parents understand, but it was hard.

Sure, major health-care overhaul was stalled, but its inevitability was throwing medicine into turmoil. As she was completing her residency at Tulane, she'd looked around and asked herself where she could go, what she could do that would make the greatest difference. She'd read everything she could find, buttonholed everyone she knew, and come to realize that the future of medicine would be decided in Washington by people who knew next to nothing about it. So maybe she could do more for her patients—and for the medical profession itself—in Washington than in the Louisiana multispecialty medical group that had offered her that attractive starting salary.

Medicine was becoming a new game now, so maybe it was time for a new kind of doctor, one who could operate comfortably in both worlds—practice medicine and still get the ear of the legislators who were making the rules. If that new kind of doctor had the skills, the drive, knew the ins and outs of how these rules were being shaped, she might develop enough respect and credibility to have a decisive impact.

Gina felt strangely sure she was that kind of doctor.

Sure enough to leave behind the man she loved to return to the area where she'd grown up to prove it.

She blinked away the memory of Peter Hanson's stricken expression the last time she'd seen him. His usually perfect brown hair had been wet from the rain, his dark eyes full of hurt and disbelief as she'd stepped toward the boarding ramp. She remembered how she'd wavered then, how she'd had to fight the urge to run back to him and throw herself into his arms. But she'd known in her heart that if she didn't give this a shot, she'd forever wonder what might have been. She didn't want to spend the rest of her life regretting, asking, "What if . . ."

All she asked now was a chance to show her stuff. The first step toward that chance was scheduled in a few hours.

She sent up a silent prayer: Don't let me blow it.

2
ON THE HILL

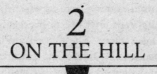

GINA CAUGHT HERSELF CHEWING A FINGERNAIL AS SHE rode the Metro escalator up to ground level at Union Station. She jammed her hand into the pocket of her jacket. Jittery. Too much coffee and just plain nervous. The next hour could decide the course of her professional life.

She looked around. No question about it, the best improvement in D.C. since her childhood had to be the Metro. Sure, the monuments had been spruced up and the Statue of Freedom atop the Capitol had been refurbished, but she'd grown up just across the river. The sights people traveled thousands of miles to see were wallpaper to her. But the Metro—*this* was progress. The three-mile drive from her apartment in the Adams Morgan section could take up to three-quarters of an hour sometimes. But with the Metro, no traffic jams, no parking hassles, just a short walk from her apartment to Connecticut Avenue, hop the Red Line near the zoo, and a few minutes later she was in Union Station.

The street-level air was warm and heavy. To her left a raggedy homeless man slouched on a wooden bench chattering away into a cellular phone. Gina doubted it was a real working telephone, but it made a great prop if you had a tendency to talk to yourself.

She remembered coming here as a child, accompanying Mama to pick up Papa after one of his regular trips to New York to visit his mother. She'd been afraid then. Union Station had been a cold, forbidding place in those days, a cavernous tomb of stained granite and shadowy corners, the area immediately surrounding it notoriously dangerous after dark.

Now it was a shopping mall with dozens of clothing and accessory shops, restaurants, a pharmacy, even a B Dalton. And the area around it had been cleaned up, with the Postal Museum on one side and the Federal Judiciary Center on the other. All the dingy brownstones along Massachusetts seemed to have been converted to restaurants.

What a change.

But she knew the magic gentrifying spell ran out of steam a few blocks east. There, out of sight of the tourists, the politicians, and their staffs, lurked the deteriorating houses, abandoned cars, poverty, and crime of the old days.

She passed the Columbus monument in the semicircular plaza in front of the station, wove between the idling tour buses—even on a sultry Monday morning the station area was packed with tourists—dodged a yellow trolley, and scooted across Massachusetts to one of the small parks that blanketed the upslope toward the Capitol. This one had an unreal feel to it: perfectly manicured grass, no litter, neat rows of trees, each labeled with its genus and species.

Welcome to Federal World.

She cut diagonally across to her left, weaving between suited federal employees and T-shirted tourists, and came out on First Street. She consulted her hand-drawn map—she'd been to the Capitol area many times as a child, but never to a Senate office building. Up ahead the white blocks of the

Russell Building sat to the right, the Dirksen Building to the left. She hurried past the Dirksen's shrub and flower-lined parking lot labeled "Federal Employees Only"—hopefully she'd have a spot there soon—and up to Constitution, then left past the Dirksen and a scruffy clutch of helmeted bike messengers lounging on the sidewalk, waiting for a call on the walkie-talkies protruding from their vests. Her destination was the adjoining block of white marble, the Hart Building.

In the white marble lobby she gave her name to the uniformed security guard and signed in. She was directed to place her bag on a conveyor belt. As it was swallowed by the X-ray box, Gina stepped through the metal detector. Just like an airport.

More white marble beyond the guards—the whole building seemed to be made of it. A short walk down a corridor lined with potted trees and she came to the Hart's huge central atrium.

She stopped, struck by the sheer mass of the enormous black steel sculpture that dominated the space. A series of jagged black peaks, stark against the white of their surroundings, thrust upward, reaching for the sunlight streaming through the ceiling beyond. Between the skylight and the peaks floated a gargantuan mobile of equally black disks.

Black mountains and black clouds in a white room. Arresting. But the tension coiled inside prevented her from fully appreciating it. Had to move, keep going, get upstairs to Senator Marsden's office.

As she passed through the atrium she noticed a man staring at her. In his gray suit he could have been any one of the thousands of Senate aides who worked on the Hill. He was good-looking, though; thirtyish, fair, tall, close-cropped blond hair, blue eyes, square jaw. But why was he staring at her like that? She wasn't dressed in any way to make her stand out from any of the other women passing through the atrium. Nothing special about her sedate, navy pinstripe suit—just a knee-length skirt and a short fitted jacket. So why was he ogling her like she was wearing a micromini and a halter top?

It made her uncomfortable. She was glad when she found the bank of elevators. She turned a corner and put some of that white marble between them.

The elevator on the end was marked "Senators Only." Gina rode one of the brightly lit peon cars to the seventh floor and began to look for SH-752—Senator Marsden's office.

The offices occupied the perimeter of the Hart Building; the hallway—actually a ramp that ran around the inner walls—overlooked the atrium and the sculpture. She noticed a gray, powdery coating on the upper surfaces of the mobile. The clouds needed a good dusting.

Down on the floor she noticed someone standing in the center of the atrium, becalmed while everyone else flowed around him. That same man, the one in the gray suit, was staring up at her.

What's your problem, mister?

She looked away and walked on. Quickly. She found 752 at the far end of the hall. A simple black nameplate on the oak door said *Sen. H. Marsden.* Vertical blinds blocked her view through the full-length windows that flanked the entrance. She reached for the door, then hesitated.

This is ridiculous, she thought, blotting her moist palms on her skirt. I've been through premed, med school, internal medicine residency, I've brought people back from the dead, I've been up to my elbows in blood and guts, and here I am nervous as a sixth grader outside the principal's office.

She grabbed the handle and stepped into the front office.

I know her.

Gerald Canney continued to stare up at the seventh-floor

walkway where that attractive brunette had disappeared from view.

But from where?

He prided himself on his ability to remember faces and match them with names. Part of it seemed to come naturally, part from his training at the FBI Academy in Quantico. Special agents had to spot faces through extra hair, dark glasses, any sort of disguise.

Only with this gal, no disguise. Her face had been there right in front of him, all but daring him to recognize her. Why couldn't he?

Could she be in some way connected to the case? The late, great Senator Richard A. Schulz used to have an office in Hart—still did, in a way, until his successor was named. Gerry had just been up there, sifting through the senator's files.

He sighed. The Schulz case was something of an embarrassment to the Bureau. They'd been tipped that the good senator was laundering honoraria; since Gerry was attached to the public corruption unit, he'd been assigned to the team looking into it.

Schulz was suspected of various other dealings of questionable legality. The corruption team was tightening the noose when he dropped to his death from his apartment balcony.

Did he fall or did he jump? The Bureau did not know. They were reasonably sure that he was alone in the apartment when he went over the balcony rail.

How could he fall? The railing was four feet high. He'd have had to climb onto it to fall, and there was no logical reason for him to climb—no plants to water, no hanging decorations that needed attention.

That left a jump. Had he heard about the investigation and decided he couldn't stand the heat? Not likely. Gerry had interviewed both his current mistresses—neither of whom knew about the other. One was listed on his office payroll as an "assistant" for forty-one thousand dollars a year. No one on his staff knew what she looked like; she'd never been to the office. The other was a lobbyist for an electronics trade association. Many members of Congress could be accused of being in bed—figuratively—with certain political interests; Schulz apparently took the phrase literally. Neither woman said she'd noticed the slightest sign of stress or apprehension in the senator at any time before he died. Even his physical therapist, who gave him an ultrasound treatment on his back only an hour before his death, said he seemed to be in excellent spirits.

So what had happened to Senator Schulz?

Gerry didn't know. Which was why he'd been at Schulz's office this morning. That office was right down the same hall the mystery girl had been traveling a moment ago. And Schulz had been quite a womanizer, a *legendary* womanizer in his time.

A third mistress?

No. Gerry didn't think that was it. Schulz's office had been sealed since his death. No point in anyone going there. She couldn't get in.

But this gal didn't work here. Gerry could tell by the uncertain way she'd walked through the atrium, gawking at the sculpture, looking for the elevators; this was her first time in the Hart Building.

So who was she?

Easy enough to find out. Just go over to the visitors log by the Constitution entrance and check out the names. But that would be cheating.

Hey, I'm a trained special agent, he told himself. I can solve The Mystery of the Strangely Familiar Foxy Brunette without stooping to checking the visitors log.

So FBI special agent Gerald Canney stood in the center of the atrium and flipped through his mental files. After five minutes he walked over to the visitors gate and showed the guards his ID.

"I'd like to see this morning's visitor sheet."

The woman slid a clipboard across the table. Gerry scanned through the names, picking out the female ones. If he saw it, he'd know it. No doubt. It would click.

He slid past one and jumped back to it.

Regina Panzella.

Regina Panzella . . . why did that ring a bell? Panzella sounded familiar, but not with that first name. Not Regina . . . not Gina . . . What went with Panzella?

Pasta.

Oh, Christ! Pasta Panzella. It couldn't be. Absolutely no way. Pasta had been . . . well . . . fat. That was how she got the name. A real chubette. This gal was anything but fat.

And yet . . .

Something about her face . . . slim down the rounded cheeks he remembered, do something with Pasta's wild tangle of hair, and it could be. It had been ten years or more since he'd last seen her, but yes, it could damn well be Pasta.

Gerry glanced at his watch. He was supposed to be back at the office soon to meet with Ketter on the Schulz case, but they hadn't set a definite time for the meeting. Maybe he'd hang around here for a while and see if he could get another look.

Pasta Panzella . . . it was almost too much to believe.

"Okay," said Joe Blair, Senator Marsden's chief of staff. "Enough about the office. Let's talk about you."

Really? Gina thought. You're finally going to stop talking about yourself and actually interview me? Can you stand it?

Blair was about her age, with thinning brown hair, brown eyes, pale skin, and a wispy mustache. He wore a short-sleeve white shirt, a nondescript tie, and dark blue slacks. He looked too young to be a U.S. senator's chief of staff, but from the stories he'd been telling her—all starring a certain Joseph Blair—he'd been on the Hill for the entire eight years since his graduation from Cornell with a poli-sci degree. This was the third senator he'd worked for, and to hear Joe tell it, he'd written more legislation than any of the members he'd staffed for.

What a guy. Reminded her of some of the orthopedic residents in Tulane.

Gina had been under the impression that she was going to be interviewed by Senator Marsden himself.

"The senator is on the floor," Joe Blair had told her.

Gina had looked around. "I don't understand."

"That means he's in the Senate," Blair said with a condescending smile. "*On the floor* of the Senate."

"I see." She did her best to hide her disappointment.

"Besides, the senator doesn't do the hiring and firing. I do."

Oh, great. Her disappointment was swept away by a wave of apprehension. She had the distinct impression that Blair didn't like her.

Blair gave her a quick tour of the office. She'd already seen the small front section with its two receptionists—one male, one female—and its antiseptic, dentist's waiting-room ambience. The rear space was much larger and sloppier, looking like a real working office with modular work spaces, cluttered desks, sagging bookshelves, glaring computer monitors, empty coffee cups, papers and folders lying on every available horizontal surface. And phones. Phones everywhere, each bearing a little U.S. Senate seal.

The staff occupied two floors that communicated via a central stairway. The two-tiered space offered more room than most senators had, but Marsden represented one of the larger states, and she knew "appropriation by population" was religious dogma on the Hill.

The second floor was pretty much like the first except for a small lounge and the computer room that housed the central processor for the office's LAN. The striking feature of the second floor was the mail room with its bins—*many* bins— of letters. Blair told her anywhere from ten to fifteen thousand pieces of mail were sorted, filed, and answered on a weekly basis by the staff's legislative correspondents.

Blair decided to interview her in the senator's office. Gina was surprised at the Spartan decor. She'd expected heavy oak paneling, plush carpeting, indirect lighting, a big leather chair, a huge impressive desk sporting a U.S. Senate seal and flanked by state and national flags—the works. Apparently Marsden wasn't impressed by the trappings of his office. The desk and its straight-back chair were of some nondescript wood, looking plain and slightly battered in the late morning sunlight that poured through the high windows. Files were stacked on the desk and floor. A few plaques and diplomas adorned the walls along with pictures of his family. A single bookcase was overflowing. A miniature basketball hoop was set up over the wastepaper basket.

Gina had a pretty good idea right then that she was going to like Senator Marsden.

But first she had to get past his chief of staff.

She and Blair settled themselves on opposite sides of the coffee table in the sitting area of the office. Blair spent another ten minutes or so talking about his prowess in helping guide the senator's bills through the many pitfalls of the legislative process, his gaze all the while drifting between her legs and her breasts. Gina drew the skirt hem closer to her knees.

She had decent legs and wore a 34-C bra. What else did he want to know?

Maybe she should have worn a pantsuit.

Finally he began shuffling through her résumé.

"Very impressive," he said, "but I don't see anything here about party affiliation."

"I'm an independent," Gina said.

He glanced up at her as if she'd burped, then cleared his throat. "Party affiliation is very important. We have to know whom we can trust."

"If I'm on your staff, you can trust me. If you want a straight answer, I'll give it to you. If I don't know an answer, I'll find out."

He stared at her. "I don't know . . . the senator was impressed that a practicing physician, especially a young one, would apply for a position as a legislative assistant on the Guidelines bill. Tell me: What do you think you can bring to the committee that we don't already have?"

Finally, here was the question Gina had been waiting for.

"I can bring a lot of things. First off—"

"You know the history of the committee, don't you?" he said. Gina did, but that wasn't going to stop Blair. "Well, back when you were still in training, before a national health-care program and universal coverage became hot topics, Senator McCready, a ranking member of the Committee on Labor and Human Resources, introduced his Medical Practice Guidelines Bill in the Senate at about the same time Congressman Allard introduced a very similar bill in the House. In a rare show of cooperation a joint committee was formed. Senator McCready chaired the hearings but died before the bill could be sent to the floor of either house. With one of its chief sponsors gone, the bill died in committee."

Gina nodded. "But earlier this year the president stepped in."

"Yes. He *personally* asked Senator Marsden to revive the McCready committee. But he wanted the legislation to include not only practice guidelines, but mandates on medical ethics as well."

"And that's why you need me," Gina said, rushing in before Blair could drone on further with his recitation. "I'm a board-eligible internist who came through the medicine and public policy residency at Tulane. I'm a fully trained physician who's well versed in public health issues. You're going to be collecting reams of testimony, much of it conflicting. You'll need someone like me to sift through it and separate the wheat from the chaff. If Senator Marsden—"

"Quite frankly, I don't share the senator's enthusiasm for having a doctor on board," Blair said, staring at her. "I think it could cause too much confusion, maybe even dissension. So, what can you say or do that will change my mind?"

Gina's skin crawled at the way he looked at her when he said that. She decided to ignore it.

"I think you need all points of view to draw up a well-balanced plan. I can provide the senator with a valuable perspective, one he's not seeing now, one he has little access to. The best generals always keep abreast of the conditions in the trenches. I can offer—"

Blair glanced at his watch. "Look at the time. We've already carried this over the limit I'd set for it." He closed her file and stood up. "Well, thank you, Dr. Panzella." He walked to the door and opened it for her. "I'll discuss your application with the senator. We'll be in touch if he decides to hire you." His expression was perfectly flat, his eyes empty. "Can you find your way out?"

"Of course," Gina said, forcing a smile.

Her heart sank as the message came through loud and clear: Don't call us, we'll call you.

Gina let the smile fade as she wound past the cubicles and out through the reception area. What a nightmare of an interview. She couldn't imagine how it could have gone worse. What was Blair's problem? Was he threatened by her? Or was he looking for something from her? *What can you say or do that will change my mind?* What was *that* all about? What had he expected her to do, lift her skirt?

She felt her jaw muscles bunch in anger. A little man with a little power equaled a big problem. Was this the way it was going to be?

She had the elevator down all to herself. She leaned against a side wall and fought the disappointment. Okay, so she probably wasn't going to get on the chairman's staff. She'd been prepared for that—not for a screwup like this, but for the real possibility that the senator wouldn't think he'd need her. There were six other members—no, check that: Congressman Lane had died in that car accident a while back. So at the moment there were five other legislators who were members of the Guidelines committee. As the ranking House member, Congressman Allard was the next obvious choice. Gina had set up a fail-safe appointment with him on Wednesday morning. Looked like she'd be keeping it.

She left the elevator and rounded the corner into the atrium. That was when she heard a man's voice from her left.

"Excuse me, but does the word 'Pasta' hold any special significance for you?"

She froze. It was a name she hadn't heard since high school. A name she'd never wanted to hear again.

Gina turned. Him again. Or still. The blond guy in the suit. She now saw some fine linear scars across his forehead and down his right cheek that she hadn't noticed before. He was edging closer, staring at her face like the kids in pediatrics stared at "Where's Waldo" puzzles. What was his problem?

But then she was struck by something familiar about him. If she imagined his hair four or five inches longer . . .

He stuck out his hand. "My God, it's really you. I don't know if you remember me from high school, but I'm—"

The name leapt into her mind. "Gerry!" She grasped his hand. "Gerry Canney!"

"Right! I'm flattered you remember."

Remember? How could she forget? Cocaptain and quarterback for the football team, captain of the swim team, and an honor student to boot. She'd had a monstrous crush on Gerry Canney all through Washington-Lee High in Arlington. She remembered positioning herself in the hall outside social studies after third period every day just to watch him stroll by. The scars on his face had wrought subtle changes on his looks, but he was still gorgeous.

"You're flattered I remember *you?"* she said. "I'm flabbergasted you remember *me."*

He grinned. "I've got a great memory for faces. And who could forget a girl with a name like Pasta."

He'd said it again. She'd have to nip this in the bud.

"It's Gina, Gerry. Gina."

He blinked. "Got you. I don't think I ever knew your real first name. Gina it is. But I barely recognized you. You look great." He winced and waved his hands in the space between them, as if trying to erase the words. "Wait. That didn't come out right. I didn't mean—"

"It's okay," she laughed, placing a hand on his sleeve. "I understand. I'm not half the girl I used to be. And you . . . last time I saw you, you had huge sideburns and hair over your ears."

He rubbed his clean-shaven cheeks. "Yeah. The seventies. Can you believe how we dressed back then? But tell me: What've you been doing with yourself?"

"I just finished an internal medicine residency."

"You're a doctor? That's great!" He glanced at his watch. "Look, I've been waiting down here to meet you since you walked in. I mean, I just had to see if it was really you. But now I'm late for a meeting and I've got to run. But let's get together soon."

"That'd be nice."

"How about tomorrow night? Are you free?"

She sensed he was asking about more than just time.

"Tomorrow? No, I'm moonlighting Tuesday night." She started a twelve-hour shift at Lynnbrook at eight.

"Wednesday night?"

"Sorry. Moonlighting again." But she didn't want to turn him down flat. "Maybe we could get together for an early bite before I go on duty. Or wait till Friday."

"Friday's a long way off. An early bite it will be. Anyplace special you'd like to go?"

"You choose."

"Okay. I will." He pulled a small leather folder from his pocket and gave her two cards along with a pen. "Give me your number and I'll call when I think of an appropriate place."

She wrote down her number and handed back the cards. He returned the bottom card to her.

"That one's for you. Call me any time you witness a federal crime." He waved and moved off. "I'll call you tonight or tomorrow."

And then he was hurrying through the glistening marble whiteness toward the exit. Gina glanced at his card: *Gerald Canney, Special Agent, Federal Bureau of Investigation.*

She smiled. Gerry was an FBI man? Amazing. She'd always imagined him going into business. Who'd have ever thought? And now the former major heartthrob of Washington-Lee High wanted to take her out. Who'd ever believe *that?*

She just hoped they didn't wind up at a pasta place. That wouldn't be funny.

Pasta . . . when had she picked up that name? Freshman year? Somewhere around the time her hormones had begun to flow. Overnight she'd seemed to balloon. It was horrible.

She couldn't squeeze into her clothes. Her breasts were growing, which was fine, but so were her thighs and hips and waistline. She hadn't changed her eating habits but her body seemed to have stopped burning off the calories she'd once been able to pack away. She'd gone from slightly above average to obese in less than a year. She'd wanted to *die.*

Her father couldn't see a problem—"There's more of you to love!" was definitely *not* a solution to her misery. Mama understood, and together they started a diet, but already it was too late. The school comedians couldn't resist "Pasta" Panzella.

She changed internally as well, becoming moody and reclusive. Looking back now, from the far side of a medical education, Gina realized Pasta had sunk into a clinical depression. She'd tell people she didn't care about her weight or what anybody called her, and to prove it, she'd binge. Especially on lonely weekend nights. Primarily on chocolate. Pasta *loved* chocolate. Chocolate cake, chocolate donuts, Hershey's with almonds, and Snickers. God, she loved Snickers. And bingeing only made her fatter, which made her even more depressed.

Pasta missed the junior and senior proms, and lots of other high-school activities in her self-imposed exile. The only bright spots in those dark days had been her novels and her part-time job in Dr. Lathram's office. Her grades began to slip but not enough to keep her out of the Ivy League.

The summer before going off to college she realized that she had a chance to start all over again. The kids in Princeton had never heard her called Pasta. She vowed that none of them ever would. She began a strict diet—no bulimia, no starvation, no trading one problem for another; just low fat and calorie restriction, plus a grueling exercise program. She remembered the constant hunger, the burning lungs, the aching legs as she forced her body to jog one more mile . . .

just one more. By the time she registered at Princeton she was proud to be merely overweight. According to her charts, her weight hit the fiftieth percentile for her age, height, and sex during sophomore year; as a junior she overshot and got too thin, so she backed off. When she graduated she was the person she wanted to be: She had her BS in biology, was on her way to U. of P. med school, and she liked what she saw in the mirror.

She'd maintained that weight through four years of med school and three years of residency. Pasta Panzella was gone.

Well, almost gone. The ghost of Pasta still haunted her, and every so often she'd propel Gina to the chocolate section of a candy store, and Gina would give in and let Pasta have a Snickers. But only once in a while, and only one.

And now Gerry Canney was asking her out. Strange how things come full circle.

She frowned. Hadn't she heard somewhere along the line that Gerry was married?

She wanted to get to know Gerry—she certainly hadn't known him well in high school—but she wasn't into games.

Pasta Panzella had been a vulnerable adolescent.

Gina Panzella, MD, was anything but.

"Sorry I'm late," Gerry said as he burst into Marvin Ketter's cramped office on the E Street side of the Bureau building. He was puffing a little and he'd broken a sweat on the rush up from the parking garage. "Took me a little longer than I planned."

Which was true. It had taken Pasta—no . . . *Gina*—a long time to finish her business in the Hart Building. And all the way back here his mind had been on her instead of Senator Schulz. God, she was beautiful now. The metamorphosis from Pasta to Gina fascinated him. Reminded him of the time as a kid he'd left a caterpillar in a dry aquarium and returned after a weekend away to find a graceful butterfly fluttering against the glass. He'd let it fly around his room, watching it in awe for hours before opening the screen to let it glide out the window.

"Well, you've had all mornin' to scratch," Ketter said. "Find any worms?"

Marvin Ketter had ten years on Gerry. His dark curly hair was just starting to gray at the temples and he wore it very very short. His eyebrows were his outstanding feature—enormous, bushy, Groucho-league tangles that were longer and thicker than the hair on his head. Give him a wide black mustache and a cigar and he could join Harpo and Chico without a hitch. Until he opened his mouth. Groucho didn't have a Georgia accent.

Ketter was SSA—supervising special agent. One notch above Gerry. Gerry wanted his job. He didn't want to kick him out or make him look bad—he liked Ketter—but when Ketter moved up, Gerry wanted to move into his chair. Not simply as a career move or because he'd been a field agent long enough; there were other, more important reasons.

"Found a few goodies, but I don't know if they mean anything. And the more I learn about our boy, the less I like him. I mean, there didn't seem to be anything too small for this guy to steal."

"Plenty like him down here."

"So I'm beginning to see. Hell, I used to think I had few illusions about what really goes on up there on the Hill, but I'm beginning to think I've been a Pollyanna."

He'd learned more than he wanted to know about Washington's honoraria industry.

Years ago the Senate had voted to cap the amount of honoraria each member could collect in a year. This did not deter senators from accepting "speaking engagements," however. They continued to be flown to plush resorts, put up in lavish suites, wined and dined for days before and after their "speech"—usually a few after-dinner remarks to the corporate sales conference attendees—and then flown back to Washington loaded down with gifts. The thousand-dollar honorarium for speaking? That was donated—very visibly— to a charity.

The all-expense-paid vacation and gifts were enough of a haul for most of the legislators, but not enough for Senator Schulz. He accepted every speaking invitation that came along, demanded high honoraria, but graciously donated every dime to a church in his hometown where his uncle was minister. Gerry's investigation had uncovered evidence that the minister was keeping only a quarter of the donations for the church and funneling the rest back to Schulz.

But then Gerry had come across a connection between Schultz and Representative Hugo Lane. Both were cozy with one of the Japanese auto lobbies. A Japanese auto corporation had bought an $800,000 condo in Palm Beach. It was registered in the company's name, but its use was reserved exclusively for Schulz and Lane. Whenever they wanted some fun in the Florida sun, it was theirs. They simply had to work it out between themselves so they wouldn't arrive at the same time.

Congressman Lane had died in a car crash—ran it into a deep ravine in Rock Creek Park—two weeks before Schulz's death.

A connection? Maybe. Gerry was looking into that. So far he'd come up with zilch, but he was still looking.

"One interesting note," he said to Ketter. "I came across a fat canceled check for plastic surgery."

"Let me guess: drawn on his reelection campaign funds."

"Of course."

"So what's the point?"

"Well, seems to me people who're looking to end it all

don't drop a bundle on cosmetic surgery. Sounds more like someone who's looking toward the future."

"Possibly. Or someone who's unhappy with himself, tries plastic surgery to improve his looks, finds out it doesn't make him feel the least bit better, so he dives for the dirt."

"Spoilsport," Gerry muttered.

"Leave the second-guessing to the shrinks. Got anything concrete?"

"Yes. An odd little correlation popped out of the database. What if I told you that both Lane and Schulz had plastic surgery this summer?"

Ketter shrugged. "So?"

"And what if I told you they both used the same surgeon?"

"Same response. These Old Boys go to the same dentist, the same chiropractor, eat at the same restaurants, have the same personal trainer, sometimes the same mistresses. So why not use the same plastic surgeon? Who's the doc?"

"Duncan Lathram."

Ketter stared at him a moment. "Well now," he drawled. "Seems I've heard that name before. And I do believe I heard it from you. Or am I wrong?"

"No, you're right."

"Seems to me you had yourself a bit of a hard-on for this Doc Lathram a while back."

"We had a disagreement. That's all."

More than a disagreement, actually. Duncan Lathram had flat out refused to operate on Gerry's face after the car accident. It had been a very bad time for Gerry. The worst. And Lathram's brush-off had almost put him over the edge. He still smarted from the sting of that rejection.

"You seemed pretty heated up at the time, if I remember."

"Look. The computer spit out the correlation on its own. I didn't go looking for it. But you've got to admit it seems a little strange that a congressman and a senator both die a month or so after plastic surgery performed by the same doctor."

"One in a car accident, the other in a fall. I don't exactly see a trend here."

"Neither do I. Just mentioning it as a curiosity."

"Fine. So basically we've got no evidence of foul play in the Schulz death."

"None."

"Okay. Then let's fold up that tent and move on without muddying the water with plastic surgeons."

"Will do."

But Gerry's interest was piqued. It might be nothing—doubtless *was* nothing—but he'd keep an eye out for any other Lathram patients who wound up in the morgue.

Just for the sheer hell of it.

3
SURGERY

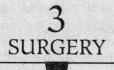

"DR. PANZELLA?"

Gina sat before a computer terminal, completing a pre-op physical, summarizing her evaluation of a patient's cardiopulmonary status and suitability for surgery. At least that was what she was supposed to be doing. Actually she was staring at the screen ruminating about yesterday's disaster at Marsden's office and that officious little—

Don't think about it.

She looked up. A young black woman, dressed in surgical scrubs and cap, had poked her head and upper body through the door of the record room and was looking at her expectantly.

"He's ready to scrub," said Joanna, the surgicenter's OR nurse.

"Be right there," Gina said.

She hit F10 to save the H and P, jotted down the file name so she could finish it later, and headed upstairs for the operating suite. Even on a VIP morning, with only one very important patient, Duncan Lathram did not like to be kept waiting. She hustled.

Not that she had that far to go. Lathram Surgical Associates sounded like a multicenter medical group, but actually it was one surgeon at one location in Chevy Chase. That location was an old single-story stone building, somewhat Gothic looking, that had once been a bank. Duncan Lathram and his brother Oliver, also a doctor, but a PhD in pharmacology, had maintained the old facade while completely gutting and refitting the interior into a state-of-the-art private surgicenter. The main floor offered a two-room operating suite, a large recovery room with six cubicles, a private VIP recovery room, an examination/consultation room, and Duncan's office. The records room, lounge, and Oliver's lab took up the basement.

Gina rushed into the scrub room, shucked her white coat, tucked her unruly black hair under a disposable cap, and joined Duncan at the sink. His forearms were already coated with tan lather.

"Morning, Duncan."

Since her first day here he'd insisted that since she was now a full-fledged physician, she must call him by his first name—"Call me 'Doctor Lathram' once more and you're fired." But she had to make a conscious effort to say Duncan. He'd been her hero since she was ten.

He grunted and nodded absently as he continued working the Betadine into his skin with the disposable brush.

Hmmm. Preoccupied this morning.

Gina watched him out of the corner of her eye as she adjusted the water temperature with the foot controls and began her own scrub. Assisting Duncan Lathram at surgery—still hard to believe it was true. Simply being alongside him like this never failed to give her a warm tingle.

She'd been working with him for months now and still marveled at how good he looked for a man of sixty-two. Neat as the proverbial pin, with dark, glossy, perfectly combed hair graying at the temples; piercing blue eyes over a generous nose set in a longish, rugged face that creased deeply when he smiled, which wasn't all that often. Six feet, maybe six-one, with a weathered Gary Cooper–Randolph Scott look, more like a saddle hand than a plastic surgeon. Long, lean, and close to the bone: a rack of baby-back ribs.

The image made her smile and took her back to her childhood when she worked in the family's Italian deli and meat market. Her dad made a practice then—still did, no doubt—of labeling certain customers with the names of cuts of meat or one of his Italian specialty dishes. Mrs. Fusco, who always had to touch everything, was a *calamari;* potbellied Mr. Prizzi was a pork loin; Mrs. Bellini, who'd always leave her shopping list home and could never remember what she needed, was *capozella;* and once when he'd thought she was in the front of the store, Gina had heard Dad ask one of the butchers if he'd got a load of the cannolis on Mrs. Phillips.

Little Gina adopted the practice and began categorizing the kids she knew by cuts of meat. Duncan Lathram was definitely a rack of baby-backs.

But Duncan's hands didn't quite go with the rest of him—long, delicate, agile fingers that could perform miracles, do medical origami with human tissues.

She felt awkward even thinking it, but the old guy was sexy.

Listen to me, she thought. He's older than my dad.

But no getting around it: Duncan Lathram was an attractive man. Not that she felt any libidinous tugs toward him. God, no. But from a purely esthetic standpoint, he was pretty hot for an old dude.

Must be our history, she thought. We go back a long way. And I've got the scars to prove it.

The big guy was quiet today. Duncan almost always had something to talk about. A news junkie. Read all the District papers, plus the *Baltimore Sun* and the northern Virginia rags. Had them strewn all over his office every morning. Never missed *MacNeil/Lehrer* and *Meet the Press.*

And never failed to find something to tick him off.

Duncan had his Permanently-Ticks-Me-Off list and his Ticks-Me-Off-Today list. Always had something to talk about.

But not today.

The silence was starting to get to Gina.

"Hear about Senator Schulz?" she said.

She thought he seemed to stiffen at the name.

"Schulz?" Duncan's voice was smooth, deeply melodic. "What about him?"

"According to the TV there's rumors that his cause of death is being investigated."

Duncan began to rinse the honey-colored foam from his arms and hands.

"The scuttlebutt on Schulz is that he jumped. And with reason. He was—please excuse the demotic—crookeder than most, and his scams were unraveling." Duncan shook his head sadly. "Twenty stories straight down, flat on his face." He sighed. "All that exceptional plastic work, all those hours of toil, wasted."

"Duncan!"

"Well, it's true. If I'd known defenestration was in his future, I wouldn't have taken such pains with him."

Gina thought she was used to his dark sense of humor, so often skating along the line between mordant and sick. But sometimes he did veer over the line.

He pressed his elbow against a chrome disk in the wall and the OR doors swung open. "Hurry up. Another of the kakistocracy's finest awaits us."

Gina glanced at the clock. Another minute to go with her scrub. She felt a warm flush as she remembered yesterday's chance encounter with Gerry Canney, and wondered if he'd call. Not the end of the world if he didn't, but it would certainly be nice. She reviewed the obscure words she'd collected to spring on Duncan today, and then her thoughts probed the enigma that was Duncan Lathram.

When they first met nineteen years ago he wasn't a plastic surgeon.

At age ten she woke up in a hospital with everything hurting. Struggling through the maze of her jumbled thoughts was the memory of horsing around with two of the neighborhood boys, proving to them that she could ride a bike as well as they could, and matching any dare they wanted to try. Suddenly she was in the middle of Lee Highway with a panel truck screeching and swerving toward her. She remembered the pale blurs of the driver's bared teeth and wide, shocked, terrified eyes through the dirty windshield as he stood on his brake pedal and tried to miss her.

Pain shoved the memories aside . . . pain and fear. . . . Where was her mama and who were these strange people bustling around her? Who was this big doctor bending over her and pressing his fingers into her tummy? Some deep part of her subconscious must have felt her life slipping away. She remembered asking him if she was going to die, and how he'd looked so shocked that she was conscious. Most of all she remembered the giant doctor going down on one knee beside the gurney so that his face was only inches from hers, squeezing her hand and saying, "Not if I've got anything to say about it. And around here, what I say goes."

Something about his supreme confidence soothed her. She believed him. She closed her eyes and slipped back into unconsciousness.

That big doctor had been Duncan Lathram. And Duncan Lathram had been a vascular surgeon then. Not just a run-of-the-mill type who spent his days doing varicose-vein strippings, but a gonzo with a scalpel, unafraid to take on any vascular catastrophe, the messier the better. Like hers. The impact with the truck had ruptured her spleen and torn her renal artery. Duncan had removed her spleen and repaired the gushing artery, saving her kidney *and* her life.

Gina remembered being absolutely infatuated with the man. He became a demigod in her eyes. From age ten on she sent him a card every Christmas. Even went to work for him at sixteen as a part-time clerk in the record room of his office in Alexandria. She learned how hard he worked, putting in fourteen- and sixteen-hour days in the hospital and office, and often being called to the emergency room at one or two in the morning to repair leaking or severed arteries damaged by everything from atherosclerosis to car wrecks to knife fights. He could be gruff, self-absorbed, even arrogant at times, but Gina didn't mind. After all, wasn't that part of being a demigod? His stamina amazed her, his dedication and boundless enthusiasm for his work inspired her so much that when she registered as a freshman at Princeton, she chose premed biology as her major. The course of her life had been set.

Eleven years later she returned to the D.C. area as a board-eligible internist and was shocked to learn that Duncan Lathram was no longer the gung-ho, life-saving surgical whirlwind she had left behind; somehow he had metamorphosed into a cosmetic surgeon who devoted his abbreviated workdays to prettifying the rich and powerful of Washington society.

From gonzo to dilettante—or something close to a dilettante. What had happened during those seven years? Gina had tried to piece it together but got nowhere. No one who knew was talking.

Only Gina seemed to care. Something was missing. Duncan used to fight bleeders, now he fought wrinkles. If he'd been specializing in tummy tucks instead of vascular repair nineteen years ago, she might not be here today. So Gina's perspective differed from all the youth-chasing ninnies who flocked to Duncan to help them turn back the clock. They worshiped this man who could help them escape the unsightly dues that nature, nurture, genetics, and lifestyle demanded they pay.

Duncan had become someone else's god.

"Morning, Gina," said a voice behind her.

Over her shoulder she saw Duncan's younger brother Oliver delivering a sterile tray of implants to the OR. He smiled and waved as he passed.

If Duncan was a rack of baby-backs, Oliver was a roast beef: rounder, heavier, with thinning hair, thick horn-rimmed glasses, and a protective layer of fat. Also softer, gentler, far more easygoing than his older brother. A sweetheart. He made sure all the women on the staff received flowers on their birthday. And when Joanna's son got arrested for joyriding, Oliver was there to bail him out. Everybody loved him.

Gina rinsed, shook, and entered OR-1 just as Marie, the nurse anesthetist, said, "He's out."

Gina took in OR-1 as Marie tied her mask and Joanna helped gown and glove her. Smaller than anything at Tulane, but the skill and professionalism here could hold their own against any tertiary medical center. Odorless—the laminar airflow kept it that way—and cold. Duncan liked to work under almost arctic conditions.

She approached the table where a middle-aged man, fiftyish or so, lay supine, his face covered except for the lips, chin, and throat, which were prepped for surgery. He looked something other than human with his skin stained yellow-brown from the Betadine and his chin and throat all marked up with the lines Duncan had drawn to guide his surgery.

Gina had met him last week when she'd done his pre-op

history and physical: Senator Harold Vincent. Another member of the recently revived joint committee.

Like Congressman Allard.

She was struck by the coincidence, but only for a moment. Hell, half of Washington's officials or their wives had been Duncan's patients at one time or another since he'd started in plastic surgery, and the other half probably were on the waiting list. Not surprising, really. His technical skills were second to none and he saw to it that people who considered themselves VIPs were treated accordingly; they got absolute discretion, and, thanks to his brother, he had exclusive use of an innovative technique that halved the healing time.

"Ready to begin, Gina?" Duncan said. "The senator is getting impatient. He's got a bunch of lobbyists camped out in his office with pockets full of cash. We don't want to keep them waiting, do we?"

Joanna tittered behind her mask.

Duncan made his first incision under the chin, carefully following the natural lines of cleavage, then began the delicate task of dissecting away and trimming off portions of the stretched muscle—the platysma—that gave the senator's neck a sagging, aged look. Senator Vincent had a particularly large amount of excess tissue, giving him a Tom-turkey wattle that fluttered when he spoke and flapped back and forth when he walked.

"Senator Impatience here couldn't wait," Duncan said as he worked. "An 'emergency,' he told me. Had to have it immediately. Anyone care to guess what the emergency is?"

"Has to be TV," Marie said from her spot at the top of the senator's head.

"Bingo. Give that woman a cigar."

Marie didn't miss a beat: "Not while the O-2 is running, thank you."

"It's the Joint Committee on Medical Ethics and Practice Guidelines, of course," Duncan said.

Gina stifled a groan. *Here we go again.* The joint committee was on Duncan's Permanently-Ticks-Me-Off list. He hated it and everything it was set up to do. He could go on for hours. Today the subject was a particularly uncomfortable one for Gina, what with no word from Senator Marsden's office, and her pending interview with Congressman Allard tomorrow.

"I've seen Senator Vincent on TV plenty of times," Gina said, sponging the blood that began pooling in the incision.

"Sure. C-SPAN. But who besides you and I watches C-SPAN? This boy has his eye on a much larger audience. Suction. Daily sound and video bites for all the network news shows, even looking for some live prime-time coverage. And our self-styled 'Champion of the Working Person' wants to look pretty for the nation. Clamp."

Gina glanced at Joanna who rolled her dark eyes as she slapped the handles of the clamp into Duncan's gloved palm. *He's off to the races.*

All right, so Duncan had a few fixations. Everybody had one or two. His just happened to be the Old-Boy network in the federal government and its intrusion into the practice of medicine. But even from his ramblings you could learn something.

"Some champion," he continued. "Voted himself a thirty-one-thousand-dollar pay raise during the recession, not to mention a government-issued Diners Club Card. Hand me the curved hemostat. That's the one. Here he is, vocal supporter of the Equal Pay Act, the Age Discrimination in Employment Act, the Occupational Health and Safety Act, and the National Labor Relations Act, as he'll remind you at every opportunity. But what he doesn't say is that behind closed doors he voted to keep the U.S. Senate exempt from all those acts. Suction."

He was silent as he made another incision. Gina continued to marvel at the grace and precision of his scalpel work. He made it look so easy. Gina knew it was anything but.

"But I'm thankful I'm only his plastic surgeon. Can you imagine being his proctologist?" He looked up and winked at her. "I mean, where to begin?"

Marie guffawed.

"As always," Duncan said, "laws imposed to assure fair play among the constituency do not apply to the kakistocracy."

Gina didn't want to, but felt compelled to ask. "All right, I give up. What's this kakistocracy you're always talking about? I can't find it in the dictionary."

"You won't unless you use an unabridged edition. The kakistocracy reflects the anomie of our times."

"Oh, that helps a lot."

"It is rulership by the worst."

Perfect time to spring one of my own words for the day, Gina thought.

"I guess then you might say that the members of the kakistocracy excel at casuistry."

She saw Duncan smile behind his mask. "Very good!"

Marie turned to Joanna. "Great. Now neither of them are speaking English."

Gina said, "I'm merely participating in the lingua franca."

Two! she thought. I got *two* of them in!

Duncan's eyes sparkled as he turned to Marie and Joanna. "Casuistry is the rationalization of matters of conscience, but I wonder if we can presume that the Senator Vincents of the world even have a conscience." He held out a gloved hand. "The implant, Gina. Time's a-wasting."

"Oh sure. Sorry."

Joanna uncovered the sterile tray, revealing the implants: tiny cylinders, soft, shiny, and slightly curved, looking like sausages or hot dogs. Hot dogs for a Barbie Doll. They came in all sizes. These on the tray were the mediums: twenty millimeters long, maybe five millimeters in diameter, each filled with Oliver's "secret sauce," an enzyme solution that promoted healing, reduced edema, and retarded scar formation.

Here was the real key to Duncan's phenomenal popularity. He had the best hands in the business, but that was only part of his appeal. These implants did the rest, allowing his patients the fastest recovery time, speeding them back into circulation to show off their new faces.

The brainchild of Duncan's younger brother, the implants were a crystal-protein matrix consisting of magnesium and albumin. Shortly after Gina came on staff, Oliver had shown her serial magnetic-resonance images of the implants after surgery. Each successive MRI showed a shrinking, shriveling membrane as the implant released its enzyme contents into the subcutaneous tissues to reduce scarring and post-operative edema. The final MRI a few weeks post-op showed nothing: After the implant had done its work, the crystals dissolved and the body's enzymes broke down the albumin to its component amino acids; those were absorbed along with the magnesium into the surrounding tissues and eventually into the bloodstream, leaving no trace.

With a probe, Gina nudged one of the implants onto the special narrow, oblong spoon Duncan had custom-made after too many implants ruptured in the grip of an ordinary forceps. She reached over and gently deposited it in the incision. Duncan used a probe to position the implant where he wanted it, then signaled for another. When he had four of them placed deep in the incision, he moved his field closer to the surface.

"He looks younger already," Gina said.

Right, Duncan thought as he trimmed a wedge of platysma. Just what I want to do: make this bastard look younger.

What he really would have liked to do was restructure Vincent's features into a configuration that reflected the man within. Not too hard with Vincent . . . slant the eyes, tilt up the nose, spread the nostrils, flare the lips . . . and find some way to make him say *oink*. Senator Harold Hogg, potentate of the pork barrel.

He smiled under the mask. He'd had so many of Congress's Old Boys on the table, he could have changed the face of American politics by now—literally.

I could be Dr. Moreau in reverse. Instead of vivisecting animals into men, I'd recast pols into the animals and reptiles they emulate. I could wear a mask and skulk through the halls of the Capitol: Duncan Lathram—the anti-Moreau, demon doctor of devolution, Phantom of the Longworth Building, scourge of the Senate shuttle.

A peal of insane laughter now and I'll be ready for Hollywood.

He sighed. Nothing so melodramatic for Senator Vincent. But Duncan did have definite plans for him.

Don't worry, Senator. You'll get yours. Trust me.

As he was placing the final implants he heard Gina's voice but didn't catch what she said.

"Hmmm?"

"I said, what is it exactly that so irks you about the joint committee?"

Gina's dark, dark eyes were fixed on him expectantly, as if his answer mattered very much to her. Under that cap and mask was a sultry Mediterranean beauty with wild, glossy black hair, full lips, high cheekbones, and flawless skin. A narrow waist and a perfect bust.

Nothing at all like the pimply, pudgy adolescent who'd worked in his file room a dozen or so years ago. In fact, when she'd shown up last June looking for part-time work as a physician, and told him who she was, he'd half considered having her investigated as an impostor.

The ugly duckling had returned as a swan. A dark swan. A cygnet.

But if he had been twenty minutes later in getting to that emergency room nineteen years ago, she wouldn't be anywhere now. That had been the great perk of his former life: saving someone who might make a difference in the world.

And he loved the way she'd started coming up with new words for him. One day she'd stump him, but that was all right.

Seems I did us all a favor when I put your insides back together, Gina.

Not for the first time, he questioned having changed his field of practice, but only for a heartbeat. The choice had been made for him. No going back.

But where was Gina going with all her brains and hard-won education?

"What irks me?" he said slowly as he began restructuring Vincent's trimmed platysma. "I don't think too much of the Joint Committee on Medical Ethics and Practice Guidelines." He made a point of enunciating the committee's name in its entirety. Simply saying the joint committee didn't do justice to the pretentiousness of its title. "I don't like its name, I don't approve of its mission, and I think it is staffed with arrivistes, parvenus, Pecksniffs, and bumptious yahoos."

He watched Gina's dark eyes crinkle at the corners.

I made her smile.

"Hey, don't hold back," she said. "Tell me what you really think."

He would have liked to tell her the truth, about what they did to his life, his family, but that would serve no purpose.

Never complain, never explain.

"Do you know what they're up to?" he said.

"Well, I understand it was the president's idea to revive the old McCready committee."

Duncan straightened and paused in his suturing. He didn't trust himself with a scalpel in his hand and McCready on his mind.

"Alas, our dear president didn't get his health-care plan, so he's taking it out on the medical profession. A medical guidelines bill wasn't good enough, wasn't *broad* enough. No. Now it's mandates on medical ethics."

Duncan closed his eyes to control his fury.

"Can you imagine it? Mark Twain said there's no distinct American criminal class except for Congress. And yet this collection of edacious, minatory pharisees is going to deliver ethical guidelines to a profession that has had a code of ethics since the time of Babylon."

"We're not all so perfect, either," Gina said.

"If all you've got is larceny in your heart, you don't spend four years in premed, four years in med school, three to ten years in postgraduate training working hundred-hour weeks at slightly more than minimum wage, all for the privilege of being six figures in debt by the time you hang out your shingle."

"Of course not," Gina said. "You do it so you can work seventy-hour weeks for the rest of your life."

Duncan smiled and felt his muscles relax. My dear cygnet. It's good to have you around.

He'd finished resecting and tightening the platysma. Time to close. He asked for 6-o gut on a curved needle. Using a continuous subcutaneous technique, he began suturing.

"Anyway," she said, "since Senator Marsden is McCready's successor, he's been asked to chair the joint committee. Got any dirt on him?"

Why was she so interested?

"Actually, no," Duncan said. "But he hasn't been around all that long. Give him time. You know what the committee's up to, don't you?"

"Holding public hearings to gather information to help them write the bill?"

"Their stated purpose—at the president's behest—is to set rigid standards for medical practice. What they're really out to do is parade a bunch of horror stories before the public, present a lot of one-sided testimony on the worst cases of negligence and medical malfeasance they can find, and paint the whole medical profession as a cartel of reckless, irresponsible, knife-happy, moneygrubbing brigands who must be brought to heel."

"Um, don't you think you sound just a little paranoid?"

With good reason, he thought.

"Even paranoids have real enemies, Gina. They're out to get us—pure and simple. I know how that sounds, but that's how I see it. They're at the bottom of the heap in public confidence—and they want to draw attention away from their own unwillingness to police themselves."

"But their ethics committees go after people all the time."

Duncan laughed. "Congressional ethics—there's an oxymoron for you. Only on those rare occasions when the press turns up the heat, only when their backs are to the wall and they have to do *something*."

"Well, whether we like it or not, I kind of think the shape of medical practice in the future is going to be decided at these hearings. So I'd like to be an aide on that committee. In fact, I had an interview at Senator Marsden's office yesterday morning."

Duncan froze and stared at her, and found Gina staring right back.

Gina's insides were wound into a Gordian knot. She'd waited until he'd almost closed the incision before mentioning this.

Why did I tell him? she wondered. I may not even get the job.

Duncan said nothing as he finished closing the incision, leaving not a single stitch on the surface. Only a hair-thin line remained along the underside of the chin.

Gina had seen him do this a hundred times at least, but still it awed her.

When he was done he looked up at her again.

"You *what?*"

"I—I had an interview with—"

"You are incomprehensible. You have a brilliant mind, an excellent medical education, and you want to be a Hill rat?"

"Only part-time. I just—"

"How can you even *think* of cooperating with that committee?"

"Doesn't someone have to make sure they get their facts straight?"

"Facts? Since when is Congress interested in facts?" He stepped back from the table and began ripping off his gloves. "I thought I was working with a doctor, not a Hill-rat wannabe."

That hurt—stung like a slap in the face.

"Duncan—"

"You can't have it both ways, Gina. When you decide which one you want to be, let me know."

He tossed his gloves on the floor and stormed out.

Gina had feared he might be a little upset, but she hadn't expected anything like this. She stood in the suddenly silent OR, with Marie and Joanna avoiding eye contact. She wondered what would have happened if she'd mentioned her appointment with Congressman Allard tomorrow morning. As it was she felt as if the floor had opened beneath her.

4
RECOVERY

WITH THE MORNING'S TRUNCATED SURGERY SCHEDULE
finished, the halls were quiet. Too quiet. Gina's stomach was
still tight as she completed her dictation on Thursday's
scheduled procedures.

Why did you open your big mouth?

Because he had to know sooner or later . . . especially
when she began asking for extra time off.

But you may never get the job, dummy.

Right. Too right.

She finished the last H and P, logged off her terminal, and
sat there.

Now what?

She had to face him. Had to clear the air. Had to find out
where she stood. Was she still welcome here as a pre-op
evaluator and surgical assistant, or was she to be cast into the
outer darkness?

Only one way to find out.

She gathered her courage and hurried upstairs to the main
floor. From there a short walk down the hall.

Duncan's slim, pretty, blond receptionist-secretary guarded the door to his office.

"Hi, Barbara. Is he in?"

She smiled up at Gina. "Just missed him. Said he was going to look in on the senator, then—"

"—head for the golf course," Gina said. That was Duncan's routine.

"He may still be here. If you hurry—"

"Thanks, Barb."

She hurried toward the VIP recovery room. Along the way she saw Sharon Collins, the recovery RN, standing in the hall and talking to Joanna. She slowed as she passed.

"Excuse me, Sharon. Aren't you—?"

"Doing recovery on the VIP?" She was short, dark, and built like a Ninja turtle, but one sharp nurse. "Yeah. Dr. D. told me to take a break while he double-checked his needlework. I'm just about to head back."

"Good. Maybe I can catch him."

"You sure you want to?" Joanna said.

Gina flashed her a smile. "No."

She scooted around the corner to the VIP recovery room— a plain, unmarked door—and knocked gently. When there was no answer she tried again.

"Duncan?"

She pushed the door open.

Noon brightness filtered through the full-length beige drapes across the picture window. Carpeting instead of linoleum, mahogany instead of Formica. A veneer of luxury for the sort who craved it, but very functional beneath.

In the bed, Senator Vincent snored softly, sleeping off the general anesthetic. But no Duncan.

Damn. She'd missed him. He couldn't have got that far. She was half turned to leave when she saw Senator Vincent move his leg. An unfolding length of sheet revealed a spot of red on the white over his thigh. She leaned closer.

Blood.

Just a tiny spot. No more than a drop. But there shouldn't have been *any* blood down by his leg. On his pillow, maybe, but not there.

She lifted the sheet and looked at the senator's leg. A small, semicircular puncture wound, less than a quarter inch in length on the outer aspect of the thigh, slightly toward the rear.

She probed the area around it and the senator moved again. Within the bandages his lids struggled open. His glazed eyes stared at her, then closed again.

"Shot," he mumbled.

"What?"

"Gafe me shot."

"Who gave you a shot?"

"Docker Lafram." He opened his eyes again and smiled. "Summin special. Only choice patients."

The senator smacked his lips and closed his eyes. He began to snore.

Gina stood over him. A shot? Since when did Duncan give injections? Never. It was unheard of.

Vincent had to be wrong . . . and yet there definitely was a puncture wound in his thigh.

She adjusted the covers back over him.

Weird. Very weird.

A noise behind her made her turn. Collins was slipping through the door. She glanced around.

"He's gone?"

"Gone when I got here. Did Dr. Lathram say anything about giving the senator an injection?"

Collins checked the order sheet. "No. Just the usual— Tylenol #3, two P-O q four P-R-N."

"No, I mean himself—giving the senator an injection himself."

Collins's wide face broke into a grin. "Dr. D.? Giving

meds personally? No way. That's what us RNs are for. Where'd you get an idea like that?"

"There's a puncture on his thigh and he said something about Dr. Lathram giving him a shot."

Collins stepped over to the bed and examined his thigh.

"Hmmm. Where'd that come from? Looks more like a tiny cut than a needle mark."

"He said—"

Collins gave Senator Vincent's shoulder a gentle shake.

"Senator? Are you awake?"

He snorted and his eyes fluttered but didn't open.

"Okay, Mom," he said.

Collins grinned again. "You see? I'd sooner believe the Man in the Moon gave him an injection than Dr. D. And besides, where's the syringe? Where's the injection vial?"

She had a point.

"You're right." Gina turned and headed for the door. "I'm out of here. See you Thursday."

It was strange, it didn't add up, but Gina pushed it out of her mind. She had other things to think about. Like her appointment with Congressman Allard tomorrow morning. Another of Duncan's patients, by the way. She'd assisted on his abdominal liposuction a while back.

And if he didn't work out, she could come back to Senator Vincent.

She hadn't realized it when she signed on here, but here was one of the perks of working with Duncan: If they had juice and they wanted cosmetic surgery, Duncan Lathram was the man to see.

5
DUNCAN

DUNCAN LATHRAM, MD, STOOD AMONG THE EARLY morning regulars at the self-serve coffee counter at the rear of the 7-Eleven on F Street off Fifth. Not exactly his purlieu. He felt a little out of place in his pale blue oxford shirt, blue blazer, and tan slacks, but no one seemed to pay him much mind.

He considered the array of partially filled glass urns before him.

They leave the pots on the heaters, he thought. Barbaric.

Grimacing, he reached for a medium-sized cup—foam, no less—emblazoned with the red-and-green corporate logo, and poured himself a cup of the *soi-disant* coffee.

He could tell from the color—he was sure he could read the morning paper through it—that they were stretching the grounds by adding too much water. The aroma—make that *smell* . . . this acrid effluvium did not deserve three syllables —testified that it had been sitting on the burner far too long.

He'd always drunk his coffee black and, even though he

knew he was going to regret this, he wasn't about to change now. He blew steam off the dark surface, sipped . . .

And shuddered. It tasted like . . . like . . .

Words failed him.

He watched the man in the blue flannel shirt next to him lighten his coffee with half-and-half, then spoon in three sugars.

"Does that kill the taste?"

The man glanced up at him, apparently startled at being spoken to. "Uh, sorta. I don't really like coffee, but I need it to get going in the morning."

"Yes. You might say I'm abstemious in all matters except coffee. What we won't do to render ourselves properly caffeinated, ay?"

He got in line at the cash register. The flannel shirt followed him. Ahead of him, Duncan watched a steatopygous woman with rollers wound into her orange hair dump three cans of Arizona Iced Tea and twenty creamsicles onto the counter, then ask for two packs of Parliament—boxes, please.

Half turning to the flannel shirt, Duncan said, "I've always believed that one can augur the course of a civilization through observation of its indigenous cuisine, don't you agree?"

The flannel shirt said, "What?"

"Exactly."

Then it was Duncan's turn to pay.

"Anything else?" said the Middle Eastern gentleman behind the counter.

"Sorry, no," Duncan said. "My doctor won't allow me more than one medium-size kerosene a day."

"Yes, sir," the man said and took his money. "Have a nice day."

Outside he walked south, crossed Constitution and

strolled up the Mall, gingerly sipping the coffeelike substance as he approached the Capitol. Here it was Wednesday, a no-surgery day. He should have been relaxed, but a fine tremor from his hand rippled the surface of the liquid in the cup. He knew it wasn't the caffeine.

Admit it, he told himself. If you were wound any tighter you'd implode. But why shouldn't you be? This is an important day. Even more important for a certain congressman.

He distracted himself by admiring the scenery.

He rarely got downtown anymore. Too bad. It had rained last night, and now a fine mist hazed the air and the grass coruscated in the early morning sunlight. Starlings managed to make themselves heard over the growing thunder of the stampeding herd of arriving federal workers. He'd forgotten how beautiful the Mall could be before the tourists arrived.

The last time he'd ventured this way had been a big mistake. He'd come down in May during the annual invasion by busloads of eighth graders from everywhere east of the Rockies. The National Gallery had been acrawl with roving, cachinnating packs of barely bridled hormones wrapped in scabrous, whelk-laden skin to whom the epitome of true art and intimate self-expression was spray painting the name of their favorite heavy metal group on a wall.

But then, one of the central pieces on exhibit at the National Gallery at the time had been a huge mural, ten feet high, twenty long, all stark white except for a beige vertical stripe two feet from the left edge.

Maybe the kids were onto something after all: *Megadeth Rules* indeed.

Duncan hadn't been back since.

Further on, a dirty, unshaven man approached him, wearing a black trash bag; he had the drawstring around his waist, his head and arms poking through appropriately placed slits.

"Got some spare change for an old soldier?" the tatterde-malion said.

Duncan stopped and reached into his pocket. "Which war was that?"

"Which one were *you* in?" the man said.

"The Korean Conflict, as it is now known."

Not true. He'd been in college then—premed. But he wanted to see what this "old soldier" would say.

"Me too."

Duncan had to smile. "What if I'd said Vietnam?"

"Was in that one too. I'm the Unknown Soldier."

Duncan figured he probably meant Universal Soldier but then again, it was very likely that he couldn't remember his name.

"Clever rain gear you've got there, soldier. The latest from the House of Hefty, if I'm not mistaken."

"Does the job."

Duncan handed him a twenty-dollar bill. The man glanced at it, then did a double take.

"God, man! Thanks! Thanks a million!"

"Why not? I expect this to be a good day for me. Might as well be a good one for you too."

The fellow began backing away, most likely trying to put some distance between them before Duncan changed his mind. "I'll spend this wisely, I assure you, sir."

Duncan laughed. "I'm sure you will."

"And you have a good day."

"I assure you I will. A very good day."

If all goes according to plan this time.

Anxiety nibbled at his stomach lining like hungry fish. Timing was everything here, but with so many variables beyond his control, luck was a considerable factor as well. And Duncan hated to depend on luck.

He walked on until he spotted the camera crew setting up

on the House side at the base of the steps leading up to the west portico of the Capitol.

"Something big happening?" Duncan asked.

"Just an interview," the bearded cameraman said. "Congressman."

"Which one?"

"Allard."

"Not Kenneth Allard! *The* Kenneth Allard? Here? Right here?" Duncan clapped his hands. "He's one of my favorites!"

The cameraman grinned at the soundman. "First time I ever heard anyone say that."

"Oh, he's a great statesman. A wonderful intellect. An isle of probity in a sea of venality."

"If you say so."

Obviously the cameraman had lost what little interest he'd had in talking to Duncan. Not that Duncan could blame him.

Make sure that camera's working, Duncan thought. You're going to see the end of someone's career.

He headed up the four flights of granite steps that led to the Capitol. He had to get to Congressman Allard before Allard got to the camera.

Last night he'd heard a TV newsreader mention that they'd be interviewing Congressman Allard today on the revival of the Joint Committee on Medical Ethics and Practice Guidelines. Duncan had decided then to be here bright and early. This was too rare an opportunity to miss.

He climbed to the top of the Capitol steps and gazed back along the green expanse of the Mall. A mile and a half away, past the Capitol Reflecting Pool, past the towers of the Smithsonian and the museums and galleries that lined the Mall, the obelisk of the Washington Monument gleamed like a spearhead in the morning sunlight and cast a narrow shaft of shadow toward the white rectangle of the Lincoln Memorial behind it. Above them, the Delta shuttle glided toward a landing at Washington National.

Flanking the Mall to the right and left, Pennsylvania, Constitution, and Independence avenues were thick with traffic, all heading this way.

And all around him a steady stream of men and women— mostly men—dressed in suits and carrying briefcases or attaché cases, scurrying up the steps. They obviously were not tourists—no Bermuda shorts, cameras, and "I ♥ Washington" caps—and he knew they weren't senators or representatives or staffers. The people who worked here, who belonged here, moved back and forth between the Senate and House office buildings on underground shuttles. These were lobbyists, armed with checkbooks loaded with the grease that keeps the wheels of Congress turning.

The kakistocracy was in session.

Duncan sighed as he watched their hurried, purposeful climb toward the House and Senate chambers. God, there were an awful lot of them.

The Congress of the United States, he thought with a grim smile. The best government money can buy.

Far below, at the bottom of the steps, the soundman nodded as the reporter checked his mike. Good. They were ready. All set up and waiting for U.S. representative Kenneth Allard. Duncan was waiting for him too.

And then he saw him. Allard stepped out on the House side flanked by three of his aides. Pushing sixty, medium height, and on the glabrous protuberance that passed for his head, a thatch of dark brown hair that had once belonged to someone else. He had a paunch but a small one. It had been much larger before Duncan had gone to work on it with the liposuction tube. What had been protuberant and tremulose was now flattened and firm.

Not a bad job, he thought as Allard started moving toward

him across the open, granite-paved expanse, even if I do say so myself.

But a face only a bacteriologist could love.

A good many of the arriving lobbyists smiled deferentially and waved to Allard as they passed. He was something of a legend on the Hill, admired, almost revered, by his colleagues in the kakistocracy for the innovative approach to campaign financing he developed while serving on the Committee on Energy and Commerce. A couple of campaigns ago, when Congressman Allard became aware that his reelection coffers were down to their last million or two, and the PACs weren't coming up with fresh money fast enough, he introduced a flurry of bills that would have devastating impact on the coal, oil, gas, and timber industries. Suddenly the energy PACs and lumber trade associations, not to mention the associated unions that would be hit hard by the new Allard bills, were swarming around him with open checkbooks. He collected eight million in three months— some of which probably paid for his surgery. After gorging himself on the pecuniary viands, he withdrew the bills from committee. The procedure had been imitated by his colleagues many times since.

But none of that had anything to do with why Duncan was here today.

He watched Allard nod to a few of the passing lobbyists, but the congressman was more interested in conferring with his aides; he looked like a quarterback huddling with his coaches, only they were all in suits.

Duncan wondered if he was the only one on Capitol Hill wearing something other than a business suit.

"Good morning, Kent," Duncan said as he neared the group.

Allard looked up at the sound of his sobriquet and squinted at Duncan. An instant of confusion—Duncan could almost hear him thinking *Who the hell?*—and then recognition.

"Doc—" He cleared his throat. "Duncan! What are you doing up here? Welcome to the Hill." His expression was wary instead of welcoming.

Doesn't want to call me Dr. Lathram. Probably afraid someone will recognize the name and want to know what fix-ups I performed on him.

Duncan stuck out his hand and delivered his lines smoothly.

"Waiting for some relatives from out of town. Promised to show them the sights . . . tour guide for a day. You know the drill, I'm sure."

Chicklet caps flashed. "I sure do."

Casually, Duncan reached into his blazer pocket and gripped the oblong bulk of his pager. He felt the sweat collecting under his arms. He was close now, but he wanted to be closer still. Just to be sure.

"You're looking good, Kent. The cameras down there are going to love you." *But nowhere near as much as you love them.*

The smile faded. The wariness reemerged. "Thank you."

Don't worry, Congressman, Duncan thought. *I'm not going to say anything about the liposuction.*

But he couldn't resist turning the screw a little tighter.

"How *do* you stay so *young* looking?"

Allard's smile returned, but looked forced now. "Clean living."

You son of a bitch.

"I must try that sometime."

They both laughed. Duncan flipped the ON switch on his pager and it began to beep. He pulled it from his pocket. A vintage model, considerably larger than the new ones. He stared at the blank message window, trying to still the ague tremor of his hand.

"Looks like my service wants me. I'd better find a phone and see what they want."

He edged past Allard and his aides, coming within a few inches of the congressman.

This is as close as I'm going to get, he thought.

His finger found another button on his pager. The special button. But he hesitated. No turning back once he pressed it.

Old questions assailed him again. Isn't this going too far? Is it really worth the risk? What if I'm caught? And the most disturbing of all: Is this something a sane man would do?

Then he remembered what Allard had participated in five years ago . . . and today's *clean-living* remark.

Duncan pressed the button.

This time the pager made no sound, but he felt it vibrate against his palm.

Allard winced and rubbed his right thigh.

"Good luck with the TV folks, Kent," Duncan said. "And think of an eighteen-year-old named Lisa."

"Pardon?" Allard said.

"Her name was Lisa. Keep that in mind." *I want it to be your last coherent thought.*

He turned and almost bumped into a dark-haired young woman.

"Gina!"

Gina tried to speak but found her voice locked. Not from the shock of seeing Duncan on the Capitol steps, but from the look on his face as he'd turned away from Congressman Allard. His eyes, arctic cold, cobalt hard, full of rage and hatred so intense she thought they'd leap from their sockets. Never in her life had she seen an expression like that. For an instant she thought she was facing a feral stranger.

And suddenly it was gone. As soon as he spoke her name

his face changed, metamorphosed into the Duncan Lathram she knew.

And then she could speak.

"Duncan. You're the last person I expected to run into down here."

He stared at her for a few heartbeats. When he finally spoke, his voice was cool, distant.

"I might have said the same about you . . . until yesterday. How long have you been standing here?"

She'd arrived early at the Rayburn Building for her meeting and had been told that Congressman Allard would be slightly delayed because of his television interview. Rather than sit cooling her heels, Gina had opted to stroll across Independence to catch the interview live.

Staying a discreet distance from the congressman's group she'd noticed a man who reminded her of Duncan, but she couldn't be sure from the rear, and besides, what would Duncan be doing down here? She'd edged closer, had been almost on top of him when he'd turned and they'd come nose to nose.

How long have you been standing here? The answer seemed important to him. Very important.

Long enough to hear you say something very strange, she thought.

"Just a few seconds. But what on earth are you doing here?"

"Me?" He looked around. "I love the Capitol area . . . the Mall . . . the monuments . . . they're beautiful."

"Knowing how you feel about politicians—"

"Let's just say I consider it a beautiful mansion that happens to be infested by termites and all sorts of vermin." His eyes bored into her. "So why are you here?"

The question she'd been dreading. "I, uh, have an appointment with Congressman Allard this morning."

He grimaced. "You want to be on *his* staff?"

"I'll be on anybody's staff. I want to be on this committee."

He stared at her again. "Yes. Yes, I see you do. Why didn't you mention this yesterday?"

"You didn't exactly give me a chance."

He made a soft guttural sound and glanced at the old-fashioned beeper clutched in his hand—a dinosaur of a beeper, at least six inches long.

Odd, she thought. She hadn't realized Duncan carried a pager. He wasn't on emergency call, but she guessed there was always the chance of a postsurgical complication.

Suddenly he seemed in a rush. He spoke quickly.

"I want to discuss something with you, Gina, but I have to make a call and this is neither the time nor the place. I will see you in my office after lunch this afternoon. Can you be there?"

. . . something to discuss with you . . . She didn't like the sound of that.

"I think so."

"Good. See you then."

He turned and headed for one of the doors into the south wing. Gina watched him for a few seconds, then turned her attention to where Congressman Allard continued to huddle with his aides. The totaled ages of the three younger men probably exceeded Allard's by very little, yet they were doing all the talking. Good haircuts, expensive suits, six-figure incomes or close to it for many of the more experienced aides, and a smug We're-where-it's-at look.

Too many of the Hill rats she'd met seemed to adopt that attitude after a couple of years on the job. She promised—swore—that wouldn't happen to her.

No doubt doing some last-minute fine tuning of his remarks before the camera.

Finally he seemed ready. He nodded to his aides, straightened his tie, adjusted his suit coat, patted his toupee, then started down the steps.

Gina sidled to her right to where she had an unobstructed view of the steps. She watched Allard descend on an angle toward the waiting camera and reporter. His movements were smooth and fluid during the first two flights, then he stopped on the landing halfway down.

He paused and rubbed his eyes, shook his head as if to clear it, then continued down. At the top of the last flight he stopped again.

A warning bell sounded in Gina's brain. Something was wrong.

Allard leaned against the bronze handrail and pressed a hand over his eyes. Even from here Gina could see that the hand was shaking.

He lowered his hand and began to sway. He grasped the rail and turned around to stare back up at the Capitol. His expression was frightened. He looked lost, confused, as if he didn't know where he was. He took a faltering step to his left but wobbled backward instead.

God, he's going to fall!

As his arms windmilled for balance, his aides cried out and rushed down to him. But Allard was already toppling. He managed to twist around but could not break his fall. He hit the granite steps and began to roll.

Shouts now from the TV crew as the reporter rushed toward the falling legislator. The cameraman followed her, taping all the way. A couple of Capitol Police started running from the other end of the steps.

Gina was already on her way down as Congressman Allard landed in a heap at the base of the steps and lay still, arms akimbo, his toupee skewed so that it hung over his left ear. His aides, the TV crew, and the cops converged on him from three directions.

Gina reached the growing knot and forced her way in.

"I'm a doctor," she said. "Let me through."

The onlookers made way for her and soon she was kneeling at Allard's side. He was on his back; his face was a mess, blood everywhere. Gina dug her index and middle fingers into the side of his throat, probing for a carotid. She found it, pulsing rapidly, but strong and regular. She saw his chest moving with respirations, small bubbles of saliva fluttering at the corner of his bloodied lips as air flowed in and out.

Pulse and respiration okay. Good. But he did seem to be in shock.

"All right," she announced to the onlookers. "His heart's beating and he's breathing. No need for CPR. But nobody move him. He may have a spinal injury." She looked around. "Is somebody calling an ambulance?"

One of the Capitol cops pointed to his partner who was babbling into his radio. "We're on it," he said.

Gina returned her attention to Allard. She couldn't do a neurological evaluation here, but if she had to bet she'd put her money on a stroke. Maybe he'd flipped an embolus to his brain.

She glanced up and saw someone standing at the railing along the edge of the west portico, looking down. She blinked. It was Duncan. She couldn't read his expression. He stood there staring for a moment, then turned and disappeared from view.

Duncan? she thought. Aren't you going to help?

6
COFFEE

GINA DIDN'T GET BACK TO THE SURGICENTER UNTIL shortly before noon. She'd hovered by Congressman Allard's side until the EMTs arrived. She watched them bandage his face, strap him to a back board, load him into their rig, and howl away toward G. W. Medical Center. She stopped back at Allard's office to let them know what had happened, and after that she'd been at loose ends, wandering around the Capitol area, thinking, wondering . . .

Duncan had acted so strange this morning, and he hadn't shown the slightest concern for the fate of the congressman, who wasn't just some stranger—he was one of Duncan's patients.

And who was this Lisa he'd been talking about to Allard? It had seemed like such a non sequitur.

She took the Metro Red Line up to Friendship Heights and walked the rest of the way, still thinking, still wondering.

By the time she reached the surgicenter she still didn't have an answer.

"He wanted to see me," she told Barbara as she paused at her reception desk.

"He mentioned it, but right now he's conferencing with another doctor. Strict orders not to disturb."

"Really? Anybody we know?"

Barbara shrugged. "All he tells me is to block out half an hour for 'Dr. V.' Now you know as much as I do. But he's *very* good-looking." Barbara's eyebrows oscillated as her voice took on a Mae West tone. "This is his second visit, and I hope it's not the last."

Why so mysterious about the name? A doctor who wanted cosmetic surgery maybe?

Gina shrugged. Not her business.

"Let him know I'm here."

"Will do."

A few minutes later she was sitting in the basement lab across the workbench from Oliver, diffidently watching him fill the next batch of a dozen or so implants for tomorrow's surgery. She already had a headache, and the residual olfactory tang of solvents was conspiring with the bright overhead fluorescents to make it worse. She should have been working with Oliver, learning the technique, but she couldn't muster the concentration.

Her chin rested on her hands and her elbows were propped on the marred black counter. She felt leaden, as if someone had siphoned off all her energy . . . the aftermath of the morning's events, and the certainty that Duncan was going to fire her.

"He's not going to fire you," Oliver said.

She glanced up at him. He sat calmly in his white coat, his pudgy hands folded in front of him. But she read genuine sympathy in the round, pale face and in the blue eyes behind the thick horn-rimmed lenses. Hard to believe he and Duncan shared the same gene pool.

"How can you be so sure?"

"He tends to fly off the handle lately. Ever since they reconvened that darn committee."

"What is it with him and that committee?"

"Well, years ago he had a bit of trouble . . ." His voice trailed off.

"What sort of trouble?"

"Nothing. Forget I said anything."

Gina wasn't forgetting anything. Especially after this morning. Another question was burning through her brainpan.

"All right then. Tell me this: Who's Lisa?"

"Lisa?"

"Yes. I heard Duncan mention something about a Lisa this morning."

The implant Oliver was filling suddenly burst.

"I . . . I don't know. He had a daughter named Lisa."

"Had?"

"Yes, well—"

The phone rang. Oliver picked it up and listened.

"She's right here," he said, then handed it across to her.

Duncan's voice: "Gina, please come to my office."

Her mouth went dry. "Okay. Sure."

The other end clicked dead. That in itself was not indicative of anything—Duncan rarely said hello or good-bye on the phone—but she could feel her insides coiling into knots.

She handed the receiver back to Oliver.

"He wants to see me."

Oliver smiled. "See? He's cooled down already."

"I wouldn't be too sure of that."

"I'll talk to him if you want."

"Thanks, but I'd better handle this myself."

With the knots inside pulling even tighter, she rose and

headed for Duncan's office. This was it. She'd been in his office before, many times, but usually just a quick stop before surgery to discuss some potential problem with one of his patients. This was the first time he'd actually called and *asked* her to his office.

He's going to fire me.

Financially, that would not be a catastrophe. She wasn't getting paid all that much here and she could take an extra shift as house doctor at Lynnbrook. But still . . .

Her throat constricted.

Fired . . . being fired by anyone from any job would hurt. But to be kicked out by Duncan Lathram . . .

Devastating.

She wasn't going to back down, though. Not when she was doing the right thing. But how to explain it to him? From what she could see, the days when doctors could focus solely on their patients and ignore what Washington was up to were gone. Dead as the Jurassic age.

For their patients' sake as well as their own, doctors had to get involved in the process. And any doctor who thought otherwise was a dinosaur, already extinct but simply unaware of the fact.

Sure, she thought. That's it. Tell Duncan he's the best surgeon alive, but he's a dinosaur. He'll definitely want to keep me on then.

Gina forced a smile as she approached Barbara's desk.

"He's expecting me."

"I know," Barbara said. "He told me to hold his calls."

Oh, great.

Gina hesitated at the door, then pushed through.

Duncan's office was a spacious quadrangle with floor-to-ceiling glass along most of the far wall. The last of the morning sun was slipping from the room but still shining brightly on the oriental rock garden and koi pond outside.

Very little of the off-white walls was visible; the few sections not obscured by mahogany bookcases filled with medical texts and surgical journals were studded with plaques, degrees, diplomas, and certificates from licensing and special-ty boards. An oversized antique partners desk stretched before the window-wall. A glorious Persian rug covered most of the hardwood floor.

The wall on the far right angled to a large cabinet custom-built for the narrow corner. Duncan had the cabinet open and stood before it now, his back to her, engrossed in whatever he was doing.

He half turned as she closed the door behind her.

"Good. You're just in time." He motioned her closer. "Come watch this."

A little off balance from the casual greeting—he seemed a changed man since this morning—and more than a little unsure of herself, she complied. As she approached she heard a whirring noise, like an electric drill. When she reached his side she was startled to see what he was up to.

Grinding coffee.

"Just got these in," he said. "Costa Rican La Minita Tarrazu. A superb batch of beans."

He dumped the ground coffee into the open end of a chrome funnel set in the top of an insulated carafe.

Gina didn't see any white inside the funnel. "You forgot the filter."

"Don't worry. It's in there. I use a gold mesh filter. Paper soaks up too many of the oils that give a coffee its character. Remember that. Always use a gold filter. And here's some-thing else to remember."

He reached into the little microwave to his left and removed a half-quart Pyrex cup full of steaming water. He took two tablespoons of water and added them to the cone.

"Always wet your grounds first. Give them about thirty

seconds to swell, then add the rest of the water. But not *boiling* water. You don't want scalded coffee. Bring the water to a boil and let it sit for about a minute, then pour it over the damp grounds. But not just any water. Use spring water. Don't use that chemical-laden junk from the tap.''

He emptied the Pyrex cup into the cone, then rubbed his hands in anticipation.

''You're about to have a real experience, Gina. Just possibly the best cup of coffee in the world.'' He turned to her. ''Any news from Marsden's office yet?''

''No. I'm not terribly sanguine about my chances.'' *Sanguine?* She never used that word. Must be Duncan's influence. ''My interview wasn't with Senator Marsden, you know. It was with his chief of staff. We didn't exactly hit it off.''

''Shot down by the senator's satrap, ay? And I guess you didn't get your chance to impress Allard either.''

''Hardly. That was some fall he had. Lucky to be in one piece after the way he hit the sidewalk.''

''Right in front of the TV cameras. They've been replaying it all morning on CNN. Too bad.''

Too bad? He'd been there, watching, and hadn't helped. Or didn't he want to admit that?

''Had some nasty facial lacerations. Chances are he'll be calling you to fix him up.''

''He can save his dime,'' Duncan said. ''You ought to know by now I don't operate on people who need surgery— only those who want it. By the way, sorry about my outburst yesterday morning. You didn't deserve that.''

Just like that: Oh, by the way, sorry I damn near gave you a heart attack.

But relief blotted out his offhandedness. The bunched muscles in her shoulders and the back of her neck began to uncoil.

"You mean I'm not fired?"

He laughed. "Hell, no! But I do want to talk to you." His smile faded. "I want to know why a bright, talented young woman like you wants to get involved with the Harold Vincents and Kenneth Allards of the world."

Oh, God, she thought as she took a deep breath. Here we go.

"*Some*body's got to, Duncan. They're calling all the shots. But when they want to know what's going on with doctors and medical care, look who they ask: insurance companies, AMA officers, public service doctors, VA doctors, whoever's handy."

Duncan grimaced with distaste. "Or even worse: Samuel Fox."

Gina nodded, remembering sitting around with her fellow residents and laughing at Fox's asinine statements during a Donahue appearance a couple of years ago. But he had a knack for PR and had parlayed his alarmist books and press releases into a position of credibility with Congress.

"Exactly. Congress gets its input from doctors who aren't physicians."

"Stands to reason," Duncan said. "*Real* doctors are out in the trenches practicing medicine. They've got too many sick people on their hands to hang around Capitol Hill."

"Too true. But that's got to change."

Duncan's jaw jutted at her. "Why?"

"Because the government's got its sights on health care. The big reform package didn't fly, but that doesn't mean the government's going to go away. It's going to keep inching in, the old salami-slicing method. Nothing's going to stop it."

Duncan sighed. "Yeah, I know. Don't get me wrong. I'm not opposed to everyone having some sort of coverage. I hate the thought of anyone, especially a child, going untreated. But I loathe the idea of the kakistocracy designing and administering the program, imposing guidelines for medical decisions that should be a matter solely between doctor and patient." His voice took on a TV announcer's tone: " 'And *now,* from the people who brought you the House Post Office scandal and the S and L debacle: *Health care!* ' " He shook his head. "I don't think so."

"Doesn't it make sense to standardize medical care and costs across the country?"

His gaze was hard as steel. "Don't you think we've got enough guidelines already?"

She thought of old Mrs. Thompson at Lynnbrook Hospital. "Well . . ."

"What this bill will do is enforce cookbook medicine. The real thrust of all this legislation isn't quality assurance—it's cost control. They'll save a few bucks but the human costs will be huge."

"It doesn't have to be that way. We—"

Duncan glanced at the carafe and held up a hand. "Coffee's ready."

He lifted the cone from the carafe and placed it in the small chrome sink next to the microwave. Then he filled two thick white diner-style mugs with the fresh, steaming coffee. He handed one to Gina.

"Now *this* is coffee. Taste."

Gina sniffed—the aroma was fabulous—then sipped. Usually she drank her coffee black with a little sugar. This didn't need sugar. The flavor was so deep, so rich . . .

"It's . . ." She struggled for words. "It's like I've never had real coffee before. This is amazing."

Duncan beamed. "It's worth the trouble, isn't it? An anodyne for *weltschmerz*. I'll grind you up some beans to take home. But use them soon. And if you use a regular drip machine, never—*never*—leave the pot on a heater. Always decant the coffee immediately into a carafe. Even the best coffee gets bitter when it's overheated."

"Thanks. I'll remember that."

Gina had had no idea Duncan was such a coffee connoisseur. The rituals, the rules . . . it was like a religion. But the result was awfully good.

They sipped in silence for a moment. Gina wandered along the glass wall and admired the koi pool, the rock garden, and the dwarf shrubs that lined it. She continued on, passing his desk. The top right drawer was open. Inside was a glass injection vial filled with a clear amber fluid. Something else too. Something metallic, almost like a large trocar . . .

Suddenly Duncan was beside her, sliding the drawer closed.

"You were saying?"

"Where was I? Well, the point I was trying to make is that if I can get on a committee member's staff, I can see to it that he gets some straight dope on how these guidelines will affect patient care. And if I can influence him even a little, won't it be worth it?"

Duncan stared at her, slowly shaking his head. "For some time now I've been worrying that you had no direction. I was afraid you were just going to drift, make a career of moonlighting and locum tenens work. Now I almost wish that were the case."

Had he actually been *thinking* about her? "Maybe I'll simply devote myself to lexiphania."

Duncan appeared taken aback. Had she stumped him? Lexiphania—the tendency to use obscure and unusual words. The irony would be rich. How wonderful to catch him with a word that described himself.

Duncan laughed. "Where'd you find that one?"

"Wasn't easy, believe me."

"All right. I plead guilty to compulsive grandiloquism, to singlehandedly trying to correct for the entire language's drift into banality."

Damn. He did know it.

She said, "I don't think it's working."

"More's the pity." He gazed at her, smiling. "Lexiphania . . . that's wonderful. How can I stay angry at you? But seriously, Gina, you've been trained for a higher sort of work than being legislative aide to some pretentious pinhead pol. I hate to see you wasting your talents."

For a moment she was struck by how much he sounded like Peter. He'd said almost exactly the same thing when she'd told him she was leaving Louisiana to get involved in medical politics.

Focusing on Duncan, Gina bit her tongue and thought, I could say the same about your face-lifts.

As if reading her mind he smiled crookedly and said, "Not that I'm one to talk about wasting training."

For an instant there was real pain in his eyes. Her heart went out to him.

"Duncan . . . whatever—"

He held up the coffee carafe. "Refill?"

"No, thanks. Can I ask—?"

"I don't envy you, Gina." Obviously he didn't want to talk about Duncan Lathram. "I wouldn't want to be starting out in medicine today and facing the terrain that's ahead of you."

"All the more reason to get *involved*." Why couldn't he see that?

"But what do you hope to accomplish? What is your goal down there on Capitol Hill?"

"Fair guidelines. *Realistic* guidelines we can all live with."

"Never happen," Duncan said. He sighed. "I hope you know what you're doing, Gina."

"I've given it a lot of thought."

"Have you? They're a pretty corrupt bunch, Gina, and—"

"And I'm so impressionable?"

"No. It's not that. It's just that, well, as doctors, we're a different breed. Our values are different. We don't speak the same language. We don't walk in the same shoes as other people."

"That sounds just a little elitist to me."

He shrugged. "Maybe. But sometimes I think the weight of the life-and-death decisions doctors have to make sets them apart from the rest of humanity. When you've felt someone's life draining through your hands, and you've reeled him back in and sent him home to his family, it does something to you. You've seen things that regular folk will never see, done things they'll never do, glimpsed them at their most vulnerable, when they're stripped of all their pretenses. You've been master of life and death, and that can't help but change you. It leaves you one step removed from everybody else."

Gina had run up against this gods-who-walk attitude all through her residency.

"It's time we ditched the god thing, don't you think? We're not gods, and it's damaging to us and our patients to foster that kind of reverence. We can do extraordinary things, seemingly miraculous things. But we're not gods. We're just people."

He was sullen as he sipped his coffee in silence.

Finally Gina said, "Doesn't look like we'll ever see eye to eye, does it?"

"No, it doesn't."

"Can we agree to disagree, then?"

"I don't suppose I have much choice."

"You could fire me."

"I don't want to do that. But don't expect my blessing."

"I never did." *But I want it, dammit. I wish I didn't, but I do.* "I don't even know if I'll get the job. But if I do I'll have to adjust my schedule to—"

"Cassidy can take up the slack. We'll work it out."

Gina felt a trickle of warmth seeping through her. This was a blessing of sorts, wasn't it? If not, it would have to do.

"Thank you, Duncan. I didn't expect—"

"I want to keep you nearby . . . where I can keep an eye on you."

The warm trickle became a chill. What was *that* supposed to mean?

"Just don't let us down, Gina," he said, his blue eyes burning into hers. "Don't betray us."

He held her locked in his gaze a moment longer, then turned away.

"I'm glad we had this talk, Gina. The first of many, I hope. I'm sure you've got some dictation to catch up on."

"Yes. Sure. I'll see you later."

"Be sure to let me know as soon as you hear from Marsden. As for me, I'm off to the links." He pulled out a key ring and matter-of-factly locked his top drawer. "Surgery tomorrow at eight."

Idly wondering why he bothered locking the drawer, Gina waved and left him.

This was turning out to be one strange day.

7
GINA

"EASY NOW," OLIVER SAID SOFTLY, WATCHING OVER HER shoulder, coaching her. "That's it. Just go easy . . . easy . . ."

Gina hadn't felt like being alone this afternoon. No word from Marsden's office, or from Gerry, so she'd arranged to spend a couple of hours in Oliver's lab practicing her implant-filling technique. She'd learn and get paid for it.

She smelled garlic on his breath and wondered what he'd had for lunch. Nothing low cal, she was sure. Oliver had a weakness for Italian food and didn't seem to care what effect it had on his waistline. Probably linguine and clam sauce, don't spare the garlic—

Better forget Oliver's dietary indiscretions. She needed to concentrate on what she was doing.

Gina had the 26-gauge needle of a tuberculin syringe inserted in the end of one of Oliver's medium-size membranous implants and was injecting it with normal saline. Had this been for real, she'd be working under sterile conditions and filling the implant with Oliver's "secret sauce."

Staring through the magnifying lens centered in the round head of the fluorescent examination lamp, she watched the half-inch-long tubular membrane swell and stretch. Like filling the world's tiniest water balloon.

"It's full now," Oliver said. "Feel that back pressure?"

She hadn't felt any until now—which was why half a dozen membranes lay ruptured on the side of the tray. But this time she did feel a hint of resistance on the plunger.

"Believe it or not, I think I do."

"Swell! Now it's time for the zapper."

Gina repressed a smile as she reached for the cautery handle. Did anyone else on earth still say *swell?* Oliver had to be the last.

He was a bit of an enigma. Didn't seem to have much of a life outside his lab. No wife or family. No significant other that she knew of. He'd had the staff over to his house for a dinner party one night and Gina had felt she knew less about him afterward than before.

"Okay," she said. "I'm ready."

"You know what to do. Just take your time."

Gina had seen Oliver do this a hundred times but had never got this far. She readied the flattened tip of the cautery unit in position near the puncture site, slowly withdrew the needle, then stepped on the round power pedal near her left foot. A tiny blue spark arced from the tip to the implant, searing and coagulating the protein membrane around the puncture.

She watched through the magnifying lens, waiting for a telltale bead of fluid to form, signaling the need for another zap. But the membrane remained dry. She'd sealed the opening.

Success. Finally. A tiny triumph. Hardly made up for the fiasco in Marsden's office Monday or Allard's accident this morning, but right now she'd take anything.

Gina looked up and found Oliver's round face grinning at her.

"It's going to be swell having someone else around who can fill these things. I'm sick to death of it."

"Why don't you just hire an assistant or two to help with the scut work?"

"There's really not all that much to be done at this stage of the studies. And I'd like to limit the number of people who know what we're working with."

"And just what *are* we working with?"

"Secret sauce."

"Oliver, come on. Don't you think I have a right to know?"

He thought a moment. "All right. Fair enough. But keep it under your hat. This solution is not patentable, so I don't want anyone stealing my thunder by beating me to market with it."

"Mum's the word," she said.

"I'm sure I can trust you," he murmured as if he'd just now realized it.

He removed his thick, horn-rimmed glasses as he sat down next to her. He began to talk, rapidly, as if someone had opened a valve. Gina realized he must have been dying to expound on his secret sauce.

"Are you familiar with the work done by the Department of Cell and Structural Biology in the University of Manchester in England?"

"No. Not a bit."

"Not many clinicians are. Okay then, how about fetal surgery? Have you seen any of that?"

"Some down in Tulane. It wasn't part of the internal medicine rotation, obviously, but I picked up some information by osmosis."

"Good. Then you know that a fetus can have surgery in utero and be born months later completely scar free."

"Yes, I remember a couple of OB residents talking about that. This high-risk baby they'd delivered had had a mass removed from its abdominal wall at about sixteen weeks' gestation and was born without a trace of an incision."

"Exactly. But the surgery has to be performed during the first five months. Any procedure done later leaves a scar just as it would on an adult. Cellular biologists have wondered about it for years. What's happening in there? What's different? What prevents the usual excess amount of collagen from being laid down and forming the scars we all know so well? The folks at the University of Manchester came up with the answer a few years ago."

Gina snapped her fingers. She remembered something . . . where had she seen it? "Some sort of growth factor, wasn't it?"

Oliver clapped his hands. "Excellent! Transforming growth factor beta, to be precise. They identified three types of the growth factor, and found that the third, beta type 3, falls off sharply at the end of the second trimester of pregnancy. The type-three molecule—I call it beta-3 for short—has been synthesized since then and that's the key ingredient in the secret sauce."

"So that's the secret behind Duncan's incredible results."

"Uh-uh," Oliver said, wagging a finger. "Duncan has the eyes and the hands that do the remodeling. Even without a drop of beta-3 his patients would have minimal scarring. All I've done is find a way to gild the lily."

"But why the implants? Couldn't he just coat the incisions with beta-3?"

"No. You need it in the final phase of healing. Remember the three stages of wound repair: inflammation, proliferation, and remodeling? Beta-3 does its work in stage three where scar tissue forms to replace granulation tissue. At suturing time, beta-3 would accomplish nothing. You need a means of delayed release."

"Enter the implant."

Oliver smiled. "A classic case of synchronicity. There I was, slaving away, testing antidepressants on rats in Skinner boxes as a psychopharmacologist at GEM Pharma during the day, and at night working in my home on a continuous delivery system for medication. Norplant was the hot topic then, but the Norplant implants have to be removed after five years. I thought I could improve on that, develop an implant that would deliver its medication in a metered dose for five years, maybe longer, and then dissolve. Great idea, no?"

"I take it that didn't happen."

"Not completely. I developed a soft, flexible, crystal-protein matrix that would indeed dissolve without a trace. However, it was nonpermeable. Wouldn't allow a drop of anything on one side to pass through to the other—until it dissolved, and then it would dump its entire contents into the surrounding tissues. I'd come up with nothing more than a very elaborate and expensive way of giving someone an injection. I was terribly discouraged."

"And then along came Duncan."

"Right. After his . . . well, after he left vascular surgery, I heard about Manchester's results with transforming growth factor beta type 3 and saw how my imperfect slow-delivery membrane might be perfect for delivering something else. The FDA approved us for clinical trials and the results have been astounding."

Gina had seen patients on postsurgical follow-up visits and only with a magnifying glass was it possible to tell they'd had surgery. Suddenly Gina was struck by the enormous potential for Oliver's implants.

"But plastic surgery is just icing on the cake," she said. "Think of what you could do in general surgery."

Oliver was nodding excitedly.

"Of course. The implants would have the most value in trauma cases, but they'll become routine in procedures like hysterectomies and appendectomies. A few weeks post-op you could wear your bikini—heck, you could even go to a *nude* beach if you wished—and no one would even guess you'd had surgery."

Gina's hand strayed to the front of her blouse. Through the fabric she could feel the upper end of the thick, numb, puckered ridge of scar that ran the length of her abdomen. Duncan's scar.

Bikini? she thought. I've never owned even a two-piece. Never even considered it.

"But the biggest benefit I see is in pediatrics," Oliver was saying. "Kids scar more than adults, and some of those scars, depending where they are, can be disabling because they don't stretch as the rest of the body grows."

Tell me about it.

"That sounds wonderful."

"It will be. And the word is out. Other surgeons want to try the implant. Companies are calling every day wanting to license it and the FDA has put it on the fast track for approval. And that's only the start. Duncan came up with an innovative idea on how to enhance the implant, and I've just about got the bugs worked out of the new, improved model. And . . ." He raised his hand and wagged his index finger in the air. "*And . . .* someone very important has taken a *very* personal interest in the implant procedure."

"Who?"

"Sorry. I can't tell you. Not yet, anyway."

She didn't want to care, but the way his eyes shone with excitement piqued her curiosity.

"Come on, Oliver. You just told me about beta-3; you can trust me with this too."

"No. Duncan would kill me. It's his secret after all. And it's *big.*"

"Okay," she declaimed with her best forlorn sigh. "I guess I'll just have to read about it in the papers."

"Oh, dear. I hope you never do that. But I have a feeling Duncan may tell you himself when the time comes."

"Speaking of Duncan, you started telling me about the daughter Lisa he 'had.' Does that mean what I think it does?"

Oliver nodded glumly. "She was just eighteen when she died five years ago."

From her days as a teenaged file clerk in Duncan's office, Gina vaguely remembered an occasional mention of his two children, a boy and a girl, both younger than she.

"Five years ago . . . I was away in medical school then. I never heard about it. What happened?"

"A fall. She never regained consciousness. It was terrible. Duncan was devastated. It was the straw that almost broke his back."

"Why? Was there something else?"

"I've said enough. If Duncan wants you to know, I'm sure he'll tell you. He's put it all behind him." His gaze wandered away. "He's put a lot of things behind him." He took a deep breath. "But as for the here and now, why don't you solidify your technique by filling a few more membranes? Then call it a day."

"Will do," she said, and patted his shoulder. "One thing's for sure, Oliver, it looks to me like these implants are going to make you a very rich man."

"Oh, I hope so."

"What are you going to do then?"

"Get as far away from here as I can."

"Really? Where? Hawaii?"

He sighed. "Anyplace where I don't have to watch Duncan wasting his talents like he is . . . prettifying twits and playing . . . *golf!*"

And then he hurried out with his white lab coat flapping around him. Gina stared after him in shock.

8
DUNCAN

DUNCAN GRIPPED THE LITTLE GIRL'S CHIN BETWEEN HIS thumb and forefinger. He tilted her head up, then down, then rotated it left and right.

Her name was Kanesha and she was six. She wouldn't meet his gaze directly, and her hand kept rising and fluttering about the left corner of her mouth, hovering there like a hummingbird that had found a nectar-loaded blossom. Only there was nothing sweet or flowerlike about the thick wad of scar tissue massed at that corner of her mouth.

Her skin was a glossy milk chocolate, her eyes huge and a deeper brown, the color of espresso. She had big white teeth and a smile that would have been knockout beautiful if not for that scar, fusing the lips at the corner, cutting every smile in half.

Her skin was scrubbed, her hair was braided, her shirt and shorts had been ironed. Kanesha and her mother had dressed up for her visit to the doctor.

Duncan liked that, not simply because it showed respect for him, but for themselves as well. Some of the people he saw in the clinic had estranged relations with all species of the soap genus and didn't give a damn. What the hell, it was a free clinic, right?

Right. The maxillofacial clinic occupied a fifth-floor corner of one of D.C. General Hospital's older buildings. The seats and fixtures in the waiting room were worn but clean; the examining room smelled faintly of the bleach that had been used to wipe the counters; its sickly yellow paint was chipped, its examination table needed reupholstering, but the staff was efficient and, more important, they cared.

Duncan turned to Kanesha's mother. "When did this happen, Mrs. Green?"

No father was listed on the intake form, but Duncan had never been able to adjust to the noncommittal "Ms." Cindy Green was young, barely into her twenties, probably little more than a baby herself when she'd had Kanesha. The intake form said she worked as a waitress. She was very pretty in a round-faced, full-lipped way. Duncan studied those lips. Kanesha's mouth would look exactly like her mother's if not for the cicatricial deformity.

"About four and a half years ago. When she was seventeen months old. Happened before I knew it."

How many times had he heard that one?

But he kept his voice neutral: "They're a handful at that age, aren't they."

"One minute she was sitting on the floor playing with the pots and pans. I turn to clean the sink and I hear her scream. I turn around and she . . ." Her throat worked and her voice grew thick. "She was knocked out and her mouth was smoking. I knew she was teething but I never dreamed she'd bite an electrical cord."

"Happens more often than you'd think."

Which was true. Obviously it happened more often in neglected kids, but he didn't think Kanesha was neglected. Just one of those tragic accidents.

Near tragic, actually.

Duncan could fix it.

He was mapping out the incisions now . . . debride the scar tissue, restore the mouth to full width, evert some mucosa for the lips . . .

This wasn't the first time he'd reconstructed an electrical burn on a child's face, and it wouldn't be the last. Kanesha was a lucky one. She'd survived without brain damage, and she had a mother who cared. And now she had him.

A shame he couldn't use the beta-3 on her, but a clinic was no place for an experimental protocol. The hospital didn't want the hassles, and he couldn't blame them. As soon as free-clinic patients heard the word "experimental" they started thinking *Frankenstein* and feared someone was going to use them as guinea pigs.

"Can you fix her, Dr. Duncan? When I saw what you did for little Kennique—"

"Who?"

"Kennique LeFave . . . you know . . . her cheek was all—"

"Oh, yes. Of course." The names people came up with these days. But he certainly remembered the three-year-old who'd fallen from a window last year and ripped the right side of her face to the bone. That had been a real challenge.

"All her mommy does is sing the praises of Dr. Duncan, Dr. Duncan. So I knew I just had to bring Kanesha to you. Do you think you can . . . ?"

Duncan nodded. "It will take a couple of procedures, but yes, I think we can fix her up good as new."

The mother's eyes were intent on Duncan's. "Can you? Can you really?"

"Is that a note of doubt I detect?"

"No, it's just—"

"Smile for me," Duncan said.

"What?"

"Go ahead. Smile."

The mother smiled—a lovely smile, even when forced.

Duncan reached out and grasped her chin just as he had Kanesha's.

"I'd like to make your daughter's smile look just like yours."

"You can do that?" the mother whispered.

Yes. He could. This was the age of miracles, and he was a miracle worker.

But still . . . never promise too much. Better to give them more than they're expecting.

"A certain amount depends on Kanesha. Not everyone heals the same. So . . . a smile like yours . . . that'll be okay?"

The mother smiled softly, hesitantly, but genuinely this time. "Yes. That will be okay."

"Good!" He pressed a buzzer on the wall. A heavyset black nurse entered. "Marge, see if we can set up Kanesha for a facial reconstruction—left upper and lower labial—for late Wednesday morning."

"Next week?" the mother said.

"Too soon?"

"Well, no, I just . . ."

"She's had that scar long enough, don't you think?"

The mother looked at him, staring into his eyes, looking for assurance there.

"Yes," she said finally. "Too long."

As Marge led them out, Cassie Trainor stepped into the room and slipped behind him. She was tall, blond, and well proportioned; her uniforms were tailored to maximize the effect of her ample bust. Midforties, trim, and sexy. She gripped his shoulders and began to knead the muscles at the back of his neck with her thumbs.

"How's Dr. Duncan today?"

Duncan had everyone at the clinic refer to him as "Dr.

Duncan." It was a legitimate moniker and it obscured the Lathram name. He didn't want it getting around that Duncan Lathram was doing charity work. He'd made such a point of refusing to deal with insurance companies—private, government, or whatever—and about performing no surgery that was necessary, that he didn't want to have to explain why he was fixing up ghetto kids for free.

He had stopped explaining.

"I'm fine, and that feels *good*."

"So, what're you doing after we finish here? Ready to buy that drink you've been promising?"

Duncan tried to keep his shoulders from tightening. He'd been ducking Cassie for months now. Not long after his divorce they'd had a little fling. Very hot. Too hot not to cool down, as the song went. She was an excellent nurse and uninhibited under the covers. He remembered one night when . . . no, now was not the time to relive that, not with her fingers kneading his shoulders. Eventually, they'd gone their own ways, but every now and again Cassie seemed to like to fan the embers of old blazes. Duncan knew there were plenty of old blazes in Cassie's past. Too many for comfort nowadays when casual sex had stopped being a recreational sport and metamorphosed into serious business, *grim* business, requiring research and background checks, especially with someone with such a busy and enthusiastically varied history as Cassie Trainor.

He hated that something so basic and so wonderful as sex had become a source of paranoia and anxiety, a new religious sect with purification rites and latex Eucharists.

What a world. What a goddamn screwed-up world.

Casual sex was all he had the heart for these days, and casual sex was like Russian roulette. No time or heart to invest in a lasting relationship, and no desire to pursue one, not after what had happened to his marriage.

What had happened to him since the divorce? Where had

his passion for life gone? He'd withdrawn from all his old friends. Not consciously. He hadn't even realized what was happening until it was done. He spent a lot of time alone now, but that didn't seem to bother him. He didn't know this preoccupied, isolated man he had become.

Maybe Lisa hadn't been an aberration. Maybe it ran in the family.

Whatever the reason, he realized he'd become a man who feared intimacy more than solitude.

But at least today he could tell Cassie the truth.

"I'd love to, Cassie, but I'm meeting my son for dinner."

"Too bad. How old is he now?"

"Twenty-one last month." Lisa would have been 23 last spring, already graduated a year. "Starting his senior year in college. We're trying that new Italian restaurant in Georgetown."

"Il Giardia?"

Duncan laughed. "Not funny. Il Giardinello. I'd ask you along but we're going to talk about *the future.*"

"I getcha. Okay. Maybe next time."

"Definitely."

She glided away and he watched the white fabric of her uniform slide back and forth over her buttocks; an urge rose within and he almost changed his mind, almost called her back. Instead he looked at his watch. He'd have to pick Brad up soon at the house.

The house . . .

Used to be his house too. Now it was just Diana's. He wondered how she could live there, walk through that foyer where . . .

Duncan rubbed his eyes and rose from the chair. When things finally fell apart, he didn't contest the divorce action. So while it wasn't exactly an amicable dichotomy, it never got vicious. He let Diana have what she wanted, agreed to generous alimony payments, and, of course, he'd seen to it that Brad had whatever he needed. He loved his son, wanted to stay close to him, and most of all, wanted to spare him the spectacle of his parents hissing and clawing at each other.

And Duncan got . . . what?

What did I get besides out?

He and Diana still were on speaking terms, but only on neutral, practical matters, never anything personal. And he would never set foot in that house again.

He tended to heal slowly, sometimes not at all. He had no implant full of beta-3 for the soul.

Which was why he had been on the west portico of the Capitol yesterday morning. Trying to heal himself by balancing the scales, by closing the circle, by imposing a symmetry on the chaos his life had become. Only then would this cancerous rage cease its relentless metastasis and allow him to get on with his life.

He barked a laugh in the empty room. His *life?* What life?

Marge poked her head in. "Dr. Duncan . . . you all right?"

"Fine, Marge. Just fine."

That's a laugh, he thought, waving her off. Nothing at all is fine.

Yesterday morning . . . another failure. Why wasn't anything ever simple? Why couldn't things go the way he planned?

Neither of the other two had gone the way he'd intended either.

Lane and Schulz, both dead, one in a car, the other in a twenty-story swan dive.

And yesterday . . . Allard was supposed to crack up in front of the cameras, not crack his skull on the Capitol steps. Duncan hadn't wanted him physically hurt. Hell, any hired thug could do that. He'd come prepared to see Allard mortally embarrassed, terminally humiliated, politically ruined; he'd wanted his credibility bloodied, not his head.

Damn! All the planning, the exquisite timing, wasted. Now Allard was just a victim of a bad fall, pitied, pathetic, an object of sympathy instead of ridicule.

Duncan wondered at his own coldheartedness, but only briefly. He had plenty of warm emotions left, but they were already spoken for. No leftovers for the likes of Congressman Allard.

Allard, at least, was still alive.

Next time . . . next time he'd get it right.

Duncan rubbed his eyes. He'd started this for a payback in kind, not to kill or maim. Merely devastate their careers, their marriages, their reputations, and let them live among the ruins. A living death.

Like mine.

Although not his intent, the fatalities didn't particularly bother him. After all, Lisa was dead because of them, and she was worth ten, twenty, a hundred of them.

Gina's presence yesterday had been another complication, one of those perverse coincidences that might one day trip him up and expose what he'd been doing.

Slim as it was, the possibility of exposure knotted his gut. Indictment for murder, a circus of a trial, then jail. The scandal . . . what would it do to Brad? His son was one of the few things left in his life that mattered to him.

He'd do anything to avoid that. Anything.

But where was the risk, really? He had a virtually untraceable toxin, and an all-but-invisible means of delivery. The only one who might put it together would be Oliver, but his preoccupied brother tended to take little notice of events outside his lab. The only other real risk was someone like Gina. Someone who knew the patients, knew about the implants, and was bright enough to put all the pieces together.

Remote as it was, he grimaced at the possibility. What a frightful quandary that would be. What would he do if Gina stumbled onto him? He'd have to find a way to neutralize her. He couldn't allow her to . . .

He shook off the grim train of thought. It wouldn't happen. Vincent would be the next to last. One more after him and then Duncan would close this chapter of his life.

But the last one would be the big one. The biggest.

9
MARTHA

GINA DELAYED HER RETURN TO THE APARTMENT. SHE didn't want to hear any bad news. And no news was bad news as far as the Hill was concerned. The capper would be a message from Gerry telling her he had to call off their dinner plans; or worse yet: no call from Gerry at all.

Gimme a break, she thought. Something's got to go right this week.

So she got off the Metro at the zoo and did a slow walk along Calvert Street across the Duke Ellington Bridge into her neighborhood.

Adams Morgan was sometimes described as funky, sometimes eclectic, but most times just plain weird. Gina loved the area. A big triangle on the hill sloping down toward Dupont Circle, roughly bordered by Calvert Street and Florida and Connecticut avenues, where you could find ethnic jewelry, folk art, and cutting-edge music while breathing the exotic aromas of an array of cuisines that could rival the entire United Nations for diversity. Where else in the District could you find an Argentine café flanked by a top-notch French restaurant and a Caribbean bistro? Even Ethiopian restaurants. Who'd ever heard of an Ethiopian restaurant? Yet there were three in her neighborhood.

Gina browsed an African bookstore, did touchy-feely with some Guatemalan fabric, tried on some Turkish shoes, then decided she'd delayed the inevitable long enough. She walked to her building, an old brick row house on Kalorama between Columbia and Eighteenth; it had a tower on its downhill side and was painted sky blue. She let herself into her third-floor apartment.

The rental agency had listed it as "furnished." Gina thought "not unfurnished" would have been more in line with most truth-in-advertising laws. The rickety furniture had been varnished so many times that the type of wood underlying all those coats was a mystery. Sometimes she suspected the varnish was the only thing holding some of the pieces together. But it was clean, and she loved her front bay window high over the street. She'd had a new mattress delivered and added a few of her own touches—a bright yellow throw rug and her three posters of Monet's *Les Nymphéas*. She kept meaning to brighten up the place, maybe with some new curtains. As soon as she had the time.

She went straight to her bedroom where the answering machine crouched on the nightstand. The message light was blinking. A good start.

The first call was from her mother, wanting to know when Gina would be able to come over for a family dinner.

"Soon, Mama," she said aloud. "Soon." Her schedule didn't leave her much free time, but she made a point of getting back to the old homestead in Arlington at least twice a month.

The next voice was Gerry's.

"Hi, Gina. It's Gerry. Look, uh, things aren't working out quite the way I'd hoped for dinner."

Oh, great. What's the excuse?

"But I'd like to try to get together with you tonight. It's just that we'll have to eat a bit more down market than I'd planned. Can we meet at a, uh, Taco Bell? There's one up your way on Connecticut, near Veazey, I think. It's a long story and I'll explain it all when you get there. *If* you get there. Which I hope you do. But if you can't make it I'll understand. Just let me know if you're not gonna show, otherwise, see you there at six. *Hasta la vista.*"

Gina pressed the repeat button. Yes, she'd heard it right: Taco Bell. Truth was, she liked Taco Bell, but it didn't quite make her short list of restaurants for a rendezvous with an old high school crush.

On the bright side: at least he hadn't stood her up.

But Taco Bell?

Gina hunted for a parking space amid the flow of D.C. workers heading home to Maryland. Connecticut Avenue was mostly residential at its northern end—strips of street-front shops interspersed with low-rise apartments and an occasional office building, all flanked by magnificent oaks and elms. Only three or four miles from Capitol Hill but like another country.

She found a spot up the street from the Taco Bell and turned off the engine.

Now what?

She scanned the curb and sidewalk around the storefront. No sign of Gerry. She didn't know what his car looked like. She didn't feel like going inside just to stand around, waiting. In fact, she didn't like any of this. Where was his wife, if he still had one? Why Taco Bell? Why had she even come?

Lighten up, Panzella.

Five minutes of watching a steady stream of bodies of all races and ages in and out of the door and no Gerry.

All right. Let's get this over with.

She went inside and looked around. This storefront Taco Bell wasn't as heavy on the southwestern motif as its freestanding kin she'd seen in Louisiana; it sported a few adobe touches, but the service counter, the soft drink machine, the booths and tables were all generic fast-food decor. Nothing generic about the aromas, though. The air was redolent of onions and spices. Gina realized how hungry she was.

She heard her name, turned, and saw Gerry waving from the other side of a partition. He stood as she approached but when she reached his booth she saw that he wasn't alone. Another female occupied the opposite bench. She was adorable, with short, wavy blond hair and huge blue eyes. She looked to be about five and was working on a burrito half the length of her arm.

"I'm really sorry about this," Gerry said. "My sitter had unbreakable plans for this evening. This is my daughter Martha. Martha, say hello to Gina—I mean, Dr. Panzella."

Martha waved and smiled around a mouthful of burrito.

"Martha's a vegetarian," he said.

Gina stared at her. "Get out."

He raised his right hand, palm out. "True. I swear. I could put you on and say it's an ethical position but the fact is she just doesn't like meat. Never did. Even as a baby she used to spit out her junior foods if they were so much as flavored with meat."

"But she'll eat tacos?"

"Bean burritos. *Loves* bean burritos—with green sauce and extra cheese. Right, Martha?"

The little blonde looked up and nodded vigorously. Obviously she'd been following every word. "And hold the onions," she added in a squeaky voice.

Gerry beamed at her. "Right. Always hold the onions. So that's why we're here. Miss Fussytummy has a very limited palate, so there was no point in bringing her anywhere else. I hope you don't mind. I'll make it up to you, I promise."

Gina had been taken completely by surprise by Martha but was charmed and touched by the warm father-daughter bond she sensed.

"Don't be silly. I'm glad you brought her. In fact, I'm honored to meet her."

"Great. What can I get you?"

"How about two bean burritos with extra cheese . . ." She winked at Martha. "And hold the onions."

Martha grinned and scrinched up one side of her face in a grotesque attempt to return the wink. Gina laughed and sat down opposite her.

"Are you a real doctor?" Martha said, cocking her head and looking up at her. Her cheeks were pink roses, her skin flawless.

"Yes, I am."

"Do you give shots?"

"Sometimes."

"I don't like shots." She held up a pair of fingers. "I had to get *two* shots before they let me into kinnergarden."

What a darling. So relaxed, so comfortable with a stranger. Obviously she liked people, and that spoke volumes about her home life.

"Shots keep you from getting sick."

She gave a Jackie Mason shrug. "I still get sick!"

Gina was saved by Gerry's return.

"I brought you a Mountain Dew. Through extensive research and experimentation, Martha and I have determined that Taco Bell food goes best with a Dew."

"Mountain *Deeeew!*" Martha said and raised her cup. Gerry clicked his own against it, then Martha waited, eyeing Gina expectantly. She clicked her own cup against Martha's, then they all sipped.

"Sorry there's nothing higher octane available," Gerry said.

"Since I have to play doctor in less than two hours, Mountain Dew has all the octane I need."

Gina watched across the table as Gerry slid in next to his daughter. She saw the resemblance between the two—same blond hair, same blue eyes, same nose and smile. And the way that little smile flashed for Gerry . . . here was a little girl who loved her daddy.

Gina was intrigued, maybe even fascinated. She'd been looking forward to this time with Gerry as a way of tying up one of her life's loose ends. A date—if you could call it that—with the big man on campus, something she'd dreamed of all through high school. But Gerry was so much more than she'd expected. He was warm, he was open, and he was a doting father. She liked that. Liked it a lot. She wanted to know more about him. The closure she'd sought here was opening to something new.

Between bites and sips they caught up on the decade or so since high school. Gerry told her about joining the FBI after graduating UVA with a criminology degree but never mentioned marriage or where Martha came from. It took all her will to keep from asking. He nodded encouragingly as Gina took her turn and skimmed through her education, but his head snapped up when she mentioned Duncan Lathram.

"You work for Lathram? The celebrity surgeon?"

"He's not the celebrity, just his patients."

"Yeah," Gerry said sourly. "And you've got to be a celebrity to be treated by him."

Gina wondered at the sudden note of hostility in his voice.

"Every day he treats people no one's ever heard of."

Gerry leaned forward and pointed to the hairline scars on his face. "He wouldn't take me."

"How . . . ?"

"MVA." He glanced quickly at Martha. "Tell you about it sometime."

Motor vehicle accident. So that explained the scars.

"Whoever worked on you did a nice job."

"Dr. Hernandez is tops. But I requested Lathram first and he wouldn't even give me a consultation."

"Duncan takes only certain kinds of cases."

"The insurance company was footing the bill, so it wasn't a question of money. Why wouldn't he help me?"

She was tempted to say, Because he won't operate on anyone who needs him, just people who want him. Just vanity surgery, the more fatuous and narcissistic, the better. No trauma repair. But how could Gina explain what she herself didn't understand? Better not to get into it.

"I don't know, Gerry. He's got some strange ideas about who he takes as patients."

"And some of his patients have had some bad luck lately."

"You mean like Congressman Allard?"

Gerry stiffened in his seat. "That guy who fell this morning? On the Capitol steps? He was a Lathram patient too?"

"What do you mean, 'too?'"

Gerry didn't answer immediately. His eyes took on a faraway look. What was he thinking? And how did the FBI know—and why should they care—who was and wasn't Duncan's patient?

His mind racing, Gerry stared past Gina at the chicken fajitas poster on the window behind her.

Allard was a Duncan Lathram patient too. That made three . . . three Lathram patients with fatal or near-fatal accidents in the past month or so. What could—?

"Gerry?"

He shook himself free of speculation and focused on Gina again.

God, he was drawn to her. All that glossy black hair and deep brown, almost-black eyes, and he loved the way her mouth curved up at the corners when she smiled. He'd never noticed any of that when she was an overweight kid. But then, he'd never looked at her much when she was Pasta.

That had to be part of it. They had a history. He'd known her when, back in the Bad Old Days when she was a homely chubette, and again, now, when she was sleek and turning heads.

But he hadn't known her then, not really, and he certainly didn't know her now. But he sensed things about her, strength and confidence surging within her, and that was as sexy as anything external.

She'd remade herself—decided how she wanted to be, *who* she wanted to be, and become that person.

And now that person was waiting for an answer.

He said, "Two powerful legislators have died in the past month. Congressman Lane and Senator Schulz. Both were—"

"Patients of Duncan Lathram. I know. But they were accidents. Weren't they?"

"That's what they appear to be so far."

"How did you know they were both Duncan's patients?"

He narrowed his eyes and said, "Vee haf vays . . ." while his mind ranged ahead, calculating how much he should and could tell her.

"I'm serious, Gerry."

She seemed upset. Why? Lathram was just her boss. Or was there more to it?

"It just happened to come up in the investigations."

"I heard about the investigations. Why?"

"Two political bigwigs? Violent deaths within a few weeks

of each other? The Bureau investigates. If there *is* a connection, we want to be the first to know."

"Oh," she said, leaning back. "I guess that makes sense."

"Allard's accident wasn't fatal, but he won't be doing much legislating for a while."

"What do you mean?"

"Apparently he's been babbling nonsense since he came to in the hospital."

"Really?" she said, her brow furrowing. "Must be some sort of postconcussion syndrome. Poor guy."

"Must be."

Three disabling mishaps—two permanently so—and all patients of Duncan I'm-sorry-but-the-doctor-doesn't-handle-posttrauma Lathram. Gerry wondered what other links the three men might have to the good doctor.

"'Scuse me, Dad."

Gerry looked around as Martha nudged him with her hip.

"Where do you think you're going, miss?"

"Need another Mountain Dew."

"Think you can handle it yourself?"

She rolled her eyes. "Da-deee!"

"Okay, but only half a cup." He slid off the bench to let her out. "Got enough money?"

Another roll of the baby blues. "Free refills, Dad!"

"Right. I knew that."

He sat down again but never let her out of his sight as she made her way to the drink dispenser. She knew exactly what to do, and half of her fun in coming here was holding the cup under the ice dispenser and letting the cubes clunk into it, then filling it from the Mountain Dew spigot. So he let her do it on her own. But Gerry was watching her and everybody around her. Anybody got the least bit frisky with Martha and he'd been on them like a pit bull on a T-bone.

"She's a doll," Gina said.

"That she is," he replied, never taking his eyes off her.

"You never mentioned her mother."

He glanced at Gina's intent expression, then back toward the drink dispenser.

"Remember Karen Shannick? The tall blond?"

"The cheerleader? Sure."

"Well, she went to UVA too. We got serious in college and were married right after. Martha came along about a year later."

"You still together?"

He pointed to the scars on his face and spoke quickly to get the story out before Martha came back.

"These are from a windshield. A rainy night on 50. Truck jackknifed in front of us. I was driving, Karen was in the passenger seat, Martha in her car seat behind me. We slid right into the truck. Martha was fine, my face was hamburger, and Karen . . . Karen didn't make it."

Out of the corner of his eye he saw Gina's hand dart to her mouth.

"Oh, my God! I'm so sorry!"

Not as sorry as I was.

"The really sad part is, Martha doesn't remember her mother. We have pictures, but that's all Karen is to Martha. I wish . . ."

His throat constricted. Karen had been the careful one, and she'd been wearing her seat belt; Gerry hadn't bothered with his that night. Yet Karen was dead and Gerry was alive.

Wasn't fair.

He saw them sliding across the wet pavement, swerving out of control, his hands hauling on the steering wheel as he rammed the brakes to the floor, watching the rear corner of the truck loom in the passenger window before it smashed through the glass into Karen. . . .

Not fair.

He'd been an emotional basket case afterward, and his cut-up face only added to the misery. Martha hadn't recognized him, screamed whenever she saw him. He looked like the Frankenstein monster. And Dr. Duncan Lathram had refused to treat him . . .

He blinked and saw Martha hurrying back to him with her brimming plastic cup of Mountain Dew clutched between her little hands. She'd never finish it all, but so what? She'd gone and filled it herself.

"So Martha and I are managing on our own," he said as he helped her back into her seat. "And trying to spend as much time together as my schedule permits."

Which wasn't nearly enough for him. But what could he expect as a field agent? This wouldn't last much longer, he hoped. As soon as he was offered an SSA spot, he was taking it—no matter where it was—so he could get on a nine-to-five schedule and be with her more. Right now she went to kindergarten, then after school to Mrs. Snedecker's. Thank God for Mrs. Snedecker.

He smoothed Martha's blond bangs and adjusted her Minnie Mouse barrettes. Incredible how much he'd learned. He could bathe Martha, shampoo hair, wash clothes, iron dresses, buy tights. His mother had helped some, but last year her heart had given out.

So it was Gerry and Martha. And God he was glad to have her. She'd filled some of the void Karen had left in his life. He might have gone to pieces but he'd had to hold together for Martha.

He still saw Karen. She came to him in his dreams. He'd ask her how he was doing with Martha but she never answered.

How *was* he doing?

Martha smiled up at him and he kissed her forehead.

"But enough about me," he said to Gina. "What were you doing in the Hart Building today? It's not exactly a doctor hangout."

She told him about her quest to have a say in the

Guidelines bill, her lackluster interview with Senator Marsden's chief of staff, and her aborted interview with Allard.

"All that medical cramming and you want to hang with the pols?"

She laughed. "You sound like Duncan."

"Well, maybe he's got a point."

"It's not *all* I want to do—just a part. And I *am* going to do it. All of it." She rattled the cubes in her cup. "I think I could use a refill too."

Gerry reached for her cup and started to rise. "Let me—"

"Thanks," she said, holding it out of his reach, "but I may want a different flavor this time."

Gerry watched her stroll to the drink dispenser, watched most of the other guys in sight follow her progress. Yes, she was definitely worth a second look. Even a third.

And I am going to do it. All of it.

The fiery determination in her eyes made her even more attractive. A self-made woman. She'd gone from a girl who could only be described as a schlub, to a woman with limitless possibilities.

"Martha," he whispered, "I do believe I'm becoming infatuated."

Martha didn't look up. "That's 'cause there's beans in this stuff."

Gerry laughed out loud.

"But don't worry," Martha said. "We can tell Gina about it. She'll make you better. She's a doctor."

"No, no," Gerry said, gently pressing a finger over her lips. "We won't tell Gina anything about it. At least not yet."

10
DUNCAN

DUNCAN AND BRAD STEPPED OUT OF IL GIARDINELLO INTO
the sulfurous air of Georgetown's M Street. The traffic
streaming in from Virginia was stop-and-go, and the carbon
monoxide from the idling cars mixed with the light fog
drifting up from the nearby Potomac. The concoction hung
in the still fall air like a toxic pall.

They turned east and headed back toward the car, passing
a gallimaufry of restaurants, bars, bistros, upscale clothing
and jewelry stores, alternative music shops, and, yes, even a
condom shop.

"Not a bad meal," Brad said.

"No, not bad at all if you like your pasta overcooked, your
veal practically raw, air thick with smoke, and acoustics so
bad you can barely hear yourself think. The service was
dilatory and indifferent at best, the decor was like one of the
Borgias' bad dreams, the wine list wouldn't pass on the
Bowery, and the espresso . . ." He shuddered. "Execrable."
Suddenly he smiled. "I must remember to recommend the
place to your mother."

Brad gave his father a gentle punch on the shoulder. "Come on, now. None of that."

"All right."

"I guess we won't be back here real soon."

"Of course we will. As soon as it changes its name, owner, and chef."

Brad only shook his head, smiling.

Duncan loved this boy, this young man, this good-natured twenty-something with his open face and guileless blue eyes, his long, lean body, his too-long brown hair, the way he never wore socks and never cinched his tie all the way up and never fastened the top button on his shirt.

Memories swirled around him like the leaves starting to drop from the trees—swimming lessons in grammar school, middle school science projects, the trauma of not making the varsity cut for the high-school basketball team, all the ups and downs of raising a child.

Somehow, he thought, we did all right with Brad. We weren't the best parents, what with our preoccupation with Lisa and all her problems, my own self-absorption, but somehow, in spite of everything, Brad turned out all right. A testament to the primacy of nature over nurture.

Impulsively, Duncan threw an arm around his son's shoulder and pulled him close. He wasn't given much to outward displays of affection, but God he loved this boy.

"Thanks for tolerating me."

Brad put an arm around Duncan's waist. "Somebody has to."

Each with an arm still around the other, they crossed Wisconsin and followed M Street's gentle down slope toward Rock Creek.

"So you're not disappointed?" Brad said.

"What do I have to do," Duncan said, "have it tattooed on my forehead? No. En-oh. I am not disappointed."

"That's such an awesome relief, I can't tell you."

Brad had told him he wanted to get together and talk about the future—his plans for his own future. Duncan had suggested dinner. It turned out Brad hadn't so much wanted to discuss what he planned to do with his future, as what he planned *not* to do.

And he did not plan to go to medical school.

Years ago, before his public lapidation by the Guidelines committee, before managed care snared the medical profession in its tendrils, Duncan would have been bitterly disappointed.

But tonight he was almost thrilled.

"Why should I be upset because you don't want to spend another eight-to-ten years in brain-busting study for the privilege of answering to panels of political appointees? The only thing medicine's got going for it anymore is job security."

"Yeah. People will always need doctors, I guess."

"That they will. But the doctor-patient relationship is eroding. There used to be an almost sacred bond between a doctor and a patient that no one could break. The examination room was the equivalent of a confessional. The intimate secrets that used to be hieroglyphically recorded in our crabbed shorthand and hermetically sealed behind the inviolable walls of our offices are now open to any government or insurance company hireling who wants to see them."

"So I've got to be careful what I tell my doctor."

"Damn right. And for your sake he's got to be choosy about what he sets down on paper."

"Sounds pretty grim. But none of that's why. The main reason is it's just not my thing."

He gave Brad's shoulder a gentle squeeze. "Just what *is?*"

"I don't know, Dad. I just don't know."

Duncan sighed. So many of this so-called Generation X seemed to have no idea what they wanted or where they were going. Duncan couldn't understand that. All his life he'd wanted to be a doctor. He'd set a course for it when he was a child. Never could he recall even an instant of uncertainty.

Maybe that was why he felt such kinship with Gina. She was as determined to do things her way as he'd been at her age. Her way wasn't his, but he could forgive her that—she'd see the error of her ways. She was almost like a daughter. Maybe he'd subconsciously slipped Gina into the empty place within that he'd reserved for Lisa. Yes . . . like a daughter. After all, he'd given her life in a way, sewing her insides back together.

But not knowing the next step . . . the anxiety that had to cause. What uncertainties roiled through Brad when he lay in bed at night, asking the dark where his life was headed?

"Whatever you decide, I'm behind you. Any time you—"

"Faggots!"

Duncan started at the word and glanced around. To his right, three shadowy figures slouched in predatory poses in a darkened recessed doorway, each with a bottle or can of some sort in hand. Light from the street reflected from their bare scalps. He kept walking.

"Skinheads," Brad whispered and began to pull his arm from around Duncan's waist.

Duncan grabbed his wrist. "Don't you dare."

"Dad, they think we're—"

"Are you going to let them be the arbiters of how a father and son can walk down the street?"

"I know how you are with the never complain, never explain stuff, but these guys are crazy."

Duncan reached his free hand into his jacket pocket and wrapped his fingers around the metal cylinder there.

"Maybe I'm crazier."

The M Street–Wisconsin Avenue area had always been the tacky section of Georgetown. A farrago of trendily overpriced boutiques, bars, clubs, and evanescent restaurants ranging from upscale ethnic cuisine to Little Tavern Hamburgers, peopled by roaming demimondaines and boulevardiers in search of something called fun. Folksingers had peopled the cafés in the early sixties, giving way to the hippies at the end of the decade. Discos came and went in the seventies. Through it all, the Georgetown street people had upheld a noble tradition of remaining determinedly dissolute but generally good-natured.

Until lately. Strolling the area these days was like navigating a third world bazaar. The boutiques bedizening Wisconsin's terminal slope were cheaper and gaudier, nobody seemed to speak English or be on speaking terms with a bar of soap, and lumpen denizens panhandled on every corner. The slovens of the grunge cadre were as unwashed as the hippies of old, but they lacked the latter's sense of style and humor. The atmosphere was as blowzy as ever, but the mood had turned grim.

Despite a new mall and brighter lighting, the Georgetown street scene, like everything else, was changing for the worse.

What a world. What a screwed-up world.

They moved out of the pedestrian traffic and turned right onto 29th; Duncan had parked the Mercedes on the hill that fell away toward the C&O Canal. He was just turning the key in the lock when something whizzed by his head and smashed on the sidewalk half a dozen feet away.

"Faggots!"

The light wasn't as good here as up on M, but he had no trouble recognizing the skinheads. The three of them were trotting down the hill. They must have belonged to some sort of gang because they all wore jeans, black leather jackets, and fingerless black leather gloves. One carried a Budweiser can, one was empty-handed but repeatedly pounded his fist into his palm, and the guy in the lead carried some sort of metal pipe.

"Shit, Dad," Brad said. "Let's get out of here."

Duncan's mouth was dry. His legs urged him to run but

his feet seemed anchored to the pavement. The thugs were too close and moving too fast. No time to get in the car, get it started, and maneuver out of the parking spot. His heart began to hammer as he pulled the little cylinder from his pocket and held it down by his thigh, out of sight.

"Time to make some faggo-burgers," said the leader, grinning as he raised the pipe and charged. His two companions were close behind.

"Hey, listen!" Brad shouted. "We're not—"

"Quiet, Brad."

Duncan's thumb found the trigger atop the little cylinder. It slipped and swiveled in his sweaty palm. His hand shook wildly as he raised the canister and shot a stream of liquid at the leader's face.

It missed, arcing past the raised pipe to splash against the throat and upper chest of the second in line. As that one gagged and turned, throwing his arms across his eyes and mouth, Duncan adjusted the stream and caught the leader square in the face. He dropped the pipe and fell to his knees, choking, clawing at his eyes. Meanwhile the third skinhead had run into the second, who had skidded to a stop and doubled over. The two went down in a tangled heap.

"Fucking Mace!" screamed the third.

Duncan caught him square in the mouth with a squirt and that was the last he heard from him.

Duncan sagged back against his car, gasping, panting as if he'd run a marathon. He could feel his underwear sticking to his sweaty skin. How long had it taken? Three seconds? Five? Seemed like so much longer. Whatever the interval, the three attackers had been reduced to writhing, wheezing, groaning, gagging, cursing lumps of blind flesh.

"Thank God, Dad!" Brad said. "I didn't know you carried Mace."

Actually it was pepper spray—five-percent capsicum. Duncan had never had occasion to use it before now. He was impressed. And almost giddy with relief. He held it up to the light.

"Not exactly a John Wayne thing, I know," Duncan said. "But since I'm not exactly a street fighter, I figured it was the prudent thing to do." He slipped the canister back into his pocket. "Maybe we should—"

The rattle of steel on concrete made Duncan turn. One of the skinheads had picked up the pipe and was on his feet, careening their way. His eyes were puffy slits, streaming tears. He couldn't see. He had to be homing in on their voices. Duncan lurched out of the way as he saw the bar swing wildly in his direction. It left a chipped dent in the car fender near where he'd been leaning an instant before.

Rage flared in Duncan. Impulsively he grabbed the steel shaft of the pipe and ripped it from the staggering skinhead's grasp. Then he swung it like a bat, catching him on the side of the head, sending him sprawling into his two companions, who had struggled to their hands and knees.

Duncan found himself standing over them, flailing away with the pipe, "You . . ." muttering through clenched teeth ". . . dirty . . ," as he cracked a head, ". . . filthy . . ." broke a rib, ". . . rotten . . ." crushed a nose ". . . lousy . . ."

Then someone had ahold of his arm and a familiar voice was shouting in his ear.

"Dad! For Christ sake! *Dad!*"

He turned. Brad's face was inches from his, staring at him with wide, frightened eyes.

"Dad, you're gonna kill them!"

Duncan looked down at the squirming, bloody tangle of their attackers. He dropped the steel bar and turned toward the car.

"Let's get out of here." The keys rattled in his shaking hand as he fished them out of his jacket pocket. "You drive."

The next few minutes were a blur, a fugue state in which

he was vaguely aware of the car moving, pulling away, joining the flow of traffic on M Street. He sat in the passenger seat, shaking, shivering, trembling with the aftereffects of the adrenaline that had surged into his system moments before. High-pitched beeps brought him around.

Brad was punching the buttons on the car phone.

"What are you doing?"

"Calling nine-one-one."

Duncan gently pulled the phone from his son's fingers and turned it off.

"No police. Let them crawl back to their cave and lick their wounds. Maybe they'll think twice or even three times before they jump another 'faggot.'"

"Shouldn't we report—?"

"If we involve ourselves, you know what will happen? *We'll* be on trial for assaulting *them*. That's the way our legal system works."

They drove in silence for a while before Brad spoke again.

"Why wouldn't you tell them?"

"Tell them what?"

"That we're not gay."

Gay. He hated that term. He couldn't imagine anything gay about being a homosexual. And he was a little disappointed in Brad. He just didn't get it.

"That's not the point. If I want to put my arm around my son's shoulder, that's my business. I don't need anyone's permission but yours. I will no more allow myself to be dictated to by these troglodytes on the street than by the decerebrates on Capitol Hill. Once you start backing down, you've got to keep backing down. So you don't start."

"But what happened to you back there, Dad? I've never seen you like that."

"That's because I've never *been* like that."

He was nonplussed at the volatility of the rage seething within him. He'd long been aware of its presence, had felt it percolating through him for years, but he'd thought he had it focused now, slowly bleeding off in the direction of the proper targets. He hadn't realized it was so near the surface, so ready to break free and hurl him at the nearest target.

"You're a scary guy, Dad."

He nodded. "Sometimes I scare myself."

11
GINA

GINA HAD JUST FINISHED CHECKING A PATIENT WITH chest pain on Three North at Lynnbrook. She couldn't help thinking about Gerry and what a nice time she'd had with him and Martha earlier at that little Taco Bell. Dinner at the Palms wouldn't have been half as warm. She'd hated to leave.

As she passed the nurses station she spotted Dr. Conway leaning on the counter, writing orders. She was surprised to see him. It was almost midnight, and usually she was the only doctor in the house at this hour.

He looked up and smiled as she took a seat on the other side of the counter. He tapped the chart in front of him.

"Hey, Panzella. If I'd known you were in the house tonight I'd've let you handle this guy."

"Maybe you should have. You look beat." She wasn't exaggerating. He had circles under his eyes. "Go get some sleep."

"Soon as I finish this progress note, I'm gone."

Gina spotted Harriet Thompson's chart and pulled it out of the rack. "I see your favorite little old lady is still here."

"Harriet?" He nodded and sighed. "Yeah. And still not ready to go home, unfortunately. 'Weak as a kitten,' she says."

Gina flipped through the chart. "All her numbers still look good."

"Perfect."

"You think there might be some secondary gains here? Like maybe she gets more attention here than at home?"

"No. She's a real independent old lady. Hates it here. I think she's got some sort of postinfection asthenia. I've seen it before, especially after a pneumonia like hers. You can't see it, can't touch it, there's no lab test to confirm it. Mostly a diagnosis by exclusion."

"The administration still on your back?"

"That's only half the story." He shook his head wearily. "It's getting a little ugly. They've brought in reinforcements. I've had calls from the head of the family practice section and from the chief of staff himself. Nothing's been said in so many words, but they've dropped broad hints that I might have a rough time moving up to full attending here if I don't prove myself to be 'a team player.'"

No wonder he looked harried.

"You can't get any family involved?"

"Called the daughter in San Diego. Talked to her myself. She can't get away. It's 'not a good time' for her."

"So what's your next step?"

"Same as ever. Screw 'em. She stays till she's ready to go."

He closed the chart in front of him, left it where the charge nurse could review it, and pushed away from the counter.

"See you, Panzella."

"Hang in there," she said as she watched him go.

Gina was worried. He could be headed for trouble here if he didn't back down soon.

Her thoughts drifted back to Gerry and what he'd said earlier about Duncan's patients. Lane, Schulz, and now

Allard . . . Gerry seemed to suspect a connection. What would he think if Gina told him that Duncan had been on the Capitol portico this morning, talking to Allard just before he fell? That he'd mentioned his dead daughter's name as a parting shot?

But how could she describe the frightening look in Duncan's eyes as he'd turned away from the congressman. The memory still gave her a chill.

This was silly. What connection could there be between Congressman Allard and Duncan's daughter? She died five years ago. Gina was pretty damn sure from the presurgical history and physical she'd done on the congressman that he'd never met Duncan until he'd come in for a surgical consultation.

But still . . . it bothered her. She promised herself that when she had some time she'd do a little independent research on the late Lisa Lathram.

Gina was just stepping out of the stairwell on the first floor when she got paged again. She called the switchboard from the doctors lounge.

"Personal call," said the operator. "Long distance."

Who, she wondered, would be calling her here, long distance?

"Gina?" came a familiar drawl. "Gina, is that you?"

"Peter! How did you find me here?"

"Wasn't easy."

She sat on the bunk and leaned back. Peter Hanson's dark eyes and strong, angular features floated before her.

"It's so good to hear your voice."

"I miss you, Gina."

"Oh, and I miss you."

She felt almost guilty now about dinner with Gerry tonight and enjoying it so much. They were two different types, really—

Why was she thinking about Gerry with Peter on the phone?

He was talking about how empty their old apartment was without her, how lonely he was.

"We really could use another internist here, Gina. Some-one with your talent, your personality, and, being a woman to boot, I guarantee you'd have a beautiful practice in three months. We need you, Gina. *I* need you."

Needed . . . wouldn't that be nice. No one seemed to need her around here.

She'd spent the last two years of her residency with Peter. He joined a multispecialty medical group in Baton Rouge. Gina had had an offer from the same group but turned it down. She'd felt she had to come to Washington and wanted Peter to come with her. They'd gone around and around with it until she'd finally left to return east.

As she listened to his voice she realized how much she missed him, missed Louisiana with its slower pace and rich, spicy food. And Peter.

And now, after the cool reception at Senator Marsden's office and still no call, it was so tempting to call it quits here and run back to New Orleans.

She ached to be with him but she couldn't go back. Not even for a visit. She might never leave, might never have the strength to say good-bye again.

"Peter, I need to see if I can work things out with this committee."

"You don't need a damn committee, Gina. You need to be practicing medicine."

They'd had this conversation dozens of times and it always ended the same: Peter angry and Gina upset.

How could she say it without hurting him?

I still care very deeply for you, Peter, but the power here, the enormity of the decisions being made every day . . . it's an adrenaline buzz like nowhere else in the world. It's, well, it's intoxicating.

She opted for her old standby instead.

"We've been over this so many times, Peter. I'm not ready to commit myself to a practice yet. There are a few things I want to try first, and this is the only place I can try them."

"How long am I supposed to wait?" he said with a hint of an edge in his voice.

"I'm waiting, too, Peter. I'm going half crazy waiting."

He sighed. "Fine. Keep me hanging. Let me know when you find out what you're going to do. As *soon* as you find out."

"I will. And I'm sorry."

"That makes two of us. Bye, Gina. Call me soon."

She sat in the doctors lounge for a long time with the phone in her lap, wondering how she could be right if everyone else thought she was wrong. Her beeper chirped before she came up with an answer.

They wanted her on Two South.

THE WEEK OF SEPTEMBER

24

12
GINA

OVER A WEEK NOW SINCE THE INTERVIEW AND STILL no word from Senator Marsden's office. Chances of a call from Joe Blair seemed slim to none but Gina kept hoping the senator himself might intervene. Because throughout her meeting with Blair she'd got the impression that he was deigning to interview her only because his boss wanted it.

The waiting was affecting her concentration. She had to resist the urge to call her answering machine every hour. The Guidelines committee started hearings in another week. Time was getting short.

True to her promise, though, she wasn't forgetting about looking into Lisa Lathram. The question was how. She had a feeling Oliver had said all he was going to say, and she couldn't very well ask Duncan.

Wouldn't the sudden death of the daughter of a prominent local warrant some newspaper coverage?

Yes, it would. She called the D.C. Public Library and they connected her with their periodicals section. They were most cooperative but could come up with only one reference to Lisa Lathram. In the August 17 issue of the *Washington Post:* her obituary. Gina stopped in the main branch on G Street and found it on microfilm.

No help there. Except for mention of the survivors, it might as well have been a high school yearbook entry.

Gina would have liked to surf through the microfilm but she was due at Lynnbrook to do her house-doctor thing, so she left that for another day.

She wasn't giving up on this. When Gina had left for medical school, Duncan was a top Virginia vascular surgeon with a wife and two children; when she returned from residency he was a divorced Maryland plastic surgeon with one child.

Something had happened in that interval to turn his life upside down. Lisa's death? Maybe. Or maybe that was just a part of it. There had to be more. And Gina made up her mind to find out what it was.

While on Three North at Lynnbrook she passed Mrs. Thompson's room and decided to stick her head in the door to see how she was doing. She saw the old woman shuffling between the chair and the bed. She tottered forward and would have fallen if she hadn't caught hold of the metal footboard.

Gina stepped into the room as Harriet eased herself onto the bed.

"You should call for a nurse before you try anything like that," Gina said as she helped her under the covers.

"I'm practicing. I've got to go home. I don't want to get Dr. Conway in trouble."

Curious, Gina sat on the end of the bed. "What makes you think he's in trouble?"

"I overheard two of the nurses talking. They said the TRO and the hospital were on his back because of me."

"That's *PRO*—Physician Review Organization. And don't you worry about Dr. Conway. He can take care of himself. You just worry about getting stronger."

"Don't worry. I'll be strong enough to go home real soon. You can count on that. Real soon."

"Good for you," Gina said. "And remember: Call the nurse when you need to get up. You fall and break a hip you'll never get out of here."

"That will never happen. I'll not be a burden on anyone. I'll be out of here sooner than you think."

"That's the spirit."

Gina liked the old woman's determination. Maybe things would work out for Dr. Conway after all.

A September storm was drenching the city when Gina dragged herself into her apartment around half past eight. As she passed the bedroom she noticed the message light on her answering machine blinking. Probably Gerry again. She'd been playing telephone tag with him since Taco Bell. Their schedules weren't meshing. When he was free, she was moonlighting. But they'd managed to connect last Friday when Gerry delivered on his promise to take her out to "a real restaurant for a real dinner."

That turned out to be a delightful evening. A little French place on Massachusetts. Good wine, good food, and good conversation. They talked and talked, lingering over coffee until the maitre d' informed them that the place was closing. She learned that Gerry Canney was not only a dedicated father, he was a dedicated FBI agent as well.

She yawned. Tired. This was no way to live. The rest of the city was up and about and starting the day while hers was just finishing. Luckily she didn't have to assist Duncan today.

She sat in the bay window, watched the rain splatter and run down the panes, then sifted through her mail. Mostly "Occupant" fliers and the throwaway medical journals that had tracked her down and followed her from Tulane. The pile yielded two letters, both from medical headhunters looking for board-certified or board-eligible internists or family practitioners to fill primary-care slots. She averaged half a dozen offers a week.

"Tired of being on call? Need a change of scenery?"

As a matter of fact, yes.

"Move to sunny Nevada."

She read on. A new Las Vegas megahotel was opening an on-premises clinic for its ten thousand employees.

No thanks.

The other letter played coy with the precise location, but guaranteed $120,000 plus benefits to start as the fifth member of a family practice group "located just ninety minutes from beach, mountains, and D.C."

Gina thought about $120,000 to start . . . wouldn't that be nice. The profession had been running low on primary-care docs for years, probably because they occupied the bottom rung in prestige and income. But the growth of managed care had created a sudden demand for the lowly generalist. Over twenty-three hundred dollars a week, probably for fewer hours than she was working now. Tempting.

But not yet.

She dropped the letters into her lap and gazed down at the street, watching the fallen yellow leaves swirl as they floated down the gutter toward 18th Street. Was she kidding herself? Was this whole idea of hooking up with the Guidelines committee a fool's errand? Was Peter right? Wasn't she wasting her training by doing presurgical medical clearance on Duncan's patients when she could be in a real practice treating her own patients?

Maybe. But this wouldn't last forever.

She spoke silently to the city beyond her window.

I know it looks like I'm just treading water, folks, but trust me: I really do have a direction. It's just that lately the current always seems to be running against me. But don't worry. The tide will change.

At least she hoped it would.

I've got the blues, she thought. And why not? It's a damp, chilly, crummy morning, I've been up all night, my energy has bottomed out, and I'm overtired.

Not the best time to make big decisions.

She tossed the headhunter letters and occupant mail into the wastebasket, and put the journals aside to skim later. Then she hit the button on her answering machine. It would be good to hear Gerry's voice.

But instead of Gerry it was an unfamiliar woman's voice.

"Ms. Panzella. This is Senator Marsden's office. Mr. Blair asked me to call and inform you that Senator Marsden wishes to personally interview you tomorrow afternoon at four P.M. If you cannot make it at that time, the senator will not be able to reschedule. Please call to confirm that you will be there." She left a number and an extension.

Gina realized with a start that the message had been left sometime yesterday. "Tomorrow" was today.

She replayed it. She'd only met Joe Blair once, but she could smell him all over that message. "Ms."—incapable of calling her "Doctor." The arbitrary time and no rescheduling. She could almost hear his voice: Do or die, Panzella.

She sensed some sort of a power struggle. What was it? The senator choosing new staff and his chief of staff resisting an intrusion into his bailiwick? That could make for a tense atmosphere. Did she want to get caught in the middle of that? Come in on the wrong side of Joe Blair and have to buck him from the get go?

She'd love it.

Smiling tightly, Gina reached for the phone and jabbed in the number. After confirming her meeting, she strode back to the window and looked out on Kalorama Road.

See, folks? What'd I tell you? The tide's turning.

13
DUNCAN

"I'M AMAZED," SAID SENATOR VINCENT. EVEN IN THE close confines of a doctor's examining room he spoke as if he was delivering a speech. "I'd been told how incredibly rapid your surgery healed, but didn't appreciate exactly *how* rapid until I'd seen it with my own eyes. Truly amazing."

Duncan refrained from reacting to the man's condescension and continued inspecting the hairline incisions under the chin through an illuminated magnifier. Yes, the beta-3 was doing its work. Only a week post-op and, except for some fading ecchymosis, virtually all traces of the procedure were gone.

Too bad I couldn't have done the Hogg reconstruction. Then you'd really be amazed.

Sometime since the surgery, Vincent had had his hair permed. It stuck out from his head in frizzy tendrils, making him look like one of those Chia Pets they hawked on TV.

Duncan backed up, examined Vincent's throat from the left, then the right. *"Damn,* I do good work!"

Vincent laughed nervously. "So I guess it will be safe to go on TV next week."

"Oh?" Duncan said with all the ingenuousness he could muster. *"Face the Nation?"*

"No. More important. The hearings. On the Guidelines bill."

"Next week? I didn't realize you'd be getting started so soon."

"Oh, yes. We're pressing on without Lane and Allard. The first hearing is Wednesday."

Got your sights set on any particular targets? Duncan wondered. Who's life are you going to ruin this time around?

"You know," Duncan said slowly, "I've never been to one of these hearings. Do you think you could get me in to the opening session?"

Senator Vincent scratched his head. "I don't know. It's a pretty hot ticket. And the hearing room's not that big . . ."

"Well, I have other patients on the committee who'll take care of it. No problem."

"You do?" the senator said, his tone warbling between pique at Duncan's implication that there was someone on the committee with more juice than he and voracious curiosity as to who else was getting fixed up for the hearings. "Who?"

Duncan wagged a finger. "Now, now. You should know that's privileged information."

"Yes, of course. But if you truly want a seat, Dr. Lathram, you've got one. I'll have my legislative director call you tomorrow. No problem."

"Thank you, Senator. I knew I could count on you. It promises to be quite a show. And I bet yours will be a household name from the very first day."

I guarantee it.

* * *

Later, Duncan stopped by Oliver's lab. He had to get down to D.C. General for the surgery on little Kanesha Green, but first he wanted to check his brother's progress on the latest refinement of the implant.

He found Oliver seated with a number of empty implants in a tray on the counter before him. He handed one to Duncan who rolled it back and forth in his palm. Light as a feather.

Duncan said, "How long can we count on the new model to sit in the subcutaneous fat without dissolving?"

Oliver shrugged. "How can I say? Six months, two years, forever. We haven't tested them. We'll have to do animal studies. I mean, really, Duncan, we haven't even finished the clinical trials on the regular implants, and here you've got me working on a whole new type."

"Got to stay ahead, Oliver. If we don't keep innovating, the intellectual slovens and me-too artists will plunder our work."

"But why this new model? I thought the whole idea was to have it dissolve shortly after surgery."

"Because I foresee a time when I may want an implant that dissolves when I *tell* it to. In trauma cases, for instance, with wide, deep wounds, premature release of beta-3 could prove counterproductive."

He had to choose his words carefully. Oliver was bright but he hadn't the faintest idea what lay behind Duncan's insistence on an implant that would dissolve on command; and no inkling of what Duncan had already done with it.

Duncan flipped the empty implant into the air and caught it.

"But you do think it's possible one of these things could nest in the fat for a couple of years?"

"I guess so. But I couldn't imagine why anyone would want it to sit there that long. The time when its dissolution would be of any benefit would have long since passed."

Not exactly, Duncan thought. Not if it was filled with the right substance and hidden in the tissues of the right person.

"Just wondering," Duncan said.

Oliver's eyes lit. "But you mentioned trauma repair. Are you thinking of returning to *real* surgery?"

Duncan laughed. "You mean vascular surgery? God, no. Why would I want to go back to being on call twenty-four hours a day and getting rousted out of bed at all hours of the night? For what? What good would that do me?"

"You're a great surgeon, Duncan. You'd be putting your talents to their best use. It wouldn't just be good for others, it would be good for you as well."

Moved by his brother's concern, and afraid Oliver might see something in his eyes that he shouldn't, Duncan looked away. Oliver was a good soul, the most decent of men. Complaisant, assiduous Oliver; his irenic presence, his lambent insight were a balm on Duncan's soul.

And he so admires me.

At times like these Duncan hated himself for putting Oliver's discovery to uses that would horrify him. And Duncan himself was horrified by the knowledge that if his machinations were ever brought to light, Oliver's fulgent, indefectible character would be tainted.

But that doesn't stop me, does it.

Again he wondered what he'd do if Oliver found out. Or Gina. How far would he go to protect himself?

He tried not to think about it.

"Why would it be good for me, Oliver? You know what happened when I was in vascular surgery. The same thing might happen again. Why should I make myself vulnerable again? Look at me now. I'm working fewer hours, I have no calls to speak of—whoever heard of an emergency tummy tuck in the middle of the night? I'm earning far more now with half the effort."

"You never cared about money."

"The public did."

"And you were saving lives then."

"But while I was saving or improving all those lives, I was publicly stoned for unalloyed greed. Remember that time, Oliver? Remember?"

Oliver nodded. "I remember."

"Now I rake in seven figures simply for resuscitating the vanity of the local gentry, and no one says a word. No one even lifts an eyebrow. Truly we live in a remarkable society, Oliver. A *remarkable* society."

What a world, Duncan thought, straining to hide the lava of rage erupting in his chest, flowing through his gut. What a goddamn world.

Oliver was staring at him. "You shouldn't have let them drive you out, Duncan."

"Now, now, Oliver. We've been over this countless times. I *chose* to leave vascular surgery. And it's the best thing I ever did."

"But you could have gone into another surgical field where your work actually meant something."

"But you had this new membrane you'd discovered, and then the Brits came up with beta-3. The writing was on the wall: cosmetic surgery was it."

Actually, he had decided never again to deal with insurance companies, or governments, or any mixture of the two. Cosmetic surgery was perfect. Only a rare insurance policy covered it anyway, and he could limit his patients to those who *wanted* it and exclude those who *needed* it.

"If that's the case," Oliver said, "then I wish I'd never developed this membrane."

Duncan gripped his brother's shoulder. "Don't ever say that, Oliver. These implants are going to transform a host of lives. People all over the world, mothers of children who'd otherwise be scarred for life will bless your name. And as for me, I've made peace with the past. Trust me, Oliver. I'm at peace."

"I hope so," Oliver said, searching Duncan's face. "I find it hard to believe, but I hope it's true."

Duncan glanced at his watch. "Oops. Time to run. Got to get over to the club."

Oliver's expression was dismayed. "You can't play golf today. It's pouring."

"Poker, Oliver," he said, nudging his brother's ribs. "When it rains we play poker. Want to join in?"

"No," he sighed, turning back to his implants. "I've got work to do."

For a moment Duncan was tempted to tell his brother where he was really going. It would make Oliver's day—make his *year*. But dear Oliver was a blabbermouth. He'd be explaining to anyone who'd listen that his brother really wasn't the coldhearted, cash-up-front bastard he pretended to be. He was a saint in hiding.

No, Oliver would have to go on being disappointed in the older brother he had once admired. And Duncan prayed he never found out about how he was using the new implants.

"See you tomorrow, then."

Duncan hurried across the wet parking lot, jumped in the Mercedes, and started the engine. But instead of putting it in gear, he sat staring at the hub of his steering wheel.

I've made peace with the past. Trust me, Oliver. I'm at peace.

How easily the lies come now. Peace? What was peace? He hadn't known a moment of it since the day he'd found Lisa lying in the foyer in a pool of blood.

If only . . .

Bright light in Duncan's eyes brought him back to the present. The sun had broken through the clouds. He shook off the memory and threw the Mercedes into gear.

I was all right, he thought. And I'd have stayed all right if not for the president's resurrection of the damn Guidelines bill. It all came back—all the pain, the rage—because of him.

But he'll get his. His turn is coming.

14
ON THE HILL

SENATOR MARSDEN MADE HER WAIT ONLY A FEW MIN-
utes, then Gina was ushered in.

The office was pretty much as she remembered it—the
stacked files, overflowing bookcases, photos, plaques, and the
miniature basketball hoop over the wastepaper basket.

Joe Blair was there, again in a white, short-sleeve shirt, a
different but equally nondescript tie, and dark slacks.
Strangely, he greeted her warmly, a smile beneath the wispy
mustache as he moved forward to shake her hand and lead
her toward the senator's battered old desk.

Gina wasn't sure what to make of the uncharacteristically
gracious behavior. An act for his boss? It was in Blair's honor
that she had worn a longer skirt today.

Senator Hugh Marsden leaned forward over his desk and
extended his hand. He was average height, sixtyish, balding,
portly, but possessed a commanding presence. It was his eyes,
Gina decided, intensely, piercingly blue; they caught her and
held her as firmly as his hand gripped hers. His voice was
deep and commanding as well.

"Dr. Panzella. Welcome."

A third person was in the room, a short, compact, dark-haired woman of about forty. She introduced herself.

"Hello, Dr. Panzella," she said, extending her hand. She had a warm, easy smile and bright brown eyes. Gina liked her immediately. "I'm Alicia Downs, the senator's press secretary."

"Gina. Please call me Gina."

"All right, Gina," the senator said. "Pull up a chair. I hope you don't mind if we get right down to business. Senator Moynihan moved a five o'clock budget briefing up to four-thirty, so time is short."

He seated himself in the straight-backed chair behind the desk and cleared the files from his desk blotter. Gina took one of the two chairs on the other side of the desk; Alicia took the other. Blair stayed on his feet, hovering. Positioning himself where he could get a good look at her legs, maybe?

"I can't help being intrigued by the fact that a young physician with your qualifications would want this position," he said. "I'd say you were overqualified. What is it you hope to accomplish here?"

Here we go again, Gina thought.

She went into her spiel of how she thought the impact of the Medical Ethics and Practice Guidelines Act would be so far-reaching, so important to the future of medical practice, that she couldn't sit idly by without attempting to have some input.

"You can't have guidelines that smother individuality," she concluded. "Do you want all doctors to be exactly the same? I hope not. Minimum standards of training and care, sure. But then allow variety in style of practice. Each practice should have its own personality, otherwise you've deprived patients of a critically important choice."

The senator studied her a moment in silence, his blue eyes

intent on her. Gina was beginning to feel uncomfortable when finally he spoke.

"You realize that this is a part-time position for which I doubt we'll be able to squeeze twenty thousand—if that—out of the budget."

"I explained that to her, Senator," Blair said. He seemed vaguely anxious; while not actually moving, he seemed to be pacing in place.

"The money's not important," she said. "I've got the rest of my life to make money. This is a chance to *matter,* to be part of something that will affect the rest of my professional life. If I were already in practice, with a mortgage, kids in school, I wouldn't be able to drop everything and devote months to this committee. But I'm not. There's only me to worry about. This is something I want to do, something I *can* do—and do well. And if I don't do it now, I'll never do it. And . . ."—dare she say it?—"your committee will be poorer for it."

"Is that so?" Senator Marsden said, a faint smile tugging at the corners of his mouth.

Out of the corner of her eye she saw Blair bite his upper lip and ever so slightly shake his head.

Had she overplayed it? "At least that's my opinion."

"Yes, well, you may have a point there. Will you give me a day to make a final decision?"

"Of course." *Do I have a choice?*

"Fine." He glanced at his watch, rose, and extended his hand. "Sorry to cut this short, but that budget briefing, you know."

Gina smiled as she shook his hand. "I understand."

"I'll walk you out," Alicia said.

Gina glanced back as she exited and saw Joe Blair leaning over the senator's desk, yammering in a low voice.

"I don't think your chief of staff is in my corner," Gina said as she and Alicia wound through the cubicles.

Alicia snorted. "Joe's a dickhead. He's pissed because he already told the senator you're not right for the job but the boss wanted to meet you anyway."

"So he's back there now trying to scuttle me?"

"Maybe. Don't take it personally. He's a control freak. Wants it to be *his* staff—handpicked by Joe Blair."

"Fair enough, I guess," Gina said with far more equanimity than she felt.

"Maybe, but he's still a dickhead."

"Gina!"

She was almost to the elevators. She turned and saw Joe Blair hurrying after her.

"Glad I caught you," he said as he reached her.

"What's up?" she said, watching him closely. "Has he made up his mind?" She didn't trust this guy. And there was something in his eyes . . .

"Despite my strong recommendation, the senator's still undecided. More of a budgeting problem than any difficulty with your qualifications." He unfolded the piece of paper in his hand and passed it to her. "But we need to figure out how to respond when he sees this."

We? Gina thought. Since when are we a *we?*

She looked at the sheet and suppressed a groan. It was a Xerox of an article she'd written for the *New Orleans Times-Picayune* during the second year of her residency. She'd been in a particularly grouchy mood after reading that paper's series on what was wrong with American medicine. She'd fired off a long letter vehemently disagreeing with their delineation of the problems and the proposed solutions. The paper told her if she'd expand it they'd publish it as an op-ed piece. Giddy with the prospect of having an audience, Gina had fired all her guns, sparing no one. It was a diatribe Duncan himself would have been proud of.

But . . . a very negative, even strident article, with no attempt at a balanced argument, and she'd cringed when she'd reread it on the day it was published. If only she'd put it in a drawer for a week before sending it in, she certainly would have leavened some of her remarks.

She hadn't given it much thought since, and yet here it was, resurrected and staring her in the face.

"This isn't really me," she said.

"I'm sure it isn't." Blair touched her hand solicitously. "But we've got to do some brainstorming to assess our options if it reaches the senator's desk."

She backed up an inch and his hand broke contact. There it was again: *we*.

"What do you suggest?"

"Oh," he said so casually, "how about my place? Tonight. And wear something nice."

Gina felt her hands close into fists. She wanted to ram one of them into his nose, and then yank out that wimpy mustache one hair at a time.

"Sorry," she said calmly, moving her jaw so she wouldn't be talking through gritted teeth. "I've got plans for tonight."

"Tomorrow night, then. We haven't much time."

We have no *time.*

She regarded him coolly, levelly. "Nope. Sorry. I'm busy. Tonight, tomorrow night, every night."

He stared back at her, obviously confused. Then his eyes narrowed, but only for a second. He shrugged carelessly and turned away.

"Okay," he said over his shoulder. "Your loss. But don't say I didn't offer to help."

"I won't," she said softly as she stretched a trembling finger toward the DOWN button.

She dammed up the rage and humiliation as she waited. It wasn't supposed to be like this, wasn't supposed to work this way.

The car finally came; the doors closed behind her and the box began its slow fall. Alone, sealed off, she wanted to scream, wanted to sob. She did neither. She wiped a single tear from her right eye and whispered one word.

"Damn."

She found Gerry waiting for her in the atrium. She forced a smile and hoped her eyes weren't red.

"What are you doing here?"

"Waiting for you. What else?"

He looked good. Even at the end of a workday with a little five-o'clock shadow stippling his cheeks, he looked damn good. But the excitement Gina had felt the last couple of times they were together was missing today. She didn't want to be with anyone now.

"But how did you know?"

"You told me. Remember? On the phone? Maybe five hours ago?"

"Oh. Right." Her mind wasn't working too well at the moment.

"So how about a drink?"

A polite demurral began in her throat but she held it back. She'd been injured and her instincts urged her to retreat to a corner and be alone. But that was what Pasta would have done.

"Sure. I'd love one."

"Great. I know just the place. We'll take a shortcut." He took her arm and led her toward the rear of the Hart Building. "A celebratory drink, I hope."

"No," she said slowly. "I'm afraid not."

"You're kidding. What—?"

"I'll tell you about it."

* * *

Gerry clenched and unclenched his fists under the table as Gina told her story.

They sat at an isolated table near the window. He'd brought her to the Sommelier, a little wine bar on Mass, because he'd learned that she preferred wine to liquor, and had a fondness for Italian reds.

Gerry preferred Irish sipping whiskey, preferably Black Bush. But if wine was the only thing, he usually toughed it out with white zinfandel. No wine snob he.

He could see Gina was hurt. She spoke softly, almost matter-of-factly, over her glass of valpolicella, swirling then sipping it, swirling and sipping. Her voice was steady, as were her hands; she looked perfectly composed. But Gerry sensed the pain.

As his mood darkened, he wished he hadn't brought her here. The gleaming surfaces of the polished brass and chrome and marble of the Sommelier were too clean, too bright for the story she told. They should have been in a seedy cocktail lounge.

No. This was better. Clean and shiny suited her. Here it was only the third time they'd been together and already he was feeling protective. And so attracted. He hadn't felt this way since college, when he and Karen had started dating and getting serious. A good, warm feeling. Thoughts of Gina were beginning to intrude on his work. He'd find himself thinking about her at the most inconvenient times, wondering what she was doing, wondering if she was thinking about him.

And now he was sharing her anger, her anguish. She had expected better of a U.S. senator's office. She *deserved* better.

Sometimes he hated this goddamn town.

"That's the way it is here," he told her after she finished. "Not just with you. With everything. It's a mind-set."

"So I shouldn't take it personally?" Her eyes flashed. "Is that what you're saying?"

"Yes and no," he said slowly. Had to choose his words carefully here. He didn't want to wind up a lightning rod for that anger. "You should be offended, angry, even feel humiliated, but realize too that Blair is simply doing what comes naturally on the Hill. He's just playing by the rules as he's learned them."

"Hill rat," she said, shaking her head. "Boy, if ever a term fit someone. But aren't there laws——?"

"Yeah, probably written by the Hill rats themselves, and passed by their bosses. But for other people, for the constituents. They don't apply up here on the Hill. You've entered an ethical *Twilight Zone*."

"You seem so casual about it."

Was he? Was she right? Had he been investigating political corruption long enough to take it for granted?

Maybe. He didn't like that answer.

But he wasn't talking about blatant graft here. No, it was more of an atmosphere, an ambience. A different set of values.

"I can't be casual about you being hurt."

She gave him a little smile. He loved the way her lips curled up at the corners. Her eyes said thank you.

He reached across and gripped her hand. She didn't pull away.

"Look, Gina," he said. "If you want to be a part of the doings on the Hill, you're going to have to play by their rules. The people up here aren't going to change for you."

"I never expected them to, but——"

"Think of yourself as having entered the world's largest bazaar, where everything is for sale but no prices are marked. The currency is influence, and the best hagglers walk away with the fullest shopping carts."

"That's pretty damn grim, Gerry."

"Gina," he said, leaning forward, "I'm sure you see influence peddling in hospital politics, but that's penny-ante stuff. This is the major leagues. This Blair guy, he's got influence with his senator to get you something you want; you, in turn, have got something he wants. Sounds as if he's experienced at the game, very circumspect in his hallway negotiation, and that's just what it was: a negotiation. And don't think that it occurred in an empty hallway by accident. No quid pro quo proposition, just a generous offer to help you deal with a possible hitch in your appointment. And no witnesses. Very smooth."

"You sound as if you almost admire him."

"I will admire my fist in his face if I ever meet up with him," he said.

Gerry was rewarded with another smile, this one big enough to reveal the glistening white of Gina's teeth.

"Don't get yourself in trouble on my account."

"It's a good account."

"Does that mean I can make a professional request?"

"Professional?"

"Yes. Police-type stuff. I'm trying to find out about Duncan Lathram's daughter."

Gerry felt his insides tighten as they always did at mention of Lathram's name, but he remained impassive. Obviously she was tired of talking about Joe Blair.

"What about her? She in trouble?"

"No. She died in an accident five years ago."

"What kind of accident?"

"A fall at home."

"You're suspicious about something?"

"Oh, no. Not at all. I just can't find out anything about her. Nobody's talking."

"It's just idle curiosity, then?" He could tell from her manner it was anything but. She was holding something back.

"No. I don't know what it is, really. I was just wondering if you could get hold of a copy of the death certificate."

Now *there* was an odd request. But not a difficult one if you knew who to call. And perfectly legal. Death certificates were public records.

"No biggee. Just have to know where she lived at the time. The rest is easy."

"Alexandria, I believe. Northern Virginia for sure."

"Okay. Have it for you in a day or two." And he would. But first he'd give it a thorough going over himself. His curiosity was piqued. "Unless there's a rush."

He watched her closely as she answered.

"No. No rush."

That settled, he could almost see her drift away as she lapsed into silence. She sighed.

He said, "What are you thinking?" Was it about Lisa Lathram, or about this Blair character, or something else?

"Maybe you and Duncan are right. Maybe I'm not cut out for this town."

So . . . it was back to Blair. An ache grew within him as he sensed the disappointment in her voice, watched discouragement etch lines around her frown. He wasn't sure what, but he was going to do something.

"Don't give up hope," he said. "Things have a way of working out."

"Maybe sometimes," she said. "Not this time."

He drained the white zinfandel.

"You never know, Gina. You never know."

Gerry stood in the wide, fresh-smelling, brightly lit hallway outside the apartment door in the Watergate-at-Landmark, a high-rise condo complex in northern Virginia, and waited for his ring to be answered.

He knew Blair was home—a hang-up phone call had confirmed that. Maybe he was eating. Gerry hoped he was alone. If he wasn't, Gerry would have to improvise. But one way or another, he was going to make this creep see the light.

As soon as he'd left Gina at her car he'd hustled up Pennsylvania to the Bureau. He ran a check on Blair, but no criminal record. Too bad. That would have made things easier.

So he'd have to bluff.

Gerry shrugged some of the tension out of his tight shoulder muscles. This sort of unofficial visit could land him in a serious load of official trouble if Blair called his bluff.

But Gerry knew how these highly placed Hill rats operated. They couldn't vote, but lots of times they had control of the line by line wording of a bill, and that could be more important than a Yea or Nay. The lobbyists courted them with trips, gifts, and honoraria for speaking engagements, just like their bosses. Gerry remembered one case, still mentioned by Hill rats in awed tones, of two staffers, John Michaels and Bill Patterson, who netted a total of twenty-eight thousand dollars from a host of lobbyists in forty-eight hours.

Blair no doubt had dreams of topping that record.

Gerry meant to disturb those dreams.

Because if Blair planned to cash in all the influence chips that would accrue from the Guidelines bill, the last thing he wanted was a ticked-off FBI agent watching his every move.

But Gerry didn't have much time. Mrs. Snedecker had said she'd keep Martha a couple of extra hours today. Gerry would have to get to it with Blair right away.

The condo door opened and a pale face with a see-through mustache cautiously peered at him through the opening. This was a gated building. Drop-in company was not the norm.

"Yes?"

Gerry held up the same badge that had got him past the doorman.

"FBI, Mr. Blair."

Blair opened the door a little wider for a better look. He squinted at the badge.

"What is it? What do you want?"

Gerry flipped the leather badge folder closed and stepped closer, quietly wedging his foot against the bottom edge of the door. He slipped the badge into his pocket.

"Don't worry. It's not official business."

"Then what—?"

Gerry put a hand against Blair's chest and gently pushed him back into his apartment. There were times when subtlety was called for and times when it wasn't.

"You and me, Blair. We're gonna have us a little talk."

15
GINA

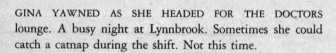

GINA YAWNED AS SHE HEADED FOR THE DOCTORS lounge. A busy night at Lynnbrook. Sometimes she could catch a catnap during the shift. Not this time.

Not that she would have got much more sleep if she'd stayed home. What a state she was in. Worse than waiting to hear about her residency match. Almost as bad as the months waiting to hear if she'd been accepted into medical school.

She ran into Dr. Conway again.

"I see Mrs. Thompson finally went home. That must be a relief."

"I guess so. Everybody's making nice-nice now that they think I caved in. Actually, she made a dramatic turnaround. Almost miraculous. One day she's dragging around, next day she's chipper and demanding to go home."

A warning bell sounded in the back of Gina's brain.

"When was that?"

"Wednesday."

"I wonder," Gina said uneasily. "I had a talk with her just the night before and she said she'd heard you were in trouble because of her. I remember her saying something like, 'I won't be a burden to anyone. I'll be out of here sooner than you think.'"

Conway stared at her. "Christ. That'd be just like her."

He picked up the phone and called medical records. He got Mrs. Thompson's phone number and dialed. And listened. He redialed and listened again. Then he hung up.

"No answer. I'm going over there."

"She could be out," Gina said.

"At seven A.M.? A seventy-eight-year-old lady?"

"I'll go with you."

"You're on duty. I'll let you know how it goes."

Gina spent the next hour wondering what Conway would find. When she wasn't thinking about that, it was back to the committee. At one point she found herself dialing her apartment, readying to activate the remote playback on her answering machine.

What am I doing? she thought, and hung up.

It was too early. No one from a senator's office would be calling before ten. Before noon, more likely.

She was about to leave when she was paged by the emergency department. Dr. Conway was asking for her assistance.

Gina found him standing by the Xray box, studying a chest film. She took one look at the opacified right lung field and said, "Not Harriet, I hope."

Conway nodded. "Found her on her back steps, barely conscious, a bunch of bread crusts in her hand. Looked like she'd gone out to feed the birds last night and collapsed."

"She was out all *night?*"

"Sure as hell looks that way. She's shocky, hypothermic, and hypoxemic, plus"—he tapped the chest film—"three fractured ribs and I'll bet that's a hemothorax. I called in Fielding. He's going to intubate her and put her on a respirator, then it's up to ICU." He snapped the film off the view box. "Damn! I never should have sent her home!"

"She told you she was fine. What else were you going to do?"

"I should have seen through that. I believed her because I *wanted* to. I was so damn glad to get the PRO and the rest of them off my back I jumped at the chance to discharge her."

"Don't be so hard on yourself," Gina said. "Where is she?"

Conway jerked a thumb over his shoulder at one of the curtained-off alcoves. Gina wasn't sure which way to go until she saw Fielding, the pulmonologist, step through a set of curtains and approach the nurses station. She slipped behind the curtains.

Harriet Thompson was almost unrecognizable. The right side of her face was swollen and purple where it must have struck pavement. A ribbed plastic tube curved from the corner of her mouth, connected by a larger tube to a hissing and puffing respirator. Her eyes were half open but they weren't seeing anything. Gina gripped her hand and gave it a squeeze.

"Hang in there, Harriet," she said. "You're in good hands."

There wasn't much Gina could do. Between Conway and Fielding and the ICU staff, all bases were covered. When she came out, she patted Dr. Conway on the back and wished both him and Harriet good luck.

She got behind the wheel of her Sunbird and rubbed her burning eyes. She was scheduled to assist Duncan this morning. Despite her fatigue, that had its up side: Time would move faster. But first a shower.

She noticed the message light blinking on her answering machine. She hurried over to it but her finger hesitated, hovering above the replay button. Dread and anticipation swirled through her. Was this it? The big turn-down?

She shook herself. She was going off the deep end. No way it could be Marsden's office.

She hit the button. It was Gerry. A rush of warmth filled her at the sound of his voice. He'd been so sympathetic yesterday.

Hi, Gina. It's about eleven now. I forgot you were moonlighting tonight, so you probably won't hear this till tomorrow morning. Just want to remind you to call me as soon as you hear from Marsden's office. It's a good bet you'll be hearing early. When you get word, call me at home. I won't be leaving till around nine. Good luck, but it'll be their good luck to get you. Bye.

How sweet, she thought, smiling as she hit the erase button. And how naive. She wouldn't be hearing early from anyone.

Funny, though, how sure Gerry seemed about the early call. And he was anything but naive.

Gina heard the phone ringing as she stepped out of the shower. Still dripping, she wrapped a towel around herself and rushed to the bedroom to grab it. It was Alicia Downs.

"You're in, Gina."

Gina was stunned, speechless for a moment.

"Hello?" Alicia said. "You still there?"

"Yes. I'm here. I just can't believe this. I'm in?"

"You are. I heard Blair telling one of the secretaries to call you and give you the word. I'm doing it for her."

"But how—?"

"Don't ask me. I put in my vote for you. I don't know about Blair. All I know is that sometime between last night and this morning the senator made up his mind. You're our new legislative assistant on medical affairs."

She felt weak. "This . . . this is wonderful. Thanks for the call. And for your support."

"Don't thank me. I mean, I think you're a nice person and bright and I'm sure you'll do a good job and all, but I want you for other reasons. You'll be a good PR asset."

"An asset. Wow."

Alicia laughed. "Hey, you're not just a doctor, you're a bright, attractive, *female* doctor fresh out of training. You're not Washington. An outsider, no connections to the bureaucracy. You're *now*. Your presence shows the senator's got a mind open to fresh ideas from the medical profession."

Gina felt herself going cold, and not from the water dripping down her legs.

"Look, if I'm just going to be window dressing, you can tell—"

"No way. Not with this senator. He wants you for your medical expertise. *I'm* the one who's concerned with appearances."

"That's a relief. I think."

She laughed again. "Relax, Gina. You're in. And you're in with one of the good guys. I've been earning my living up here for twenty years now, and Senator Marsden is the first guy in a long time to restore my faith in the electoral process. I can't tell you what a joy it is to polish the image of a guy you really like."

"That's good to hear. Really good."

"Then I take it you accept?"

"Of course I do."

"Great. Our staff is meeting here tomorrow at ten A.M. sharp. I hope you don't have any major plans for the weekend."

"Well, nothing firm." She'd been hoping she and Gerry might get together.

"Good. With the hearings opening next week, you can

expect to work through the weekend. Welcome aboard. See you tomorrow.''

Gina hung up and stood in the center of her bedroom, grinning foolishly, absently toweling herself off as she let the reality sink in.

"I'm in. I . . . am . . . *in!*" She pumped her fist into the air.

"Yes!"

As she dried her hair, she began to dance around, shuffling into the front room, blindly turning, gyrating, undulating her hips in time to a reggae tune on the radio.

Here she is, ladies and gentlemen! The latest, the greatest, the hottest legislative assistant in the nation's capital, dancing under her stage name, Pasta Primavera, with her own exclusive interpretation of the Hill Rat Hustle!

Gina lowered the towel from her hair and found herself in front of the bay window, standing nude as a jaybird over Kalorama Road.

"Whoa!"

She ducked away and hurried back to her room. As she pulled open her underwear drawer she caught sight of herself in the full-length mirror. She turned to give her body a closer look, twisting this way and that to get different angles on her breasts and hips.

The hips were a little more generous than she liked. But her abdomen was nice and flat. She ran her hand lightly over the puckered scar of her old incision, then traced a fine line of hair down to the dark tangle over her pubes. Time for another bikini wax.

Not too bad, she thought. Not too bad at all for an old broad looking thirty in the eye.

She had two careers now. Why not go for a third as Pasta Primavera—exotic dancer? No . . . there was another term for it, a Duncan word. What was it . . . ?

Ecdysiast flashed into her mind.

Right. Regina Panzella: doctor, legislative assistant, and ecdysiast.

She tried a little bump and grind before the mirror.

Pretty lame.

Ah, well.

She turned away and began picking through her underwear.

Once she was dressed, her high spirits were brought down by the thought of Harriet Thompson. She called the Lynnbrook ICU and learned she was stable. Okay.

Then she called Gerry. He seemed genuinely happy for her, but not as surprised as she'd expected.

"See," she told him. "Sometimes things work out. It doesn't do you any good to be cynical all the time. Hard work and persistence still pay off."

"*I* knew all along you were the best person for the job. Now I guess this guy Blair and the senator know it too. But what's really great is that it means you'll be down in my neighborhood a lot more often."

"That's right, isn't it?" She hadn't thought of that. "I'm glad of that too."

She liked Gerry more each time she saw him. Maybe an FBI agent wasn't as glamorous as a high-powered internist like Peter, but she sensed something deeply caring in Gerry. If this kept up . . .

"By the way," he said. "I located a death certificate on Lisa Lathram in Fairfax County."

Gina felt her breath catch. One part of her wanted to tell him never mind, leave the dead alone; another part wouldn't rest until all her questions were answered. She tried to keep her tone casual.

"That was quick. What does it say?"

"It's on its way. I'll let you know when I get it."

"Thanks, Gerry. You're becoming indispensable."

"I hope so."

"I'm afraid I'm going to have to cut back some of my hours here."

She and Duncan were halfway through a tummy tuck. Gina had a wide retractor hooked around a six-inch layer of abdominal wall and was positioning it where Duncan could resect the redundant layers of yellow fat. She hadn't planned to tell him until the surgery was over, but he'd begun talking about tomorrow's surgery schedule and it had simply popped out.

"Oh?" he said. "And why's that?"

"I . . . I got the job on Senator Marsden's staff."

There. I said it.

She watched him closely, remembering his explosion last time. How was he going to react this time?

His blue eyes glanced up at her for a second or two, then returned to the surgical field.

"Congratulations. When do you start?"

Gina didn't answer immediately. She'd been steeled for anger. This quiet acceptance was almost as intimidating.

"Uh, this weekend."

"So you're leaving us high and dry."

"Cassidy said he'd fill in."

"I hope you'll still find *some* time for medicine."

"I'll have to cut back, but I don't want to quit."

"Good. I don't want to lose you. Your work here has been excellent."

"Thank you," she said, basking in the rare praise.

"The Hill will be educational for you," Duncan said. "Give you a chance to see the kakistocracy at work. You'll witness firsthand the rampant sophistry of the congressional solipsists. They'll—"

Marie the anesthetist groaned. "Oh, no. Here we go."

Joanna glared at Gina in mock anger. "We were breezing along here. Did you have to get him started?"

"Sorry," Gina said.

"All right, all right," Duncan said, glancing around and smiling behind his mask. The skin around his eyes crinkled with amusement. "Despite your bumptious insubordination, I'll spare you all a lecture this time. But let me just say this—"

Marie groaned again.

"Wait now," Duncan said. "All I'm going to say—and I want you all to listen and remember that you heard it here first: I predict Gina will not last a year on the Hill before she throws her hands up in disgust."

"There's always a chance of that," Gina said, thinking of Joe Blair, "but I know these hearings are going to be interesting. I can't wait till they begin."

Duncan glanced up at her. "Neither can I, my dear. Neither can I."

Gina stared back at him. Something in those bright blue eyes . . . something almost feral, reminding her of how he looked on the Capitol portico with Congressman Allard. An icy tendril traced a chill up her spine.

Gina left the Lathram office early and put in another call to the ICU when she got back to the apartment.

"She's having some BP problems," the charge nurse said. "Real shocky. Dr. Conway's here. Want to talk to him?"

"No. Don't bother him. Just tell him I was asking about her."

Gina hung up. Damn. That didn't sound good.

She called her folks next. Her mother answered and Gina told her the good news.

"Is this what you want, Gina?" Mama said.

Why did everybody ask her that?

"Yes, Mama," she said patiently. "For the time being."

"Then good. I'm happy for you. We'll expect you about six."

"Expect me where?"

"Here, of course. We'll celebrate. We'll open some spumante, and I'll make you your favorites: stuffed shells and three-cheese lasagna."

Gina's mouth began to water. But she was so tired. And this was the stuff that had turned little Regina into big fat Pasta Panzella.

"I'm really beat, Mama. I was up—"

"Gina, Gina," she said in that voice that always got to her. "You haven't been here in so long. You live a few minutes away and yet you never visit your family. Are you going to forget your Mama and Papa?"

Gina repressed a sigh. "What time again?"

"Your father will be home by six. Get some sleep and we'll see you then."

Gina collapsed on the bed and let sleep take her.

16
FAMILY

GINA PULLED UP IN FRONT OF THE FAMILY HOME IN
Arlington and stared at its aged brick front. During the first
dozen years of her life it had been a two-story brick box
sitting on a rise along with all the other brick boxes in this
little postwar development. She remembered learning to ride
a bike on that gently sloped driveway, watching the cars go
by from her bedroom window up there on the second floor,
helping Papa pull dandelions from the lawn every spring.
Papa and his lawn, she thought, looking at the flawlessly
green, precisely manicured front yard. Still perfect.

As Papa's butcher shop grew to an Italian specialty food
store, and a little money was left over to play with, they
added a screened porch to the front, enlarged the kitchen and
master bedroom in the rear, and built on a deck. A nice,
roomy, comfortable house now. Thirty years her folks had
lived here, and probably intended to stay another thirty.
They weren't exactly into change.

Gina shook her head. Change? They were both born in
America; her father was barely into his fifties now, her

mother just fifty last April, yet they were old-world Italian in so many ways. Attitude-wise, they were barely into the twentieth century.

They'd actually arranged a marriage for her when she was two. Thank God that hadn't been mentioned in years. Apparently the fits both she and her intended had pitched during their adolescence had caused both families to reconsider.

She climbed the two steps to the front door and walked in without knocking. The delicious odor of sautéing garlic enveloped her. God, she loved that smell.

Her father sprang from his chair in front of the TV. He was only an inch taller than Gina, with broad shoulders and muscular arms; his full head of black hair was a little grayer every time she saw him, but he still had the vitality of a twenty-year-old.

"Gina!"

He wrapped her in his bear arms and twirled her around. "How's my little *scungile?*"

She hugged him around the neck and kissed each cheek. "Fine, Papa."

He released her and held her at arm's length. "So, being a doctor's not enough for you, eh? Now a politician too?"

"I'm not—"

"Gina!" It was Mama, wiping her hands on her apron as she trotted in from the kitchen. More hugs and kisses.

It was always this way. Gina came home for dinner and family affairs every two or three weeks, but each time they acted as if she'd been away for a year. She supposed an only child had to expect that.

Soon the three of them were standing around in the kitchen, sipping spumante, sneaking pieces of bread into Mama's sauce, laughing, reminiscing, talking about the future.

So good to be here. Times like this made her wish she

visited more often. She loved the warmth, the security. She'd be taken care of here. She didn't have to prove anything here, she wouldn't be so tired all the time, she wouldn't have to be running in four different directions trying to do too many things, trying to learn where she fit, trying to make her life matter.

She fit here. She mattered here.

And she knew it was a velvet trap. As much as she loved her folks, she knew she'd go crazy here. Despite all the hustle and running and stress of her life now, she knew deep down she wouldn't want it any other way.

But the main thing was that her folks still didn't quite get it. As proud as they were of her, Gina knew they wondered when she was going to have time to give them grandchildren—bambinos to bounce on their knees. She knew in the backs of their minds they felt their daughter would be better off being married *to* a doctor than being one—a nice *Italian* doctor, of course.

They knew something about Peter, but had no idea that they'd been living together.

Oh, God. Peter. She should have called him and told him about her new job. She'd have to do that first thing when she got home.

Peter . . . how could she have forgotten?

Stuffed from the food, logy from the spumante and the special Chianti Papa had broken out for the occasion, Gina got back to her apartment around half past ten. She washed up, brushed her teeth, and headed straight for the bedroom. But before hitting the sack, she dialed the ICU at Lynnbrook.

"Hello, this is Dr. Panzella. I just wanted to check on Mrs. Thompson."

"Who?" said the ward clerk.

Gina was suddenly queasy. "Harriet Thompson. Dr.

Conway's patient. She had a hemothorax and was on a respira—"

"Oh, yeah. Here it is. Sorry, Dr. Panzella. I just came on. She was pronounced a couple of hours ago. Nine-thirty-four, to be exact. Dr. Conway was here."

Gina felt her throat constrict. She managed a faint "Thank you" and hung up.

She pounded a fist on the mattress. Damn, damn, *damn!* Harriet Thompson's death certificate probably would list her cause of death as respiratory failure due to hemothorax due to fractured ribs due to complications of accidental trauma.

But it hadn't been any of those.

What had really killed her were administrators who hadn't examined her and didn't even know her but made decisions about her medical care, who had been more concerned about the bottom line than the patient.

Harriet Thompson had died of guidelines.

Gina pulled down the covers and slipped between the sheets. Senator Marsden was going to get an earful this weekend.

One last thing to do before sleep: that call to Peter.

He was in, he was awake—after all it was an hour earlier in Louisiana—and he was glad to hear from her. At least he was at first. His voice changed when she told him about getting the spot on Marsden's staff.

"Is this really what you want?"

She was getting fed up with that question. The only one who seemed to be on her side completely was Gerry.

"You know, I wish people would stop asking me that."

"If you're hearing it that often, maybe there's something to it."

"Look, Peter, I don't want to argue—"

"Aren't we good together, Gina? Are there any people better together than us? Remember those nights wandering around the Quarter, drinking wine and listening to the street musicians, and then afterward going back to the apartment and—"

"Please, Peter." Those had been good times, wonderful times. "I'm lonely enough here as it is."

"We're *both* lonely. Isn't that dumb? Come back, Gina. This is where you should be. You know that."

So tempting, and if she'd been turned down by Marsden's office this morning she might be pulling out her suitcases and starting to pack. But . . .

"I know that I've got an opportunity here that I can't pass up. I may never forgive myself if I do. Can you understand that, Peter?"

There was a prolonged silence on the other end. Peter's voice was thick when he finally spoke.

"I guess this is it, then. I'd been hoping you'd run up against a wall with these senators and finally come to your senses and get back where you belong. Back with me. But I guess that's not going to happen now that you're on somebody's staff."

"Peter . . ."

Gina found she couldn't get words past the lump swelling in her throat. He was right. She hadn't seen that becoming part of Marsden's staff would put a match to her last bridge back to Peter.

It was over. Whatever they'd had had been moribund for months, but tonight, without realizing it, she'd officially pronounced it dead.

"I'm sorry, Peter."

"Me too. Good-bye, Gina."

And then he hung up.

Gina cradled the receiver, turned out the light, and pulled the covers up to her chin.

God, I hope I'm doing the right thing. I hope it's worth it.

Then the sobs and the tears started. It was Peter, but

maybe it was Harriet Thompson too. She hadn't cried herself to sleep in a long, long time. Not since her Pasta days.

"Wha . . . ?"

Gina opened her eyes. Dark. And noisy. A bell ringing. Loud. Almost in her ear.

The phone.

She picked it up and heard a familiar voice.

"Gina? It's Gerry. Sorry to call you at this hour but I'm in a jam."

What hour is it?

She glanced at the clock: 2:33.

"Something wrong?" she said. The urgency in Gerry's voice dispersed the fog of sleep.

"We've had a break in a kidnapping case and I've got to go out."

"What kidnapping?"

"I can't say. We've kept it out of the papers. But the thing is, Mrs. Snedecker can't come over and I struck out with my backups. I was wondering, hoping . . ."

"I'll be right over."

He gave her directions to his apartment complex in Arlington. She smiled ruefully at the irony. Just four hours ago she had been only a couple of miles from him.

Gina found Gerry standing outside the front door of his duplex, keys in hand. Apparently he'd shaved, put on fresh clothes, and was alert and ready to go. Even at this unholy hour he looked good.

Better than I do, she thought. She knew she looked rumpled—she *felt* rumpled in her flannel shirt, jeans, and raincoat—but she'd got here as quickly as she could.

"You made great time." He kissed her; a friendly peck on the cheek. His voice was a machine gun. "I can't tell you how much this means to me. I'd never have imposed if I'd had any other place to turn."

"Don't be silly. I—"

"Martha's upstairs. She's a sound sleeper. You can just sack out yourself. I'll be back as soon as I can get free, but I don't know exactly when that'll be."

"Take your time," Gina said. "I'll stay as long as you need me. I don't have surgery today."

He kissed her again—on the lips this time. "You're the greatest. See you soon."

And then he was sprinting for the parking lot. When he reached his car he turned and called to her.

"Oh, by the way. I left something for you on the kitchen table."

Gina watched him drive off, then went inside and locked the door behind her. Shucking her raincoat, she wandered through the living room of the duplex and into the adjoining dining room, wall-to-wall carpet in the former, an area rug in the latter. Danish modern furniture. Neat, clean, functional. Not much personality. No lingering telltale odors to identify the cook's favorite food. Hard to tell if anyone really lived here until she got to the kitchen. A miniature art gallery there. Everywhere she looked—on the walls, on the cork bulletin board, on the refrigerator—the room was festooned with a child's drawings. A riot of colors. Martha, it seemed, believed in using every crayon in her box, and it had to be quite a box. Nor was she exactly traditional in her color designations. In one drawing green people might stand on yellow lawns next to pink trees under orange skies; in the next drawing the color scheme would be completely different.

A munchkin van Gogh. With a father who obviously adored every squiggle she put to paper.

She looked in the fridge. Lots of prepackaged meals in the freezer. Just what she'd expect with a single father on the go.

Then she remembered what Gerry had said about leaving something for her on the kitchen table. She turned and saw nothing on the table . . . except a sheet of paper. She recognized it before she picked it up. A death certificate.

Lisa Lathram was typed on the name line. Gina noted that the certifier was Stanley Metelski, MD, Fairfax County coroner at the time of the accident. Which meant Lisa's death had been a coroner's case. Of course it would be. Any eighteen-year-old dying suddenly is an automatic coroner's case.

She scanned down to the cause-of-death section.

Immediate cause of death: Intracerebral hemorrhage.

Due to or as a consequence of: Left parietal skull fracture.

Due to or as a consequence of: Intentional drug overdose.

Gina nearly dropped the sheet. *A suicide?*

Suddenly shaky, she lowered herself into a chair and leaned on the table.

Oh, God. Poor Duncan. No wonder no one wanted to talk about it. He must have pulled some heavy strings and called in a lot of favors to keep that last line from getting out to the public.

Was that why he ended his marriage, closed up his practice, stopped being a Virginia vascular specialist and became a Maryland cosmetic surgeon?

Or was there more?

The drug overdose . . . why? The fall . . . obviously the coroner thought it was a result of the overdose. Was it?

Gina had thought the death certificate would answer some questions, but it only raised more.

Rising, she dropped it back onto the kitchen table and wandered toward the front of the duplex. She pushed Lisa Lathram to the back of her mind and brought Martha

Canney front and center. Gina had a sudden urge to look in on her.

She crept upstairs. Two bedrooms and a bath there. She peeked in the first. In the dim light seeping up from the first floor she could see Martha's little head framed by her pillow and the covers. Lots of Disney characters on the walls and shelves. Gina stepped closer and snugged the covers a little more tightly around her shoulders. As she turned away she spotted a framed photo standing on Martha's dresser. She picked it up and angled it toward the light.

A pretty young blond. Although they'd moved in entirely different circles during their high school years, Gina recognized Karen Shannick. The late Mrs. Gerald Canney. Martha's mother.

God, she'd been beautiful. Classic, clean, all-American-girl looks. She married an all-American guy. And they'd had a child. A *Happy Days* life until . . .

She thought of Harriet Thompson, also gone, but who'd had seventy-eight years. Poor Karen had had maybe a third of that. And what a shame she couldn't see the doll she'd brought into the world.

Life really sucked sometimes.

Gina stared down at Martha for a moment and was struck by the realization that this was Gerry's child. His alone. This little person was totally dependent on him, and he was completely responsible for her. She wondered how that would feel.

Scary, she thought. Very scary.

She replaced the photo on the dresser but the leg that angled out of the back of the frame collapsed and it fell flat on the dresser top.

Gina winced. Not a loud noise, but it sounded like a gunshot in the little bedroom.

"Daddy?"

Oh, no.

Quickly Gina turned and knelt beside the bed. Martha was sitting up, rubbing her eyes, not quite awake yet. She looked at Gina.

"Where's my daddy?"

"He had to go out," Gina whispered. "He asked me to stay with you. Remember me? Gina? From Taco Bell?"

"You're the doctor."

"Right. What a great memory you have."

"Where's Mrs. Snedecker?"

"She's away. That's why I'm here."

Am I doing this right? she wondered. If Martha were sick Gina would know exactly what to do; but she'd never had any younger sibs, so she wasn't too sure of herself here. Getting her back to sleep seemed like the best thing. She straightened the covers.

"Here. Why don't you just lie back down and close your eyes. I'll be right downstairs. If you need anything, you just call and I'll be right here. Okay?"

Martha didn't say anything as she lay back and pulled the covers up. Gina adjusted them around her and then, on impulse, leaned over and kissed her cheek.

"Good night, Martha."

As she rose and turned toward the door, she heard a sob from the bed. She knelt back down again.

"What's wrong, Martha?"

"I get scuh-scared when my daddy's not here at nuh-nuh-night." She started to cry.

"He'll be home soon, Martha," she said, searching for a way to comfort her. "What if I stay here with you?"

Martha sniffed and sat up. "Can you?"

"Sure. It'll be fun."

"Will you get under the covers?" She wriggled over to make room. Her fears seemed to have evaporated. "This'll be like a sleep-over."

Gina hesitated, then shrugged. Not much room in that

little bed, but what the heck. She kicked off her sneakers and slid under the covers. Martha immediately nestled into the crook of her arm and snuggled against her. In minutes she was asleep.

Gina lay there and listened to the gentle sound of Martha's breathing. She stroked her soft hair and felt strangely content, at peace.

Peace . . . what a strange sensation. It seeped through her like warm water through a dry sponge. Throughout her brain and her body she sensed all the various engines that were driving her begin to downshift, finally going into neutral, idling.

And through the peace crept an ancient need, long unnoticed amid the adrenalized buzz of her day-to-day life.

She squeezed Martha closer. Is this what I'm missing? Isn't this what it's all about? Her throat tightened. A child of my own? God, I'll be thirty next year . . .

Damn! Where are my priorities? What is better than this?

Gerry pulled into his parking space in front of the house. Night was leaching from the eastern sky. Dawn wasn't far off. Somewhere in the trees a bird called.

He headed for his front door, bounding over the curb and up the steps. He was pumped. And relieved. A successful operation tonight. At the last minute the Bureau had called out every available agent—the kidnapper had made a mistake—and they got the little Walker boy back safe and sound. Gerry could have stayed and celebrated with the rest of the guys, but this case had made him anxious to get back to his own child.

And it reinforced his determination to move up to a position with regular hours. And soon.

"Gina?"

Gerry stood inside his front door and surveyed the empty living room. Gina's raincoat was there, but where was she?

"Gina?" A little louder.

Upstairs with Martha? Had to be. But an unreasoning fear made him pad up the stairs, taking them three at a time as silently as he could, hurrying to Martha's bedroom. He stopped at the door, struck dumb by the sight of his child curled up under Gina's protective arm. Both were asleep, both faces so smooth, so relaxed, so innocent in the growing light.

He'd taken a chance asking Gina tonight. He hadn't known how she'd react, how it would work out, but he'd sensed a rapport between Gina and Martha during their first meeting and, well, he'd longed to see her. And who better than a trained physician?

But this?

He stood staring, captured by the *rightness* of the scene. It was as if their little duplex, his and Martha's little world, had changed; their fragmented family briefly made whole again.

He realized that tears were sliding down his cheeks.

You belong with us, Gina, he thought.

He wiped the tears away and had to fight the urge to crawl in with them. Besides, there was no room left in that tiny bed.

So Gerry pulled up the rocker Karen had bought for nursing Martha and sat there watching the two women in his life until the sun came up.

THE WEEK OF OCTOBER

1

17
THE HEARING

"RELAX, GINA," SENATOR MARSDEN SAID AS HE GATH-
ered the papers on his desk. "You look as if you're about to
jump out of your skin."

His desk was piled high with folders, reprints, charts,
graphs, and detailed analyses of medical statistics. Joe Blair
had been in earlier, reviewing his last-minute strategies on
networking with other chiefs of staff. He was cool and
professional toward Gina but decidedly distant. And Alicia
was a whirling dervish, darting in and out of the office like an
overweight hummingbird. She'd conscripted a couple of the
office's legislative correspondents to field the endlessly ringing
phones. This was her big day and she seemed to thrive on the
pressure.

The past four days had been a whirlwind of activity. Gina
felt as if she'd moved into these offices. She'd met Charlie and
Zach, the other two legislative aides assigned to the Guidelines
committee, and had been impressed with the amount of
research they'd collected. They had copies of guidelines and
codes of ethics from every state medical board in the country.

The amount of material to be reviewed and absorbed was daunting. But she'd waded in with the rest of them.

"I'll be fine," Gina told the senator.

And she would be. It was just that not only was this her first day of actually attending a congressional hearing as a participant, but the chairman of the committee would be depending on her medical knowledge to interpret the testimony being given, all of which would occur before cameras broadcasting the proceedings to the nation.

Nothing to it.

Right. That was why her hands were cold and her palms were sweaty and her stomach had shrunk to a walnut-sized knot.

But she was all set to go: She had a pad, a supply of pens, and she had her brand new photo-ID badge slung on a chain around her neck.

"I know you will. Remember: Your job is to listen and take notes. Alert me immediately—pass me a note, tap me on the shoulder and whisper—whenever you think someone's blowing medical smoke my way. And I do mean immediately. I don't want to find out days later that someone was running double-talk by me. Your responsibility is to keep the medical testimony honest."

She held up her steno pad and pens. She didn't know shorthand but the steno pad was a convenient size.

"I'm ready."

She hoped she sounded confident. She was beginning to feel the weight of the responsibility she'd taken on. And she'd be shouldering it in public.

She'd watched congressional hearings on TV before and seen aides passing notes or whispering in committee members' ears; hard to believe people would be watching her doing the same today. Her father was staying home from the store this morning to watch C-SPAN.

Senator Marsden winked at her. "And maybe when this is

over you can write a more evenhanded op-ed piece for the
Times-Picayune."

Gina stiffened. "You know about that?"

"Sure. Joe showed it to me shortly after the interview. It's
his job to background anyone joining my staff."

"I was afraid it might put you off."

He rose and tucked a bulging file folder under his arm.

"I spent forty years in business. I learned the worst thing
you can do is surround yourself with yes-men. That's why I
like to keep a devil's advocate around."

Gina felt a burst of warmth for this man. Alicia had called
him "one of the good guys" and now Gina believed her.

"I'll be it."

"Then let's go."

The hearing room was gorgeous, paneled floor to ceiling in
gleaming mahogany. The carved ceiling would have been at
home in Versailles—nearly twenty feet high, white with
delicate, hand-painted blue designs. Rich red carpet
stretched wall to wall. Three tall windows ran almost to the
ceiling and were trimmed with black crepe in honor of the
committee's departed member, Congressman Lane. Set between the windows and all around the room were giant brass
sconces, designed like ornate torches that would not have
been out of place in the Roman Senate. Each flared a wedge
of light against the paneling above it. All the furniture—the
curved dais where the committee members sat like knights of
the semicircular table, the witness table, the visitor chairs—
was fashioned of mahogany perfectly matched to the paneling. The red leather on the seats and backs of the chairs
arranged in neat rows for visitors and witnesses and lined
against the wall behind the dais for the committee members'
aides matched the carpet, as did the leather inlays in the tops
of the press tables flanking both sides of the room.

Chaos reigned. Photographers were jockeying for position in the space allotted them, reporters were weaving through the mix of legislators, witnesses, and visitors, looking for comments, sniffing for rumors, while the C-SPAN technicians made final adjustments on their cameras, one near the front and the other midline at the rear.

Gina followed Senator Marsden to the dais—why did it feel so special to stroll past the "Staff Only" sign?—and staked out a chair behind his spot at the apex of the semicircle. Zach would be with her. Charlie had stayed behind at the office. While Marsden began arranging his papers, she looked out over the milling crowd and was shocked.

Duncan.

"Senator, do I have time to talk to someone?"

"Of course," he said, glancing up at the disorder before him. "We won't come to order for at least another ten or fifteen minutes."

As she stepped off the dais, someone tapped her on the shoulder.

Another familiar face—one she was *very* glad to see.

"Gerry! What are you doing here?"

"Just stopped by to say hello."

"But how'd you get in?"

He flashed his FBI ID. "Never underestimate the power of the Department of Justice. I knew this was your big day and I just wanted to wish you luck. I'd've brought flowers but—"

"Oh, I'm glad you didn't. I wouldn't have known what to do with them."

He leaned forward and kissed her on the cheek. "Knock 'em dead, Gina."

She gave him a hug. "Thanks. That means a lot."

And it did. No one else had wished her luck, or thought she should even be here. She watched him go, then spotted

Duncan on the far side of the room. He was talking to one of
the committee members: Senator Vincent. Both looked to be
about the same age, wore suits of similar cut, but Duncan's
trim figure and aristocratic bearing somehow left the senator
looking like a poor relation. And what had the senator done
to his hair? A permanent?

She tapped Duncan on the shoulder.

"Excuse me, sir," she said in an officious voice. "Do you
have a pass?"

Duncan greeted her with a warm smile and threw an arm
around her shoulders.

"I was wondering when you'd show up. Senator Vincent,
I'd like you to meet Senator Marsden's newest assistant, Dr.
Gina Panzella. Also my surgical assistant. In fact, she assisted
me on your procedure."

Senator Vincent glanced around uncomfortably as he
shook Gina's hand. "I wish you wouldn't—"

"Don't worry, Senator," Duncan said. "Gina is the soul of
discretion, just like everyone else on my staff. You know
that."

"You look great, Senator," Gina said, and she meant it.
Except for the hair. But as far as the surgery, the improvement was remarkable. Amazing how all that redundant flesh
under his chin had aged him. He looked at least fifteen years
younger.

But that hair. Ugh.

"So I look okay? No sign that I had—that anything was
done?"

"Not a bit," Duncan said. "I predict you'll be the next
bright star in the C-SPAN firmament."

Senator Vincent laughed nervously.

"I'm serious," Duncan said. "After your performance
today, you're going to be on all the networks. Mark my
words."

Just then a beeper sounded. Duncan had his hand in his coat pocket. Gina watched him pull out his oversized pager, the same one he'd had on the west portico of the Capitol . . .

. . . the day Congressman Allard fell down the Capitol steps.

He grunted and said, "Now, who could this be?"

He looked at the display window and pressed a button. At that moment the hearing room's PA system began a feedback howl, and Gina noticed Senator Vincent wince and begin massaging the outside of his right thigh.

"Something wrong?" she asked him.

"I don't know," he said. "For a second there it was almost like a bee sting. But it's better now." He glanced at the clock high on the rear wall. "We'll be starting soon. Excuse me."

Gina turned to Duncan as Senator Vincent wandered off. "Anything important?"

Duncan had already pocketed the pager. "One of my golf foursome. Probably checking on our tee time. And may I ask, who was that man with whom you were engaging in a public display of affection?"

"Gerry Canney. An old friend from high school. He's now an FBI agent."

"And I suppose you embrace all your old high school friends whenever you see them?"

Gina felt herself blush. "He's a little more than a friend."

"I see," Duncan said, raising his eyebrows. "Well, I'm happy for you."

Gina regarded him. Something different about Duncan this morning. He seemed wound up. Like a Thoroughbred owner before a big race.

"Three guesses who's the last person I expected to see here this morning."

His eyebrows lifted even higher. "Me? I wouldn't miss this show for the world."

"It's the hottest ticket in town. How'd you get in?"

"Consider for a moment the names in my patient files, Gina, and tell me who in this Circus Maximus is better connected than yours truly." He cocked his head toward Senator Vincent. "Actually, it was the good senator himself who saw to it."

"You'd probably be better off watching it on C-SPAN."

"Nothing like actually being there." He sniffed. "Catch that, Gina? The effluvium of naked power waiting to be unleashed. Heady stuff."

Gina laughed. "Tell me about it." She glanced at the dais and saw the committee members seating themselves. "Got to run. Enjoy yourself, Duncan."

His smile was tight. "I hope to."

Her palms were moist by the time she regained the dais. She hoped she didn't look a tenth as nervous as she felt.

Let's stop fooling around and get this thing started, folks.

She knew she'd be fine once the hearing was rolling; it was the waiting that was killing her.

She checked out the dais. All the attending committee members except Senator Vincent were in place. Where was he?

She searched the floor of the hearing room and spotted him, standing next to Duncan again. She saw Duncan say something to him and turn away. She couldn't see Duncan's face, but Senator Vincent's wore a baffled look.

Gina had a sudden sense of *déjà vu* . . . Duncan . . . his beeper . . . a parting comment . . .

Gina chewed her lip as the senator gained the dais and approached his seat. She knew it was all coincidence but she wanted to know what Duncan had said to him.

Now wasn't the time, however. But right after the hearing she'd find a way to ask.

* * *

Duncan sat quite literally on the edge of his seat, his hands clutched tightly between his knees. He struggled for outer calm, to hide the surging adrenaline within.

No glitches today. This one *had* to go according to plan. The setting was absolutely perfect.

He'd waited to see where Senator Vincent was sitting before choosing his own place. When he spotted Vincent settling himself three seats to Marsden's right, Duncan found a chair halfway back with a clear view of the senator.

He glanced at his watch.

Won't be long now.

He watched Gina sitting tense and stiff against the back wall as Marsden brought the room to order. The senator made a few brief opening remarks about the missing committee members, offering condolences to the Lane family and hope for Congressman Allard's speedy recovery. Out of respect, he said, their nameplates would remain before their places until their replacements were chosen.

Duncan knew he was tempting fate to do this with Gina here, but he had little choice. Another of those perverse twists that dogged his heels lately. Still, there was no way Gina could connect him to what was about to happen to Senator Vincent.

Ah, Gina, he thought. Look at you, my naive cygnet, thinking you can have some effect on these proceedings. But it's all preordained. The real decisions as to whether or not American medicine will be practiced via government-issue cookbooks, and whether your fellow physicians will be suffocated under mountains of regulations where they'll spend more time dodging fines and penalties than attending to the health of their patients, will not be made here but in back rooms and hallways, where a vote for the Guidelines act will be traded for a bridge or a highway spur.

The first witness was called: Samuel Fox, MD.

Typical, Duncan thought. Congress's favorite pet doctor, the physician-hating physician.

Fox styled himself as a consumer advocate but was little more than a grandstanding autolatrous worm. This hearing was proceeding exactly as expected.

As the notoriously prolix Fox began reading a prepared statement, Duncan kept his eyes fixed on Vincent, watching for the first signs.

His thoughts wandered back to the day Congressman Hugo Lane had shown up at his office. That had been earlier this year, shortly after the president had instigated the anabiosis of the committee. Lane the notorious lush had come to him for removal of the spidery blemishes sprouting all over his face and upper trunk. Supposedly from too much sun. Duncan recognized them immediately as arterial angiomas, known in the trade as boozer blossoms. They meant a fatty, cirrhotic liver. Too much sun? Too much Johnny Walker.

It had required enormous control not to slam the man back on the examining table. The flagitious toper! Lane had been a member of the original McCready committee, a participant in the savaging of Duncan's career, his *life,* and he didn't even remember him.

Like the old song: *Am I That Easy to Forget?*

He'd been part of the process that had killed Lisa and he had never even heard her name.

Duncan remembered staring dumbfounded, thinking, We have this history together, the most traumatic time of my entire life, and you have no inkling.

If Duncan had not been in a towering rage over the revival of the committee, if Lane had not been reappointed to it, Duncan might have simply explained who he was, what he and his cronies had done to his life, and thrown the bastard the hell out.

But circumstances being what they were, Duncan had said, Yes, Congressman. No problem. We can take care of all those unsightly areas of sun damage. Cautery of the central vessel of each with an ultrafine laser. Easy as pie. Barbara will arrange a day and time for the procedure.

While I arrange a little something extra for you.

So Congressman Lane had been the first.

Duncan's plan had been to have him make an ass out of himself at the French embassy. Duncan had been there, had watched and waited, but Hugo Lane had behaved as usual: drank too much, ate too much, and talked too loud. Maybe all the alcohol in his system was to blame, maybe his fatty liver wasn't working up to snuff. Whatever the reason, Lane was apparently his usual self until he was driving home. Witnesses said he wove all over the road before crashing through a barrier and rolling down an embankment in Rock Creek Park.

Duncan had been shocked and dismayed. He hadn't intended for Lane to die—just go crazy in front of a roomful of his peers. And maybe stay crazy for a few years.

No worry about being found out. Lane's blood-alcohol level was explanation enough for the accident. But even if the ME had looked for other causes he would have come up empty. Toxicology screens can find only what they're looking for, and no one would be screening for what Duncan had put into Lane. Only a handful of people had ever known it existed.

Schulz had been next. This procurante, too, had no memory of the doctor his committee had flagellated years past, no knowledge of the teenage girl who'd died because of it. Duncan realized then why they didn't remember him: He'd never been important to them. Duncan Lathram was a name on a piece of paper handed to them by one of their aides five years ago. They'd reviled him when the microphones were on, but never gave him a thought between hearings, and forgot about him after a couple of weeks.

Schulz . . . a vain, strutting, womanizing roué whose diligent efforts over the years to keep a year-round tan had left his face a mass of wrinkles. On the recommendation of his good friend Congressman Lane he'd come to Duncan for a solution. He'd already tried Retin-A but to no avail. His myriad wrinkles seemed baked in. Could Duncan help?

Of course, Senator. Duncan had smoothed his rugose hide, and given him something extra.

Duncan hadn't yet decided on the time and place for Schulz when the shocking news reached him that the senator was dead. Duncan had been baffled until he'd learned that a physical therapy session had been the penultimate event in the good senator's life before he took a dive from the balcony of his high-rise town house. That probably explained it.

Or maybe Schulz simply had a guilty conscience.

Not likely.

Again, no loss to the world. But once again he'd been deprived of the catharsis he craved.

Allard had come the closest to what Duncan had planned for him, but that, too, had fallen short.

Today was going to be different. Duncan could feel it in his bones. And when he noticed the corner of Senator Vincent's mouth begin to twitch, he was sure of it.

Gina leaned forward in her seat and placed another note in front of Senator Marsden. She'd been culling one question after another from Dr. Fox's parade of dubious statistics but was passing only the more flagrant errors forward. There wasn't time for the senator to consider all of them.

As she slid back she noticed a small fleshy bump atop the auricle of the senator's left ear. Smooth with a pearly surface.

On a sun-exposed area, that was a basal cell carcinoma until proven otherwise. She wasn't his doctor, and it was sometimes touchy to point out a potential health problem to someone who hadn't asked, but she decided to mention it to him later.

She heard a pencil drop. She looked up. No, it was a pen. It had fallen near Senator Vincent. He must have dropped it, but he didn't seem to notice. She was forcing her attention back to Dr. Fox when she noticed Senator Vincent jerk in his seat. She watched and he did it again. A spasmodic movement, as if someone had jabbed him with a pin, or a violent chill had passed through him. The room was cool but he seemed to be sweating. He ran a trembling hand through his frizzy hair.

Is he all right? she wondered.

She watched him a moment longer and he seemed to be calm; no more jerks or twitches. But he was still sweating, and gripping the edge of the table as if it might float away from him—or he from it.

Concentrate on the testimony, Gina, she told herself. That's your job here. Not Senator Vincent's hangover or whatever's bothering him.

She focused on Fox's words and was in the middle of another notation when . . .

"Just a minute, please. P-Please, excuse me."

Gina jumped at the sudden interruption. Senator Vincent, kissing his mike and popping his P's, had broken in at peak volume.

"Yes, Senator?" Senator Marsden said softly. "Shall we allow the doctor to finish his statement before questioning him?"

"No!" Vincent shouted, slamming his fist on the table. His eyes were wild as he glared along the table at Senator Marsden. "We shall do no such damn thing. Not when this son of a bitch starts slandering my wife!"

Gina was rocked by that. Fox had been talking about overutilization of services. She saw heads snap up all around the hearing room. Both C-SPAN cameras had swiveled toward Vincent, and the still photographers were screwing their lenses back and forth as they focused on him; the previously somnolent reporters had come alive and were now scribbling on their pads or jabbing away at their laptops.

And on the dais she watched the other members exchange puzzled glances. Marsden looked the most concerned of all.

He cleared his throat. "Senator Vincent, I don't believe Dr. Fox mentioned anyone's wife. He was discussing—"

"Don't you tell me what he said or didn't say, you greenhorn!" Vincent shouted. "I was taking testimony when you were pissing your pants. And don't you side with him against me, either!"

"Senator," Dr. Fox said from the floor. His expression was wounded and confused. "I assure you I never said or even implied anything—"

Vincent leapt to his feet. He was off mike now, but his harsh voice cut through the hearing room as he pointed a trembling finger at Fox.

"Don't lie to me, you little shit! Of course you did!" He swayed as he swept the room with his hand. "They all heard you. Every word of it." He stared at the wide-eyed, gawking visitors. "Didn't you? *Didn't you?*"

Silence . . . except for the clicks of camera lenses and the whir of advancing film.

Vincent began to nod his head. "Oh, so that's it. You're *all* in on it. Well that's just fine. I'll just—" Suddenly he whirled on Senator Marsden. "What did you say?"

Gina saw Senator Marsden cringe back. She didn't blame him. The naked fury in Vincent's eyes was frightening.

"I—I didn't say anything, Harold. Maybe we should call a recess until—"

"No! No recess!" Saliva flecked his lips and began to spray

as he shouted. "We're going to settle this right here. Here and now! We're—"

Suddenly he stiffened. His arms went rigid, his head snapped back as his spine bowed. Gina saw his eyes roll up and knew he was going to convulse. She was out of her chair and halfway to him when he dropped to the floor and began a tonic-clonic seizure.

Gina crouched beside him, cradling his jerking head. His eyes were open but he was seeing nothing. She listened to the air hissing in and out between his clenched teeth. Good. As long as that kept up, she knew he hadn't swallowed his tongue.

"Somebody call the emergency squad!" she cried.

She loosened his tie, folded it, and worked it between his grinding teeth. The senator was going to need a dose of diazepam soon.

She looked up and saw Samuel Fox in the encircling huddle of anxious faces and camera lenses—those damn clicking, whirring cameras.

"Dr. Fox. How about a little help?"

Fox didn't budge. He shook his head. "I can't! I . . . I've never practiced."

"Great," Gina muttered.

Suddenly Senator Marsden was at her side.

"The EMTs are on their way. What do you want me to do?"

Gina gave him a quick, grateful smile. "Just grab his arms and steady them. Don't try to pin them down, just blunt the wild movements, keep him from flailing around too much and breaking a bone."

"Will do."

It took another minute or so—it seemed much longer— before the seizure abated and Senator Vincent's limbs relaxed. His body slumped, his eyes closed. He began to snore.

"Does he have a history of seizures?" Gina asked Senator Marsden as they released their hold.

"Not that I know of. But then again, that's not something you broadcast in public life."

Right. Voters were probably funny about voting for an epileptic. But what about the bizarre paranoid behavior just before the seizure?

The EMTs arrived then. As they started an IV drip and loaded Senator Vincent on the stretcher, Gina told them he'd suffered a grand mal seizure and suggested they call ahead and have a neurologist waiting.

"Have ten milligrams of diazepam ready to go IV push if he starts again," she told them as they were leaving.

She turned to Senator Marsden. "Thanks for your help."

He nodded absently, then surveyed the milling, murmuring crowd around the dais.

"Nothing like starting off with a bang," he said with a sigh.

"Are you going to call a recess?"

He nodded. "An indefinite one."

"What do you mean?"

His expression was bleak. "I opened the hearings this morning two members short. Now I'm *three* short. I've got half a committee now. Even if Senator Vincent recovers soon, I don't see him appearing before the cameras again for quite some time. Do you?"

"No. Can't say as I do."

"So I'm going to have to wait until at least one of those empty seats is filled."

"How long will that take?" Gina said, her heart sinking. She'd just started this job last week, now it was evaporating before her eyes.

"Could be a while."

Gina's expression must have revealed her dismay. He smiled and put a hand on her shoulder.

"Don't worry. I want you around doing background during the hiatus. I like the way you handle yourself. And who knows? We may not have a long wait if I can get the president involved. He wants this bill before the end of the year. Maybe he can twist a few arms."

He returned to his seat on the dais, banged his gavel twice, and announced that hearings were suspended until further notice.

Gina suddenly thought of Duncan. She searched the crowd for him but he was gone.

Twice now, Duncan had been present when some catastrophe had befallen one of his legislator patients.

What had he said to Senator Vincent down on the floor . . . minutes before the senator went crazy?

Gina had a strange feeling that he'd told him to remember someone named Lisa.

Later, Gina returned to the Hart Building via the underground shuttle and was surprised to find Gerry waiting for her in the atrium.

"Am I glad to see you."

She needed someone to talk to, needed to ventilate the morning's events. She gave him a hug and felt the tension in his muscles. Gerry didn't seem to be in a listening mood.

"We need to talk," he said. His expression was serious, almost grim.

"Is something wrong?"

"Something might be. Can I tell you about it over lunch?"

"Nothing about Martha, is it?"

He stared at her, then put his arm around her shoulder. "No. Nothing at all to do with Martha."

They walked down to Mass. Gerry tried to make small talk but didn't do a very good job.

Summer wasn't letting go just yet. The sun was high and

the air warm. Gerry pointed to an array of red-and-white Tecate umbrellas on a patio in front of a converted brownstone about a block and a half down from Union Station.

"How about T-Coast?" Gerry said.

Gina looked at the sign: *Tortilla Coast*. Mexican food. "It's not a Taco Bell, but I guess we can make do."

She was too wound up to eat, but just sitting in the sun would be good.

They took a corner table near the sidewalk.

"So what's the problem?" she said as the hostess left them with their menus.

"I heard about Senator Vincent."

"It was terrible."

"You realize, don't you, that he's the third member of your committee to bite the dust."

"Yes. Senator Marsden and I were just discussing it. But what—?"

"I did some quick background on him. Checked if he'd had any surgery recently." He paused, staring at her. "You know what's coming next, don't you."

It wasn't a question. What was he getting at? Why was the FBI interested?

"Duncan."

"Right. That makes four."

"Four what?"

"Four dead or disabled legislators—two senators, two congressmen—all Lathram patients. Three of them on the Guidelines committee. Could your Dr. Lathram have it in for that committee or something?"

Gina suddenly felt a little queasy. He was echoing her own crazy thoughts.

The waitress arrived then. Gina agreed to share Gerry's nacho platter and ordered a Pepsi. Considering what the morning had been like, she could have done with a brew—she'd acquired a taste for Dixie while at Tulane—but she didn't want to show up at the senator's staff meeting this afternoon with beer on her breath.

"He was there this morning, you know," she said when they were alone again.

"Who?"

"Duncan. And he was on the Capitol steps when Allard took his fall."

"You were there? You never told me. How close was he?"

"You mean, did Duncan push him? Come on. But he . . ." She hesitated, wondering if she should mention it, then plunged ahead. "Duncan's last words to Allard were something about Lisa."

"His daughter? The one who—?"

"Committed suicide. I think so. He said something about 'an eighteen-year-old named Lisa.' Had to be her."

Gerry was silent a moment, then, "On the subject of Lisa, I dug a little deeper after reading her death certificate. Got a copy of the coroner's report."

Gina's heart kicked its rhythm up a notch. "You have it with you?"

"No. It's back at my office. But I read it through a couple of times. It summarized her whole medical history. Let me tell you, Lisa Lathram was one troubled kid."

"You mean she tried it before?"

He nodded. "Twice. Once with pills. Once with a razor to the wrists."

Gina slumped in her chair. "How awful."

"Apparently neither attempt was that serious."

"But she got it right the third time."

"That was the real tragedy. According to the report, Lisa had been doing extremely well on Prozac, which I understand was pretty new at the time. Then suddenly—*boom*—something happened and she went over the edge. Gulped all the old antidepressants she'd squirreled away over the years. But the worst part was she didn't take enough to kill her.

Just enough to make her dopey and clumsy. She toppled over a balcony and landed on a hard tile floor. Doctor Lathram came home and found her.

"Oh, God. Poor Duncan."

That explained it then—the sudden radical change in Duncan's life. Everything must have fallen apart for him.

But it didn't explain his mentioning Lisa to Allard two weeks ago.

"Any hint in the report of a connection between Lisa and Congressman Allard?"

Gerry shook his head. "Not that I saw. Of course, I wasn't looking for one. I'll make you a copy. But in the meantime . . ." He leaned forward. "I understand Lathram's putting some sort of implants into his patients."

"How . . . how'd you know about that?"

He shrugged. "It's no secret. The FDA has him down as approved to do a clinical study. What's in those implants anyway?"

"Just some enzymes and such to reduce scarring."

"Well, could there be something wrong with—?"

She gave in to a sudden urge to defend Duncan. "Gerry, he does a dozen or more cases a week. Very visible people. If there were something wrong with the implants, there'd be nobody left to go to all those embassy parties."

"What if he puts something different in certain implants . . . so he can get to certain people . . . ?"

"Do you hear yourself, Gerry? Dr. Duncan Lathram is lacing his implants with some mystery substance that causes people to get drunk and wreck their car, commit suicide, fall down steps, or have seizures. That's one hell of a versatile drug."

"Who says it has to be one drug?"

"All right. I'll give you the benefit of the doubt on that. But let's take Senator Vincent today. You're saying that Duncan has such control over whatever drug he supposedly used that he can make it go into effect on command, right in the middle of a committee hearing. Is that what you really think?"

Gerry leaned back in his chair. Gina could feel the frustration pouring out of him.

He sighed. "Does sound pretty far out, doesn't it?" He was silent for a while, then he leaned forward again. "But something doesn't smell right, Gina. I can't tell you how I know, or why, but my gut tells me something's going on here."

"I know what you mean, but it's just a string of coincidences. Duncan has his eccentricities, but he's not . . . he isn't . . ."

"Look, just to shut me up, could you bring me a sample of whatever it is he puts in those implants?"

"No, Gerry. I can't. That's Oliver Lathram's concoction and it's not patentable. What do you want to do, have it analyzed?"

"Just to see if there's anything toxic in it."

"I can assure you there's nothing toxic in that solution."

"Ever hear of a binary poison?" Gerry said.

"No. I don't know much about poisons."

"They come in two parts. Neither half is toxic by itself, but when they meet in the bloodstream and bind—wham."

"Very interesting. But I'm still not getting you a sample. I couldn't. It would be a breach of trust."

He nodded slowly. "Okay. I can respect that. But keep your eyes open up there. And be careful. I don't want anything happening to you."

Something happen to *her?* Absurd.

Gina tried to lighten the mood by smiling and saluting him. "Aye, Captain Queeg. And how would you like your strawberries, sir?"

Finally a smile broke through. "You think I'm crazy, don't you?"

"No crazier than I."

"See? We were made for each other. Have dinner with me tonight?"

"Sure. How about my place? I'll cook."

His eyes lit. "Really?"

"Bring Martha."

A little of that light faded in his eyes. "Oh. I thought maybe you—"

"Surely you've figured out by now that I only put up with you so I can see Martha."

"I can live with that," he said. "Whatever it takes."

Gina was touched. She reached across and laid her hand on his. He gripped her fingers.

And then the nachos arrived.

But as Gina watched Gerry pile his plate, she heard, *Could your Dr. Lathram have it in for that committee or something?*

Why had those words come back? Duncan *did* have it in for the Guidelines committee. He ranted against it at every opportunity.

But at one time or another, Duncan ranted against just about everything and everyone in the government. That didn't mean he was waging war on it.

Did it?

She shuddered briefly. An absurd thought.

Not Duncan. Even if it were possible. And it wasn't. So why even consider it?

But come to think of it, Duncan had disappeared right after Senator Vincent's seizure. With no offer of help. Just like when Allard had fallen. No imagining there. Those were facts.

And they bothered her.

18
GINA

FRIDAY GINA WAS BACK IN THE LATHRAM OFFICE. SHE'D spent most of the morning assisting Duncan with a particularly difficult composite rhytidectomy, in which all the underlying facial tissues are lifted as one piece. Normally it would take five or six weeks for the facial swelling to resolve from such an extensive procedure. With the help of Oliver's implants, this particular sixty-two-year-old Washington doyenne would be back in the social whirl well before then.

Duncan had been in a particularly chipper mood through the surgery, humming, joking. "No jeremiads about the lamentable state of the nation today, ladies," he'd said, sounding apologetic. No one had complained.

Later Gina wandered into Oliver's lab with a cup of coffee, looking to kill a little time before starting on her presurgical exams for next week's cases. She noticed he had a tray of large implants sitting on the counter. The empty syringe and the bottle of normal saline solution sitting next to the tray explained why the implants looked full.

She bent over the tray for a closer look. Were these the new model Oliver had mentioned? Looked just like the old model.

"Hi there, Gina."

She looked up. Oliver was coming through the doorway, pushing a wheeled cart ahead of him.

"What've you got there?"

"An ultrasound unit."

She gave it a closer look. Not the diagnostic or imaging kind used in pregnancy. This type was for deep-heating subcutaneous tissues. A big difference in power: The former measured output in megahertz, the latter in watts.

"Going into physical therapy as a sideline?"

He chuckled. "No. Just testing out the latest batch of the new, improved implants."

He'd lost her. "With ultrasound?"

"Sure. Just give me a second to set up and I'll show you."

He set the unit on the counter, plugged it in, adjusted a few dials, then picked up the handle.

"Watch."

Oliver took the implant from the end of the row and moved it away from the rest, placing it on the counter a couple of feet from the tray. He positioned the ultrasound head over it and pressed the button on the handle. Immediately the implant began to quiver; an instant later it dissolved, leaving a spreading puddle on the counter.

He placed another implant in the puddle and held the ultrasound head farther back. The implant dissolved, the saline puddle enlarged.

He did this repeatedly, each time backing farther away with the handle, each time enlarging the puddle until finally it ran over the edge and dripped onto the floor.

Gina watched in wonder.

"That's incredible," she said.

She stepped to the counter for a closer look. Only minute

shreds of the implant membranes remained floating in the puddle.

"How does it work?"

"I altered the crystal-protein matrix," Oliver said as he unplugged the ultrasound unit. "I made it more stable, more resistant to the body's tissue enzymes, but I rigged it so that at a certain ultrasonic frequency, the crystals vibrate and dissolve the matrix. As a result, the implant membrane collapses and releases its contents."

"Brilliant."

"Duncan's idea, actually."

Somewhere in the rear of Gina's mind, a bell chimed a sour note.

"Duncan's?"

"Yes. He wants more control over when the implants dissolve. As he says, why leave the timing up to the vagaries of the circulatory system and the tissue enzymes? Let's develop implants that empty when we tell them to."

She remembered what she'd said to Gerry after the Guidelines hearing earlier in the week. *And not only can this miracle toxin do all these different things, but Duncan has such control over it that he can make it go into effect on command.*

It had sounded so absurd then, but the means were staring her in the face.

"Is . . . is Duncan using these yet?"

"Oh, no. The FDA approved us to do clinical trials with the original implants only." He flashed a smile. "The Original Recipe, you might say. We'll have to go through the whole approval process again for the new membrane."

"Oh. So these are brand new."

That's a relief. Duncan couldn't have used the new implants if they hadn't existed at the times of the surgeries.

But the relief was short-lived.

"Not really," Oliver said. "I've been working on them for most of the year. And they're still not perfected yet."

Gina swallowed. "Looks like they work pretty well to me."

"Not good enough yet for Duncan. He wants a more stable membrane, one that will last almost indefinitely until hit with the right ultrasound frequency."

"Do you see any clinical purpose in that?"

Oliver shook his head. "No. But Duncan's the doctor, not me. He knows what he wants."

Gina helped Oliver mop up the saline with paper towels, but all the while her thoughts were looping in wild circles. She slowed them down, straightened them out. She had to approach this logically, like a diagnostic puzzle. Lay out the facts first, then draw conclusions.

All right: Duncan did have the means to implant a toxin of some sort inside his patients and release it at will.

No, not at will. He had to zap it with ultra-high-frequency sound. If Duncan had been responsible for what had happened to Senator Vincent, he'd have had to wheel an ultrasound machine into the hearing room and point it at the senator.

Ridiculous.

Still, the ultrasound demonstration left a residue on her thoughts, a sour mental aftertaste.

She went looking for Duncan. She'd forgotten to check with him about putting in a few extra hours here until the hearings got underway again. And she needed to talk to him, to reassure herself.

"Oh, he's gone," Barbara told her as Gina went to knock on Duncan's office door.

"Out with the mysterious Dr. V., I suppose?"

"No. Dr. V.'s not due back for a while. Dr. D. said he was heading for the golf course."

"Damn. I wanted to catch him before he left."

"He's not gone all that long. I'll try his car phone."

Barbara punched in some numbers, waited, then hung up. "No luck there. I can page him for you."

"No. I don't want him coming off the golf course just to talk to me. It's not that important. What's the number of his club? Maybe he's still in the clubhouse."

"Want me to call for you?"

"No, thanks. I'll call him myself."

Barbara looked it up and wrote it down.

Gina used the records-room phone. First she tried the club dining room, but he wasn't there. Then she tried the pro shop. Maybe she could catch him before he started his round.

"Doc Lathram?" said the chief caddy. "Haven't got a tee time for him."

"Maybe he's playing with someone else."

"Maybe, but I ain't seen the Doc 'round here for months."

"Are you sure?"

"Missy, I'm here just 'bout every day. Doc Lathram's been a member here forever, but it must be six months since I put his bags on the back of a cart. But if he shows up I'll give him a message if you want."

"No," Gina said. "Never mind."

What's that all about? she thought as she hung up. When he hasn't been bitching about the kakistocracy, it's been about his golf, his slice, his bogies, complaining about the condition of the greens.

So what's he been up to?

Not golf, obviously. What else had he been lying about?

Gina was uncomfortable. She didn't like the idea of Duncan lying, to her or anyone else.

On impulse she went back upstairs and returned to Duncan's office.

"I left some papers on his desk," she told Barbara as she breezed by her.

Great, she thought as she swung the door open. Now I'm lying too.

Tense and uneasy, feeling like a sneak, she went to the big partners desk and tugged on the top drawer. It wouldn't budge. Locked. Damn.

She dropped into his chair and slouched there, swinging back and forth, wondering what to do.

What, if anything, was going on here? And what should she—could she—do?

Most likely it was all just nothing, but she had to ask herself: Did Duncan have anything to do with those four dead or damaged legislators?

Probably not. Their deaths, accidents, and illnesses weren't really linked . . . just one of those weird coincidences that sometimes occur . . . the kind of coincidence that gets conspiracy theories started.

Still, why was he lying about where he went when he cut out of here early every afternoon? Did that really matter?

But she had seen an injection vial of something in Duncan's top drawer; also some sort of trocar. Why were they there? What was in that bottle? Why did he keep the drawer locked?

Damn! She hated doubting Duncan like this. But why wasn't he where he'd said he'd be? Where the hell was he?

Duncan removed the dressing from Kanesha's face and studied his work. He gripped her chin and gently turned her head back and forth.

Reflexively her hand fluttered up to cover the area of the surgery.

Duncan gently pulled the hand away and pressed it against her hip.

"No need to do that anymore, Kanesha."

The thick, stiff wad of scar tissue that had held the left side of her mouth prisoner was gone. In its place were a pair of healing hairline incisions and a normal-looking angle of the mouth. Duncan was pleased. But now the most important test.

"Smile for me, Kanesha."

Again the hand came up and covered that corner of her mouth. She looked at her mother. Her expression said, Get me out of here.

"C'mon, Neesh," said her mother. "Smile for Dr. Duncan."

Duncan pulled the child's hand down again and stood her on the chair. He turned her toward the mirror on the wall.

"Look at that girl in there," he said. "What do you think of her?"

Kanesha stared at herself in silence for a moment, then leaned forward for a closer look. Her left hand came up again, this time not to cover, but to touch, to confirm that what she saw was real.

Duncan watched her, waiting for a smile. And the smile was important. Kanesha's had been a tougher piece of surgery than he'd anticipated. The scarring had gone deeper than usual; not only had he had to free up all the subcutaneous layers, but he'd had to do a partial reconstruction of the perioral musculature. A smile was the only way he'd know how successful he'd been.

"Well?" he said. "Don't keep me in suspense, little girl. Has Kanesha Green got something to smile about or not?"

He poked a wiggling finger into her flank, tickling her. She giggled, and with that giggle came a smile. An enormous smile—bright, even, symmetrical.

She stopped giggling and stared. The smile faltered for a heartbeat as she leaned forward, her eyes wide, then it returned full force.

She turned to Duncan, grinning, joy and wonder dancing in her dark eyes. Her mother burst into tears and reached for her daughter, but Kanesha did the unexpected. She leaned forward, threw her arms around Duncan's neck, and hugged him. An instant later her sobbing mother had her arms around Duncan as well.

"Oh, thank you, Dr. Duncan! Thank you so much!"

This was getting a mite sticky.

"Now, now, ladies," he said, extricating himself from the tangle of limbs. "We've made a big jump, but we're not finished yet."

"Not finished?" the mother said, wiping her eyes. "She's beautiful!"

"Of course she is. But she's not fully grown yet. And some scarring might redevelop in the deeper tissues. In a few years I may want to do one more procedure—to make her perfect."

"She looks perfect now! Oh, Dr. Duncan, if there's ever anything I can do to repay you, anything at all, just—"

Duncan put his hand on Cindy Green's shoulder. "Just keep her smiling."

"No, I'm serious."

"So am I. Keep her safe, keep her healthy, keep her smiling. Daughters are . . ." His voice caught. He cleared his throat. "Daughters are precious. I don't want to find out I did that surgery for nothing."

"I will," she said, putting her hand over his. "I promise."

"Good!" He straightened and lowered Kanesha to the floor. "Stop at the desk on your way out. The nurse will have some ointment and instructions for its use. I want to see Kanesha next week."

Cindy Green was puddling up again. "Dr. Duncan . . ."

"Come on, come on," he said, ushering them toward the door. "You're wasting time. Get her home and let her show off that smile."

That'll teach you to doubt me, he thought as he watched them go.

"Okay, Marge," he called out. "Who's next. Let's keep moving."

He didn't have all day.

It began as a whim, which soon evolved into a compulsion, and by midafternoon Gina found herself in the periodicals section of the Alexandria Public Library.

Lisa Lathram . . . there had to be more on Lisa Lathram. And where better to find it than in the town where she lived and died?

Disappointingly, the *Alexandria Banner*'s obit was identical to the one in the *Post*. But a short news blurb about her death made an offhanded mention of her father being under investigation by the Virginia State Board of Medical Examiners.

Gina went rigid in her seat. Duncan? Investigated? For what?

She began buzzing backward through the microfilmed issues of the *Banner*. Fortunately it was a small paper with a low daily page count. Whenever she found mention of Duncan she photocopied the page and put it aside. When the Lathram references petered out, she assembled the copies and read through them in chronological order.

The first story appeared about three months before Lisa's death. Half the *Banner*'s front page was devoted to Duncan, citing him for billing Medicare over a million dollars in vascular surgery fees the preceding year. An editorial in the same issue categorized him as a prime example of "unchecked greed in a profession run amok."

Gina shook her head in wonder. A million . . . a lot of money, even for a vascular surgeon. But billing Medicare for a million didn't mean you received a million. It only paid a fraction of what was billed. And even if it paid dollar for dollar, so what? She'd seen how Duncan worked when he was a vascular surgeon. If he billed a million, it was because he'd *earned* a million.

The follow-up article described how a patient's rights group was circulating petitions calling for an investigation of Dr. Lathram to determine how much—not *if*, but *how much*—unnecessary surgery he was performing. The petitions were forwarded to the Virginia State Board of Medical Examiners. Soon the *Banner* was announcing on its front page that Duncan Lathram, MD, was under investigation for suspicion of malfeasance and fraud by the state board. Then came an article revealing that Medicare's fraud unit was conducting an audit of Duncan's office and hospital records.

God, how awful, she thought. How humiliating to have all those investigators pawing through your records, probably while patients sat in the waiting room.

Then Lisa's death.

And after that . . . nothing.

Where was the resolution? What was the outcome? She couldn't find a single mention anywhere. Had Duncan lost his Virginia license? Was that why he was in Chevy Chase now?

One way to find out. She glanced at her watch. Still time to call the Virginia state board.

It took four calls, but Gina finally tracked down the executive secretary, a Mrs. Helen Arnovitz. She asked if Duncan Lathram was still licensed in the state; and if so, had any disciplinary action ever been taken against him?

Helen put her on hold and returned a minute later.

"Yes, he's still licensed and no action was ever taken. However, I remember the case well. The board did conduct an investigation for the possibility of fraudulent billing and performing unnecessary surgery."

"And?"

"The charges were found to be groundless. The board was obligated to investigate due to some adverse publicity Dr. Lathram had been receiving, but found no malfeasance. When the results of the Medicare audit came back clear, we completely exonerated him."

"So it was all much ado about nothing."

"For us, but not for poor Dr. Lathram."

Gina stiffened. "Really? Why not?"

"His practice dwindled to the point where he had to close his office. I understand he's doing quite well now in Maryland, but it was a shame that Virginia had to lose such a fine vascular surgeon."

"I'm sure it was. Thank you."

Gina hung up, leaned back, and closed her eyes. Her heart went out to Duncan.

Public humiliation, the death of his daughter, the closing of his practice, the breakup of his marriage . . . all in the same year. Why had it happened? What had started it all? It was enough to drive anyone . . .

. . . crazy.

No. That wasn't fair. Duncan was anything but crazy. And none of this had any connection to Schulz, Lane, Allard, and Vincent. At least none that she could see.

So why didn't she feel relieved?

There was more to this. Had to be. But where to look?

No time for that now. She was due at Lynnbrook tonight. She'd hoped this mini-research-trip would ease her mind but it hadn't.

Only one thing to do. And she hated herself for doing it.

Gerry slouched in the cubicle that served as his office, staring at Martha's drawing of an orange horse—truly a horse of a different color. He should have been devising a way to snare Senator Schulz's uncle as an accomplice in laundering honoraria. Instead he was thinking about the loss of three members from the same committee. What were the odds of that happening by chance? Especially when they'd all had surgery from the same doctor.

His phone rang. The receptionist down in the visitor area.

"There's a Dr. Panzella here to see you."

He damn near dropped the phone.

"What? Dr. Pan—she's there? Now?"

"Yes. Standing right in front of me."

"I'll be right down."

Gerry grabbed his suit jacket and headed for the elevators. He pressed the down button but none opened immediately so he took the stairs. Only three floors. Nothing to it.

He burst through the doors and found Gina standing in the center of the lobby. Her features were tight.

"Gina? Is something wrong?"

She handed him a package—something wadded up in a brown paper lunch bag.

"Here. This is what you wanted."

"I wanted?"

Baffled, he wormed his hand inside the bag and produced a test tube filled with clear fluid; a sheet of computer printout came with it.

"I don't get it."

"It's what Oliver Lathram puts in his brother's implants."

"Oh, hey, I didn't—"

"Analyze it, Gerry. Satisfy your curiosity, resolve your suspicions, and then let me know what you find. That's a list of what's *supposed* to be in the solution. See if the analysis matches it."

She was so stiff, her expression so grim.

"Gina, what's wrong?"

"I don't like what I'm doing, Gerry. I'm not proud of myself for sneaking this out of Oliver's lab."

"But you didn't have to. I was only—"

"You started me thinking, you got me worried. So now I want to know too."

"I'm sorry."

She started to say something, then seemed to change her mind. It looked as if she'd been about to say, *You should be,* but she said, "It's okay. You're just doing your job."

He offered the tube to her. "You can have this back."

She shook her head. "Too late now."

The tension was so thick between them Gerry doubted even a Ginsu knife would cut it.

"Dinner was great the other night," he said. "You're a super chef."

"I'm glad you liked it."

No thaw yet. He'd have to pull out the big guns.

"Martha loved it. And she loves you."

Gina's features softened. Finally.

"And I love her," she said. Then she pointed to the test tube. "But let me know about that stuff as soon as you hear, Gerry. It's important to me."

"Don't worry. As soon as I hear, you'll hear. But in the meantime, what are you doing for dinner tonight?"

She shook her head. "Moonlighting at Lynnbrook." She turned and started walking away. "You *will* let me know, won't you?"

Gerry raised three fingers, Boy Scout style. "Promise."

Damn right I promise, he thought. *Because I can see you're going to be a basket case until I do.*

As he headed upstairs to get a lab requisition form, he didn't know whether he should be elated or depressed. He had a sample of Duncan Lathram's solution, but he'd also made Gina terribly upset. Was the prize worth the cost? If analysis turned up a toxin, how would he tell her?

But he would. And pull her out of Lathram's place so fast her head would spin.

* * *

Gina ran into Dr. Conway as she checked into the doctors lounge at Lynnbrook. He was on his way out. She nodded absently. Duncan and Oliver's secret sauce was on her mind and Conway was almost gone before she realized she hadn't seen him since Harriet Thompson's death.

"I heard about Harriet Thompson," Gina said. "Sorry."

"Yeah," he sighed. He looked depressed. "Me too. But there's some lawyer in town who's real happy about it."

"Oh, no. You're getting sued?"

He nodded. "For gross negligence. The daughter in San Diego who couldn't get free to come look after her mother for a few days managed to find a lawyer as soon as she got to town. Probably called 1-800-SUE-DOCS or whatever number the ambulance chasers are using today. Never miss an opportunity to cash in, right?"

Gina could understand his bitterness. "Why doesn't she sue the PRO?"

"Don't you know? Physician Review Organizations are immune from malpractice suits. That leaves me."

Gina felt awkward and angry. Not knowing what else to do, she put a hand on his shoulder.

"Don't worry. You'll win."

"Sure," he said. His smile was humorless. "Bet you just can't wait to get into practice." He walked out.

THE WEEK OF OCTOBER

8

19
ON THE HILL

"YOU'RE GOING TO HAVE TO LEARN TO PLAY THE GAME, Hugh."

Gina slowed as she passed the closed door to Senator Marsden's office. Her mind had been far away, wondering what the analysis of Oliver's secret sauce was showing. She'd die if there was anything incriminating in it.

The waiting was consuming her. She could barely concentrate on anything else. But the condescension in the voice slipping through the senator's transom pulled her up short. She knew Senator Kramer had arrived for a meeting. Their voices weren't raised but even out here she could sense the tension.

Senator Marsden's voice sounded tight. "When I start thinking of the Senate as a game, I'll know it's past time to quit."

Kramer chuckled. "I was pretty self-righteous too when I was a freshman. But I learned. And if you want to get things done in this town, you'll learn too. You don't, you get left out in the cold."

"I'm not in favor of loosening up on offshore drilling at the moment. I don't think we need it now."

"I'm sorry to hear that, Hugh. Because it's important to my people."

"Do I take it that my position on easing offshore drilling restrictions will affect your vote on the Guidelines bill?"

"Oh, I wouldn't put it that way. Let's just say I'm reserving my judgment until your bill gets out of committee."

"I see."

"It's horse trading, son," Kramer said, getting folksy all of a sudden. "It's what makes the wheels turn. I'm obliged to keep the home folks happy and prosperous. Remember: One person's pork-barrel project is another person's wise investment in the local infrastructure."

"How about simply casting a vote for something because it's the right thing to do?"

Gina heard a chair scrape against the floor.

"Because what's right for you isn't necessarily right for me. We'll talk again sometime, Hugh."

Not wanting to get caught with her ear to the door, Gina hurried off.

She related the conversation to Alicia on their way to the Senate cafeteria in the basement of the Dirksen Building. The Hart and Dirksen buildings were attached, but the walls down here were brick, the doors a dark oak, in sharp contrast to the antiseptic decor of the newer Hart. They passed the Senate Post Office, then turned into the caf.

"I'm not surprised," Alicia said. She picked out a tuna salad and a diet Pepsi. "A lot of the people on the Hill don't think he's for real. And the ones that do are leery of him."

Gina took a turkey on rye and a Mountain Dew.

"Care to explain that?"

Alicia scanned the tables. "Let's see if we can get off by ourselves and I'll give you the true facts."

"True facts? You mean as opposed to the other kind?"

"Exactly."

They found an isolated corner table. Alicia sat with her back to the wall and watched the room as she spoke.

"First off, you should know that Senator Marsden ruffled a lot of feathers right off by coming to town with a self-imposed term limit. He said depending on how much he accomplished, he might serve only one term, and absolutely positively no more than two. That was a no-no."

"What's wrong with that?"

"Because term limits is a *very* touchy subject around here. The members like to think of themselves as elected for life."

"How can they? Congressmen have to run every two years."

"Well, as I heard one member say to another back in the eighties, 'You have to be a real bozo to lose this job.' Incumbents average a ninety-five-percent reelection rate."

"Wow."

"I tell you, Gina, nobody wants to leave this place once they get here. And can you blame them? You're part of the most powerful government in the world. And the most expensive. Salary, perks, and privileges come to more than two million bucks per member per year. No other government even comes close. And the few bozos who somehow fail to get reelected don't go home—they hire out as lobbyists. It's called Potomac fever. I understand it's incurable."

"Do you think Senator Marsden will catch it?"

"Maybe," she said. "You never know. I think he's sincere when he says he doesn't intend to stay here more than two terms. But I'm in the minority. Just about everyone else on the Hill thinks it's a pose. A holier-than-thou act that he'll use to squeeze the PACs for big bucks later. They're all watching, waiting to see if it works."

"That's sick," Gina said. "Why do you put up with it? Why've you been at it for so long?"

Alicia shrugged. Her smile was shy. "Potomac fever. We staffers aren't immune either. Who knows? Maybe you'll catch it too. Maybe you already have."

Not me, Gina thought. I'm immune to that sort of thing. She felt a twinge of uneasiness. At least I hope I am.

Gina was straightening up her work area, preparing to call it a day as a legislative aide and change into her doctor hat. Another frustrating round of writing reports on referral and utilization patterns and wondering if anyone would read them. She was also sneaking in time on a freelance report, using the Harriet Thompson case as a paradigm of how treatment guidelines can backfire. She hoped the story's poignancy might raise a little consciousness as to the human cost of well-meaning guidelines when they were mechanically implemented.

Maybe in the process she could help Dr. Conway.

Alicia bustled by then.

"Got a maybe from Senator Hirsch," she said as she passed.

"Just a maybe?" That surprised Gina. Hirsch always seemed to have something to say about health-care policy. "I thought he'd jump at the chance."

Alicia slowed but kept moving. "It's a joint committee, not a permanent thing. Too ad hoc. It might screw up his ranking position on his other committees, ones that guarantee serious, long-term PAC attention."

Gina couldn't hide her annoyance. "Is everything about money, dammit?"

"Senator Mark Hanna said something you should keep in mind when you're working on the Hill: 'There are two things that are important in politics. The first is money . . . and I can't remember what the other one is.' That's from the horse's mouth. But what this place is really about is influence. And influence brings in campaign donations. And campaign donations help you come back for another term."

"So you can increase your influence," Gina said without enthusiasm.

Alicia laughed and gave her a thumbs-up. "Now you're getting it!"

"I'm afraid I am," Gina muttered as Alicia disappeared down the hall.

Then her phone with the seal of the Senate rang. It was Gerry.

"The report's back."

Gina lowered herself into her chair. "I thought you said not until tomorrow."

"Your list helped. Much easier to identify compounds when you know what you're looking for. And besides, I told them it was for someone very important. So they rushed it."

Gina couldn't help smiling as a warm rush washed through her. She liked this man more each day.

"And?"

"And the analysis matches the list perfectly. Nothing in there that isn't supposed to be there."

Gina sagged in her chair. She felt weak all over. She was so damn *glad* she could have cried right then.

"Gina? You still there?"

"Yes," she said softly. "Thank you, Gerry. You don't know how good that is to hear."

"How about dinner tonight? That sound good?"

"Tonight's a Lynnwood night, I'm afraid." A thought struck her. "But I've got a great idea. Come with me to my folks' house on Thursday night. It's Columbus Day and my father always makes a big deal of it. It's crazy. You'll love it. And bring Martha. There'll be plenty of pasta with no meat."

"You're on."

A few minutes later Gina was on her way out of Senator Marsden's office, feeling as if the weight of the world had been lifted from her shoulders. Duncan and Oliver were in the clear.

One less thing to worry about.

20
COLUMBUS DAY

GERRY AND MARTHA WERE WARMLY RECEIVED INTO THE
folds of the Panzella clan's Columbus Day celebration. Gina
knew the welcome might have been a bit more guarded had
her folks realized that Gerry was more than just an old high
school friend she'd run into again.

Gina had already explained to her folks about Gerry's
being a widower. It probably wasn't necessary, but you
never knew. Papa had a tendency to verbalize whatever was
on his mind, especially after he'd been celebrating for a
while. She could just hear him asking Gerry where Martha's
mother was. Papa was looking forward to meeting him. He
vaguely remembered his name from the Washington-Lee
football team, and was intrigued by the fact that he was an
FBI agent. Mama wanted to know all the details of his
widowerhood, clucking and tsking and *Madrone*ing as Gina
told her.

What she hadn't explained was how she felt about him,
the growing need, the building heat between them.

It went swimmingly. Papa and Gerry hit it off immediately, and Uncle Fiore used to be a cop so he wanted to talk shop with the Fibby. And Martha . . . well, Martha charmed the women immediately and before Gina knew it, the little five-year-old was in the kitchen, draped in an apron almost as big as she was, standing on a chair at the counter helping Mama and Aunt Maria roll meatballs and stuff shells.

Gina passed her Aunt Terry and her Aunt Anna in whispered conversation.

". . . killed in a car accident. A terrible tragedy."

"And I understand he's raising that little girl all by himself."

"And doing a good job, I'd say. Isn't she darling?"

Gina moved on, smiling.

She had hoped that as the evening wore on it would become apparent to anyone who saw them together that she and Gerry were more than just friends. She knew she had succeeded when she overheard Mama in serious conversation with Gerry.

"And now your name. I'm not sure how you spell it. Is that with an 'i' at the end?"

"No. With an 'e-y.' 'C-a-n-n-e-y.' It's Irish."

"Is it now? 'At's a-nice."

Gina almost laughed aloud at Mama's sudden reversion to an Italian accent. She was born in Baltimore.

But Gerry earned a place in Mama's heart by eating everything she put in front of him—from stuffed calamari to stuffed shells—and coming back for more. How could she stay cool toward anyone with a big appetite who loved her cooking? And Martha . . . Martha actually ate a meatball, a little one she'd made herself.

Gina was careful what she ate. Pasta had awakened inside her and was urging her to fill her plate, but Gina turned a deaf ear. She stayed on the move, sampling and nibbling, and made sure to leave something on each plate she used.

After dessert Gina spotted Gerry in a corner doing shots with Papa, Uncle Fiore, and Uncle Dom. Gerry caught her eye, lifted his glass of pale liquid, and winked at her. God, he looked great. And she loved the way he seemed to fit right in, going with the flow of the party, not standing on the side watching, but jumping right into the heart of the festivities. She realized right then how much she wanted him.

She wondered if she should warn him about what he was drinking. If that was what she thought it was, he was going to be sorry. But why be a wet blanket? Let him have his fun.

The dishes were washed and racked and the festivities were waning when Gina, Gerry, and Martha made their way toward his car. Mama, Papa, and a couple of the aunts and uncles were standing on the front stoop waving good-bye.

"I think you two were a hit," Gina said. "Did you have fun?"

"I think I had too much fun," Gerry said. He held out the keys. "Do you mind?"

He seemed fine, steady on his feet, his voice clear, but Gina took them, glad he could admit when he'd had too much.

"Not at all."

"Mama said I could come back and help her cook anytime," Martha said.

Gina had to smile. Her mother must have really taken to Martha if she told her to call her Mama.

"And I know she meant it," Gina told her. "It's been a long time since she had a little girl around to help her cook."

She remembered with a pang all the holidays she'd stood on a chair at the very same counter and helped her mother prepare the feasts. She wondered if Mama felt abandoned by the daughter who went off to become a doctor. Without sons there'd be no daughter-in-law to take under her wing.

I wonder if she knows how much I love her? Gina thought.

But when was the last time I told her?

She couldn't remember. That shook her. She took it for granted Mama knew, but everyone needed to hear it once in a while. Gina vowed to start doing just that on a regular basis.

Why not start now?

She ran back to the front steps and threw her arms around her mother.

"I love you, Mama. You're the best." She kissed the stunned woman and then hurried to the car. A glance over her shoulder showed Papa beaming and Mama smiling and wiping her eyes.

After strapping Martha into the backseat, Gerry slumped into the passenger seat.

"What was that your father was pouring at the end?"

"Grappa," Gina said.

"I was fine up till then. I mean, I'm Irish. We can drink just about anything that won't kill us. But that stuff . . ."

"Grappa won't kill you," Gina said with a smile. "But if you're not used to it, it can make you wish it had."

Martha's bedtime was long past but she was wired, talking at light speed about filling cannolis and grating cheese and how ugly the calamari were before Mama cleaned them. Gina was glad it hadn't been Easter. How would Martha have reacted to *capozella?* If she and Gerry were still seeing each other next spring—and she hoped they would be—Gina would have to prepare Martha for the sight of a sheep's head in the kitchen.

Martha talked nonstop right into the parking lot by their apartment, but was sound asleep in her father's arms by the time they reached the front door. Gina went upstairs and helped put her to bed.

Downstairs, Gerry put his arms around her. She snuggled against him.

"Thanks, Gina," he whispered. "This has to be the best Columbus Day of my life."

"It's not over yet," she said, and kissed him.

He leaned back and looked at her for a second, then they kissed again, long and passionately. Gina didn't want this night to end yet.

They tumbled to the couch and before long were fumbling with each other's buttons, shucking off their clothes like old skins until there was nothing between the new skins. And they didn't need much foreplay because he was ready and God knew she'd been ready all night.

She didn't want to ask, but she forced herself to say it. "I don't have to worry about you, do I?"

"What? Oh, you mean . . . no. Well, two women, both very straight. We thought something might be there but nothing came of either. How—how about you?"

"One guy for most of my residency."

"What happened?"

"I came here, he stayed there. It's over."

"Good."

And then he was above her and in her and he rode her furiously, bringing her to the peak . . . and then leaving her there.

"I'm sorry," he said when he'd caught his breath a moment later. "It's been so long, and I've wanted you so bad. I just . . ."

She put her arms around his neck and held him close. "It's all right," she said. "I understand. There'll be other times."

Physically, she was frustrated—here she was with Gerry Canney, her high school dream man, her very much *now* man—and her pelvis felt as if it were ready to explode. It wasn't supposed to be like this. He was supposed to be the perfect lover and she should have been drifting on ecstatic clouds of delight. But another part of her was charmed. She'd sensed he was a straight arrow, and this confirmed it in a way. If he'd performed like a stud tonight she might have wondered about him.

She did wonder about herself. Did she really feel this deeply about Gerry, or was it a rebound thing, someone to fill the void left by Peter?

No, she decided. This is real. This has been a long time coming.

As they cuddled, he ran a hand over her abdomen and traced the long, puckered scar that ran from the lower tip of her sternum straight to the left of her navel.

"What's this?"

"The reason you'll never see me in a bikini."

"No, really."

She told him about being hit by the truck, her torn-up insides, and how Duncan had put her back together.

"Ah. Now I see why you're so devoted to him. I guess I owe him."

"What for?"

"For saving you for me. Let me show you a couple of my scars. Here's my appendectomy . . ."

"Mine is bigger than you-ors," Gina singsonged.

And somewhere along the way as they compared scars, she noticed that he was ready again.

"It *really* has been a long time, hasn't it?" she said.

"Forever."

But this time she took charge, straddling him, riding him, controlling the tempo, and when she climaxed it was as if the almost-orgasm of before had been waiting in the wings and had jumped in at the last minute to explode with the new one. She moaned and he reached up to cover her mouth and she bit down on his hand and thought she was going to pass out.

Later, as they sprawled exhausted on the couch, she saw that his hand was bleeding.

"Oh God, I'm sorry. Look what I did. I didn't mean to."

"I know. I just didn't want anything to wake Martha."

God, she'd forgotten all about Martha.

"But you said she's a sound sleeper."

"She is. And she's probably sleeping like the dead after that party tonight, but still . . ."

"Even in the throes of passion, you don't stop being the protective father."

"It's not a hat I can just take off when I want to. I hope that doesn't offend you."

"Not in the least," she said and kissed him to make sure he understood. "It tells me something about you—something good."

She loved this man. She felt so at home with him. They shared a past, and she sensed they shared a set of values. Here was something that could really last.

With that thought bright and warm in her mind, Gina dozed off.

Gina was almost dressed when Gerry woke up. Dawn was moments away. He winced at the light. She could tell he had a headache.

"What're you doing?"

"Got to get home and get showered. Surgery this morning with Duncan."

"At least stay for coffee. I can put on—"

"I think it's better if Martha doesn't find me here when she wakes up."

"Maybe you're right," he said, "but I won't be getting her up for a while yet."

"Still, I've got to go."

They embraced. She didn't want to let go, didn't want to leave. She wanted to spend the morning with Gerry having coffee and bagels and then making love again and showering together and then, maybe only then, think about assisting on cosmetic surgery.

"My place next time. We can scream and shout all we want. Nobody in Adams Morgan notices that sort of thing."

On her way home, the sun was just peeking over the horizon and silhouetting the spire of the Washington Monument as she crossed the Arlington Memorial Bridge.

Again she worried that she was rushing things with Gerry. But no . . . this felt *right*.

Does it get any better than this? she wondered. She was assisting Duncan Lathram, she was legislative aide to Senator Marsden on health-care matters, she was making love to Gerry Canney. Finally, all the pieces of her life seemed to be falling into place.

No. It did not—could not—get any better than this.

21
CONSULTATIONS

▼

MRS. JABLONSKY WANTED A BREAST REDUCTION. SHE SAT topless on the examination table, lifting her large, pendulous breasts and letting them drop . . . lifting and dropping . . .

"I'm sixty-eight years old," she told Duncan. "I've had these since I was fourteen. I used to be proud of them, but now they're quite literally a pain. They're weighing me down, making me stoop-shouldered, giving me backaches. I want them gone."

"Surely not gone," Duncan said.

"No, of course not. Just less of them. If they droop any farther I'll be able to tuck the damn things into my waistband."

Duncan laughed. "That doesn't sound too comfortable. We'll trim them to a more manageable size for you. But what . . . ?"

He'd noticed a large number of white and pink lesions all over her trunk. He touched one, then another. They looked and felt like the aftereffects of cryosurgery.

"Oh, those. That's Dr. Sauer's work. You know—the dermatologist? He's been removing my lesions."

"Your lesions?"

"That's what he calls these things." She pointed to a half-inch area of seborrheic keratosis on her upper arm. "He says they're not cancerous but they could change anytime."

"These things? He said they might turn cancerous?"

"Yes. And I had *loads* of them."

Duncan felt his jaw muscles tighten. "How many of these 'lesions' has he removed?"

"Oh, fifty at least. He had me coming back every week to take off a few more. We're just about done. It's been quite a trial, but it's such a relief to know I won't have to worry about skin cancer anymore."

"Must have cost you a fortune."

"Oh, no. He just billed Medicare. He accepts insurance. Not like you."

"You're right there, Mrs. Jablonsky. I'm nothing like Dr. Sauer." He lowered his voice and muttered, "Probably graduated from the Ingraham."

"I beg your pardon?"

"Nothing."

Duncan ground his teeth. The medical mountebank. Freezing off perfectly benign keratoses and billing for removal of precancerous lesions.

What a world. All a doctor had to do was practice straight, ethical medicine, and he was guaranteed a decent living. But that wasn't enough for the avaricious slugs who left a trail of slime across the profession. It drove him up the wall.

Congress had no exclusive on greed. There were doctors who deserved an implant as well.

Duncan's thoughts began to wander a new path, wondering if there might be a way . . .

He shook it off. No sense in letting matters get completely out of hand.

He scheduled Mrs. Jablonsky for surgery, then went on to the next patient. The chart sat in a pocket on the outside of the exam-room door. He glanced at the intake sheet as he reached for the doorknob—and stopped. *Hugh K. Marsden.* Could it . . . ?

His gaze jumped a couple of lines down to the occupation box: *U.S. senator.*

Duncan leaned against the doorjamb. This was too much. The chairman himself?

Could it be . . . was someone on to him? Was he being set up?

But they'd never use a U.S. senator to try and trap him. Still . . . hard to believe Marsden's presence was mere chance.

Well, he'd pretend not to recognize Marsden and see how the consultation played out.

"Mr. Marsden," he said, entering and extending his hand. "Dr. Lathram."

Marsden's handshake was firm. And he didn't correct Duncan's failure to address him as Senator.

"Glad to meet you, Doctor. You come highly recommended."

"That's always good to hear." He pretended to glance through the medical history on the intake form he'd already perused outside the door. "Looks like you've been in pretty good health. What can we do for you here?"

Marsden turned his head and touched the top of the auricle of his left ear. "I have it on good authority that this needs attending to."

Duncan stepped closer and saw the pink nodule in question. He touched it: smooth, firm. He pulled an illuminated magnifying glass from a drawer and bent for a closer look. Fine capillaries crisscrossed the opalescent surface. A positive Tyndall effect with the light. He palpated it again, pressing around the edges. It was bigger than he'd initially thought.

"Your authority is a good one. You've got a basal cell carcinoma there. No risk of distant spread, but if left to its own devices it will continue to grow and eventually ulcerate and bleed. My advice is to have it out now, while it's small."

"That's why I'm here."

Duncan placed the magnifier on the counter.

"Sorry. I don't do therapeutic surgery; only cosmetic work. But I can recommend—"

"*You* were recommended."

"I won't argue with that, but I don't do what you need done."

"But I *do* need a cosmetic repair. I don't want a notch out of my ear."

"I appreciate that, but—"

"Dr. Panzella told me you're the best."

"Gina? She sent you to me?"

Why? he wondered, irritably. She should know better.

"Not really. It seems we have something in common: She works for each of us. She spotted this thing on my ear—called it a 'lesion'—and told me to have it looked at. Since many of my colleagues on the Hill speak highly of you, and since Gina seems devoted to you, I figure you're the man."

Duncan's mind raced. He felt awkward. But this explained Marsden's presence: the Gina connection.

All right. Maybe it was time to stop playing completely dumb and move to slightly dumb.

"Marsden . . ." he said slowly. "Good Lord, you must be Senator Marsden. Forgive me for not making the connection. Of course. You're chairing the"—he snapped his fingers—"the . . ."

"The Guidelines committee."

"Right! The Joint Committee on Medical Ethics and Practice Guidelines."

Marsden smiled. "You know the full title. So few people do."

"I read a lot. You're group has had some trouble recently, it seems."

"Yes. Poor Harold. He's quite ill, I'm afraid."

"Any idea as to if or when he'll be back?"

"No. No definite word yet."

Marsden was playing it close to the vest. Not revealing anything. As he should do. Duncan was trying to sort out his feelings for this man. He had nothing personal against him. If he weren't chairing a committee that had no right to exist, he might even like him.

"A bit of bad luck, wouldn't you say?"

"Quite a lot more than a bit. It's almost as if some sort of curse was hanging over this committee."

"You don't know if any of your members went poking into a pharaoh's tomb, do you?"

Marsden's smile was wan. "You'd almost think so, wouldn't you?"

"Does that mean you're now out of the Guidelines business?"

"Only for a little while. I'm doing my damnedest to fill those empty seats. We should be rolling again in no time."

"Will you now?" Duncan said, feeling his jaw muscles bunch. "How interesting."

"But back to the matter at hand," Marsden said. "I'd like you to do the surgery. And the reason is, quite frankly, cosmetic. I understand you have a method that heals many times faster than regular surgery. I need that."

"Do you?"

"Yes. Depending on the president, the hearings could be up and running again in a matter of weeks. I don't want to be there on national TV with a cauliflower ear, or an ear that looks like someone took a bite out of it. You know the press. There'll be speculation about it; and once they find out, there'll be story after story on my skin cancer; then TV specials on the prevalence of skin cancer and how to avoid it."

"Nothing wrong with that."

"No. But I don't want the press to center on me and my minor skin disorder. They should focus on the Guidelines committee and what we're trying to do."

Just what *are* you trying to do? Duncan wanted to ask.

Marsden continued: "With your reputed skill and accelerated healing methods, I believe you're just the man for the job."

Oh, I am, Senator, Duncan thought. I am that.

"Very well, Senator. Because of your connection with Dr. Panzella—who speaks very highly of you, by the way—I'll make an exception. But I will not make an exception about not dealing with any insurance company. You pay my outrageous fee up front. In return you will get the finest cosmetic surgery in the world, with absolute discretion. Ours is a doctor-patient relationship. It does not involve Medicare, Medicaid, Blue Cross, HMOs, PPOs, IPAs, or any of the rest of the alphabet soup. I do not fill out forms, talk to utilization committees or quality assurance coordinators or nurse-bureaucrats insisting on a second or third opinion. I speak to you, you speak to me. No other parties involved."

Marsden's expression reflected fascination rather than consternation.

"I take it then that you're not a participant in any of the managed-care systems."

"You're looking at an endangered species, Senator."

"If you want, I can have you put on the Department of the Interior's protected list."

"Too late for that, I think."

"Well, the sale of my company left me with a bit of money. I can afford to spend some of it on my ear."

"Good. I'll turn you over to my secretary, who'll arrange all the releases. How does next week sound?"

"Thursday would be the best for me."

"I'll see what we can arrange. But if you want me to use the accelerated healing procedures, you'll have to watch a videotape and sign a stack of release forms. The implants I employ are still considered investigational at this point."

"Whatever you say."

"Excellent."

As Duncan led him out into the hall, he spotted Gina passing by.

She glanced his way, then did a double take.

"Senator Marsden!"

Something flickered across her face. Somewhere in the moment between her surprise of recognition and smile of greeting her features twisted with an odd expression. Was it fear, concern, or consternation? Whatever, it was plain that Gina was anything but happy to see the senator here.

Why?

She'd seen nothing but good results—*excellent* results—during her time here. Why on earth should she have the slightest concern about her senator's having surgery here?

Unless . . .

No. How could she suspect? How could she even guess?

It had to be something else. Maybe he'd misinterpreted her expression.

But he didn't think so. Something there, something very much like fear.

Duncan tried to shrug off the feeling but it wouldn't let go. Why on earth should the sight of him with Senator Marsden strike terror into Gina?

Unsettling thoughts whirled through Gina's mind as she watched Senator Marsden sign the consent forms, thoughts about three members of Marsden's committee, all Lathram patients, all either dead, damaged, or demented . . .

She did her best to keep calm.

"What a surprise to see you here," she said after Duncan was gone.

He tapped the tip of his ear with his finger. "Well, it seems it's unanimous that this has got to go. And didn't you say he was the best?"

"Yes, but I never meant you should come here . . . I mean, he doesn't take cases like yours."

"He said he'd make an exception in my case."

Gina felt a cold lump form in her stomach. Duncan never made exceptions.

"Really. I'm surprised."

"Maybe you should be flattered. He said it was because of you." He clapped her on the upper arm. "See. I knew I'd be glad I hired you."

I hope so, Senator, she thought. She made what she hoped was a graceful exit and hurried away. She had someplace to go.

She sat in the periodicals section of the D.C. Public Library's main branch on G Street. She'd remembered something Oliver had said about the Guidelines committee . . . shortly after Duncan had exploded at the news that she was looking for a post on the committee.

. . . *years ago he had a bit of trouble* . . .

Trouble with the Guidelines committee? How many years? Oliver wasn't talking. Maybe the microfilm would.

She ran a search of the *Washington Post* the year of Lisa's death, looking for Duncan.

The earliest was dated May 7th, about a week before the first anti-Duncan article in the *Alexandria Banner*. Front page, lower right corner.

Gina's stomach lurched as she read the heading: "Committee Decries 'Gross Overcharging' by Surgeon."

She scanned the article until she spotted his name, then backtracked.

From his seat beside the committee chairman, ranking member Senator Harold Vincent said his staff had uncovered a case of "flagrant abuse of the current system, right here in our own backyard." He went on to excoriate Dr. Duncan Lathram, a vascular surgeon in Alexandria, for collecting over a million dollars from Medicare last year. "This sort of gouging is a prime example of a profession running wild, lining their pockets with millions of taxpayers' hard-earned money. If ever there was a doubt that the medical profession needs guidelines imposed on it, that doubt should be banished by the likes of Dr. Lathram."

Gina sat rigid in her seat before the microfilm screen, shocked not only by the words, but by their speaker. Senator Vincent . . . Duncan had operated on him just a few weeks ago, they'd been bantering in the committee hearing room moments before his seizures. And though he'd attacked Duncan in public five years before, neither had ever mentioned it. Had they both forgotten?

No. Not Duncan. Vincent, maybe. In a quarter century on the Hill, this was simply another in an endless series of remarks prepared by one of his aides and tossed away after they were read into the record.

But Duncan . . . those words no doubt were branded on his brain. He'd never forget something like this. Nor would he forgive.

She went back and read the article from the beginning. Vincent had attacked Duncan from his seat on the Committee for Medical Practice Guidelines—the *original* Guidelines committee under Senator McCready. The article listed the other members of that first committee. Besides Vincent and McCready, it named Lane, Allard, and Schulz.

Schulz! Schulz had been on the original committee. Gina hadn't known that.

"Oh . . . my . . . God," she whispered. That was the connection between the four dead or injured legislators—all had been members of the McCready committee.

She found another mention of Duncan, deeper in the paper, a week later. This time it was Congressman Allard pillorying this price-gouging surgeon and calling him "the tip of the iceberg." Something must be done on the federal level. He demanded a Medicare audit of Duncan's office and hospital records.

Gina leaned back. So this was where Duncan's hell had begun, ignited by a spark from the original Guidelines committee. He must hate these men . . . yet he'd done cosmetic surgery on four of them.

And now those four were either dead or hospitalized.

It was all circumstantial, all four cases were different, and she couldn't see how any grand jury could indict on the available evidence . . . yet only a fool could deny the obvious and terrifying pattern.

But where was the connection to Lisa?

And did it matter?

At the moment, no. What did matter was that Senator Marsden was going under Duncan's knife next week.

She remembered him signing the surgical consent forms a few hours ago. Wasn't there an expression about signing your life away?

22
GINA

GINA DIDN'T WAKE UP SATURDAY MORNING. SHE DIDN'T have to. She never got to sleep.

A night of endless tossing and turning. She'd tried everything short of a sleeping pill. She didn't have one around and it probably wouldn't have worked anyway. Her racing mind was stuck in overdrive and refused to downshift.

Something's going to happen to Senator Marsden.

The thought had ricocheted off the walls of her brain like a racquetball. She'd countered it with every explanation she could dredge up. It all came down to the fact that despite a seemingly obvious pattern, all the evidence was circumstantial. Yes, the committee had initiated a series of events that had ruined Duncan's practice, but it would take more than that to set him on a murderous vendetta.

Yet every time she thought she'd laid the fear to rest, some dark, formless dread from her hindbrain, that ancestral home of primal instincts, would rear up and slam it into wild, random motion again.

So now she sat in her bay window and looked down on the

Saturday-morning quiet of Kalorama Road. God, what was she going to do?

She'd have to do something.

Stop the surgery? How? What reason could she give? No, she'd have to find a way to ease her mind so she wouldn't go crazy waiting for something to happen.

But anything bad that happens to Marsden after the surgery, even if he gets hit by a meteor while raking leaves in his front yard, I'm going to blame on Duncan.

Gina could handle just about every question except the one about Duncan's desk drawer.

She had seen the vial and the oversized trocar. And she couldn't explain them.

What was in that vial? What was a trocar doing in there?

Only one way to find out. Did she dare?

She headed for the bedroom to throw on some clothes.

Gina let herself into the surgicenter through the private rear entrance and coded off the alarm. She felt more than a little guilty about this. After all, Duncan had entrusted her with a set of keys and here she was sneaking in to snoop through his desk.

It's not as if I'm going to steal anything, she thought. I'm just going to borrow a little reassurance.

She locked the door behind her, then set up her excuse for being here. Not much chance that anyone else would be in on a Saturday, and her car was in the rear lot, hidden from the street, but you never knew. So, first thing, she trotted down to the records room and left her Senate ID badge on the floor under the dictation desk. Should anybody ask, that was why she was here: looking for her lost badge.

Back upstairs, she let herself into Duncan's office. She noticed her hands were sweaty. What if Duncan popped in

and caught her here? Not likely. He couldn't wait to get out
of here weekday afternoons, so why would he show up on a
Saturday? Oliver was a different story. But he'd mentioned a
trip to Virginia Beach for the weekend, so it was unlikely
he'd show up.

Through the picture window she saw that the rock garden
was half in shadow. The shrubbery shielded her from anyone
outside, but also blocked her view of the rear parking lot, so
she left the office door open to hear anyone unlocking the
private entrance.

She moved to Duncan's desk, praying she'd find the top
right drawer sitting open.

No such luck.

Okay, another prayer that he'd forgotten to lock it. She
pulled on the handle. The drawer wiggled but wouldn't slide.

Damn! She slapped her palm against the drawer. She
wanted this over with. She couldn't stand it.

She slumped into Duncan's chair and stared at the drawer.
The putting-to-bed—or God forbid, confirmation—of all
her distress lay on the far side of half an inch of wood. She
stared at the brass face of the lock. She'd seen Duncan's key
ring hanging from that lock, which meant the drawer key
went wherever he went. But maybe there was a spare around.

She went through each of the remaining drawers carefully
and did find two keys, but neither fit the lock. She tried
prying it open with a letter opener but was getting nowhere,
and she was afraid to exert too much leverage for fear of
scratching the wood.

If only she knew how to pick a lock . . . or knew someone
who did . . .

They made love first.

Gerry arrived a few minutes early and, as much as Gina
wanted to learn how to pick a lock, the sight of him standing

inside her door swept away thoughts of locked drawers. After about three words they were in each other's arms and leaving a trail of clothing between the front door and the bedroom. Nicer making love on a bed instead of a couch, and this time Gerry took charge, running his lips around her nipples, then between her breasts, down along her scar to her navel, circling that, and continuing downward. She whimpered with delight and thrust herself against his probing tongue.

Afterward, they lay breathless and sweaty in each other's arms. Gina fought the urge to fall into a contented doze. She got up, threw on a robe, and opened a bottle of merlot. They snuggled together on the couch, sipping their wine.

"That was wonderful."

"For both of us," she said, nuzzling his neck.

"By the way, did I say hello?"

Gina laughed. "That was a hectic scene, wasn't it?"

"Where's this lock you can't open?" he said finally.

Gina was uncomfortable with the lie she'd told him about a lost key, so she was glad she didn't have to remind him. She pointed to the far corner of the room.

"That little oak filing cabinet over there. I don't even know why I locked it. And now the key is gone."

She hated lying, but she couldn't tell Gerry the real reason. He was too much of a straight arrow to let her go through with her plan.

She'd chosen the little oak filing cabinet because its lock looked to be about the same size as the one on Duncan's drawer.

"No spare key?"

She looked sheepish. "I think it's inside."

That, at least, was true.

Gerry laughed as he picked up his jacket and pulled an oblong box from the pocket.

"A lock-picking kit?"

"Even better." He opened the box and showed her

something that looked like a miniature cordless screwdriver. "A battery-operated lock pick."

"Really? I didn't even know there was such a thing."

"They've been around for a while. This one's the EPG-1 Electropick. It'll open just about any pin-and-disk tumbler cylinder lock in under a minute."

"What about picking locks the old-fashioned way?"

"Let's hope that won't be necessary," Gerry said. "I never learned how. Lock picking isn't a skill required by the Bureau."

"Then why this electro-thing?"

"For when we're in a big hurry and we can't get a locksmith right away."

He tried a number of little black metal instruments in the keyhole until he found one that fit, then he fixed that into the end of the Electropick and began adjusting a thumbscrew atop the device.

"Once we find the right-sized raking tool, we adjust the up-and-down motion—a narrow range for a small lock like this—put it into the lock, and turn her on."

Gina watched the metal tool begin moving rapidly up and down inside the lock. Gerry moved the Electropick in and out a few times, then removed it.

"Okay. All the pins are in position. Now I just insert this tension bar"—he slipped a fine, L-shaped metal rod into the keyhole—"and twist."

She heard a click. He removed the tension bar and gestured toward the drawer.

"Okay. Give her a tug."

The cabinet drawer easily pulled open. She kissed him.

"My hero! A man of many talents."

He held up the Electropick. "Just me and my handy EPG-1."

"Wait a minute." She rummaged in the bottom of the cabinet drawer. "Here's the spare."

"Great place for it," Gerry said with a wry smile. "How about sticking it *under* the cabinet for safekeeping?"

"Good idea. But first . . ." She stuck the key in the slot and relocked the drawer. Then she held out her hand for the Electropick. "Let me try."

Gerry was hesitant, but then showed her how to use it. Under his guidance she unlocked and relocked the cabinet three times.

Gina knew then that she had to have an Electropick.

"Where can I get one of these things?"

"Not at Wal-Mart, that's for sure. They cost a couple of hundred bucks, but if you really want one I can give you the address of a mail-order place."

"That's okay," she said, disappointed. No time for mail order. "I mean, how many times would I need something like that?"

And then it was time for dinner. They went out to a Thai place in the neighborhood where she couldn't talk Gerry into trying fish stomachs in peanut sauce. Then they caught the new Kevin Costner flick. She could tell Gerry wasn't crazy about it, and she might not have liked it either if Kevin Costner hadn't been the star. Just watching him move and listening to his voice made up for a multitude of shortcomings in the rest of the film.

And finally it was back to the apartment for more lovemaking. Slow and deliberately languorous this time.

"Strange, isn't it?" Gina said as they lay together at the end. She was thinking how she might want to be with Gerry forever. "So much has happened to each of us since we went to high school. We hardly knew each other when we spent most of the day in the same building. And now after all those years and miles we run into each other in a city of millions and wind up like this. I don't believe in fate, but you've got to admit . . ."

"Fate," he said softly. "That has a nice ring to it."

Gerry left about 1:00 A.M. Without the Electropick. Desperate, Gina had removed it before handing him his jacket. She felt like a creep, but consoled herself with the thought that she was only borrowing it.

Gina was warm and contented as she dozed off, vowing to spend most of Sunday morning becoming an expert with the Electropick, then tackling Duncan's drawer in the afternoon.

Only a nagging apprehension about what she'd find there disturbed her repose.

THE WEEK OF OCTOBER

15

23
GINA

IT WAS TUESDAY AFTERNOON BEFORE GINA GOT A chance to use the Electropick on Duncan's drawer.

I should have been done with this days ago, she thought as she stood inside the door to the basement stairs. She was waiting for Barbara to leave her desk on one of her frequent trips to the copier or the printer, both of which were downstairs, or to the patient education room across the hall from her desk.

Sunday would have been perfect. Gina had practiced all morning with the Electropick and had become fairly adept. She'd used it on every cylinder lock in her apartment, even on her car.

Gerry had called Sunday afternoon, and they'd talked about how wonderful the night before had been. Finally he asked about the Electropick. He couldn't find it. Had he left it there? Gina told him he had and joked about it, telling him he didn't need to pull that old stunt of leaving something behind just so he could have an excuse to come back. When he mentioned stopping by later to pick it up, she begged off saying she had a million errands to run before pulling a shift at the hospital. Which was sort of true. Luckily, Gerry didn't seem to be in a big rush to get it back. They had a number of the things at the Bureau.

More practice, and by midafternoon Gina felt ready. But when she arrived at the office she found a dark blue Buick Park Avenue parked in the lot. Oliver's car. What was he doing back? And on a Sunday when he should have been home watching football? Except Oliver wouldn't know a Redskin from a Mighty Duck. All he cared about were his lab and his implants.

So Gina drove off and returned in two hours. The Buick was still there. Two hours after that it was gone but night was falling and the cleaning service had arrived. She had to call it quits. She was due at the hospital.

Monday offered no chance. Duncan stayed uncharacteristically late and Gina couldn't hang around because she had a meeting with the other legislative aides in Senator Marsden's office.

But today Duncan had stayed true to form, finishing his surgery and making a beeline for his club—so he said.

That was another thing that bothered her. Where did he really go? And who was the mysterious Dr. V. he'd been meeting with? Secrets and more secrets. How could she help but be suspicious?

She heard footsteps approaching. High heels. Only one person here wore heels. Casually, Gina stepped out into the hall.

"Hi, Barbara," she said.

The blonde started, then smiled. "Jesus God, you scared me. I thought you were gone."

"I will be in about two minutes."

Gina hurried down the hall and ducked into Duncan's office. Plenty of light from the afternoon sky filtering through the rock garden. Perfect lock-picking conditions.

"I've got to be crazy," she muttered. Tension was a cold hand tightening on the nape of her neck. She tried to shake it off.

Do it. Now.

She knew if she hesitated, if she gave herself time to think, she might allow a spasm of sanity to change her mind. She pulled the Electropick from her lab-coat pocket and knelt before the drawer. On the remote chance that it might be unlocked, she tugged on the pull. No such luck.

Okay. Electropick, do your thing.

She probed the keyhole with one of the raking tools but it wouldn't fit. She needed a smaller one. No problem. She'd spent much of Sunday switching rakes. A lot like switching drill bits, only easier. She inserted the next smaller size, adjusted the thumbscrew, then tried again.

This time it slipped in easily. Half a minute later she had the tension bar in the keyhole and was slowly twisting it. She heard a click as the little bolt slipped back inside the lock.

"Yes!" she whispered.

She extracted the tension bar and pulled open the drawer. And there they were: the oversized trocar and the mystery bottle.

She hesitated, then picked up the trocar and sighted down its bore—little more than a hollow stainless steel tube with a sharp, beveled point at one end and a hilt at the other. Something like a giant hypodermic needle. Just about big enough to hold one of those giant economy-size implants she'd seen Oliver dissolving with ultrasound. She slipped the obturator into the trocar, filling the bore with more stainless steel.

She remembered the puncture wound on Senator Vincent's thigh in recovery. It could have been made by something like this. She imagined Duncan positioning the trocar's sharp beveled point against the skin along the outer aspect of Vincent's thigh, then punching it through on an angle. He'd advance the trocar about three inches into the subcutaneous fat, then withdraw the solid obturator, leaving the hollow outer tube in the thigh. He'd slip the implant into the bore of the trocar. With the blunt end of the obturator he'd ease the implant to the far end of the bore, retract the trocar along the shaft of the obturator, then remove both instruments as one.

Leaving the implant behind, nestled in the subcutaneous fat of the thigh.

She shuddered. The whole idea gave her the willies.

She separated the trocar and obturator and laid them aside, then picked up the mystery bottle. An injection vial. She examined its top and spotted multiple punctures in the center of the red rubber stopper.

It's been used, she thought. But what's in it?

A thin, clear, amber fluid sloshed on the other side of the glass. She twisted the bottle until she could read the label. The GEM Pharma colophon huddled in the upper left corner. Two words were typed across the center:

TRIPTOLINIC DIETHYLAMIDE

"Well," she muttered, "that clears up everything."

What the hell was triptolinic diethylamide? She'd never heard of it. She studied the name, committing its spelling to memory, then she placed the bottle on the desktop and began rummaging through the drawer.

Not much there. The most prominent object was the little handheld recorder that Duncan used for his consults and operative reports. Gina's heart revved a little when she spotted a tape in it. She pressed the rewind, then hit PLAY. A tinny version of his voice buzzed forth, droning an incision-by-incision, suture-by-suture recap of the tip graft they'd done on an eighteen-year-old girl's nose Monday. She spot-checked through the tape and found only more of the same.

In the back of the drawer she found a slightly faded photo of a teenage girl. Blond hair, a forced smile, and bright blue eyes. Duncan's eyes.

Gina's fingers trembled. Lisa Lathram. Had to be. She stared at the innocent, seemingly untroubled face that offered no hint of the troubled soul harbored within. Who'd ever guess she'd attempt suicide three times?

Gina sighed and put the photo aside.

What else in the drawer? No other tapes. A few business cards, a two-year-old schedule for the Orioles, a brochure from a coffee importer, some blank index cards, and a nail clipper.

That was it.

Gina leaned against the desk, relieved, but still unsettled. Lisa's photo was here, but no legislator death list with names crossed off, no morbid collection of newspaper clippings. But still there was the trocar and the triptolinic diethylamide, whatever that was. Probably harmless . . . but why was it in his locked drawer? Maybe for the same reason an old Orioles schedule and a nail clipper were locked up along with them: This simply was where certain items ended up.

No. That didn't wash. Duncan had been a little too quick to close this drawer when he'd found her staring into it that time. And he seemed religious about keeping it locked. Obviously he wanted to keep this stuff private.

She replaced the photo and the incidental items, then the trocar and obturator; then, after one last look at its label, the bottle of triptolinic diethylamide, arranging them all as closely as possible in their original positions. Then she slid the drawer closed and was reaching for the Electropick to lock up again when she heard a voice outside.

Duncan!

She snatched up the pick, ducked under the desk, and crouched in the kneehole.

Ohmigod, ohmigod, ohmigod! Her heart pounded, her mind raced. Where'd he come from?

Thankfully the desk had a so-called modesty panel that shielded the front of the kneehole, but she knew her feet were visible in the gap between the panel and the floor. She held her breath as Duncan approached, apparently calling back to Barbara as he entered.

". . . only for a minute. I'm not staying."

Gina huddled in a ball, trembling, rationalizing with herself: What was the worst that could happen? If he discovered her, she'd be terminally embarrassed, she'd blurt something unintelligible, bolt from the room, and never show her face around here again. And that would be it. Not as if she was in any real danger. But then, considering the humiliation she'd feel, she wondered if she just might prefer death to being caught here.

She watched the carpet along the edges of the kneehole and saw Duncan's shoes appear under the modesty panel. She held her breath. Maybe she'd get through this. Hadn't he said he was only going to be a minute? As long as he didn't sit down . . .

An awful thought struck: My God, what if he checks his drawer and finds out it's unlocked?

She huddled breathless and statue-still as he shuffled through the papers on his desk. She heard him grunt, heard a piece of paper being folded, then listened to him turn and walk out.

Gina slumped back and almost sobbed with relief as she gasped for breath. She'd made it. She didn't move just yet. She stared at her watch and forced herself to wait a full two minutes.

Stiffly, she rolled from under the desk and began guiding the business end of the Electropick toward the keyhole in the drawer. Her hands trembled from the adrenaline still burning through her bloodstream. She fumbled the tool into the opening and thumbed the switch. The tool did its thing. When she felt the pins slide into line, she removed the Electropick, inserted the tiny torsion bar, and twisted. She heard the bolt snap into the lock position.

But when she tried to remove the bar, it wouldn't budge. She moaned softly. "Oh, no!"

What else could go wrong?

Her fingertips grew slick as she tried to wiggle it out. She thought she heard someone outside the office door. With one last desperate, frantic tug she wrested the torsion bar from the lock and almost landed on her back.

Sweating, shaking, she jammed the Electropick and its accessories into her pocket and hurried to the door. She pressed her ear against it and listened. Quiet. She opened it a crack and sneaked a look at Barbara's desk. Empty. Gina took a breath, stepped through, and walked out.

She passed Barbara in the hall, carrying a printout.

"You're *still* here?" Barbara said.

"Practically on my way out. Say, did I hear Dr. Lathram's voice before?"

"Yeah. But you missed him. He's already come and gone. I think he forgot something. Probably back on the golf course already."

Yeah. Right.

"Barbara, I just have to look something up, then I'm gone. See you Thursday."

She hurried to the records room. Carol the file clerk had left for the day, so Gina had the room to herself. Manila folders lined every inch of wall except for the dictation area in the corner. A computer terminal on the desk there, and a short shelf of medical reference texts. Gina grabbed the PDR and thumbed through the generic and chemical name index. No listing for triptolinic diethylamide.

Not surprising. It wasn't in a commercial container.

Next was the *Merck Index*, a weighty, small-print tome

that listed the name and formula of just about every available chemical compound. But again she struck out.

Gina sat at the dictation desk and stared at the blank face of the computer screen before her, wondering where to look next.

Okay. If the *Index* didn't list the stuff, it was either brand new or had never been reported to it.

She snapped her fingers. An investigational compound. Something in development. Had to be.

But how to track it down? The properties of new compounds were kept close to the vest during the development stages. But their formulas were registered immediately for patent protection.

Gina picked up the phone.

"Hi, Barbara. Don't we have a linkup to the FDA database?"

"Sure. And NIH, and the American College of—"

"How do I access the FDA?"

"It's kinda complicated. I've got an instruction manual somewhere around here that tells—"

"I'll be right up."

Gina trotted upstairs where Barbara made a relay team handoff of the manual as Gina passed her desk. A minute later she was seated before the records-room computer, logging herself into the FDA computer, and picking her way through the various menus until she got to investigational compounds in development.

But again no listing for triptolinic diethylamide.

Double damn. This was like chasing a phantom. But she wasn't giving up yet. There had to be some other way. The label on the bottle . . . the GEM Pharma colophon. What if she used the company as a starting point and worked back from there?

It took a good forty minutes of running into dead ends and backtracking, but she finally located triptolinic diethylamide in the vast cybernetic waste bin of discarded registered compounds on which further research had been canceled.

She downloaded the file and tagged it with her initials, *RFP* for Regina Francesca Panzella, then logged off the database. Back in the Lathram system again, she entered "TYPE RFP | MORE" and began reading from the hard drive.

A small file. Triptolinic diethylamide—referred to as TPD in the file—started off its existence at GEM Pharma as an investigational compound with antidepressant properties. Early animal trials in mice and rats were encouraging, but when testing moved up to primates, TPD was found to be toxic, inducing psychotic states. All further investigation was canceled and GEM Pharma moved on to more promising compounds.

A sudden queasy feeling rippled through Gina's stomach. Toxic . . . psychotic states . . . Senator Vincent's behavior before his seizure was certainly disturbed, might even fit the criteria for psychotic. And from what she'd heard, even though he hadn't had any further seizures, mentally he remained far out in left field.

And Duncan . . . Duncan had been there, right there in the hearing room when it had happened.

A few feet to her left, she heard the laser printer begin to hum.

And Congressman Allard . . . he'd had that nasty fall and cerebral concussion that had left him disoriented, not quite sure of who or where he was. But what if it wasn't the concussion that had scrambled his thoughts? What if his thoughts had been scrambled before the fall . . . as he was going down the steps? What if the scrambled thoughts had *caused* the fall?

Gina's own thoughts began to feel scrambled. She blinked and rubbed her eyes with an unsteady hand as the queasy feeling rippled toward nausea.

Footsteps behind her. Quickly Gina blanked the screen, then looked up to see Barbara retrieving her printout.

"You okay?" Barbara said, staring at her.

"Hmmm? Why do you ask?"

"Because you don't look so hot. I mean, you looked fine when you picked up that manual, now you look like you're gonna be sick."

Maybe I am.

Gina rubbed her upper abdomen. "My stomach's bothering me." That was no lie.

"You're working too hard. You're gonna give yourself an ulcer."

"Maybe I already have."

"I've got some Mylanta—"

"That's okay."

Barbara pointed to the FDA database manual. "You finished with that?"

"Yes. Thanks."

"I'm getting ready to leave," Barbara said as she picked up the manual. "You want me to lock you in?"

"No. I've done all I can do here. I'm on my way."

As Barbara went back upstairs, Gina shut off the terminal and got to her feet. She felt weak, confused as she trudged upstairs—ninety years old at least.

She was barely aware of her surroundings. Somewhere along the way she said good-bye to Barbara, but when she reached her car, she didn't start the engine. She sat behind the wheel and stared at the back of Duncan's office building.

Vincent . . . Allard . . . but what about Schulz? He jumped off his balcony. Was that psychotic? Maybe, maybe not. But it certainly wasn't rational. And Congressman Lane. He died in a car accident with a high blood-alcohol level. She couldn't link that to Duncan. But she couldn't rule it out, either. What if the TPD reacted with alcohol? Or what if it kicked in while he was driving? The same disorientation that could make you fall could make you drive off the road.

I hate this, she thought. She pounded her fist against the steering wheel. *Hate* it!

Duncan couldn't be involved in this. Couldn't—

Listen to me. Involved in *what?* No evidence that there was anything for Duncan to be involved *in*.

Then why the TPD? What legitimate reason could Duncan have for keeping a psychosis-inducing compound locked in his desk drawer?

Okay . . . Oliver used to work for GEM Pharma, the company name on the label. That would explain how the bottle found its way to Duncan. But why have it at all? Why keep something of no therapeutic value, something that was a proven toxin?

And what about the trocar, perfect for inserting one of Oliver's large-size implants—loaded with TPD, maybe?—under someone's skin, where it could nestle in the fat until Duncan zapped it with an ultrasound beam?

Wait a minute. Ultrasound. That was where this whole insane scenario broke down. Sure, Duncan had been at the Guidelines committee hearing when Senator Vincent went off the deep end, but Gina hadn't noticed him wheeling an ultrasound machine through the room.

And yet . . . with microchips and printed circuits, it was certainly possible to have an ultrasound transducer small enough to fit in one's pocket and . . .

Gina rubbed her throbbing temples. She hated what she was thinking. She began remembering Louisiana and wishing she'd stayed there.

If only she could *know!*

She shook herself and started the car. One thing she did know. Come Thursday morning she was going to be on duty and she was not going to let Senator Marsden out of her sight for one second.

24
PRESURGICAL

DUNCAN POURED A SECOND CUP OF COFFEE·FROM THE carafe and settled behind his desk. He liked Wednesday mornings in the cool stony quiet of the office, especially when, like today, he could get in early and have the place to himself. With no surgery scheduled, he could dawdle with his coffee, savoring the silence and the aroma as he watched his koi meander around their pool in the rock garden, and catch up on his dictation, tidy up any loose ends from Monday's and Tuesday's procedures, then have the rest of the day to himself. Maybe he'd call Brad and convince him to take the afternoon off from classes—he figured Brad would need about ten seconds of convincing. Maybe they could get in a round of golf. He hadn't played in ages.

He picked up the remote and aimed it at the TV across the room. He switched from CNN to *Today* to *Good Morning America* to *This Morning* and then back to CNN. Apparently nothing newsworthy had happened yesterday, and the morning shows seemed interested only in movie stars. C-SPAN was rerunning footage of presbyopic senators droning over-long speeches to an empty chamber in support of or in opposition to some inconsequential bill.

Time to catch up on dictating his surgical reports. He pulled out his key and inserted it into the lock. It wouldn't turn. He tried it again, wiggling it back and forth, sliding it in and out. He checked to make sure it was the right key, then tried again and noticed that the key wasn't going in all the way. Something was wrong with the lock. Jammed somehow.

Now how the hell had that happened? It hadn't been sticking or showing any warning signs that something was amiss. Goddamn. What a world. Didn't anybody make anything that worked?

He wandered out to Barbara's desk and now wished she were here. He needed to get a locksmith to get that damn thing open. He supposed he could call himself but it was probably too early. He grabbed a pen and left a note on Barbara's desk to call one as soon as she got in.

As he straightened and started to turn away, he noticed the manual for the FDA database lying on Barbara's desk. Probably Oliver had needed it. At least somebody was getting some use out of it.

He went in search of another minirecorder.

Gina levered up to a sitting position in bed.

"Oh my *God!*"

She'd been lying here, wishing she could rest easy and luxuriate. No surgery today, no moonlighting last night, and no meetings at the senator's until the afternoon. Should have been a great morning.

But yesterday's revelations wheeled over the bed like hungry vultures.

The trocar . . . the TPD . . . the information from the FDA . . . she kept trying to put a fresh spin on them, one that wouldn't make Duncan look bad. Racking her brain, going over everything, she remembered the FDA download. The "RFP" file she'd created on the hard drive.

She hadn't erased it.

She jumped out of bed and began pulling on her clothes. She could brush her hair in the car, but no time for a shower. She had to get up to the office and erase that file. If Duncan ever found it, or Oliver ran across it and asked Duncan about it, he'd know she'd been in the drawer.

She grabbed her car keys and ran out.

"All right, Doc," the locksmith said. He was thin, looked about forty, reeked of tobacco, and had *Bill* stitched on his work shirt. "You're all set."

"Excellent," Duncan said but didn't mean it. The man had spent an hour on what should have been a fifteen-minute job.

It hadn't been easy, but after twenty minutes of grunts and muttered curses, Bill finally got the drawer unlocked. Duncan had hovered over him the whole time, and as soon as the drawer slipped open, he removed the TPD and trocar and put them in one of the cabinets on the other side of the room. Neither would mean a thing to the locksmith, but Duncan wanted them safe and out of sight. As for the rest of the drawer's contents, he dumped them on the desktop.

Bill took the empty drawer out to his truck, saying he could work on it better there. Duncan figured he could also have a cigarette.

So now, after an interminable period, Bill was back.

"Had to put in a new lock."

"What was the matter with the old one?"

"I wanted to know the same thing. Had to take it apart to find out. A little strange."

Why did he seem hesitant?

"How so?"

He fished in his pocket and brought out a piece of Scotch tape. He dropped it on the desktop in front of Duncan.

"This was in it."

Duncan picked up the tape, a single piece folded on itself. Caught between the two sticky surfaces was a small shard of metal.

"How did this get in my lock?"

"Somebody left it there."

"Now why on earth—?"

"Not on purpose. It looks like it broke off the tip of a tension bar."

"A tension bar?"

"You know, something you use to pick locks with."

No, Duncan did not know. He stared at Bill as a spasm rippled through his intestines. He dropped the tape, then snatched it off the desk. Had this man actually said . . . ?

"*What?*"

Duncan's expression must have been fierce, because Bill began verbally backpedaling.

"I can't be sure, of course, but that's the first thing I thought of when I saw it drop out of the cylinder."

"But that's ridiculous!"

He realized he'd raised his voice. He hadn't meant to do that.

"Hey, okay," Bill said, making conciliatory motions with his hands. "Don't get excited. Makes no difference to me. If you ain't missin' nothin', then I guess maybe I could be wrong. But it sure looks like the tip of a tension bar."

Duncan's mind raced back over the contents of the drawer. The TPD, the trocar, Lisa's photo, the recorder, and some miscellaneous junk. All there when they'd opened the drawer.

He modulated his tone. "Well, I'm not missing anything.

And I don't keep anything in there worth stealing in the first place. So I guess that means the lock wasn't picked."

Bill shrugged, averting his gaze. "You could say that. Could also say that the piece might've chipped off and jammed in there before whoever it was got the drawer open."

Duncan winced as the spasm tightened its grip on his gut. *He's right. But who in the world . . . ?*

"Yes, well, since nothing is missing, I think I'll just forget about it. But I'm certainly glad you brought it to my attention."

"Hey, no problem."

When Bill left, leaving a set of keys for the new lock, Duncan went to the appliance cabinet and checked the TPD bottle. He hadn't memorized the previous fluid level but it appeared unchanged. The autoclave envelope was still sealed around the trocar. He replaced both in the drawer and locked it. Then he leaned back in his desk chair and felt his gut slowly uncoil as he willed himself toward calm.

All right. Let's be rational. Very strange. And very unsettling. But where was the logical reason for anyone to try to get into that drawer—and by picking the lock, of all things?

And what was there, really, to worry about? Even if someone had found the TPD, what could they do? They wouldn't know what it was. TPD was an orphaned, abandoned compound. The only record of its existence was in the dead files of GEM Pharma, and in the cavernous data banks of the . . .

FDA.

Good Lord!

Duncan bolted from the chair and hurried out to the reception area.

"Barbara! Did you use the FDA database yesterday?"

"No, I—"

"I saw the manual on your desk this morning."

She leaned back from him, a startled expression on her face. He hadn't intended to speak so harshly.

"I—I gave it to Dr. Panzella yesterday. She asked for it, so I dug it out for her."

He was stunned. Gina?

"That was all right, wasn't it?"

Gina?

"What? Oh, yes. Fine." Time for a little damage control. "I was just looking for it. I have to use it . . . need some data from the FDA myself."

Barbara handed it to him and he returned to his office, shaking his head at the image of Gina attempting to pick a lock.

Absurd. Laughable.

And yet . . .

She certainly had access and opportunity. But why would she? No. No way.

And yet . . .

The jammed lock, Gina asking for the FDA manual . . . the juxtaposition was just a little too close.

Duncan returned to his desk and turned on his computer terminal. Maybe there was some way to find out just what she was after from the FDA.

Gina stiffened behind the wheel when she saw Duncan's car in the lot. Not that unusual for him to be here on a Wednesday morning, but she'd been hoping and praying he'd have done whatever it was he did and be gone by now.

Well, she couldn't let that stop her. She jumped out of her car and hurried for the rear entrance.

She'd use the old, as yet untried Forgot-my-Senate-ID-badge excuse if anyone asked why she was here. The whole procedure would take ten seconds: log into the hard drive, DEL the file with the triptolinic diethylamide data, log out, then get the hell out of Dodge.

Simple.

God, it better be.

Duncan had logged in to the FDA database but that was no help. No way to tell what Gina had done. He'd even called the FDA, but three different clerks hadn't the vaguest idea how to help him.

Seething with frustration, he exited the program and leaned back, staring at the C-prompt. There had to be a way . . . but what if there wasn't anything to find? And even if she had been searching for TPD, she may never have found it. Years back, Duncan himself had had a devil of a time accessing it and he'd known where to look. But if she had found it and simply read the information on the screen, there'd be no trail, no way for him to know. Only if she'd downloaded the file—

Duncan straightened in his chair.

Download. She'd have to create a download file, have to tag the incoming data before it could be written to the hard drive. He punched in DIR/O:D and entered it. The entire contents of the hard drive, every directory and free file, scrolled up before him at an unreadable pace. No matter. If Gina had downloaded directly to the hard drive, he'd find it here, somewhere near the end of the list. If she'd routed the file into one of the directories, he'd have to search it out, directory by directory. And if she'd erased it . . . well, then he'd just be wasting his time.

And how would he recognize it, anyway? Would she have labeled it TPD? Hardly.

And suddenly there it was, at the bottom of the screen. The last file. "RFP" followed by yesterday's date.

Regina F. Panzella. He'd forgotten what the F. stood for, as if that mattered. What was in that file?

He punched in TYPE RFP and watched the lines zip up the screen. When the scrolling stopped at the end of the file, he read the final line.

CURRENT STATUS: Further investigation of triptolinic diethylamide discontinued.

No! He squeezed his eyes shut. He didn't want to see that.

He pushed away from the chair and wandered the room, turning this way and that with sharp, agitated movements. He couldn't be still. He felt as if some unseen force were at his back, propelling him around his office. This hurt like a sucker punch. Gina had been in his locked drawer—she'd *picked* the damn lock! How could she? *Why* would she?

That was the most unnerving question. *Why?* She couldn't suspect anything. He'd been too careful. He'd used a cutting-edge system only a few people were aware of to deliver a drug hardly anyone knew existed. There had to be something else.

How much does she know?

Obviously she knows about the TPD. But what else?

And how to find out? He couldn't simply sit her down and ask her.

His peregrination took him near the door then and he heard Barbara call good-bye to someone. Suddenly he had to know who. His privacy had been violated, his little fortress had been broached. He wanted the name, rank, and serial number of everyone who walked through those doors.

He stuck his head through the door. "Who was that?"

Barbara turned. "Dr. Panzella."

"Really." He kept a calm facade as alarms clanged anew in his head. "I hadn't realized she was here."

"Oh, she just popped in to pick up something she left yesterday."

Her lock-picking kit? he wondered as he nodded and closed the door.

What was Gina up to now? What was she doing sneaking around here on her day off? Prying into more of his private affairs?

He made a fist.

Betrayed. By Gina.

He wanted to punch something.

I saved your life, child!

How could she? And what had she done just now?

A thought struck him. He stepped back to his terminal and reran a DIR on the hard drive. The scroll of directories blurred past as before, but ended in a different place.

No "RFP" file.

She must have realized she'd left the file on the disk and came back to cover her tracks. The perfidious little ingrate. What was she up to? And dammit, how much did she *know?*

He had to have answers, and soon. Before next Friday.

25
GINA

GINA YAWNED AND SHOOK HERSELF AS SHE WOVE through the traffic on Connecticut Avenue.

Tired.

Not just tired. Exhausted.

She'd done a shift as house doc last night. Tried to get out of it, tried to trade, but no one was buying.

At least she'd been able to get Jim Grady to agree to take the last two hours of her shift. But much as she'd love to, she wouldn't be using the time for sleep. She wanted to get the jump on Duncan before today's surgery. She was going to be there first, be there when Duncan arrived, and keep an eye on him until Senator Marsden arrived. After that she was going to stick to the senator like Krazy Glue: Assist with his surgery and not let him out of her sight until he walked out to his waiting car.

She turned into the office parking lot and skidded to a halt. Duncan's black Mercedes was already in his space.

She pounded her fist against the steering wheel. Damn it! All right. She'd have to adjust. If Duncan asked she'd simply say she got off her shift early but not early enough to go home first.

She pulled into one of the staff spaces and hurried to the door. Once inside she stopped. Muzak filtered through the air, a lush, inappropriate string arrangement of a Beatles tune, accompanied by the rich aroma of Duncan's fresh coffee. Gina wasn't tempted. She'd been drinking coffee all night.

Her shoes were soft-soled and made no sound and she walked slowly down the hall toward his office. She slipped past Barbara's desk and listened a moment at the open door. No sound from within. Not even the television. Duncan almost always had CNN or C-SPAN running. She tapped lightly as she peeked inside.

"Duncan?"

Empty. Except for the heavy aroma of coffee, the office was pretty much as she'd left it on Tuesday. But where was he?

As she turned to leave, a glint of light from the desktop caught her eye. She stepped closer. A bottle.

Her mouth went dry as she recognized the TPD. It sat on a metal tray. So did the trocar and obturator, now sealed inside an autoclave pouch. The assembly had been sterilized. Why? Being readied for use? Beside it lay an uncapped syringe. And a large implant. A *full* implant.

She felt sick. The room swayed and nausea rippled through her stomach.

Oh, Duncan! It's true!

Tears welled in her eyes, a sob bubbled in her throat. How could he?

Then Gina heard a door slam somewhere out in the hall. Panic bolted through her. She couldn't let him catch her in here.

She spun and ran to the door. No one in sight but she could hear footsteps approaching from around the corner. Her heart pounding madly, she scampered two doors down and ducked into the employee restroom. She stood there gasping, sweating as the nausea surged back. Then she bent over the toilet and retched. Nothing came up. As she turned and sagged against the sink, tasting the acid in her throat, she caught a glimpse of herself in the mirror: pale, sick, trembling.

Duncan . . . Duncan . . . Duncan . . . this can't be happening. This can't be you!

But it *was* Duncan. The pieces all fit. Her wildest speculations had been right on target. Duncan was poisoning these men, implanting a neurotoxin in their tissues, sending them over the edge into psychosis . . .

Where he himself already was.

Gina gripped the edge of the sink and steadied herself. She splashed water on her face and tried to focus her thoughts.

Duncan had had a breakdown.

Not a breakdown, she told herself. Let's get clinical. Use your training.

Not easy to do when it was someone so close, but she had to take a couple of steps back and look at him.

Duncan . . . some form of paranoid schizophrenia . . . taking revenge on the Guidelines committee for ruining his practice years ago . . . and now, in his mind, threatening to destroy all medical practice. Paranoid delusions were often anchored, however tenuously, in reality, but the psychosis magnified the threat. *Everyone* was a potential enemy. He could rely on no one, so his only recourse was to take drastic action on his own.

Left alone, Duncan most likely was a danger to no one but the Guidelines committee. But if challenged, if threatened, if cornered, he could be unpredictable, could become a danger to anyone within reach.

So what do I do? she asked her reflection as she dried her face.

Her color was better now. Her sick expression had faded. She felt a little more in control; but only a little. Her stomach had settled and she wasn't looking to run.

One thing she knew *not* to do: Confront Duncan. He might go wild, do something crazy. Except he's already done that. Four times. Possibly more.

With Senator Marsden next.

A violent tremor rattled through her, starting in her spine and rolling outward. An aftershock.

Get a grip, Panzella. You can handle this.

She straightened, smoothed her blouse, shook her hair back, and tried to think of a plan.

She wouldn't say or do anything this morning. Act naturally. Give Duncan no hint that she suspected a thing. She'd do what was expected and maybe a little more: assist on the surgery, sit with the senator through recovery, see him off, then leave. But as soon as she got home she'd call Gerry, tell him about the TPD, the ultrasound and trocar, fax him the newspaper clippings, and let the FBI or the Secret Service or whoever take over.

Act naturally. Right.

She stepped out into the hall and walked back toward Duncan's office, trying to look casual. Barbara's desk was empty. Still too early for her. As before, Gina stepped around and approached the door. This time there was sound from within. The TV was on.

She tapped and called Duncan's name but no one replied. She stepped inside. A quick glance around—still empty— and then her eyes went to the desk.

The desktop was clear except for the computer terminal and the usual papers and journals.

The tray with the TPD, the syringe, the trocar, and the implant was gone.

Another tremor, another wave of dizziness, but short-lived this time. She was in control again.

What did you expect? He's not going to leave that stuff on display all morning.

Locked away in the drawer now, ready for use.

She set her jaw. Not today, Duncan. Not on *my* senator.

"Well! You're early today."

Gina almost yelped with surprise as Duncan breezed by her and crossed the office to his coffeemaker.

"I got out early," she managed to say.

"Good. We've got a lot to do today." He filled a cup from the carafe and held it up. "Coffee?"

"No, thanks."

"Nonsense. It's genuine pure Kona, shipped directly from a plantation south of Kailua. You must have some. I insist."

Maybe she'd better, just to be sociable.

"Okay. Just a taste."

"You'll love this," he said, pouring and handing her a steaming cup.

He hovered as she sipped, and beamed when she nodded.

"Hmmm. This is great."

She watched him fuss with his funnel and filter. He was dressed in gray slacks, a blue oxford button-down shirt, and a maroon crew-neck sweater. He looked so relaxed, so damn *normal*. But she knew that was often the way with the paranoid schiz. Perfectly sane and normal in every aspect of their lives except the one delusional facet. She remembered a case study about a successful businessman, ran three companies, an exemplary husband and father, loved by all, one day going berserk when one of his vice presidents tapped a cigarette ash into the urn that housed the little blue man who advised him.

Duncan stopped what he was doing to stare a moment at the TV. C-SPAN was replaying an interview with the Speaker of the House. He grimaced.

"They shouldn't allow this stuff on during the day."

"Why not?"

"Children might see it," he said with a mischievous wink. "C-SPAN should be limited to late-night broadcasts. Children in their formative years should not be exposed to politicians. People whine about violence on TV, but this is far more corrupting."

Gina forced a smile. She could not find him funny now.

He continued to stare at the screen. "Where do they *find* these people?"

"They were elected," Gina said coldly. "It's the American way. They ran for office and they got the most votes."

"Yes. Tweedledum and Tweedledummer. No one you'd really like to see in public office has the bad taste to run. And if he does, he's not going to win."

"I can think of at least one exception," she said, thinking of Senator Marsden.

"A rara avis, I assure you. Think about it, Gina. On one side you've got a man of intelligence and integrity. Against his better judgment he agrees to run, thinking he might be able to do something meaningful. But he won't suck up to ward bosses, won't kiss babies or judge hog contests or put on an apron and a white cap for a bake shop photo op. He insists on being judged by his positions on the issues. On the other side, however, you've got a political hanger-on who'll promise anything to anyone, make deals left and right, and pose any time someone lifts a camera, do anything it takes, anything at *all*, to get a vote." Duncan turned to her. Suddenly he was fiercely intent. "Tell me, Gina. Who's going to win that election?"

Gina couldn't answer. He had a point, damn him.

"I repeat," he said, not waiting for an answer. "People who deserve to be elected rarely run. And when they do, they do not win. *That's* the American way."

"I don't know of a better system. Do you?"

"No," Duncan said with a sigh. "But that doesn't mean it

can't be improved. We limit the president to two terms. Why not limit the legislature?"

"Senator Marsden has imposed his own term limits," she said, getting in a plug. "Two terms and he's out."

"We'll see about that."

Gina heard an ominous ring in that remark.

"Speaking of the good senator," Duncan said, "he's last on the list this morning. And you're assisting, I believe?"

"That's right."

"By your own request, am I right?"

"Right again."

"Why is that? You've never before requested to assist on a specific patient."

"I work for the man."

He turned and eyed her. "Do you think that's wise? You're not afraid of being emotionally involved? I could call Cassidy—"

"This isn't exactly life-and-death surgery. And I'm only assisting."

Why all these questions? He'd never quizzed her like this before. Then again, aren't paranoids suspicious of everyone?

"Very well. We'll scrub at nine forty-five. Marie will have him under by ten o'clock. We should be done in plenty of time for lunch."

"Under? You're using general?"

"Of course."

"Won't local do?"

He eyed her. "You've been working here for how long? This is the first instance I can recall you questioning the level of anesthesia. Are you *sure* you're not too involved with this patient?"

General meant Marsden would be groggy after surgery. Duncan could pop that implant under his skin without the senator ever knowing.

"Quite sure," she said. "It's just that it seems like such a small lesion, I was just wondering—"

"I've got to make a wide enough incision to excise all of that tumor and leave no chance of recurrence. Then I've got to graft and rebuild the top of the auricle so it doesn't look like someone took a shot at his head and barely missed. I don't want him twitching or getting a crick in his neck and jerking his head while I'm in the middle of it. Don't you think that's justification enough for general anesthesia?"

"Of course," she snapped, the tension getting to her. "I was just asking."

A slow smile played around his lips. "A bit edgy this morning, aren't we?"

She placed her half-empty cup on his desk and started for the door.

"Too much coffee, I guess."

Out in the hall she felt her tough facade crumble. Duncan was calling all the shots. She prayed she'd be able to carry this off.

The surgery went smoothly. Duncan did a beautiful job of excising, grafting, and rebuilding the upper auricle of Senator Marsden's ear. And Gina did what she hoped was an equally skillful job of protecting the rest of the senator.

First, she personally helped Oliver fill a batch of his tiniest implants, one of which would be used in the senator's ear. As soon as the senator arrived, she saw to it that he was never alone with Duncan. She accomplished that by being constantly at either the senator's or Duncan's side until the surgery.

Strangely enough, Duncan had shown no sign of frustration or agitation. Gina had been worried that he might fly into a rage or do something rash when he found it impossible to get the senator alone. But considering the fact that she was thwarting his scheme at every turn, he appeared to be in the best of spirits.

That worried Gina even more.

So now she sat watch beside the snoring Senator Marsden as he slept off the anesthetic in the VIP room. He stirred for the second time in the past five minutes. He was coming out of it. The ordeal was almost over.

Thank God. She was dead tired. Sitting here with the early afternoon sun pouring in the window, she might have dozed off if it weren't for her bladder. The pressure in her pelvis was becoming unbearable. She couldn't remember ever having to go this bad, but she wasn't leaving this room for a second.

"How's he doing?"

She started and twisted in her chair at the sound of Duncan's voice. He stood in the doorway, leaning on the frame with one hand.

"I've never seen you so jumpy, Gina. Maybe you're right about too much coffee."

"I'm okay," she said, trying to keep the tension out of her voice. Was this it? Was this when he'd try something?

Duncan smiled. "Good. But how's the senator? He's the patient, remember?"

"Coming up. He should be awake in a few minutes."

Not true, but she didn't want Duncan to think he had time to make his move.

"Excellent." He glanced at his watch. "Look. I've got to run. The links are calling. And since you've decided to be his recovery-room nurse as well as his surgical assistant and legislative aide, you can handle him from here on. Just make sure Barbara gives him the usual instructions on graft care and schedules a follow-up appointment for next week."

Gina stared at him. Baffled. Speechless.

"Gina?"

"You're leaving?" she said.

"Is there a reason I should stay?"

"Well, no. I just . . . have a good game."

"Thanks. I will."

He waved and was gone, leaving Gina sitting and staring at the empty doorway.

Am I going off the deep end? she wondered.

Hadn't she seen the tray with the TPD, trocar, and implant sitting on Duncan's desk? Why, if he had no intention of using it today? Unless . . .

Unless she had this whole thing wrong.

What if she'd misinterpreted, misunderstood? What if—?

No. The pieces fit too neatly. Duncan was up to something.

But what? He hadn't had an opportunity to dose the senator with that implant—Gina was sure of that. She'd stymied his plan. So what did he do? He ducked out to play golf. Except he never went to his golf club when he said he did.

Gina's head whirled. She was beginning to have a surreal feeling. What was going on here?

But at least with Duncan gone, she could run to the bathroom. Her bladder was going to burst if she didn't. She stepped out into the hall and went to the back door. Duncan's parking spot was empty. She ducked into the restroom.

A few minutes later, feeling almost lightheaded with relief, she was back in the recovery room.

Senator Marsden hadn't moved. But his eyes were open. He lay on his side, blinking at her.

"Good afternoon, Senator," she said.

He gave her half a smile and closed his eyes again.

She stared at him, suddenly anxious about having left him alone for those few minutes.

I'm getting as paranoid as Duncan, she thought, but couldn't resist lifting the senator's sheet and checking his leg.

Her knees almost buckled when she saw a tiny red spot on his thigh. *Blood?* Shakily, she dropped to one knee and leaned close.

Yes . . . blood. A small, semicircular puncture wound, just the mark a trocar would leave. Just like the mark on Senator Vincent's thigh in this very room last month.

"Oh, God," she whispered as fury and terror tore at her. "Oh dear God."

Gently she poked the area around it. The senator's leg stiffened. She glanced up and found him looking at her.

"Hello, again," she said, rising, trying to keep her voice calm, her face professionally neutral. "Was Dr. Lathram just in here?"

"Who's Dr. Lathram?" He smacked his dry lips. "Could I have some water?"

Still too groggy to be of any help.

"Yes. Sure." There was a pitcher at the bedside, but she pretended not to see it. "I'll get you some."

She forced her wobbly legs to walk her out to the hall where she leaned against the wall and let herself shake.

What sort of a nightmare had she fallen into? Where was the looking glass she'd stepped through to land in this crazy place?

Duncan. Where was he now? Obviously he hadn't left. Only pretended. Probably sneaked into one of the rooms and waited for her to leave the senator alone.

And while I was relieving myself, he sneaked into the senator's room and jabbed him with the trocar.

The bastard!

Gina scampered to the front door and saw a black Mercedes like Duncan's pulling away from the curb. She couldn't see the plates and couldn't be sure through the heavily tinted glass if Duncan was behind the wheel. She watched the car disappear into the traffic.

She hurried back down the hall and found Barbara staring at her.

"Are you all right?" she said.

"I'm fine," Gina said. She had to tell someone about this, but Barbara was not that someone. "Perfectly fine."

She returned to Senator Marsden's room and found him propped up on an elbow.

"Silly me," she said. "The water was right here all along."

She filled a glass and watched him drink as she cast about for a way to go. Should she tell him? Tell him that his surgeon had just placed a toxin-filled implant in his thigh?

She studied Senator Marsden's bleary expression. He wasn't in any condition to listen or comprehend. So where could she turn? Who could she go to?

26
GERRY

GERRY HAD JUST RETURNED FROM LUNCH. HE WAS ADMIR-
ing Martha's latest Crayola masterpiece, freshly pinned to the
wall of his cubicle, when Gina's call came in. He was glad she
was calling him for a change. She'd been strangely distant all
week.

"Gerry, I need your help."

Not a good start. She sounded frazzled.

"Sure. What's wrong?"

"It's about Duncan."

Gerry suppressed a groan. Not that again. He wished he'd
never mentioned that conspiracy theory to her.

"What about him?"

"He put a toxic implant in Senator Marsden."

Gerry didn't reply immediately. Couldn't . . . too
shocked to speak.

"He did, Gerry. I know he did."

"Gina," he said, finally finding his voice. "We've been
through all that. We tested the solution, that 'secret sauce' or
whatever you call it, and it turned out to be—"

"I'm not talking about the secret sauce. This is something else. This is a drug no one's ever heard of."

"How'd you find out about it?"

Now she paused. "I found it in one of his desk drawers."

"He leaves it where anybody can find it?"

Another pause. "No. He keeps it locked up."

"So then how did you—?" And then it hit him. "Oh, no. You didn't."

"I'm sorry, Gerry, but I had to."

"Gina, you used the Bureau's pick to break into someone's office?"

"Gerry, you've got a right to be angry, but please don't be. This is too important. I didn't break into his office, only the lock on his desk drawer."

"Same thing. You could have been caught, arrested, maybe worse."

"Look, I knew you'd react like this if I told you. That's why I didn't. But I *had* to get into that drawer."

"I don't believe this. You—"

"Gerry, two people may be dead because of him. Two others are crazy. This drug causes psychotic reactions. You saw the tape of Senator Vincent on the first day of the hearing, didn't you?"

"Of course. Who didn't?"

"Was he acting sane just before he convulsed?"

"No," he admitted grudgingly. "I guess not." He reached for a pencil. "What's the name of this drug?"

"Triptolinic diethylamide." She spelled it for him. "TPD for short."

"And it makes you crazy?"

"According to the FDA it does. Research was discontinued because of psychotic reactions in primates."

"So if Lathram is dosing people with this stuff, why hasn't some medical examiner picked up on it?"

"Because nobody's looking for it. Nobody even knows it

exists. Gerry, thousands upon thousands of compounds are tested every year. Maybe one out of ten thousand ever reaches the public. It was an investigational drug that was dropped because of side effects. That's it. Good-bye. Sayonara. On to the next compound, and nobody gives the losers another thought."

"So how'd Lathram get hold of this . . . ." He glanced at the sheet. "TPD?"

"His brother. Oliver used to work for the company that was investigating it."

Gerry straightened and leaned forward in his chair. All the old suspicions he'd been trying to put to rest were dancing through his head again.

"And you think he dosed Marsden with this stuff?"

"I know it!"

"Did you see him do it?"

"No, but I saw the puncture wound in his thigh."

She went on to tell him about seeing the bottle of TPD on Lathram's desk this morning along with an implant and something called a trocar.

"But couldn't Lathram have simply given him a shot of something?"

"Not there. And Duncan never gives injections. He has one of the nurses do it. I tell you, Gerry, Senator Marsden is lying down the hall with an implant full of TPD in his right thigh. I've got to get it out!"

"Okay. Slow down for a second here and let me think."

He leaned back again, trying to remain calm, to contain the excitement racing through him. This was heavy. A prominent, well-connected area surgeon and a very visible U.S. senator. Headline-grabbing stuff. It had the makings of a major case. Or a major embarrassment.

If only Gina had actually *seen* Duncan insert the implant.

"Do you think Marsden's in any immediate danger?"

Gina hesitated, then, "No. Duncan's gone for the day. I

think he wants to choose a specific time and place. Remember how both Allard and Vincent had their mishaps while the cameras were rolling. I think that's what Duncan might be waiting for."

"But why, Gina? We're missing a motive here. Why should he want to do this?"

"He hates the Guidelines committee and what it's trying to do."

"So do lots of other doctors. But they're not—"

"No. Listen. It's personal with Duncan." She went on to tell him about the stories in the *Post* and the *Banner,* and told him that Schulz had been on the original Guidelines committee. Bingo! That was the link he'd been searching for to connect the four legislators. She also told him of her call to the Virginia Board of Medical Examiners.

By the time she finished he was convinced, but that wasn't enough. He'd have to convince Ketter.

"Okay, look. Since the senator's in no immediate danger, we can take a little time to build a case here."

"Gerry—"

"Hear me out. We'll have someone keep an eye on the senator's home, make sure nobody's nosing around it. Meanwhile, don't you do anything to alert Lathram."

"Don't worry."

"Don't give him a chance to cover his tracks. I want him to think he's in complete control, that everything's status quo. And you keep your distance. No more Nancy Drew stuff. Leave the rest to me."

He wanted Gina out of harm's way. No telling what Lathram would do if he felt cornered.

"Okay. But are you sure the senator's going to be all right?"

"Gina," he said, "right now I'm not sure of anything. But I want to get moving on this and I don't make these decisions. I've got to build a case and bring it to the SSA, and he may have to take it higher. And the sooner I get moving on it, the better."

She gave him the year and the months when the newspaper articles appeared, then said, "Keep me informed, okay?"

"Don't worry. But one thing that can't be mentioned, now or ever, is how you got into Lathram's locked drawer. Understand?"

"I got it. And I'm sorry. Really."

"Accepted. Talk to you later."

He sat for a long while after he hung up, making notes, organizing his facts, consulting his computer for the personal database he'd built on Dr. Lathram.

Gerry was wired. He knew this could mean big things for him. He wasn't going to let this one get away from him, either. This was his baby. It meant a lot of extra work in the short run, but in the long run . . . breaking a case of this magnitude could make a career.

And it looked pretty solid. The good doctor had access and opportunity. Gerry had to document his motive.

He put in a call to research for any information anywhere on Duncan Lathram, MD, with special attention to links between Lathram and any of the fallen legislators. Gerry wanted those clippings in hand when he brought the case to Ketter.

Gerry was surprised when an interoffice envelope from research appeared on his desk less than half an hour later. So soon?

Quickly he shuffled through the sheets, mostly photocopies of old newspaper articles with Lathram's name highlighted along with those of Lane, Allard, Vincent . . . and Schulz.

Here they were, villain and victims, all neatly crossreferenced in the pages of the *Post*. A long way from an open-

280 F. PAUL WILSON

and-shut case, but these plus Gina's statement about the neurotoxin ought to be enough to get things rolling.

He headed for Marvin Ketter's office.

Ketter stood at his window, staring down at the rush hour traffic on E Street. His brow was furrowed in concentration, drawing his bushy eyebrows into a continuous line. Gerry knew he was trying to make up his mind.

A cautious man, Ketter. Too cautious. Afraid of making a mistake. But no way was Gerry going to let him take a pass on this one.

"Look," Gerry said, wandering the room, looking for a way to tilt the SSA his way. "Lathram has motive, means, and opportunity. What else do we need?"

"It's all circumstantial."

"Four members of the old committee are down or out. Dr. Panzella all but saw Lathram stick one of these implants of his into Senator Marsden. How long do we wait?"

" 'All but saw' isn't quite the same as seeing. You know that, Gerry. And Marsden wasn't a member of the original committee. So there goes your motive."

"But he's chairing the new committee. Gina's right. I know she is."

Ketter's eyebrows reached for his hairline. "Gina?"

"Dr. Panzella. We went to high school together." He didn't want Ketter to know it was more than that. "That's why she came to me. Look, don't tell me you don't know in your gut there's something wrong here."

Ketter patted the sprawl of papers Gerry had put before him. "Trust me, Gerry. There's nothing I'd like better than to uncover something like this. It would be good for both of us."

Gerry took his turn at the window, watching the cars. Ketter wouldn't get off the damn fence, even though a coup like this would move him up and put Gerry in this very office. Gina would be proud of him, Senator Marsden would be grateful, and he'd have more time to devote to Martha. And to Gina.

Christ, he wanted this.

"So what do we do? Wait until Senator Marsden keels over?"

"If he does, at least we'll know what to look for, and where to look for it."

Gerry shot him a skeptical look.

"I know, I know," Ketter said. "That won't do Marsden much good. But I won't go off half-cocked and embarrass the Bureau."

All right, Gerry thought. If reason doesn't work, how about a threat?

"I know one thing, Marvin. Anything happens to Marsden, Dr. Panzella's going to be screaming bloody murder. She's on Marsden's staff. Don't think she won't tell the press and Congress and anyone else who'll listen that she warned the FBI but we ignored her. You're worried about embarrassment, think about that."

Ketter's eyebrows met again in the middle as he rubbed his jaw.

He's almost there, Gerry thought. Just one more nudge . . .

"Look," Ketter said. "If there was some way we could confirm the existence of this implant without letting either Marsden or Lathram know what we're doing, I'd go for it. But the damn thing's supposedly in his leg. What do we do? Knock him out and drag him into a hospital and x-ray him?"

Gerry turned and stared at Ketter. Yes!

Ketter said, "What?"

"I think I know how we can do it."

27
TRICKS

GERRY RAISED HIS FIELD GLASSES AS A SILVER-GRAY LIN-coln Town Car pulled out of the driveway and turned right. Senator Marsden sat behind the wheel. He felt the butterflies begin to flutter against the walls of his stomach. They'd been fluttering all night. A lot hung on this little operation. By Bureau standards it was no big deal in resources: a couple of vehicles, a couple of field agents, a couple of civilians. But it was a *very* big deal for him.

Butterflies? More like a couple of angry roosters going at each other.

Not many places to hide in this section of McLean. Mostly open horse country, zoned for high acreage, with big, sprawling homes set far back from the road. But Gerry had managed to find a stand of oaks that allowed him to pull off the road and keep an eye on Senator Marsden's driveway. Gina had called the senator's office and learned that he was expected in sometime between eight and nine.

Even if Gerry hadn't known his face, the white bandage on the left ear would have confirmed the ID. And he was wearing his seat belt. Great. A sensible man. He glanced at his watch: 8:05 Prompt too.

And as usual, he was driving himself. That had been a concern. As minor as the surgery was, there was always the possibility that the senator might order a limo to take him to his office. Fortunately he hadn't. An extra passenger or a different vehicle would complicate things.

Gerry punched two buttons on his cellular phone and it called a preprogrammed number.

"Okay. He's on his way. Using the Town Car. I'll keep you posted."

He eased his Bureau Ford into gear and followed Marsden as he wound past horse farms and meadows and turned north onto Dolley Madison Boulevard. They passed the CIA entrance and eventually fed into the traffic on the George Washington Memorial Parkway. He understood why Marsden took this route. It was beautiful. Wooded hills and vales undulated to the right, beginning their shift into fall colors, while the tranquil Potomac flowed far below on the left. Across the river the towers of Georgetown University pierced the morning sky.

Gerry's tension mounted as they passed under Key Bridge. Marsden could choose from two bridges into the District from here: the Teddy Roosevelt or the Arlington Memorial. If he'd had more time, Gerry could have learned the senator's usual route, but it had been less than twenty-four hours since the surgery. Gerry had prepared for both routes, but he was hoping for the Memorial.

He had to hand it to Ketter. Once his SSA got moving, he *moved*. They'd spent a lot of overtime last night getting approvals, securing personnel and equipment, but by seven this morning, everything was in place, waiting.

When he saw Marsden go past the off-ramp for the Teddy, Gerry relaxed a little. But only a little.

He called in again.

"Okay, folks. He's right on course. Hitting the Memorial bridge now. Everybody be ready to roll as soon as he hits Constitution."

Gerry didn't hang up this time, but kept the channel open as he passed the Seabees Memorial and cruised between the granite bald eagles that flanked the entry to the bridge. The massive white marble box of the Lincoln Memorial squatted directly ahead on the far side, and the Washington Monument loomed to his right. He followed Marsden around the Lincoln and onto the Henry Bacon diagonal to Constitution.

As a dark wedge of the Vietnam Wall in its depression slipped past on his right, he said, "Coming to Constitution. Go!"

And now those stomach roosters were really kicking up. Timing was crucial here. It had to go down within the next few blocks, but the Bureau's stunt driver had to wait for an opportunity. Not only did he have to make contact, but he had to get away.

A Nova . . . he'll be driving an old blue Chevy Nova.

Cruising with the commuters as they paced the Potomac along Constitution Avenue, Gerry's gaze roamed side to side, flicked from mirror to mirror. Then he spotted the car, weaving through the traffic behind him. He pulled over to let it pass. A brief glimpse of the driver showed a knitted cap pulled low over the forehead, an old flannel shirt with the collar up. Gerry couldn't help a nervous smile. Trevor Hendricks looked to be anything but a special agent.

"Don't miss, Hendricks," he whispered. "Please don't miss."

Gerry chewed his lip as he watched Hendricks edge nearer the senator's car, looking for his chance. He found it at 19th, across from the Department of the Interior. Marsden was just pulling up to a red light when the Nova lunged ahead and swerved into the senator's Town Car. Only a glancing blow but enough to cave in the left front fender. The Lincoln lurched to a halt while the Chevy burned rubber and peeled off down Constitution.

Gerry pulled to a halt directly in front of the senator and trotted back to his window.

"You okay?"

"Yes," said Marsden, looking a little pale and shaken, but apparently uninjured. "Did you see that crazy son of a bitch?"

Gerry stared down Constitution and saw the Nova make a right onto 17th. Hendricks would dump the car there, mingle with the tourists gathering around the Washington Monument, then walk the few blocks back to the Bureau. The car was a gift from the DEA: the unregistered, confiscated property of a drug mule.

"Saw the whole thing." He pulled a card from his pocket. "If you need a witness—say . . . aren't you Senator Marsden?"

"Yes. Yes, I am."

Gerry thrust his card through the open window. "Canney. Special agent FBI. I'll call this in."

Without giving Marsden a chance to reply, Gerry whipped out his cellular phone, flipped it open, and turned his back to the senator as he pretended to make a call.

"The police should have someone here in a second," he said, turning back to the car. "You're sure you're all right?"

"Positive. Look, we're blocking traffic here. Why don't I just pull ahead and see if I can get off the road."

Gerry looked back and saw that they'd created a minor traffic jam by reducing inbound traffic from three lanes to two. But he didn't want Marsden going anywhere.

"Don't know if that's such a good idea. Let me take a look at the damage here."

He stepped toward the front fender and bent over it. Hendricks had done a perfect job: the metal was folded in against the tire.

"I don't think you're going anywhere, sir."

As he straightened he saw Marsden starting to get out. Gerry stepped up and gently eased him back into his seat.

"Maybe you shouldn't move just yet, Senator."

"I'm perfectly all right. It was just a fender bender."

Gerry stood firm, blocking the door with his body. "Still, sir, I think it would be smarter and safer if you moved as little as possible until help arrives."

"Don't be ridiculous! I'm perfectly fine and fully capable of—"

A blue and white unit roared up then, sirens wailing, lights flashing, followed closely by an ambulance and a mobile ICU, all with the Bureau.

The senator was adamant against being taken to the hospital. He protested vigorously, but since his car wasn't going anywhere, and since the cop and the EMTs weren't taking no for an answer, and GWU hospital was only six blocks up the street, he finally relented.

As the ambulance wailed off, Gerry leaned back against the Lincoln's damaged fender and took a deep, relieved breath. The diciest part was over, and Marsden had come through without a scratch.

Did it!

Christ, what a feeling. Almost like sex. If he smoked he'd be reaching for a cigarette.

But now came the most important part: finding that implant.

Gerry hoped to God it was findable. Because if they missed it, there was going to be hell to pay.

Gina huddled in the dictation area of the records room and pressed the receiver against her ear to keep any trace of Gerry's voice from escaping.

She hadn't wanted to come in today, but Gerry had thought it best not to deviate from her routine.

"All right," Gerry said. "We've got the senator here in the emergency room. Let me just go over this again to make sure there's no mistake. We're all set up to do a magnetic resonance image of his right leg. That's what we want, right?"

"Right. An MRI with special attention to the lateral midthigh. Tell them to look for the healing puncture wound in the skin. The implant should be somewhere within a three- or four-inch radius from there."

"Okay. Just triple-checking."

"And Gerry." She lowered her voice to a whisper. "Don't let anyone use an ultrasound to find it, okay? Sometimes they use ultrasound to locate foreign bodies in soft tissue, but *don't let them.* Don't let anyone even *near* him with an ultrasound."

Diagnostic ultrasound used a tiny fraction of the power of the therapeutic modality—but why chance it?

"Okay. No ultrasound. Look, I've got to run. We should have the answer soon."

"Call me."

"Soon as I can. Once we identify it, we've got to tell Marsden and convince him it should come out immediately. That may not be so easy."

"Just save him, okay?"

"I'm doing my damnedest."

"I know you are. Love you."

He was silent a moment, probably as surprised as Gina herself that she'd come out and said that. Where had it come from?

From the heart, I guess, she told herself.

"I feel the same way," he said, and she had to smile. He probably had a dozen other agents around him. "Let's get together after the dust settles here. We need to talk."

"Think you'll be able to come over for dinner tonight?"

"I think that can be arranged. Want me to bring something?"

"Just Martha."

"Martha?"

"Yeah. I haven't seen her in a while."

"Great."

"We'll stay in. I'll cook again. How's broccoli and linguine sound?"

"Martha will love it."

"Great. Bye."

Gina sat there a moment, staring into space. She hadn't wanted to be alone tonight. With Gerry and Martha as company, maybe she wouldn't feel so terrible about all this.

Gerry had sounded both excited and tense. Gina felt only nausea. When they found the implant, Gerry's job would be done. They'd hand Senator Marsden over to the doctors for its removal and the case to the federal prosecutors.

But Gina's involvement would not end. Somewhere along the line she'd have to face Duncan.

She shuddered. She felt like a rat. He'd saved her life, given her a job in high school, and now another. He'd been unfailingly generous for as long as she'd known him, and this was how she repaid him.

But how could she let him go on doing what he'd been doing?

She'd done the right thing, damn it. Ethically, morally, legally, the right thing.

So why did she feel so rotten?

The morning's procedures completed, Duncan sat in his office, his back to his desk, a cup of Kenya AA cooling between his hands. He stared through the glass at the rock garden, idly noting that the red leaves of the dwarf five-finger maple were beginning to brown. Fall was taking hold. Winter was approaching. A winter of the heart.

Gina, Gina, Gina . . . how much do you know?

She did know something, and suspected more. Any doubts had been laid to rest by the way she'd stuck like a second skin to that senator of hers.

Duncan wondered at his growing animosity toward Senator Marsden. A decent man by all accounts, even if he was engaged in extending the domain of the kakistocracy. Was it personal? Could it be he was feeling piqued by Gina's devotion to someone else, a veritable stranger?

More crucial than what Gina knew was the question of what she meant to do about it. He couldn't get a reading from her this morning . . . she'd been unusually quiet, distant, rarely looking him in the eyes.

Something was up . . .

The intercom buzzed. He swiveled and picked up.

"A Dr. Melendez on oh-two about Senator Marsden."

An electric tingle coursed through Duncan's limbs. Melendez? Who the hell was Dr. Melendez?

He punched 02.

Melendez, it turned out, was one of the ER docs at GWU hospital. In a minimally accented voice he told Duncan that Marsden had been involved in an MVA this morning and had mentioned having surgery the preceding day. Melendez just wanted to check out if he was on any analgesics or other meds.

"Nothing stronger than ibuprofen or Tylenol," Duncan said. "Is he hurt?"

"Not a scratch. The dressing on his ear wasn't disturbed in the least."

"Good."

"If you want, I can take a look under the bandage when he gets back from radiology."

"I thought you said there wasn't a scratch."

290 F. PAUL WILSON

"There isn't. But he's getting an MRI anyway. The feds are making a big deal out of this, I guess, his being a senator and all."

"Feds?" A larval suspicion began worming through his gut.

"Yeah. Couple of FBI types lurking about. I don't get it. I mean, he's not hurt so an MRI isn't medically indicated in the least, but hey, I'm just a doctor."

"A lowly health-care provider," Duncan said, trying to keep his tone light.

"You got it."

"Well, Dr. Melendez, I thank you for the courtesy of the call."

"Any time."

Duncan drummed his fingers on the desk. An MRI? Of what? The head? Or a leg? He'd been rattled by the mention of the FBI and had forgotten to ask.

And that young man Gina had been seeing lately, wasn't he with the FBI?

His fingers stopped drumming and curled into a fist.

A little too much to be coincidence.

He snatched up the phone. Bob Rubinstein had been with GWU radiology for years. Duncan gave Barbara the job of tracking him down, and five minutes later he was on the line.

After the obligatory long-time-no-see small talk, Duncan broached the subject.

"The reason I'm bothering you, Bob, is that I understand one of my patients, a Senator Marsden, had an accident this morning and is getting an MRI. I was wondering how he's doing."

"Don't know anything about it. MR's another section. But I can find out, if you want. Can you hold?"

Duncan could and he did, listening to tinny Muzak while trying to quell the tension rising slowly within him.

Rubinstein was back in a couple of minutes.

"Just spoke to Sal Vecchiarelli, the chief of MR. Know him?"

"No."

"A good man. And is he pissed! Your senator's all right, but they're doing this MR on him anyway. It seems—this is all sub rosa, so don't repeat it, okay?"

"Trust me. Not a word."

"Okay. Seems the FBI commandeered this time for an MRI of the senator last night. Some twelve hours before his accident. Looks like they knew he was going to have it. Pretty strange, wouldn't you say?"

Duncan felt himself going cold. "I certainly would."

"Wonder what they're up to."

"I couldn't imagine. I operated on his ear yesterday. Are they—?"

"No. It's his leg they're interested in. His right leg, I believe."

Duncan closed his eyes and swallowed. His mouth was parched. He did not want to ask the next question. "Any idea what they're looking for?"

"Some sort of foreign body."

He slammed his fist against his thigh. *No! No, dammit!* He forced his voice to remain calm, steady.

"Are the results in yet?"

"Not yet. The senator's in the tunnel as we speak. Sal's fuming. He just wants to get the study done, give them a reading, and send them on their way so he can get to patients who really need the test."

"Can't say as I blame him."

"Since the senator's your patient, I can call you back with the reading if you want."

"No, thanks, Bob," Duncan said slowly as a weight grew in his chest. "Not necessary."

I already know the reading.

His hand trembled as he hung up the receiver. He stared

at his fingers. What were they vibrating with? Rage? Or heartache?

Gina knows.

He'd guessed she knew something, but until this moment he'd had no idea how much. Now there was no more guessing. Somehow she'd pieced together the who and the how, and maybe even the why.

But instead of coming to him, she'd gone to the FBI.

He wanted to break something—punch a hole in the wall, grab his chair and fling it through the picture window.

But no. He was not a maniac. He was in control. Although, looking at all this from Gina's perspective, she had to think he was psychotic. A paranoid schiz. He'd no doubt have thought the same thing if situations were reversed.

But he'd have gone to her first. He wouldn't have sneaked off and betrayed her to the kakistocracy.

Gina, my dear cygnet . . . how could you?

She'd cut him deeply today. He didn't know if he'd ever forgive her for this. But that was a question for another time. Much more pressing was the question of what was he going to do now?

28
FALLOUT

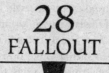

GINA WAITED, SHUTTLING BETWEEN THE DICTATION DESK and the recovery rooms, checking on this morning's post-ops. A light load today: two rhinoplasties and a thigh liposuction. She wished there was more to do. This waiting was killing her.

She glanced out the window of the main recovery room and noticed Duncan's car was gone. She stopped by Barbara's desk on her way back.

"I don't know if he's coming back or not," Barbara said. "I looked up and there he was, breezing past me. Didn't even say good-bye."

"It's not even noon yet."

Barbara shrugged. "Maybe he's got a big weekend planned and wants an early start."

Gina wondered about that. Usually he stayed later on Fridays, going over a list of things he wanted done or set up before surgery began again Monday morning. Why the change in routine today? Did he suspect something?

Got to stop thinking like that, she told herself, rubbing

her upper arms as a chill of apprehension skittered across her shoulders. *Nothing is different today. No reason to suspect a thing.*

She would have loved to leave herself, but she was required to stay on duty until the last patient went home. So she stayed on, doing everything as usual, behaving as if nothing were wrong. It hadn't been such a tough decision. The thought of sitting alone in her apartment, waiting for the phone to ring, was hardly an enticing alternative.

Lunch hour came and went without her having a bite— couldn't think of eating a thing—and Gerry hadn't called. The afternoon dragged on. Still no call. Gina was all caught up on her dictation and paperwork, and was running out of things to do. She heard Oliver puttering in his lab. She could have wandered over to help him out, but now, after what she knew, the thought of even being near those implants repulsed her. Better to try to look busy until Gerry called.

By quarter after three Gina still hadn't heard, and she was beginning to worry. They should have had the reading by midmorning. Why hadn't he called?

Unless . . . her chest constricted at the thought . . . unless the MRI showed that the implant had ruptured in the accident. They'd have had to rush Senator Marsden into emergency surgery before too much of the TPD leaked into his circulation.

What a nightmare scenario. But still, Gerry would have called to tell her.

She got up, wandered around upstairs, then came back. She couldn't sit still. What was *happening* downtown?

Finally she picked up the phone. Enough waiting. Time to make a call of her own. She dialed the FBI and asked for Gerry. After a moment on hold, the receptionist came back: "I'm sorry, but Special Agent Canney is not available now. Would you care to leave a message?"

No, she wouldn't.

Gerry wasn't back yet? Could that be? She felt her anxiety level rising. The chart-lined walls around her seemed to lean over her, closing in.

Keep calm, she told herself. Everything's under control.

Quickly she dialed Senator Marsden's office. When she asked how he was after the accident, Doris, the receptionist, said, "Oh, he's fine, Dr. Panzella. Want to speak to him?"

Nonplussed, Gina mumbled something that vaguely resembled yes.

"Gina," the senator said without preamble, "I wish you could have been with me today. If ever there was an example of the need for the Guidelines act, it was the fiasco I witnessed this morning."

"Are you all right?"

"Of course, I'm all right! There was never anything wrong with me. Yet they insisted on shoving me into this MRI machine and scanning my legs. Everything happened so fast, I was squeezed into that tube before I was sure of what was going on and had a chance to protest."

"I'm sure they had good reason—"

"They had *no* reason! Just trying to pad the bill! I'm furious."

"Maybe it was because you're a U.S. Senator," she said, trying to mollify him. This was not what she wanted to talk about. "I'm sure they don't do that to everyone."

"Wait till I get the bill," he said. "Just wait. *Then* they'll hear from me."

Gina figured he'd have a long, long wait.

"Uh, did they find anything?" she asked and then held her breath.

"Find anything? Of course not! There wasn't anything *to* find! Wasted half my morning because of a stupid hit-and-run fender bender."

Found nothing . . . hadn't they told him? Why not? What was going on?

Gina fumbled through the next minute of conversation, only half listening, replying with what she was sure were non sequiturs, and then somewhat less than gracefully ended the conversation.

Her mind spinning, she immediately called the FBI again, and again, Gerry was "not available at this time." She left her name and an urgent message to call her as soon as possible.

And then she was up and moving. She had to get out, get some fresh air. She hurried to her car and turned the heater on high. She was cold, but that wasn't why she was shivering. Dread settled around her like a tenebrous shroud.

Somewhere, somehow, something was terribly wrong.

The late afternoon had been endless. She'd taken a shower, fixed a sandwich that she didn't touch, tried to watch talk shows. She was going nuts.

When she hadn't heard from Gerry by half past six, Gina called his office again and was told he was gone for the day.

Why hadn't he called? Had he missed her message?

She called his home. He answered on the second ring.

"Gerry. Thank God!"

"Gina. Hello." His voice sounded flat, lifeless.

"I've been trying to reach you all day. I've been going crazy here. Didn't you get my message?"

" 'Going crazy,' " he said. "That's a good one."

A wave of cold formed at her center and spread outward. With the cordless phone tight against her ear, she stepped out of her bedroom and began pacing the front room.

"Gerry, what's wrong?"

"What's wrong? Gina . . . ." he sighed, then said nothing. The few silent seconds seemed to stretch into the night falling outside her bay window. "Gina, there was nothing there."

It wasn't a complete shock. Some part of her subconscious

must have expected this but hadn't allowed her to face it directly. Now she had no choice.

Still, she couldn't accept it.

Her words came in a rush. "There had to be. Gerry, I saw it. Less than an hour before the surgery he had the trocar and an implant filled with TPD sitting on his desk ready to go. I left the recovery room for a few minutes, and when I returned there was a puncture wound on the senator's thigh. It was still bleeding."

"We had that 'puncture wound' checked in the hospital. It was little more than a scratch."

"Gerry, it—"

"But it doesn't matter whether there was a scratch or a puncture *in* the skin, Gina, the fact remains that there wasn't anything *under* the skin. The MRI didn't pick up a single trace of a foreign body. Not in the right leg, and not in the left leg either, because we checked *both* of them. There's nothing under Marsden's skin but fat and muscle and bone. No implant, no nothing!"

"Gerry, that can't be. If it's not in the senator's leg then it's got to be somewhere else. I know—"

"That's the trouble, Gina. You didn't know. And you don't know now. I thought you did. I never should have—" He cut himself off.

"Gerry, I'm so sorry. I was so sure. Why else would he have that implant out and ready to go just before the senator's surgery?"

"I don't know, Gina." She sensed a growing edge to his voice. "You tell me. You're the only one who saw it . . . or that TPD stuff."

"Do you think I imagined it?"

"I don't know what to think anymore. Look, I know I started you on this, but I must have been crazy, and I made you a little crazy too. I do know that Ketter and I are the big joke around the Bureau."

"Oh, God. I'm so sorry. Look, you sound tired. When you and Martha come over we'll have some wine and you can relax while I—"

"I don't think we'll be able to make it, Gina. Not tonight."

Something in his voice made her sit down in the nearest chair. She bit her lip.

"Gerry, what's wrong?"

"Wrong? Everything's wrong, Gina." She heard the hurt, the disappointment in his voice. "I'm really not very hungry. And to tell the truth, I don't think I'll be very good company tonight."

Gina felt tears well in her eyes. "I feel terrible about this, Gerry."

"That makes two of us. Maybe you've been working too hard, stretching yourself too thin. I shouldn't have got you wired on my little conspiracy theory."

She felt as if she'd been punched. "You *do* think I imagined all this! Did I imagine all those newspaper articles?"

"I told you, Gina, I don't know what to think anymore. Maybe this isn't a good time for us to be discussing it. I know it's not a good time for me. I've got to get dinner for Martha. We'll talk some other time, okay?"

"Talking it out tonight might—"

"The last thing I need is to talk about Duncan Lathram. Frankly, if I never hear his name again, it will be too soon. What I need is to cool down and get this day over with."

"You're sure?"

"I'm truly sorry for begging off at the last minute like this, but trust me, it's for the best."

She didn't want to hang up but sensed he didn't want to talk anymore.

"Call me tomorrow?"

"Will do."

"All right. Good night."

"Good night, Gina."

And then she hung up.

Bewildered, Gina sat and stared down at Kalorama Road.

"He thinks I'm crazy," she whispered to the empty apartment.

But she'd been so certain, so damn *sure* that Duncan had stuck an implant into Senator Marsden. She'd seen it lying on his desk just before the surgery. Why else would it have been there?

Unless . . .

Unless Duncan had been setting her up.

But how? He had no inkling of what she knew. She'd relocked his desk drawer, erased the FDA download from the computer. She'd left no trail. No reason in the world for Duncan to suspect she had the vaguest clue. So why would he set her up?

Maybe he hadn't. Maybe he'd tried to jab an implant into the senator's thigh but didn't have time to complete the job, leaving a skin wound but no implant.

And maybe he wasn't up to what she thought he was. Maybe she'd misinterpreted everything.

Was that possible? Could she have been that far off the mark?

And poor Gerry. He'd stuck his neck out on account of what she'd told him. Sounded as if he'd been damn near decapitated as a result. He had a right to be hurt and angry.

But so do I, dammit.

She wandered over to the kitchenette and saw the heads of broccoli sitting on the counter, waiting to be sliced up into flowerets. Enough for three or four. And she wasn't the least bit hungry.

I've really screwed things up, haven't I, she thought as she returned to the bay window and curled up on the seat.

The streetlights were on. She stared down at the passing singles and couples. She felt utterly alone, but she wasn't going to cry.

Gerry sat in his easy chair with Martha on his lap. He had his arms around her, holding her close and warm against him in her Osh Kosh corduroys while she read him a story. It was the Martha Canney variation of *Madeline*. She couldn't read just yet, but she'd heard the story so many times that she knew it almost word for word.

So did Gerry. So his mind drifted. It would have drifted no matter what Martha was reading.

What a godawful, rotten day. If only . . .

Yeah. If only. He must have had a million if-onlys since this morning when the MRI report had come back negative.

Damn! If only he hadn't rushed it, taken a little more time to check things out. But dammit, they couldn't take too much time. Marsden was supposedly in danger.

Supposedly . . .

He'd bought into Gina's scenario completely. If only he'd been a little more skeptical.

He winced as he remembered the excruciating moment when he'd had to call Ketter and tell him that they'd come up empty-handed. The little operation that was to make them a couple of fair-haired boys had left them the big jokes of the Bureau. And then Cavanaugh, one of the assistant directors, had called them into his office and dressed them down but good. Gerry couldn't remember ever feeling so embarrassed and humiliated. He'd wanted to crawl under a rock.

But the worst of it was that lost amid all the reprimands was the fact that the operation Gerry had designed and managed had gone off like clockwork. Everything as planned, on time and under budget. Marsden's car had been hit without damage to him, he'd been whisked off to the hospital, examined, and delivered back to his office without the slightest hint that it had all been arranged.

At least the Bureau itself had been spared any public embarrassment. Thank God for that.

But no one would remember his well-oiled operation. Only that there'd been no poison pill in the senator's leg, and that Gerry Canney had to be the most gullible agent in the Bureau.

But what hurt most was knowing that any hopes he'd had of moving up to SSA soon had been dashed but good.

He held Martha closer.

Looks like it's business as usual, kid, he thought glumly. Catch-as-catch-can fatherhood for the foreseeable future.

"Daddy, you're squeezing too tight!"

"Sorry, honey. What happens to Madeline next?"

"She has her operation."

"Tell me all about it."

His mind drifted again. What about Gina? What was going on inside her? Where had she come up with that wild fantasy? *From me, dammit.* At least initially. But she'd pushed it a few steps further . . . Marsden . . . that triethyl-whatever-it-was . . . and he'd bought into it on the strength of her conviction, on the basis of his faith in her . . .

Looking back, knowing now that it had been the proverbial wild-goose chase, he couldn't believe he'd got sucked in like that. But thinking about it, he guessed he had been primed to believe anything shady about the uppity Dr. Lathram.

He wished today had never happened.

Gerry suppressed a growl as he closed his eyes. He knew he was feeling sorry for himself. He hated self-pity. Tomorrow was a new day. He'd suck this mess in, chew it up, spit it out, and get back on the job. But tonight . . . tonight he was feeling pretty goddamn low.

His thoughts ran to Gina again. He'd been pretty rough on her. Hadn't meant to be, but the bitterness was like a pressure; he'd had to blow off at least some of it. Couldn't on Ketter, who'd backed him a hundred percent, and certainly not on Martha.

That left Gina.

Maybe she needed some help. She certainly hadn't been fully connected to reality imagining that implant in Marsden.

Gina . . . he felt a need for her but didn't want to be in the same room with her. At least not tonight. Maybe he'd get past this and maybe not. Where did they go from here? The fallout from today could poison their relationship.

He shifted in the chair. Enough wallowing. He had someone very real and very important sitting on his lap. Time to focus on Martha, and on the problem of Madeline's tummy ache.

But a vision of Gina sitting alone in her apartment came to him. He wondered if she had anyone to turn to tonight. He wondered if she knew someone was thinking about her.

Duncan sat before *MacNeil/Lehrer,* sipping a scotch and soda, barely listening. He was envisioning Gina. His earlier anger was gone and now he was wondering what *she* was thinking.

Poor girl. Probably couldn't figure up from down at the moment. Probably questioning her sanity.

He sighed. He wished he could feel good about hood-winking the poor thing, but frankly, it hadn't taken much. He'd been all primed for her yesterday morning. He'd had the TPD, the trocar, and a saline-filled implant sitting on his desk where she could see them. He'd dosed her coffee with twenty milligrams of Lasix. The diuretic had achieved the desired effect: she'd had to leave Marsden's side for a trip to the john. And while she was gone he'd ducked in and given

Marsden a quick jab with the tip of the trocar. After that it was simply a matter of waiting.

All to see what she knew. Obviously she suspected something, but how much?

Now he knew.

Gina knew everything. Or at least enough to go to her fellow in the FBI and convince him to save her dear senator from the wicked Dr. Lathram.

The call from the hospital that the FBI was involved had come as a mind-numbing shock.

He sipped his scotch. But he was better now. Everything was under control again.

But poor Gina. She must have been *so* sure.

And right now she probably wasn't sure of anything at all, except that the FBI considered her an unreliable source.

He'd neutralized her without harming a hair on her head. Pretty slick.

So now she had to put this behind her. Write it off as a bad dream and let things return to normal. If he were smart he'd find an excuse to fire her. Play it safe and get her off the premises.

But he couldn't do that. He still remembered that skinny, raven-haired little girl with the huge brown eyes, wide with fright, asking him if she was going to die, and later his hands inside her abdomen, her blood pooling around his wrists as he fought to find the bleeders and mend her damaged arteries. As much as he hated to admit it, he missed those days. He missed the adrenaline rush of the emergencies, opening up a patient and searching for the leak, racing against the falling blood pressure, the falling hematocrit, the impending cardiovascular collapse and shock. Or rushing to tie off a bulging abdominal aneurysm before it blew and splashed red against the ceiling. He missed saving lives.

But McCready, Allard, Lane, Schulz, Vincent, and the rest of them had made that impossible.

He rubbed his eyes as bitter memories rushed in . . . memories of poor Lisa . . .

Lisa Lathram . . . a euphonious name, such an up sound to it. And yet Lisa herself . . .

He remembered her as such a happy child, could still hear her dulcet laugh, see her bright eyes, her effulgent smile— Lord, that smile . . . Lisa was *always* smiling—accepting everyone and everything, hugs and kisses all around.

When Brad came along, Duncan loved him equally, but as a son. There was a difference there.

Lisa remained the light of his life. At times he was sure Diana was jealous of their relationship. When he arrived home from the hospital or the office, Lisa was the first one he looked for, and she always came running when she heard his voice. How he cosseted her. Whatever she wanted, whatever she needed—a piano to play, a horse to ride, a balance beam for gymnastics practice—was hers for the asking.

But the halcyon days of her childhood evanesced as puberty took hold, and Duncan came to understand firsthand the origin of the changeling myth. As her body changed, so did Lisa's personality. At first he and Diana chalked up the moodiness to the new hormones pulsing through her. After all, what was there to be grumpy about? With her flowing blond hair and lissom figure, she was only getting prettier.

He and Diana kept hoping their adolescent agelast would snap out of it, but after a while it became clear that more than hormones were at work here. She lost interest in her friends, her piano playing, her horse. The downs kept getting deeper and longer, and there never seemed to be any real ups, only not-so-downs.

And then she swallowed half a bottle of her mother's Dalmane and had to have her stomach pumped. She was diagnosed with severe endogenous depression and the endless rounds of antidepressants and outpatient therapy began.

Nothing worked for very long. And then came that terrible

night she locked herself in her room and screamed with pain. Duncan kicked the door down and found her sitting in the middle of her bed bleeding from a slit wrist.

They hospitalized her for a month after that, and tried something new called Prozac. Lisa responded beautifully. In her case it was truly a miracle drug.

Duncan still remembered the day he came home from the hospital to find Diana standing in the foyer sobbing. Immediately his heart plummeted, expecting the worst. And then he heard it, floating in from the living room, the sound of Mozart's Piano Concerto no. 21. Lisa was playing again.

He and Diana fell into each other's arms and wept.

Even now his eyes clouded at the memory.

After that, as Lisa brightened, so did their lives. Duncan hadn't realized how his daughter's problems had tainted their entire family life. But now that she was getting back to normal, the days seemed brighter, his own step lighter. Laughter again around the dinner table as Lisa began riding her horse and hanging out with some of her old friends. Her grades turned around and she began dating Kenny O'Boyle.

They dated for months, and Kenny became the sole topic of Lisa's conversation. She and Diana would have long mother-daughter talks about him, and Diana told Duncan she was worried that Lisa might be getting too involved. She'd just turned eighteen, true, but she'd missed a lot of growing up in those black years.

Duncan wasn't crazy about Kenny. He seemed a shifty, inarticulate dolt, but then Duncan was naturally leery about any male sniffing around his daughter. Lisa adored him. And Lisa was happy. Happy for the first time in years. So Duncan decided to keep his eyes open and his mouth shut.

And then the McCready committee reared its ugly head.

He remembered the morning five years ago when it all began, in the doctors lounge at Fairfax Hospital, somebody showing him the article on the front page of the *Post*. He'd just come off two scheduled procedures, an abdominal aneurysm graft and a carotid endarterectomy, all after rushing in at 3:00 A.M. to close a torn femoral artery on a motorcyclist—"donorcyclist," as the ER staff called them. He was tired. But not too tired to be furious at Senator Vincent's public condemnation of his million-dollar charge to Medicare the year before.

Every time he turned around some baseball player or basketball dribbler was signing a contract for five or six million dollars a year. How many lives did they save in a year? Barbra Streisand can get twenty million for two nights of warbling, but you, Duncan Lathram, you moneygrubbing bloodsucker, you charge too goddamn much.

He'd wished he had some legal recourse, but how the hell did you sue a congressional committee? And what would he accomplish but call even more unwanted attention to himself?

What did it matter? he remembered thinking. The whole brouhaha would blow over in a couple of days.

But he was wrong.

His *auto-da-fé* at the hands of the Guidelines committee continued with unflagging zeal. Apparently the members thought they'd found a particularly tasty bone in Duncan Lathram and wanted to keep gnawing away at him. Then the *Alexandria Banner* picked up the story, followed by a patient's rights group demanding an investigation; so the State Board of Medical Examiners got involved, and soon Medicare had a team of pettifogging auditors formicating through his office records, pawing through his files, and swarming in the hospital records room, sifting his charts for pecuniary indiscretions. To hell with patient confidentiality. Those weasel-faced bureaucrats would know all the secrets of everyone he'd operated on in the past few years. But what did that matter? Spurred by the Guidelines committee, the government had declared *jihad* on Duncan Lathram.

Duncan was angry and embarrassed, but not too worried. His medical records were impeccable, and he'd match his morbidity and mortality stats against anyone in the country. Let them investigate. He'd come up smelling like a rose.

He just wished they'd hurry and get the whole mess over and done with.

But it dragged on, and in the ensuing months Duncan began to notice a hint of coolness from some of his colleagues at the hospital. He was getting fewer requests for surgical consults. He understood their predicament: worrying about guilt by association. They were waiting till things cooled down.

Still, he was in for a nasty shock one day as he began one of the surgical consultation requests he did receive. When he entered the patient's hospital room and introduced himself, the patient bolted upright in bed. Duncan still remembered his words.

"Oh, no. Forget it. No way I'm gonna be operated on by some knife-happy, moneygrubbing quack!"

Duncan was mortified, angry enough to punch a hole in the wall. And dammit, hurt. He consoled himself that most likely he had just experienced the nadir of the whole affair. It couldn't get any worse. The only way he could go from there was up.

Again, he was wrong.

Because all the bad press was having a devastating effect at home. Duncan Lathram, MD, was the talk of the town . . . including the high school.

And so in retrospect it seemed inevitable that he would come home one night to find Lisa sobbing in her mother's arms. She and Kenny had had a fight and broken up. The cause of the fight? What the kids were saying about Lisa's father, saying to Kenny behind Lisa's back. Kenny's parting shot? "Forget the prom! Forget everything! I ain't goin' anywhere with the daughter of no crook!"

Devastating for any teenager, but to Lisa it seemed like the end of the world.

Barely able to speak through her sobs, she wanted to know why her father hadn't said anything, why he hadn't come out and defended himself.

Duncan remembered the scene as if it had occurred only a moment ago.

He knelt before his daughter and gripped her hands. "Honey, these are lies from spotlight-hunting buffoons. The way these things work, the louder I proclaim my innocence, the guiltier I look."

"But you haven't said *anything!*"

"I'm letting my records do the talking. I've got nothing to hide, Lisa. When the bureaucrats finish their investigation, I'll be vindicated. And *they'll* be the fools."

"But meanwhile they're making you look like a crook! And making everybody hate me! And you don't care!"

"Of course I care."

He realized then that he'd misread the whole situation. He'd treated it as a brief but unpleasant interlude, another in a long series of fleeting Capitol Hill cacophonies that would die down as soon as Congress, in tune with its well-earned reputation for a short attention span, moved on to the next hot topic. So he'd done nothing to counter the accusations leveled. That had been a mistake.

Another mistake was thinking it would involve only his practice. He should have seen that his professional obloquy would have a ripple effect on his private life as well. He'd always separated the practice and the family, but there was no way of insulating the latter from the ravages upon the former, not with an assault of this magnitude.

He hurt for Lisa.

"But what could I have done, Lisa? What can I do to make this better?"

"I don't know—*something*. You could plea bargain or

whatever they call it. Something, *anything* to make them shut up and get off our backs."

"Plea bargain?" He was stunned. "You don't plea bargain when you're innocent."

Lisa tore her hands from his and ran upstairs, screaming, "Thanks! Thanks for *nothing!* My life is *over!* And all because of *you!* I might as well have *AIDS!*"

Diana followed her, glaring back at him. "She's right, you know. You could have done *something!*"

This was vintage Lisa, always taking everything too hard, seeing everything in the worst light. With her history, though, that kind of outburst could not be laid off to hyperbole and histrionics.

They increased her therapy sessions and kept an eye on her day and night. But a week later, when it became clear—at least to Lisa—that she and Kenny were through for good, she dug out a hoard of old pills she had squirreled away over the years—a potentially lethal combination of antidepressants like Elavil, Parnate, Desyrel, Sinequan, Norpramin, Tofranil, Nardil, and lithium—and took them all.

And then she fell. Over the railing. Down to the hard, cold foyer floor. Where Duncan found her.

And then she died.

And Diana blamed him.

And Duncan blamed himself.

He had never realized what grief could mean, never imagined he could mourn the loss of another human being the way he mourned Lisa. And he knew it was all his fault . . . all his fault . . .

Until the audits and investigations were completed. Then he knew who was really to blame.

The rasorial crew of Medicare auditors finished their quest for any improprieties that might grease his path to the gibbet, always in full view of his steadily diminishing patient flow, and the worst they could come up with were a few errors in the coding of certain procedures. The quality assurance examiners found no cases—not one!—of unnecessary surgery. Every single procedure met or exceeded recommended indications.

No apology, though, from the Guidelines committee and their fugleman, McCready. They'd moved on to other hatchet jobs.

Except for a few loyal patients who wrote letters on Duncan's behalf, no one had come to his defense throughout the entire ordeal. His colleagues had kept their heads down. Even some AMA paper-pusher was quoted as saying the amount Duncan billed was "excessive."

Duncan learned the meaning of alone.

The long-delayed reports finally got forwarded to the State Board of Medical Examiners. The "coding irregularities" did not result in any net gain on Duncan's part—actually he lost money—but still he was issued a warning to be more careful in the future. Since there was no evidence of fraud or negligence, or of performing even a single unnecessary procedure, the board exonerated him.

But where was *that* publicized?

In a small paragraph buried deep in the *Banner*. But the *Washington Post*, which had broken the original story that started this nightmare, never mentioned it.

The public flogging was over, but it had dragged on too long. Referral patterns had changed. Generalists who used to feed his practice had found new surgeons.

His practice was ruined. He'd been held up to national scorn and then cleared. But his reputation remained tainted.

He could have shrugged it off, all of it, if Lisa still were alive and Diana still behind him.

But Lisa was gone. Dear, dear Lisa, who left without a good-bye, blaming him for all her pain.

Diana, too, blamed him. And soon their marriage went the way of his practice.

But he wasn't to blame. He'd done nothing wrong. Couldn't she see that? It was the committee . . . that damned Guidelines committee. McCready and his claque of pharisaical louts had plundered his life and then casually moved on.

Duncan had actually entertained thoughts of buying an assault rifle and blowing them all away. But then McCready had died, and the Guidelines committee disbanded, leaving Duncan with no target for the monstrous, smoldering mass of rage, coiled and writhing within him.

But he got over it—got past it, to use the current phrase. After all, he still had his son—Brad had stuck by him from beginning to end. And Oliver, of course. Steadfast, sedulous Oliver. Without them . . . Well, he just might have shoved a gun barrel in his mouth. So he started anew—new state, new specialty, new persona.

And everything seemed fine until the president revived the Guidelines committee. It was then that Duncan realized that the rage had never gone away. Like a cancer, it had metastasized throughout his system until it now lived in every tissue.

And still he might have controlled it if so many committee members hadn't begun looking around for someone to enhance their appearance for the heavy TV exposure they expected . . . and come to him, because he had the implants . . .

The irony should have been delicious.

Make me look good for the cameras . . .

He stopped himself from hurling his glass across the room. No sense in wasting good scotch.

So now five of the original seven were gone. McCready from natural causes, four Duncan's doing, and two left . . . the two youngest who were unlikely to seek out cosmetic surgery.

Almost time to call it quits. The new committee was in

complete disarray, the Guidelines act moribund. One more strike—the biggest of all—and it would be dead.

Just like Lisa.

And he wouldn't have to worry about Gina interfering with the last target. She'd be too off balance after today. Wouldn't even know about that patient. She'd be home, enjoying a day off.

And then he'd quit. Flush the TPD and wait for his moment to dissolve the last implant.

Which reminded him: he had to move the TPD. He'd left it in his top drawer in case Gina went for another look. Now that the games were over, he'd have to find a new hiding place.

He lifted his glass.

Pax, Regina.

Mind your own business and we'll all live happily ever after.

If not . . .

Gina lay in her bed in the dark, listening to the tick of the old mantle clock from the other room. An awful night alone, grappling with her doubt, her confusion. But she'd passed through that fire, emerging with a new perspective.

She hadn't imagined this. For a while there she'd been dazed and unsure, rocked back on her heels by the way everything had gone so wrong today. But she was on her feet again.

It's not over, Duncan, she told the darkness. You're smart . . . no, you're brilliant. Somehow you got way ahead of me on this. You probably think you've won. But I know what I saw, and I know what I know.

This is not over.

THE WEEK OF OCTOBER

22

29
SUNDAY

GINA WAS GOING TO FIND OUT EVERYTHING ABOUT Duncan.

She started her engine as Duncan's black Mercedes pulled to a stop at the end of his street. She couldn't park outside his house, or even on his block. Duncan lived in an ultraexclusive Chevy Chase neighborhood of large, stately, Federal-style homes on half-acre lots in which her little red Sunbird would stick out like a garbage scow at the Potomac Yacht Club. But one of the hallmarks of the neighborhood's exclusivity was limited access. The brick-pillared entrance opened onto a secondary road near a small, upscale strip mall. Gina had camped in the mall's parking lot most of yesterday and all of this morning and no one had bothered her.

Yesterday had yielded nothing of interest. Duncan had gone out only once, stopping at a liquor store, a gourmet coffee shop, a gas station, and an electronics specialty shop. "Caliguire Electronics," read the sign over the front door. "Audio, Video, SurroundSound, Satellite Dishes, Custom

Electronics." Gina remembered Duncan talking about his satellite dish on occasion. This was probably where he'd got it.

"Boy toys," she'd muttered.

And then it struck her: custom electronics. Duncan needed some sort of miniature ultrasound transducer to dissolve his implants. Something small enough to hide on his person and aim at his victim when he got within range. Something pocket-sized—

Ohmigod! His pager. His old-fashioned oversized beeper. She remembered how he'd had it in his hand when she saw him with Allard, and how it had gone off as they were standing with Senator Vincent on the hearing room floor before Senator Marsden gaveled everyone to their places. A few minutes later Senator Vincent was convulsing behind the dais.

What if it was oversized for a reason other than Duncan's stubborn unwillingness to part with a less than state-of-the-art piece of equipment? What if his pager was a minitransducer?

Could Duncan have used this place or someplace like it to fashion one for him?

The question nagged Gina the entire time he was inside, which stretched out almost to an hour. Finally, he came out and returned home.

Gina had seriously considered the idea of returning to the electronics shop to question the owner about transducers disguised as beepers, but then Gerry's words came back to her.

No more Nancy Drew stuff.

Gerry . . . she missed him. She wished he'd call.

But it was good advice. Not only was she too old to be Nancy Drew, she didn't want to be a detective; being an internist was quite enough. And besides, questioning the folks at Caliguire might prompt a call to Duncan.

Better just stick to following him around.

Nice way to spend a weekend.

So now it was Sunday evening, the light fading, and this was the first Gina had seen of Duncan all day. She'd worried that he might have another way out of his neighborhood, but a drive by his house an hour ago had revealed the Mercedes parked at the top of the semicircular drive before the front door of his brick colonial.

Then the radio gave her the most likely reason why he'd chosen now to be on the move. The Redskins game was over. They'd lost. Again.

She put her car in gear and waited to see which direction he turned. Whichever way, she'd be close behind. She wasn't crazy—not psychotic, not even neurotic—and she wasn't going to let anyone make her think so. Duncan had secrets. He lied about where he went on his afternoons. She was going to find out where he really went. He wasn't going to be able to sneeze without her saying *Gesundheit*.

She was *not* going to drop this.

Gina watched him turn south; she let a car get between them before she pulled out and followed. When he turned onto East-West Highway, she had a pretty good idea where he might be headed.

Sure enough, he pulled into the surgicenter.

Now what? She couldn't exactly pull in behind him and follow him into his office.

His office . . . he had that rock garden with the pool and all those thick bushes outside his office window. Maybe she could get a peek.

She found a parking spot half a block down and trotted back. Homing in on the glow from Duncan's windows, she crept along a grassy buffer between the surgicenter and the neighboring office building and lowered into a crouch as she neared the rear wall of the rock garden. Duncan's office windows were just past that. If she could get a look . . .

Look at me, she thought. Creeping across lawns, spying on people . . .

This wasn't her. And hadn't she sworn she wasn't going to do the Nancy Drew thing? Was this the behavior of a stable personality?

Maybe I do need help.

The thought chilled her, but she shook off the doubts. She had to see this through.

She parted the branches of a small evergreen—from its ginlike odor she guessed it was some sort of juniper—and peered through the plate glass into Duncan's office.

He was seated at his desk. Gina settled onto her knees and watched, hoping he'd do more than just straighten papers. It was getting *cold* out here in the wind.

She caught her breath as he leaned to his right and unlocked the top desk drawer. She leaned forward, all but thrusting her face through the prickly juniper as she watched him remove the TPD from the drawer, heft it in his hand, then rise and wander about. He opened cabinets and poked inside, lifted bottles, pulled out books and journals, peered into the space they left, then shoved them back.

What's he doing?

He seemed to be looking for something.

Or some*where*.

Finally he pulled a volume the size of the *Merck Manual* off a top shelf, placed the bottle of TPD in the rear of the gap, then slid the book back in.

He was hiding the TPD.

Gina was dumbfounded.

Why would he hide the bottle when he had a locked drawer for it?

Maybe he had no further use for it. Or maybe he'd never used it. But then why was he hiding it now?

Damn! Why didn't any of this make *sense?*

Suddenly the office went dark. Duncan had turned out the

lights. Gina spun and scampered back to her car. It was good to get the heater going again. She watched Duncan's car turn back the way it had come on East-West. She gave him a good lead, then swung around and followed.

When she saw him turn into his neighborhood, she turned east and headed for Connecticut Avenue. For Adams Morgan. For home.

She'd had enough Nancy Drew for one night. In two days of trailing him she'd learned two things: one, he liked to hang out at Caliguire Electronics; two, he'd changed the hiding place of his bottle of TPD.

No answers. Just two facts which did nothing but engender a whole slew of new questions. She didn't need more questions. She had questions coming out her ears. She needed *answers,* dammit!

Maybe tomorrow. When Duncan left early to go to his golf club, Gina would be right behind him. She'd find out where he really went. Maybe a mistress. Or maybe something to do with that little bottle of TPD. Hopefully she'd be able to cross one question off her lengthening list.

30
MONDAY

"OKAY, DOC. SHE'S ALL SET."

Duncan walked over to the corner of his office where Harry stood on a small aluminum utility ladder. Dressed in a Guns n' Roses T-shirt, he was heavyset, maybe forty, with a receding hairline and a ponytail. He was positioning some of the bric-a-brac on the top shelf around the sensor. When he finished, he stepped down and pointed to it.

"Would you ever know it was there?"

Duncan scrutinized the shelf. The sensor was a small brown rectangle the size of a cigarette box. It blended neatly with the woodwork, appeared almost a part of the cabinet. The camcorder lens looked like some sort of glass bauble.

Duncan nodded approvingly. "Only if I knew exactly where to look."

"Cool. Now just stand still a moment while I get us some power." He plugged a transformer into the outlet to the left of the sink. "All right. Now move your arms."

Duncan waved his arms and saw a red dot begin to glow on the sensor.

"Smile," Harry said. "You're on *Candid Camera.*"

"What about that little red light?" Duncan said.

"That just means it sensed motion. You tripped the circuit."

"Yes, but the light is a giveaway. The whole idea is *surreptitious* surveillance, Harry. Kill that light."

"No problem."

Duncan sipped his morning coffee as Harry climbed back up his step ladder and began whistling while he removed the back plate of the motion detector.

Harry seemed to love his work. Why not? Duncan was paying him handsomely for playing at his hobby. Duncan remembered how excited Harry had been when he had challenged him to miniaturize an ultrasound transducer. That had taken weeks, but the big bill had been more than worth it.

This little chore, on the other hand, was a piece of cake.

Duncan had told him he thought one of his employees might be pilfering. He'd said he had a pretty good idea who but wanted to catch the culprit in the act. Which was true. He wanted to see if Gina would try again.

Harry had said that was cool. Yeah, what with the labor laws these days, you just about had to catch someone red-handed before you could give them the boot.

Harry's solution: a video camera activated by a motion detector.

"All right," Harry said, coming off the ladder again. "The light's disabled. Now, remember, the only time you want this thing on is when you're out of the room. Otherwise you're gonna find yourself fast-forwarding through umpteen hours of yourself sitting at your desk or making coffee or whatever."

"Mostly whatever, I should think," Duncan said. "I often engage in whatever while I'm here."

"Cool," Harry said. He laid a finger on the upper edge of the transformer. "Okay. Two little buttons here. This one turns the power off, this one on. Just before you leave, click it on. That'll arm the sensor. Any movement then will trip the sensor which'll turn on the camera and you'll be taping for the entire time someone's here until a full minute after they leave. It's also got a date and time readout that'll appear in the corner of the picture. I fixed the cam with a wide-angle lens so's you've got the whole office covered."

Duncan said, "Cool."

"You know, if you decide to make this a permanent setup, I can rig the camera directly to a VCR and—"

"Just temporary, Harry, I assure you. And here is your check."

Harry glanced at the amount, said, "Cool," one last time, packed up his tools, and was gone.

Okay, my little cygnet, Duncan thought, staring into the blind eye of the video camera. The next step is up to you.

He glanced at the clock. Perfect timing. Harry had arrived early and done his work quickly, leaving Duncan a few minutes to spare before scrubbing for the day's first surgery.

An abbreviated schedule today, mostly minor procedures. Dr. VanDuyne was due here about noon and Duncan wanted a clear field when he toured him and the others around.

He pushed the ON button, moved an empty carafe in front of the transformer, and headed for the locker room. The back of his neck tingled with the knowledge that his movement had triggered the sensor and his exit was being recorded.

Gina rushed through her dictation and other paperwork so she'd be ready to tail Duncan when he took off. She'd had to hustle. The way he'd whipped through those procedures this morning made her think he was in a big rush to leave. But once surgery was over, he seemed in no great hurry to go anywhere.

Gina was up and down the stairs, keeping an eye on Duncan's office, ready to grab her coat as soon as he looked like he was going to leave. But he seemed to be killing time. On one of her surveillance runs she glanced out into the parking lot and saw the mysterious Dr. V. and two other men get out of a gray sedan.

So that's why he's hanging around.

Twenty minutes later, Duncan was leading the trio downstairs on a tour.

"And here are the nether regions. My brother's lab and our records room."

The good-looking Dr. V. looked relaxed, but his two suited friends were as stiff and uptight as they were clean-cut. Nosy too. Peeking into every closet, every cubbyhole, asking questions in low voices Gina could not pick up.

"Just showing these gentlemen around," Duncan told Gina as they passed. "Don't let us disturb you." He didn't bother with introductions.

She followed the group upstairs and watched the two suits point to doors and windows as they conferenced with each other. Neither of them smiled once. What were they? Lawyers? Accountants? Security consultants?

Then the entire entourage, including Oliver, retired to Duncan's office and closed the door.

What was going on? She was pretty sure now it wasn't a matter of taking on a new associate. Was Duncan selling the building? He'd never mentioned moving. And why did this Dr. V. look familiar?

Curiosity was eating Gina alive. She'd have given almost anything to be a fly on a wall in that office right now.

* * *

Forty-five minutes later all five came out in a group. They stood in the hall, shaking hands. The suits looked as grim as ever, Duncan and Dr. V. were pleasant, and Oliver was quite literally beaming. Then the visitors headed for the parking lot, Duncan returned to his office, and Oliver bustled down the hall toward Gina.

"This is wonderful," he said as he approached. The overhead fluorescents gleamed from his glasses and exposed scalp. He was grinning like a man who'd just won the lottery. "This is *so* wonderful!"

"What is, Oliver? What's going on?"

"I can't tell you," he said as he hurried past her. "I wish I could, but I can't. Not now. Maybe sometime."

Gina watched him disappear into the stairwell down to his lab. She'd never seen him like this. Had he worked out some huge deal for his implants? She started to follow. She was sure she could pry it out of him.

But then she saw Duncan shrugging into his sport coat as he stood before Barbara's desk. He was talking, she was taking notes and nodding her head. Then he was on his way.

Gina ducked into the locker room, grabbed her coat and purse, and hurried after him. She'd have to put off grilling Oliver until later.

"Hey, great news," Barbara said as Gina passed her desk. "We've got a three-day weekend coming up."

Gina slowed. "When?"

"This weekend. We're going to be closed on Friday. Dr. Lathram just told me to give everybody the day off with pay. Isn't that great?"

"Yeah," Gina said, picking up speed again. "Great."

Friday off. Normally she'd assume Duncan had someplace to go this weekend and wanted an extra day. But the decision seemed to have been made right after his conference with Dr. V. and the suits. How come?

*　*　*

No surprise when Duncan's Mercedes led her away from his golf club, but she was completely unprepared for the course he took through the District. East, then down Connecticut, past Adams Morgan to Dupont Circle. From there he took Massachusetts downtown.

He's heading for the Hill, Gina thought, but he breezed past Union Station and kept going, deep into Southeast. Mass was lined with two- and three-story row houses down here, painted in bright reds, yellows, blues, greens, even orange. The neighborhoods deteriorated; on a couple of corners she saw men in rough clothes drinking from bottles in paper bags. Gina was almost afraid to stop at the red lights. And she was in a three-year-old American compact. Duncan's Mercedes stood out like a luxury yacht in a fleet of tugboats. Yet nobody was bothering either of them.

What was he doing here? He had such a haughty attitude, she could not imagine him down here among the po' folk.

And then they came to the end of Mass Avenue and she caught on. D.C. General Hospital lay spread out on the downhill slope before them. She followed Duncan along the winding driveway through the well-kept complex of a dozen or so brick and stucco buildings, past the D.C. Correctional Treatment facility to a restricted parking lot—"Decals Only" warned the sign. As Duncan turned in, Gina scooted into the nearby patient lot. She saw uniformed guards everywhere. Security seemed a major concern here.

She spotted Duncan strolling toward the doctors' entrance—a rectangular hole in the brick face of one of the buildings. How was she going to get in? She wasn't on staff.

But she could look like she was.

She grabbed an extra stethoscope from her glove compartment, hung her Senate ID badge around her neck, and hurried after him.

She wished she knew D.C. General. The brick building ahead was a big one and had a jury-rigged look. Eight stories high at the front end, six at the rear, it looked as if it had started out considerably smaller and grown by accretion—a wing here, a few extra floors there. This could be tricky.

She kept up the quick pace as she passed the guard perched on a stool inside the entrance, smiling and waving with the hand holding the stethoscope, hoping he wouldn't notice that her photo ID wasn't for D.C. General.

The guard smiled back and nodded, then went back to reading his newspaper.

About fifty feet ahead of her she saw Duncan heading down the hall. She broke into a delicate trot to close the distance between them. She knew if she lost sight of him, she'd never find him again in this maze.

He led her on a tortuous course that ended before a bank of elevators.

Gina hung back, uncertain. If she didn't get on that elevator with him, she'd lose him. She wouldn't even know which floor to search.

Only one thing to do. She tucked her Senate ID badge away and stepped forward.

"Duncan!" she said, tapping him on the shoulder. "What are you doing here?"

He turned and started when he saw her. Something flashed in his eyes. Shock? Anger? Suspicion? She wasn't sure which. Maybe all three. Whatever it was, it was gone in an instant.

He smiled. "Gina! I never expected to see you here."

Which doesn't answer my question, she thought. She felt her heart pick up tempo. What's he going to do now?

"I was just visiting a hematology resident I know. An old friend from U. of P. But how about you?"

He sighed unhappily and rubbed his jaw. "Well, I didn't want anyone to know about this. If word ever got out . . ."

Oh, God, she thought. He's sick.

Terminal diagnoses like cancer and AIDS raced through her brain.

He sighed again. "Easier to show you than explain it all." A battered elevator door wobbled open to their left. He pressed his hand gently against her back and guided her toward the emptying car. "Let's go."

He took her up to the maxillofacial clinic where the nurses beamed at him and the patients seated in the waiting room stared with wide eyes and whispered to their companions as they pointed to him. She sat with Duncan in an examining room and watched in dazed wonder as he evaluated prospective patients and inspected his handiwork in postsurgical follow-ups.

It was the postsurgical patients who got to Gina. Some were effusive in their praise, some were almost inarticulate in their gratitude, but one and all they worshiped him, all but falling down on their knees before him for what he had done for them.

And finally the last patient was gone and she was alone with him in that tiny room, watching him scribble a progress note.

So this was where he'd been sneaking off to when he'd said he was playing golf. She was baffled.

"Why, Duncan?"

"Hmmm?" He looked up from the last chart and flipped it closed.

"Why are you here?"

He shrugged. "I had a few empty hours to fill. Face-lifts get boring after a while and I like to do something different now and then."

"But this is a free clinic and you're Duncan Cash-up-front-I-don't-give-a-damn-what-insurance-you-have Lathram."

His smile was sad as he shook his head slowly. "It was never about money. It's never been about money."

"Then what *is* it about?"

"Someday I'll tell you. I'm not ready just yet."

Gina bit back her frustration. "Okay, then. Why do you keep this a secret?"

Another shrug. "When I opened up my cosmetic surgery practice I proclaimed to anyone who would listen about limiting myself exclusively to elective surgery and not accepting insurance of any type. Which was all fine at first, but quickly became stultifying." He looked away. "Despite heroic efforts to avoid it, I could not resist the urge to direct my skills toward a somewhat more meaningful application."

"Somewhat?" she said. "This is wonderful. I'm so proud of you."

He looked at her now, and again something flashed in his eyes, different this time. Almost like pain.

"Don't get carried away now, Gina. This isn't a one-way street here. I get something out of it too."

At that moment Gina felt very close to him. Her throat constricted and tears swelled against the backs of her lids. Shame made her cringe inside. How could she ever have suspected him of hurting anybody?

She wanted to hug him.

"I've got to go," she said when she could trust her voice.

"I'll walk you out."

He guided her back to the elevators. On the way down, she couldn't resist another nagging question.

"So, who were those men you were touring around today?"

"Back at the office? Just some people who wanted to look around."

"Are you selling the place?"

"I should say not."

"Remodeling?"

"They simply wanted to look around."

"Oh. Well. That clears that up."

He put his arm around her shoulder and laughed. "Gina, Gina, Gina. You always think you have to know everything. Life is full of little mysteries."

"And this is one of them, right?"

He laughed again. "Right."

He escorted her to her car, held the door for her, and waved as she pulled away.

Gina's emotions were in turmoil. She felt like a swimmer in a sea of wild and capricious currents. Where was land?

After thinking the worst of him just days ago, she now found Duncan regaining his hero status. He was almost like . . . she searched for a comparison . . . almost like Zorro. To most of the world he presented a dilettantish demeanor, like the foppish Don Diego in the story; but to the poor, scarred people at the maxillofacial clinic in D.C.'s innermost city, he was the dashing Dr. Duncan—Dr. Zorro—with the flashing blade that made things right.

Duncan probably reveled in the paradox: Insouciant, money-hungry plastic surgeon to the rich and powerful who sneaks off to treat the poor and homeless at a free clinic. But what impressed Gina most was the sneaking. Most people trumpeted their charity. Duncan kept his hidden, as if it embarrassed him. Charming.

Duncan was almost back on his demigod pedestal. Almost. He'd be at the pinnacle of her personal pantheon if it weren't for that bottle of TPD hidden in his office.

That damn bottle.

All in all, Duncan thought as he made his way to his own car, that turned out pretty well.

But nonetheless disturbing.

The inescapable fact was that Gina had followed him here and he hadn't a clue she'd been on his tail. The question now was, how *long* had she been tailing him?

Not that it mattered really. What could anyone learn from tailing him? He led a drearily mundane existence, never ranging far from home. He almost pitied anyone who had to spend days traipsing after him.

But Gina was still suspicious enough to devote an afternoon to following him to D.C. General, and that was disturbing. And she *had* been following him. Not for a second did he buy that story about an old college friend, the hematology resident. D.C. General was not in a neighborhood that invited casual visitors.

He smiled as he pulled out and headed back to Chevy Chase. But sometimes things work out for the best. What was that old saw? When somebody hands you a lemon, make lemonade.

He'd fought the impulse to launch a verbal assault when Gina had tapped him on the shoulder by the elevator, accuse her of shadowing him, invading his privacy. A wiser part of him knew that would be counterproductive. Instead, why not let her in on his little secret? It was too late to keep her out, so he might as well welcome her along.

And it had worked. She'd been completely disarmed. He could see it in her eyes as she saw the "before" photos and the living, breathing "after" results.

And why shouldn't she be disarmed? he thought. I do damn good work.

Good work . . . good works. Weren't good works supposed to be their own reward? Up to now they'd been just that. He'd found satisfaction in removing scars and correcting nature's mistakes in people who'd otherwise have no chance at proper repair.

But today they'd brought an unexpected lagniappe. His altruistic participation in the clinic had blunted, if not completely deflected, the suspicions of one very bright and very nosy young woman.

Perhaps the good men do was not necessarily interred with their bones.

But he couldn't let down his guard. Not yet. Not until after Friday.

And that reminded him of the video camera in his office.

Duncan stood alone in his office. The building was empty except for him, which was just the way he wanted it. He pushed the videocassette into the VCR and hit the RE-WIND button. The machine hummed and stopped almost immediately. Good sign.

He hit PLAY, then FFWD. A high-angle shot of his office flickered into focus and he recognized his retreating back. Then Barbara fast-walked to and from his desk to drop off his dictation; then again with his mail; then once more with what appeared to be more dictation. And then he saw himself, strolling into the room, sifting through the mail and papers on his desk. Strange to watch himself in fast motion. He looked like a Keystone Kop. Then he approached the counter below the camera's field of vision, reached forward, and . . .

The screen blanked. That was when he had turned off the power.

Very good, he thought as he rewound the tape. No sign of Gina. No snooping around, no trying to get into the locked desk drawer again.

He prayed for similar results every time he reviewed this tape.

The last thing on earth he wanted was to hurt Gina.

31
TUESDAY

"ALL RIGHT, OLIVER," GINA SAID. "ENOUGH WITH THE secrecy. You've got to tell me why those men were wandering around the building yesterday."

It was early. Gloved and masked, they were down in Oliver's lab, filling implants under sterile conditions for the day's procedures. Gina had spent half the night cudgeling her brain for a way to learn the identity of Dr. V. and the mysterious suits.

"I can't, Gina," Oliver said. "Duncan would kill me."

Poor choice of words, Gina thought, annoyed at the chill they gave her. Duncan wouldn't kill anyone. She believed that now. She had to.

"Don't be silly," Gina said. "You're his brother." She winked. "And besides, he needs these implants."

Oliver rolled his eyes behind his horn-rims. "Thanks. That does wonders for my self-esteem."

"Seriously, though. This is driving me crazy. I've caught this Dr. V. ducking in and out of here at least three times now, and I know I've seen him before. Just tell me who he is.

Not what he's doing here, just his name. Just that one little
thing, and I won't ask another question, I promise."

"I'm sorry, Gina, but—"

"I'll sneeze all over your implants."

"No. You wouldn't do that."

She sniffed. "Uh-oh. I feel one coming on now. It's
building up. It's gonna blow right through this mask."

"Gina, please don't kid around like—"

"Here it comes. Ah . . . ah . . ."

"All right, all right."

Gina shook her head as if to clear it. "Well, what do you
know. All better. For the moment. Now, who is Dr. V.?"

"I really shouldn't. I promised Duncan I wouldn't breathe
a word."

She sniffed again. "Oliver . . ."

"All right. But just his name. If it doesn't ring a bell, too
bad. Agreed?"

"Agreed."

Oliver leaned forward and Gina could tell by the look in
his eyes that he'd been dying to confide in someone. Now
she'd given him an excuse.

"His name is VanDuyne. Dr. John VanDuyne."

VanDuyne . . . Gina knew that name. It was scampering
about the back corners of her mind, just out of reach.
VanDuyne . . . John VanDuyne . . .

And then she had him. One of the guest lecturers at the
public policy seminars back in Tulane. A physician, he'd
come from Washington and he'd seemed uncomfortable
lecturing, and in his role with the government. John
VanDuyne, one of the higher-ups in HHS . . . but he was
something else too. She'd read an article or heard some other
mention of him. Dr. John VanDuyne . . .

"Ohmigod!" she cried. "Duncan's going to operate on the
president!"

Oliver tore off his mask and slumped back in his seat. He

ran his fingers nervously through his thinning hair. "Oh, no! Now I've done it!"

"I'm right, aren't I?"

He nodded resignedly, a look of astonishment on his face. "I don't believe you put it all together so fast. Just from a name. How did you do it?"

When she remembered that VanDuyne was the president's personal physician, suddenly it was obvious that the men with him yesterday had been Secret Service. And the way they'd been looking around, studying entrances and exits, peering through windows . . . why else unless they were reconnoitering before a presidential visit?

But she felt no triumph at her lightning deduction; instead, a cold sodden weight was growing in her stomach.

The president of the United States going under Duncan's knife. After yesterday, she should have felt proud that Duncan had been chosen for whatever it was the president wanted done. But she was terrified.

"He's coming Friday?"

Again Oliver nodded. His eyes looked wounded.

So that explained the day off with pay.

"What procedure?"

"His eyes," Oliver said. He slipped the tips of his index fingers under his glasses and touched his lower lids. "Wants to be rid of the bags. A lift on the upper lids, too, while Duncan's at it."

"But those baggy eyes have become his trademark. What will all the cartoonists do without them?"

Oliver shrugged. "Apparently his media consultants and spin doctors have converged and decided that his baggy lids have become much baggier and people think the president looks tired and older."

"Being president of the United States tends to do that to people."

"But they want the youth vote. That's what put him in the

first time. They don't want some younger-looking upstart to steal that constituency. They blame the eyelids for his tired, older look, so they have to go."

"Ridiculous. The election's more than a year away."

"But not the primaries. He's expecting a strong challenge, so he wants to be looking his best in New Hampshire."

"So why Duncan?"

"Why not? He's the best." He pointed to the tray of implants. "Especially with these."

Gina had to admit he had a point there. "But why all the secrecy?"

"Isn't it obvious? The president doesn't want anyone, especially the press, to find out. He's going to arrive at the crack of dawn on Friday. As soon as he's out of recovery he'll be whisked off to Camp David for a long weekend and some extra days of vacation. He'll wear dark glasses all weekend, and by the time he returns, there'll be minimal evidence of the surgery. Any slight discoloration that persists can be covered by makeup. Foolproof, huh?"

"Yeah," Gina said slowly. "Foolproof."

But was it Duncanproof?

Stop! She shouldn't be thinking like that.

"But with all the staff off, how can Duncan operate?"

"They're importing an anesthesiologist from Bethesda Naval Hospital, and Dr. VanDuyne is going to assist."

"And the Secret Service men will be guarding the hall, I suppose."

"Right. Isn't it exciting?"

"Yes. Exciting as hell."

But Gina was feeling anxiety rather than excitement. She knew what Duncan thought of the president. How many tirades about him had she endured?

Yet Duncan had agreed to do a cosmetic repair of his eyelids . . . agreed to perform a procedure designed to give the president a little edge toward reelection.

It didn't add up. Why would Duncan do anything to help this man?

Simply because he was the president and he had asked? Maybe. The office did have a mesmerizing effect on people.

Look at Oliver—beaming like a starstruck Boy Scout. He can't tell a soul, yet he's totally gaga over the idea of his implants being used on the president of the United States.

Was she borrowing trouble? Even if Duncan wanted to try something, how could he with the Secret Service watching his every move?

But in the recovery room . . . would they be hovering over him there?

Probably not.

Why was she thinking this way? She had to stop. Yesterday she'd seen a side of Duncan she'd thought long gone. She'd promised herself to revamp her thinking. And she'd be succeeding, too, if not for that damn bottle of TPD.

Was it still where she'd seen Duncan hide it?

Only one way to find out.

Now or never.

Gina wished she could call Gerry and talk to him about this, but look what happened last time she'd gone to him with a suspicion. Their relationship was stretched to the breaking point. Or maybe he'd already broken it off without her knowing it. He hadn't contacted her since Friday.

Duncan was out to lunch, Barbara was away from her desk. Gina slipped into Duncan's office and went directly to the bookshelves. She remembered it had been the far left section, top shelf. But the top shelf was too high to reach.

She looked around for a chair to stand on and spotted a small step stool over by the sink. How convenient. She'd never noticed one here before. Maybe because she'd never been searching for something to stand on. She pulled it over and stepped up to where she was eye level with the top shelf.

She thought back to Sunday night, standing outside in the cold and spying on Duncan. The book had been short and fat, with a green binding. And here it was, right in front of her. She wriggled it out and peered into the dark gap. Daylight from over her shoulder reflected off the glass of an all-too-familiar injection vial.

There it was, just inches away. But now what?

Why not just take it? a voice whispered. Take the damn bottle and rip off the stopper and pour the contents down a drain. Duncan might spend days, weeks wondering what happened to it, but so what? It'll be gone and you won't have to give it another thought.

Unless there were other vials of the stuff around.

But did that matter? This was the one she knew about. This was the one that had to go.

Gina was just reaching into the space when a voice cried out behind her.

"Jesus!"

She started and nearly lost her balance as she turned. Barbara was standing in the center of the office, her palm pressed between her breasts.

"You almost gave me a heart attack!" Barbara said. "Dr. Panzella, you've got to warn me when you're coming in here."

"Sorry," Gina said. She hoped she didn't look as shaken and embarrassed as she felt. "You weren't at your desk and I needed to look up something."

"Just make sure he knows you've been in here."

"What do you mean?"

"He likes everything in its place. So if you're going to borrow anything, better check with him first, otherwise I'll hear about it."

This isn't going to work, Gina thought. She held up the green text.

"Okay, Barbara. Watch." With a small flourish, she slipped the book back into its space. "Voilà. Right back where it belongs."

"Great. He's such a stickler for detail, you know."

Gina stepped down and slid the step stool back to its original position.

"That's what makes him a great surgeon. He sweats the details."

Barbara placed some papers on Duncan's desk and they left together. Gina gave one worried backward glance at the green book on the top shelf. She'd have another chance at it tomorrow.

Unless Duncan moved it again.

Oh, no.

Duncan could feel all the warmth drain out of him as he watched the screen. He shuddered.

The videotape showed Gina entering the office at 12:17 P.M., dragging the step stool to the bookshelves, and pulling out the book where the TPD was hidden. There had been not the slightest hesitation. She knew the shelf and the exact volume to remove.

But how did she *know?*

He felt an urge to step over to the shelf himself—it was only a few feet away—and check to see if she had taken the vial, but he could not move. He stood frozen, his eyes fixed on the screen.

He watched her peer into the space, saw her hand rise toward it, and then Barbara came in.

Thank God for Barbara.

Their voices were muted but he could make out Gina's

excuse and Barbara's comments about his tidiness. And then the book was back in its place and they were leaving. But he saw Gina's wistful parting glance at the bookshelf.

She'd be back. Dammit, she'd be back.

He fast-forwarded through the rest of the tape, but Gina did not return. That was a relief. He hit rewind and checked behind the book. Yes, the vial was still there. But how——how had Gina known that he'd moved it?

She watched me.

Of course. She'd followed him to D.C. General yesterday. She'd probably been following him since the fiasco on Friday.

He turned around and stared through the plate-glass outer wall. If she'd been tailing him Sunday night, she could have crouched out there in the darkness among the shrubs and observed his every move.

With a start he realized that she could be out there right now, spying on him.

But no. Since their encounter in D.C. General yesterday, he'd been on guard, keeping careful watch in his rearview mirror, so much so that he'd nearly caused several accidents. No one had followed him anywhere today.

But why had she checked behind the book today and not yesterday? Had something happened today to rekindle her suspicions?

He fast-forwarded to where Barbara and Gina were leaving and paused on Gina's final backward glance. He read anxiety in her expression. No question something was making her apprehensive.

A thought jolted him: Could she know about the president?

Good Lord, if she'd found out about that, she might do something rash, something catastrophic.

He picked up the phone and jabbed in his brother's number.

"Oliver," he said immediately, "did Gina mention anything to you about our special case on Friday?" He took care not to identify the president on the phone.

"Wh-what do you mean?"

The hesitation in Oliver's voice gave Duncan a terrible feeling.

"Does she have any idea who it is?"

"Um, she knows. She guessed."

"How in the world—?"

"She recognized Dr. VanDuyne, then deduced that the men with him were Secret Service. From there it was two plus two, I guess."

"Did you confirm it?"

"Well, what else could I do?"

"Damn it, Oliver! Dammit to hell!"

"Duncan, I swore her to secrecy. You know you can trust Gina. Wasn't it better to confirm her suspicions than to have her go on wondering and asking questions?"

"Well, maybe." He reined in his anger at his brother. Oliver had no idea why it had been so important to keep Gina out of this. "When did this conversation take place?"

"This morning. Maybe eleven or so. Why?"

"Nothing. I'll see you Thursday."

He hung up and began to pace the room, pausing only to hit the REWIND button on the VCR.

Damn! Gina confirmed it through Oliver at eleven and an hour later she was here meddling with the TPD.

The chance of a lifetime. The president himself, the commander in chief of the kakistocracy, would be sleeping off his anesthesia right down the hall. The man who single-handedly had resurrected the Guidelines bill, who had insisted on including medical ethics in its purview, and who would keep pushing relentlessly for the committee to get its foul job done.

So what? Duncan thought. He had nothing to do with

Lisa's death. Why not let him go and be satisfied with what I've done so far?

Because I can't. Not yet.

He was out of control and he knew it. He felt like a runaway train careening downhill. McCready had started it, and Duncan would finish it. He could not let this opportunity pass. He'd never have another like it. He would impose a symmetry on this madness . . . he would close the circle with the president.

But Gina Panzella was going to ruin it. He could see it in her face, feel it in his bones. She was going to meddle again. And he could not allow that. Not this time.

The VCR whirred and ejected the tape. Duncan pulled it out and stared at it.

Why, Gina? Why do you have to keeping sticking your nose in where it doesn't belong?

His fury rose, a pressure in his head, his chest, threatening to explode. She was leaving him only two choices: either back down or somehow neutralize her.

He groaned. She had backed him into a corner, and the only option left was to strike out at her. He might have to harm her.

And he loathed himself for it.

With a cry he hurled the videocassette to the floor and smashed it under his heel.

"Damn you, Gina!"

32
WEDNESDAY

"I'VE BEEN KEEPING SOMETHING IMPORTANT FROM YOU, Gina," Duncan said. "But I decided this morning I'm going to confide in you."

Gina sat across his desk from him, sipping a late-morning cup of one of his exotic coffees—Jamaican Blue Mountain, she thought he'd said, but she'd been feeling too tense and wary to pay much attention. She'd been up most of the night brooding about the president's surgery. Should she be as worried as she was? Should she do anything? Should she call Gerry about it?

Again, she'd decided not to call Gerry. She had even less to go on this time than the last. He already thought she was distraught. Why add fuel to that particular fire?

She'd still been debating her next step when Duncan had called her in, told Barbara he did not want to be disturbed, and shut the door. He'd handed her a cup and asked her to be seated.

So now she sat, tense and rigid in her chair, the coffee

warming her cold hands as she anxiously waited to see what was up.

"Since you are a physician in this facility, what I'm about to say falls under physician-patient privilege. Is that understood?"

"Of course."

"Good." He leaned back and steepled his fingers. "You might be wondering why I gave the staff off this Friday. The reason is extraordinary: I'm operating on the president of the United States that day."

Gina felt her jaw drop open. Duncan was actually telling her.

He smiled. "I can see by your expression that this was the last thing you expected to hear. Good. That means our security measures are working."

He went on to tell her most of what she had learned from Oliver yesterday: the nature of the procedure, the rationale behind it, the reasons for all the secrecy. Not wanting to get Oliver in hot water, she pretended it was all new to her.

All the while her mind was racing, searching for a reason why, if he was planning to harm the president, he would tell her this.

"You must be very proud," she said when he paused.

"Well, much as I dislike the man's policies, I have to admit it's an honor to be selected as his surgeon."

"Honor aside," she said carefully, "I'm a little surprised you'd do anything to help him get reelected. I mean, knowing how you feel about him."

Duncan waved his hand dismissively, as if physically brushing aside her words. "It's all media-consultant nonsense." His smile was laconic. "As if his eyelids could in any way make or break an election."

"You know what they said about Nixon's five-o'clock shadow in that television debate back in 1960."

"I saw that debate. Nixon's five-o'clock shadow was the least of his problems."

"So you are going to help him look younger."

"No. Actually, I'm going to remove his eyelids completely so he'll have this ghastly bug-eyed look."

Her heart jumped. He wasn't serious . . . was he? "Duncan, don't even—"

"Only kidding. Look, the president himself wants me to do it, so I'm doing it. As a rule I don't correct a single-feature defect like this, but the rest of his face is fairly young-looking, so I'm making an exception." He grinned. "And trust me, this is *not* a freebie."

"Who's assisting?" Oliver had already told her it would be Dr. VanDuyne, but she thought she should cover for him by asking.

Duncan leaned forward. "That's why I called you in here. I'd like you to assist."

Gina blinked. The words rocked her. What in heaven was going on?

"Me?"

"Yes, you. VanDuyne, the president's personal physician, has offered to assist. He'd probably be okay, but the more I think about it, the more I want someone who's worked with me. You've done dozens of these lid lifts with me. So, if you haven't already made plans for Friday . . ."

"No . . . no plans."

"Good. I'd also like you to handle recovery. VanDuyne was going to, but again you're more experienced. I'd feel better if you were on hand to watch over things."

"Sure," Gina said, still off balance. She struggled to get her bearings, fought not to be awed. "I'll be glad to."

"Excellent. I intend to add a fat surgical assistant's fee to the bill which will go directly to you."

Gina was going to be assisting on the president of the

United States, *and* be well paid for it. Talk about having your cake and . . .

But even more disorienting was that Duncan had *asked* her to assist him. How could he be planning any harm if he wanted her right there in OR and in recovery?

Had all her suspicions been for nothing?

No, not all. That vial of TPD still loomed in the background, but Gina began to feel the tension uncoil within her, felt her neck and shoulder muscles relax as if the weight of the world had been lifted from them.

She half listened as he went on about the anesthesiologist from Bethesda, the security measures, and the need for absolute discretion.

"You can't tell anyone: not your best friend, not your parents, not even your boyfriend in the FBI."

"We're just friends," she said. Although even that might be pushing things at this point.

"Whatever. Only the Secret Service and the four doctors in OR-1 on Friday morning will know about this. We're scheduled for seven-thirty. The president and VanDuyne will arrive at six-thirty. You, Oliver, and the anesthesiologist will be here at six. I'll come at five to open up for the Secret Service so they can secure the premises—I believe that's the expression they used. Any problem with that?"

"None at all."

"Wonderful. Oliver, by the way, is nearly delirious about this. Wants to celebrate in advance. I think it's rather silly but if we don't do something to mark the occasion he just might explode. Since we all have to be up early on Friday, and since Oliver loves Italian food, I've reserved us a table at Galileo tonight. Oliver and I would both very much like for you to join us."

Galileo. God, the four-star restaurant where the president took his Hollywood friends when they were in town. Gina was beginning to get excited herself.

"How could I say no to Galileo?"

"I'll pick up Oliver and we'll be by at half past seven to pick you up." He rose. "And now, unless you have any questions, I suggest we both get back to work."

Feeling slightly dazed, Gina nodded, rose, and made her way to the hall.

Life was certainly full of surprises.

Duncan watched Gina go, then poured himself another cup of coffee.

That went rather well, he thought grimly. Too well.

Under different circumstances he might find this sort of cat-and-mouse game stimulating. But not with this particular mouse. Plus, everything was rigged in his favor: he knew what she knew, but she hadn't the slightest notion that he was on to her.

Gina was beginning to trust him again. And he was going to use that to cut her off at the knees.

He didn't much like himself today.

He spotted a sliver of black plastic and plucked it from the carpet. A remnant of the videocassette he'd smashed last night. After that little tantrum, he'd picked up the pieces, discarded them, and slipped a new cassette into the camera. Then, with his emotions locked away where they could not interfere, he'd sat down, assessed the cards he'd been dealt, and worked out the best way to play his hand.

First, he'd lock up the TPD in his desk drawer again and see that Gina did not get another chance to pick the lock.

Then he'd take the offensive. She'd learned about the president—something he'd been desperate to keep secret. The worst thing to do then would be to retreat. That would confirm that he had something to hide. So do the opposite, the unexpected. Don't lock her out. Welcome her in. Show his hand—but only those cards that have already been exposed.

Which was exactly what he had done. He'd sounded so open this morning, he'd almost scared himself.

The result: Gina was not only thoroughly off balance, but literally starstruck at the opportunity to assist on the president's surgery. She was *honored,* for God's sake.

Maybe he'd overestimated Gina.

He shook off the irritation and reviewed the last element of his plan: keeping Oliver out of this. Oliver usually took Wednesdays off and today was no exception. But just to be sure, he'd called him and told him that he must not, under any circumstances, mention their conversation of last night to Gina. Not until Duncan had a chance to talk to her today.

This was crucial because if Gina ever learned that Duncan was aware that she already knew about the president, his credibility would crumble, and with it, his plan.

Now he had only to keep them apart until dinner tonight.

After that, it wouldn't matter.

Duncan rubbed his tired, burning eyes. If only there were another way out of this. He'd walked the floor most of the night trying to come up with one. He couldn't.

A wave of nausea rippled across his stomach.

Lord, he wished this night were over.

The phone rang. It was Duncan.

"Are you ready?"

"Of course I'm ready," Gina said. "You said seven-thirty, didn't you? Don't tell me you haven't left yet."

"I'm crossing the Ellington as we speak. I'll be there momentarily."

The wonder of the cellular phone, Gina thought as she hung up.

She assumed from the call that Duncan didn't want her to keep him waiting. The Duke Ellington Bridge was less than a minute away and no doubt he expected her to be standing downstairs in the vestibule when he arrived. Oliver would probably be glad to run up and escort her down, but why make him go to the trouble?

She checked herself one last time in the mirror. The little black dress Mama always told her to keep in her wardrobe certainly had come in handy today. When she'd returned from Louisiana she'd invested in a slinky little Donna Karan number—nicely fitted, with a jewel neckline. She'd added a short string of pearls and pearl earrings. Simple but elegant. The perfect look for all those receptions on Capitol Hill she'd dreamed of attending. So far the dress hadn't left the closet. Tonight would be its coming out. At Galileo. Not too shabby a spot for its debut.

The forecast was wet so she threw her raincoat over her shoulders and headed downstairs. Duncan's black Mercedes pulled up a moment later. He got out and opened the front passenger door for her. As she slid in she glanced in the back. Empty.

"Where's Oliver?"

"A little under the weather. That stomach thing that's going around. He sends his regrets and says, Galileo or not, he can't even think of food tonight."

"Oh, that's terrible. Let's call him right after dinner and see how he feels."

"I think he was going to crawl into bed and pull the covers over his head until morning."

"No one to take care of him?" She couldn't resist seizing the moment to satisfy her curiosity about Oliver. *Have I no shame?* "No friends to look in on him?"

"Oliver is one of the most self-sufficient people I know. He has a maid come in once a week, otherwise he's alone and quite happy to be so. No wife, no kids, no mistress, and no, he's not a homosexual."

"I never thought—"

"If you did, you wouldn't be the first."

"Poor Oliver. I feel bad for him. Didn't you say this dinner was his idea?"

"I was going to call it off but he insisted that we not stand you up. So tonight I'll have to be myself and Oliver as well."

"Does that mean you're going to be eating for two?"

"Yes. With lots of garlic."

Gina noticed that Duncan's smile seemed a little forced. He looked tense, his posture stiff. He seemed generally uneasy. Because of her? Could it be he was uncomfortable taking a young female employee out to dinner?

But Duncan rarely gave a damn what anyone else thought of him.

The Mercedes cruised down Connecticut like a battleship on a lake. She'd never been in Duncan's car before. She felt invulnerable as she watched the shops and hotels along Connecticut roll past on the other side of the tinted glass. They cruised around Dupont Circle, then turned right onto M Street. A left on Twenty-first Street and they were there.

"Galileo," he said as they pulled into the garage next door. A simple maroon canopy jutted out from what looked like an office building. "Where the effete elite meet to eat."

Gina decided to go him one better. "Where the voracious and edacious mendacious can wax loquacious while looking gracious, sedacious, and perspicacious."

There. That was two or three better.

Duncan stared at her a moment, then said, "That, my dear, was a thing of beauty."

But he wasn't smiling. His expression was strange. Almost . . . pained.

What's eating him tonight? she wondered.

* * *

Her before-dinner manhattan was perfect, the mezze lune di granachio was superb, the service impeccable, and the wine Duncan ordered—a 1984 amarone—as smooth as silk. Galileo's spare decor was not what she'd expected. No heavy Mediterranean drapes and furniture. Everything was light and understated. But the mood at their table was anything but light. At times the conversation actually dragged— something she would have thought impossible in Duncan's presence. He didn't rant, didn't launch into a single tirade. Even when Larry King and Senator Rockefeller arrived and were seated three tables away, Duncan managed only a few disparaging remarks. At times she'd find him staring at her, his eyes intent on her face; other times he'd be a million miles away. He picked at his veal and barely sipped his wine, but kept refilling her glass. She wondered if he might be coming down with what Oliver had.

She wished she could get a grip on this jigsaw puzzle of a man. Every time she thought she had him figured, a new piece would pop up requiring her to rearrange everything and start over again.

She watched him stare into his half-full glass of wine for the longest time.

"Are you okay?"

He looked up. "Hmmm? Yes. Fine."

"You seem down."

He shrugged. "Just thinking about life, the twists and turns it takes you through. The cruel tricks it plays on you."

"Some of the tricks are funny," she said.

"Sometimes we back ourselves into corners," he said, as if she hadn't spoken, "and we despise the means necessary to extricate ourselves."

What was *wrong* with him tonight?

"Do you want dessert?" he said as the waiter was clearing the dinner plates.

"I don't think I could eat another thing. But I could go for some coffee."

"Leave the coffee to me," he said. "I don't care if this is one of the best restaurants inside the beltway, their coffee can't hold a candle to mine. We'll have *real* coffee back at the office."

She considered begging off, but realized she couldn't deny Duncan his coffee ritual. Maybe it would pull him out of his funk. Besides, it was only a few miles out of the way.

After Duncan paid the bill, Gina rose and felt a little wobbly. She realized that she'd consumed most of the amarone.

As she stood staring at the languid koi in the rock garden pool beyond Duncan's office window, Gina wondered if there was any place on earth she'd feel less comfortable than Duncan's office. This was where she'd broken into his drawer, where just yesterday she'd been sneaking through his bookshelf. And here he was toiling a dozen feet away making her what he called the best coffee in the world.

She felt like such a rat.

But at least the prospect of some good coffee seemed to have cheered him up. Maybe that had been his problem all along tonight—caffeine withdrawal.

"At last," he said, turning from his drip equipment with a steaming cup. "The perfect after-dinner coffee."

Gina took it from him and sniffed. "Licorice?"

"I know, I know. You must promise never to mention to anyone that I adulterated my own coffee. But I figured that after an evening of Italian food, I'd break down and add some sambuca."

Gina sipped and repressed a grimace. Bitter. She could taste the coffee, and the licorice tang of the sambuca, but there was something else there, something she couldn't identify.

"Mmmm," she said. "Unusual."

"A special black sambuca," he told her, sipping his own. "Gives it a unique flavor. Drink up."

Gina took another sip. Definitely not to her taste, but she couldn't very well dump it after he'd gone to the trouble of brewing it for her. Rather than prolong the agony, she drank it quickly.

"Another cup?" Duncan asked.

"No, thanks," she said. "Between the manhattan, the wine, and the sambuca, I think I'm already over my limit."

That was an understatement. She was definitely woozy now.

"Maybe I'd better take you home," Duncan said.

"Maybe you'd better," she said. "I'm sorry."

"Nothing to be sorry about. You're not driving, so what difference does it make?"

A fine drizzle had begun to fall. In the Mercedes, the swirl of lights from the streets and passing cars refracting through the myriad beads of water on the windows made her stomach begin a slow turn. She squinted and breathed deeply. She would die before she'd throw up in Duncan's car.

He double-parked on Kalorama, took her keys, and walked her up to her apartment. He let her in, then stepped back onto the landing.

"Are you going to be all right?"

"I'll be fine. Thanks for dinner. And I'm sorry about . . ."

"Don't give it another thought. I shouldn't have given you that doctored-up coffee."

Something strange in his voice as he said that, but his face was unreadable. Or was that because her vision was blurred?

"Good night, Duncan."

"Good night. Go right to bed."

"Don't worry about that."

As soon as he closed the door, Gina headed for the bathroom. But she didn't vomit. The nausea was still there, but now that the world around her was no longer in motion, it seemed to have eased.

She thought about taking a shower, then said to hell with it. What she needed was sleep.

She took off her raincoat and threw it on a chair. She sat on the bed and peeled off her panty hose, then began working on the buttons of her dress. Before she reached the last she flopped back and closed her eyes. Just for a second . . . no more than a minute . . . then she'd finish undressing . . .

33
THURSDAY MORNING

GINA AWOKE WITH GLUE IN HER MOUTH, SAND IN HER eyes, and heavy metal pounding in her ears. She rolled out of bed and stumbled across the floor with her hand stretched toward the snooze button. She always left her clock radio on a hard-core metal station. Never failed to get her up. No way she could stay in bed with that stuff playing.

Only now she wished she'd spun the dial to something else—*anything* else—before passing out last night. Noise equaled pain this morning, but speed metal went beyond pain into torture. The throbbing bass and drums were piercing straight through to the center of her brain. One of these groups should name itself Torquemada.

She banged her fist on SNOOZE, then turned around and headed for the bed again. She looked down and noticed she was still in her dress. Damn! It looked like hell. So did she, most likely.

Like a falling tree, she collapsed facedown on the mattress.

Why did she feel so rotten? She hadn't had *that* much to drink last night. The combination, maybe?

Whatever it was, she didn't like it. Her stomach was queasy, and her head . . . God, her *head*.

She was just dozing off when the howling guitar riffs filled the room again. This time she got up and turned off the radio. She staggered to the bathroom, removing the dress along the way. She looked at herself in the mirror.

Yuck. Awful. Simply awful.

She turned on the shower and stripped. As soon as the water was warm, she stepped in and let it run over her head and down her body.

God, that felt good.

She began lathering herself, starting with her face and working down. The water and the scrubbing action began to revive her. She was returning from the dead, reentering the world of the—

"Ow!"

She twisted and looked down at the lateral aspect of her right thigh. She'd felt a stab of pain while scrubbing the area. Tender there.

She ran a hand over the spot and noticed a small bruise. She must have collided with the corner of a table or her nightstand on her way to bed last night.

But wait . . . this bruise was more toward the rear of her thigh than the front. The only way she could do that was by walking backward.

She braced her foot on the edge of the tub and took a closer look. More than a bruise. The skin had been broken. A little semicircular cut in the center of the bruise. Almost like the one she'd seen on . . . Senator . . . Marsden . . .

Gina's knees buckled and she grabbed the towel rack to steady herself.

No, wait, stop, she told herself as the bathroom wobbled around her and she fought to regain her balance. This is crazy. This is impossible.

But when she looked again the tiny laceration was still

there. She probed it. She could feel the fine ridge of the edge. Had to be fresh. She pushed harder. A tiny droplet of blood appeared at its center. She probed deeper around the bruise, palpating the subcutaneous fat, looking for—

Her fingers froze. Was it her imagination or was something there? Something soft like fat but too smooth to be fat. Something oblong, cylindrical. Like an implant.

The bathroom wobbled again. And even with the hot water coursing over her, Gina suddenly felt cold. And sick. She stepped out of the shower and bent dripping over the toilet and retched. Nothing came up.

Her head throbbed even more painfully as she sank to her knees. When the room steadied, she took another, closer look at her thigh. She touched the spot again, but gingerly this time. If there really was something under it, and if that something was an implant, she didn't want to disturb it or . . . rupture it.

But how could it possibly be an implant? Duncan had dropped her off, and she'd locked the door . . .

Wait. Duncan had had the keys. He'd opened the door for her and let her in. And then he'd left. Had he handed her the keys? No. Had she seen him leave them? No. She hadn't seen much of anything. The door latched automatically, and she hadn't bothered with the chain lock. All she'd wanted was to hit the pillow.

Gina pulled herself to her feet, wrapped a towel around her, and shut off the water. She shivered.

The coffee in Duncan's office last night. She'd believed the bitterness was due to some strange black sambuca he'd said he was trying. But it could have been something else. Could have been chloral hydrate.

An old-fashioned Mickey Finn.

He'd had her keys. He could have kept them, driven around the block a few times, come back, let himself in, and stuck an implant in her thigh while she was out cold.

Still dripping, she stumbled out of the bathroom and went to the front door. The chain wasn't on, but she didn't remember fastening it. And her keys . . .

She looked around and spotted them on the coffee table.

But of course he'd leave them behind after he'd finished with her. What use were they to him then?

But why? Why would he do this to her just hours after asking her to assist on the president's surgery? It didn't make sense. Unless . . .

Unless he thought she knew too much. What if he'd found out about the FBI and the staged accident and the MRI done on Senator Marsden's leg? What if Oliver had told him that she'd guessed about the president? He'd want to make sure she was out of the way. *Before* Friday. He'd—

The phone rang. Her hand trembled as she lifted the receiver. When she recognized Duncan's voice, she almost screamed.

"How are you feeling?"

Controlling her terror, the hurt, Gina forced herself to reply calmly. "Fine. A little headache, maybe."

"Glad to hear it. You were sailing last night. For a while there I—"

"Duncan!" Unable to repress them any longer, the words burst from her. "Duncan, how could you do this to me!"

"Do what?"

"You know damn well what! You stuck an implant in me last night!"

"What? Hold on just a minute."

He put me on hold! she thought. I don't believe this!

She was just about to slam the receiver down when she heard a click and pressed it back to her ear.

"Now, Gina," he said. "I don't understand this. What do you think I've done?"

"Don't play dumb with me, Duncan. I know all about it.

You slipped me a Mickey last night and put an implant filled with TPD in my leg."

"You think I broke into your apartment and did surgery on you? And what's TDP?"

"You know damn well what it is! It causes psychotic symptoms."

"Gina, listen. Think. If I wanted to dose you with something, why bother with an implant? Why not just inject you with it?"

That took her back. Why hadn't he just shot her up and been done with it? And then suddenly she knew.

"Because you were out with me last night. We were seen together. You want a comfortable buffer zone between when you were with me and when I have a breakdown."

"I fear you're having one now, Gina."

"Just what you'd like people to think, isn't it? Well, listen, Duncan—"

"Have you heard enough, Barbara?"

And then Gina heard Barbara's voice, husky with pity. "Gina, you've got to calm down. We're you're friends here. We only want to help you. Please. You've got to believe that."

Gina nearly dropped the phone. "Oh my God! Barbara! He's conning you!"

The bastard! He'd put Barbara on the line while she was on hold. Now he had a witness that she was making wild accusations before her complete breakdown.

"Just stay where you are, Gina," Duncan said. "I'm calling an ambulance to come to your place. We'll get you to where you can receive the help you need."

"NO!"

She slammed the phone down and ran for her bedroom. "Damn me! How could I be so *stupid!*"

She pulled on her clothes. She had to get out of here. She could see it all now . . .

He had set all this up, and so cleverly. First the fake-out on

Marsden. She must have made it too obvious that she suspected something. So he'd pulled a reverse on her by puncturing the senator's thigh with an empty trocar. He'd led her into making a complete fool out of herself. But that was the least of it. Now her rationality and soundness of judgment were suspect.

But how in the world did *he* know how much *she* knew? Unless he had a security camera in the office or something.

My God! Was that possible? Then he would have seen her picking the lock on his desk drawer, seen her peeking behind that book two days ago. She groaned. No wonder he wanted her out of the way.

She pulled on a sweatshirt, jeans, and sneakers, grabbed her purse, and headed for the door. She stuttered to a halt at the threshold.

Where am I going?

Home? But that was the first place he'd look for her. And she did not want to get her folks involved.

Gerry? He had awful doubts about her reliability. But this time she had proof. Right here in her leg. An implant nestled there in the fatty layer.

She leapt back to the phone and dialed Gerry's home. He'd still be there now. At least she hoped so. As the phone began to ring, she worked to keep her voice under control. She wanted to sound sane while she explained something *in*sane. How to say it all in as few words as possible? And make it believable. She had to make Gerry *believe*.

"Gerry, it's Gina."

Gerry felt a small glow of pleasure at the sound of her voice; also a stab of guilt and, in a way, relief. He'd wanted to talk to her but had been hesitant about making the call. He'd been pretty rough on her last week. He was glad she'd taken the first step. On the other hand, he couldn't help being more than a little apprehensive about what she might have to say, especially since her voice sounded strained.

"Hello, Gina. I've been meaning to call."

"I don't have much time, so please listen to what I have to say. Last night Duncan put one of those implants in my leg while I was asleep. It's still in there."

He groaned. Not again.

"Oh, Gina. You've really got to get—"

Her voice rushed on. "Listen to me, Gerry. I beg you. This isn't fantasy. There are two hard facts you can check out. One is, obviously, the implant in my leg. I know it's there. I can feel it. We can get a scan to prove it, but what I really want is someone to operate and remove it. The second is the reason Duncan did this to me: He's doing cosmetic surgery on the president tomorrow morning."

Gerry closed his eyes. Poor Gina. Duncan Lathram strikes again: first Senator Marsden, now the president.

"I know what you're thinking, Gerry," she said, "and I don't blame you. But just check it out. You've got to know someone in the Secret Service."

"Yeah. I know a couple of guys."

Bob Decker immediately came to mind. He was on the White House detail. If anyone would know the president's hour-to-hour whereabouts, it would be Bob.

"Good. Call one of them. Call them all. Confirm what I said about the surgery. Once we've established that, maybe you'll be more willing to believe that I'm not completely crazy."

"I don't think you're crazy," he said, hoping he sounded convincing.

"You're a terrible liar. But please don't leave me hanging. Check this out. Then we can get on with removing this thing from my leg and put a stop to Duncan before he does something catastrophic. Please. I'm begging you."

The note of plaintive desperation in her voice cut through all his rational objections to getting sucked in again.

She's frightened, he thought. Deeply frightened.

"Okay. I'll call the White House." It was the least he could do. And what would it hurt? "But it may take me a while to get an answer. Those guys aren't just sitting around waiting for calls. If the president's out somewhere, they'll be with him."

"It's still early. Maybe you can catch somebody."

"I'll try."

"Thanks. That's almost more than I could hope for."

She sounded not only frightened, but lost. Not a friend in the world.

"Where will you be? Home?"

"God, no. He's coming for me. I've got to get moving. I'll call you back in a little while. When I get to a safe place."

Oh, Gina.

"Do you want to stay at my place?" he said. "Martha will be in school. You could stay here till I hear from the Secret Service guys."

He wanted her safe. What should he do with her? He had to get some help. Maybe get in touch with her parents, let them know she was having a breakdown.

"Maybe later. After we get this thing out of my leg, I'll need a place to rest up. Right now I'd better keep on the move."

Gerry chewed his lip. He didn't want to push her, not in her mental state.

"Okay. Do what you have to do. But stay in touch. Keep calling in."

"You can count on that." She paused, then: "And you *will* call, won't you? You're not just humoring me?"

"I'll call. I promise."

"Thanks, Gerry." Her voice softened. "Thanks for giving

me the benefit of the doubt here. After last Friday, that can't be too easy."

"It's okay."

After he hung up, Gerry sat and stared at his phone. He didn't want to sound like a jerk calling up Bob Decker and asking if the president was having plastic surgery tomorrow. He'd yet to live down the Marsden debacle. Guys were still coming up and offering to sell him the Brooklyn Bridge.

He looked up Decker's extension at the White House and made the call. Years ago he and Decker had become casual friends after an FBI racketeering case turned out to involve counterfeiting as well and the Secret Service was called in. Every so often they got together for a drink.

He was surprised how relieved he felt when he was told that Decker wasn't in. Gerry left his office number for the return call.

Decker's call came in shortly after Gerry got to his desk. After the standard how's-it-goin' preliminaries, Gerry took a deep breath and jumped in with both feet.

"Listen, Bob. The reason I called is that I heard a rumor that the president's getting a face-lift or something tomorrow. Any truth to that?"

Decker cleared his throat. "A face-lift? Tomorrow? That's a good one. Where'd you hear something like that?"

"The usual roundabout way. Somebody heard from somebody whose second cousin's mother overheard it at the Laundromat, and so on. I thought I'd check it out with you and lay it to rest. Or if it is true, I figure you'd want to know that the word is out and spreading."

"Thanks, Gerry. I appreciate that."

"Well?"

"Well what?"

"Is it true?"

"The president's heading for Camp David tomorrow morning for a long weekend, and I'm going with him." He chuckled. "Christ, he's going to be pissed when he hears about this. I *know* he doesn't want anyone to think he's having a face-lift. How do these crazy stories get started?"

"Crazy people, I guess," Gerry said glumly.

"Well, thanks for thinking of me. You can put the kibosh on this one, but let me know if you hear any others."

"Will do."

Just great, Gerry thought as he hung up. The president's not even going to be in town.

At least according to Bob Decker. But Decker could be covering for the president. If he'd been instructed to tell no one, he'd do just that, even if the FBI was asking.

Who to believe? A week ago there'd be no contest. But after the Marsden mess . . .

Coffee splashed over the rim of his cup as Gerry pounded his fist on the desk.

Damn it, what was he going to tell Gina?

And where was she now? Racing around the city in her car? Or hunched over a cup of coffee at the rear table of some diner?

He had to get her help. And fast.

Gina sipped a cup of cappuccino and watched the street. She'd found a Moroccan coffee shop on Columbia Road with a booth that offered a view of the eastern corner of Kalorama, half a block uphill from her apartment. If Duncan or an ambulance arrived, they'd turn that corner.

So far, no ambulance, no black Mercedes. But Duncan was tricky. He'd certainly proven that in the past week. Who said he had to come in his Mercedes?

Rather than run all over the city with no definite destination, she'd left her car parked in front of her building and walked up here to sit watch. Was Duncan really calling an ambulance, or coming himself? God, she wished she knew. The only thing she knew for certain right now was that she had to stay as far as possible from Duncan Lathram.

She glanced at her watch. Time to give Gerry a call. Another good thing about this little coffee shop was the location of the phone: right inside the front door. She could call and still keep watch on the corner.

Gerry sounded tired when he said hello.

"Did you call the Secret Service?"

"Yes."

"And?"

His sigh was full of angst. "They say he's not having surgery tomorrow or any other day. As a matter of fact, he's leaving in the morning for Camp David for a long weekend."

"To recover from the surgery!"

"According to the Secret Service, there's no surgery, Gina."

"But how . . . ?" Oh, God, why hadn't she thought of that? "Gerry, of course they're going to deny it. It's all hush-hush. He doesn't want anyone to know it's being done."

"I already thought of that. Look, Gina, you can't keep doing this. You're a doctor. Don't you see a pattern here? There's no surgery on the president, just like there was no implant in Senator Marsden's leg."

"Well, there's one in mine! I can show you!"

"Gina, you need help." She heard real pain in his voice now. "Let me get you in touch with someone we use at the Bureau. Maybe he can—"

Tears of frustration welled in Gina's eyes. "I'm not paranoid, Gerry. Duncan has done a beautiful job of manipulating events to make me look that way, but I'm not. And I've got the implant in my leg to prove it."

"Gina," was all he said.

"All right. That does it." She was angry now. "You don't believe me, so I'll show you. I'm coming down there right now and I'll prove to you that there's an implant in my leg. And you leave word at the desk that I'm coming."

"I don't think that's a good idea, Gina."

"Maybe not, but it seems to be my only option now. So get ready, Gerry. I'm on my way."

"Gina—"

She hung up on him and stood inside the door trembling with anger and fright. What if she couldn't get anyone to believe her? She realized how she must have sounded. She had to stay calm and sound rational. She wasn't going to convince anyone if she kept flying off the handle.

But I'm *scared*, dammit.

And worse than the fear was the question that had begun tapping with increasing insistence on the back door of her consciousness.

If everybody thinks you're crazy, maybe you shouldn't completely dismiss the possibility they might be right.

Feeling utterly miserable, she leaned against the door and pressed her right temple against the cool glass. The caffeine and a couple of Tylenol had helped, but her head still throbbed. And the doubts only intensified the pain.

Am I sane?

Could all this be simply the fabrication of a mind sent off course because her brain had begun synthesizing faulty neurochemicals or producing the right ones in the wrong proportions? How many paranoids had she seen in her psych rounds who were utterly convinced of the veracity of their absurd claims? They'd heard with their own ears, seen with their own eyes. If you can't trust your senses and your own ability to interpret their input, who or what can you trust?

Gina rubbed her thigh, gently. Maybe that mark was nothing more than a bruise. And maybe the hangover this morning was nothing more than too much amarone and sambuca. And maybe Duncan hadn't asked her to assist on the president's surgery tomorrow.

God, what was real?

She slammed her palm once against the pay phone.

No! She wasn't crazy!

That's what they all say . . .

Something black and gleaming caught her eye. Duncan's Mercedes—or one exactly like it—was passing on the street. It turned onto Kalorama.

Abruptly the doubts were gone, the fatigue and the headache forgotten. She ducked back to her booth, threw a couple of dollars on her table, and returned to the door. The car was out of sight now. She stepped outside. The cool, damp air refreshed her. A drop of water hit her forehead. She glanced up. The low, gray, moisture-laden clouds seemed to be sinking under their own weight.

She begged the rain to hold off a few more minutes.

She hurried across Columbia and trotted downhill to Kalorama. She stopped under the front canopy of an apartment house on the corner and craned her neck to peer down the street. She could see her building from here.

Duncan, looking very dapper in his blue blazer and charcoal slacks, was on his way up the front steps.

She watched him step inside the front door. Unless someone let him in—unlikely because everybody worked— he'd spend the next few minutes waiting for her to answer his rings. As soon as he left, she'd jump in her car and head straight downtown to the FBI Building.

She waited. What was he doing in there? Why didn't he come out?

Then she glanced up at the third floor and gasped when she saw a man standing in her bay window.

Duncan! He had a key. He must have had a copy made last night. Sure. He establishes with Barbara that Gina's acting irrationally, so he rushes down, supposedly to see what he can do. He finds her, zaps the implant in her leg, and then reports that the poor girl was sitting there drooling and babbling incoherently when he found her.

Well, guess what, Duncan, Gina thought as her jaw muscles bunched. Gina's not there. And she's not letting you within striking distance.

It began to rain. Only a gentle drizzle now, but cold.

Great. What else could go wrong? She was wearing only jeans, an old Tulane sweatshirt, and no hat. If her hair and her clothes got wet, how convincing would she be if she looked like a drowned rat when she got to Gerry?

Duncan gazed down at the street from the empty apartment, his right hand gripping the ultrasound transducer in his pocket.

What am I doing here?

He hated this. He'd regretted implanting Gina with the TPD almost as soon as he'd done it. But performing the act was like burning a bridge behind you: Once done, there was no going back. He had to follow through and dissolve it.

He seemed to be spiraling out of control. It was never supposed to turn out like this. But he couldn't stop himself. He had to keep going until he got to the president. After that he didn't care.

The situation was deteriorating, as well. Gina had been scheduled to show up at the surgicenter this morning; they were to go through their usual routines, then, somewhere around lunchtime, he'd intended to give her leg a burst of ultrasound and leave for the day. He'd have been miles away before she began to show the first effects. Maybe some visual hallucinations, maybe auditory, maybe both. She'd become disoriented, incoherent, might even start pulling at her hair and screaming. Or she might simply withdraw into a catatonic state, curled in a fetal position and drooling in a corner of the records room.

The images nauseated Duncan. He swallowed back the acid creeping up from his stomach.

Why couldn't you have stayed out of this, Gina?

Bad enough he'd have to pull the trigger on her. But she'd somehow discovered what he'd done to her last night. So now he had to hunt her down. That implant was a two-edged sword. Knowing it was there, she could use it against him—*if* she could get someone to believe her. He had to catch up with her before she had it removed.

Where was Gina now? Couldn't be too far. Her car was parked on the street below. Maybe she was out there, watching him, waiting to see his next move.

He nodded slowly. Yes . . . that would be just like her. Let him find her gone, then return to her place and ponder her next move calmly and in comfort while he ran around in circles.

All right. He'd do a circle. Circle the block and see if he could catch sight of her.

Lord, he hated this. The whole idea sickened him. He wanted to have it all over and done with.

And after that he'd have to find a way to live with himself.

Gina watched Duncan hurry down her front steps and get into his car.

Where to now, Duncan? A little worried, perhaps, now that your pigeon has flown?

She watched him drive away. She waited until he turned off Kalorama onto 18th, then she sprinted for her Sunbird. She jumped in and started her up.

The drizzle graduated to full-fledged rain as she headed down Kalorama, following Duncan's path. Only she wasn't following him. He was probably on his way back to Chevy Chase; she was headed downtown.

She peered up and down 18th, very possibly the most colorful street in the District. No sign of Duncan. She made a right and raced down to Florida where she hung another right. That brought her to a red light at Connecticut Avenue.

Gina searched Connecticut uphill and down, but no sign of Duncan. She allowed herself to relax. She had to forget about Duncan for the moment and figure out a way to convince Gerry that she—

Gina jumped in her seat as she glanced in her rearview mirror. Through the rain and the slightly fogged rear window she saw a black Mercedes ease to a stop two cars behind her. She stared at the Mercedes's windshield, but the rain and the sweeping wipers prevented her from seeing the driver.

She swallowed. Her mouth was dry. She couldn't make out the plates, but that could be Duncan back there . . . could easily be Duncan.

But why would he be following her? Had to be more than simply to see where she was going. What did he have in mind? Running her off the road? Hardly. She was sure the last thing he wanted was to be placed in her vicinity. So what was he up to? What did he hope to—

Ultrasound.

An icy hand clamped down hard on the back of her neck as she remembered the specialty electronics store he'd visited. Did Duncan have a device that could send an ultrasonic pulse into her car and dissolve the implant? She didn't see how. What she knew of the physics of sound said it wasn't possible, but a lot of events connected with Duncan didn't seem possible. Maybe he had a way . . .

Another glance in the rearview mirror.

How convenient to have her begin to hallucinate while driving.

The Honda directly behind her gave a polite toot. She

looked up and saw the light was green. She also saw the NO LEFT TURN sign. One way to find out if that Mercedes was following her . . .

Gina floored the Sunbird and swung left onto Connecticut. She saw the startled face of the driver of a yellow VW coming the other way as Gina dodged in front of him. The VW stuttered to a halt with an angry horn blast as Gina swerved past. She felt her back end slip a little on the wet pavement but the front-wheel drive pulled her out of it and seconds later she was speeding downtown.

Another glance in the rearview showed no Mercedes— didn't show much of anything through the rain and fogged-up glass. The traffic behind her was a mass of blurred gray shapes. He could be anywhere.

Dupont Circle was dead ahead. She could see traffic slowing, backing up. A perfect spot for Duncan to pull up alongside and . . .

Her hands became slippery on the wheel as she began to weave through the traffic. Had to get through the circle. She made a few reckless moves, earned a few more angry horn blasts, but moments later she was cruising toward the circle. She blew through an amber light and then slowed to get her bearings.

As she swung around the curve she checked the rearview again. She twisted left and right, peering out the side windows. No Mercedes.

She leaned back in her seat and took a deep breath. Maybe it hadn't been Duncan after all. Lots of big black Mercedes in this town. The diplomats loved them.

She swung off the circle onto Connecticut again.

Okay. She was on her way. With a pang she suddenly realized where she was. Only a few blocks from Galileo. Seemed like so much longer, but only a dozen hours had passed since she'd been dining with Duncan, feeling happy, carefree.

Now she was running for her life. Or if not her life, her sanity.

She put the painful memory aside and concentrated on the now. Not far to the FBI Building from here. Had to calm herself, gather her wits. Couldn't act as frazzled as she felt. Had to be convincing. Had to . . .

In her left sideview mirror . . . rising out of the Dupont Circle underpass like some dark demon from the netherworld . . . looming ever larger, ever closer . . . a black Mercedes. And this time she could make out the MD plates.

Duncan!

He'd bypassed the circle by going under it. Now he was nearly on top of her.

Her heart raced ahead of her engine as the Mercedes pulled in behind her and began riding her rear bumper. She sprang ahead, darting in and out of the traffic, squeezing her smaller car through openings where the Mercedes could not hope to follow, especially on this wet pavement. She pushed the lights, gunning through intersections whenever one threatened to turn red.

It was working. Slowly but steadily she increased the distance between them.

But she was coming to the end of Connecticut. The traffic lights of K Street loomed ahead. Green now. Traffic was flowing through. Good. Where to now? Normally she'd swing onto Seventeenth past Farragut Square and head down to Pennsylvania, but Duncan was only two cars back. And just ahead, the light was turning amber. Again, NO LEFT TURN hung over the intersection.

It hadn't worked before, but maybe this time . . .

But then the BMW in front of her began to brake for the light.

"Oh, no!" she cried aloud. "You *wimp!*"

Instead of slowing, Gina set her jaw, punched the gas, and wrenched the steering wheel to the right, swerving around the Beamer and into the middle of the intersection. Then she yanked it back into a hard left to head east on K.

She cried out as she hit a puddle and felt the tires begin to slip sideways on the wet pavement. She floored the brake pedal but the car didn't slow. It was completely out of her control. She saw the curb and the sidewalk careening toward her.

"Oh, God, no!"

Gina braced herself for the impact as the Sunbird slammed into the curb. The right rear wheel bounced over onto the sidewalk and the car tilted and threatened to tip over. Gina's head hit her side window as the car fell back onto four wheels. She shook her head to clear it. The window was okay and the car, thank you, God, had finally come to a halt without hitting anybody.

Gina wanted to cry, wanted to be sick, but she didn't have time for that. Except for a bruised scalp she was all right. Her seat belt had kept her from being tossed about the inside of the car. Horns were blaring all around her, frightened pedestrians were staring and either pointing fingers or shaking fists her way.

And her engine had stalled. She restarted it and tried to turn back into traffic, but her wheels were locked. She couldn't turn the steering wheel. She got out and ran around to the other side of the car and gasped when she saw the front wheel. The tire had been knocked off the rim and the wheel itself was bent, canted under the car. She didn't know if that meant a broken axle or what, but she did know her little Sunbird wasn't going anywhere without extensive repairs.

She was at the top of Farragut Square, a block of grass and shrubs and park benches with a statue of the admiral at its center. A wide-open area. She felt exposed. She looked around and saw Duncan's Mercedes pull into the curb on the other side of Seventeenth Street.

With a small cry she turned and bolted into Farragut

Square. Her sneakers slipped on the wet grass as she ran. She found a walk and slowed enough to look over her shoulder. No sign of Duncan's car back at the curb. Good. That meant he wasn't following her on foot. But where was he? She'd feel better if she knew. Because she didn't know the effective reach of whatever ultrasound device he might be carrying.

Ahead and to her right, across Eye Street, she spotted a Metro sign. Immediately her spirits lifted. The Orange Line would leave her a couple of blocks from the FBI Building. She picked up her pace and cut across the grass toward the entrance. She was less than thirty yards from it when a black Mercedes pulled up and Duncan stepped out.

"Oh, no."

He stood by the Metro stairs, looking around. When he spotted her, he started walking toward her with a determined stride. Gina made a sharp right turn and hurried on an angle back toward the corner of K and Seventeenth. A glance over her shoulder revealed that Duncan must have changed his mind about following her on foot. He was heading back to his car.

Gina broke into a run and turned down K. She had to get off the street. She was a sitting duck out here. She passed a CVS and ducked inside. As good a place as any to hide. Big and crowded with other people getting out of the rain.

She moved toward the side wall and wandered among the nail-care items hung on the Peg-Boards. She pretended to be shopping but all the while her eyes were fixed on the front doors. She migrated toward the rear, near the pharmacy counter where the first-aid items were stocked. She ducked behind a condom display as she saw Duncan walk past the front windows—under an umbrella no less. She hung there with her nose poking among the party-colored boxes. Anyone watching would have thought she had a hot time planned for tonight.

When she thought she'd waited long enough, she stepped

out into the aisle and made her way toward the front of the store. Halfway there she saw Duncan on the sidewalk outside again. Only this time he didn't pass. This time he pushed through the door and came inside.

Gina dropped to a crouch. In case anyone was watching, she quickly untied and retied her shoelace. She glanced around. No one was paying her any attention. She half straightened and looked around. Her heart tripped over a beat when she saw Duncan heading her way, his head rotating back and forth like a radar dish as he roamed the aisles.

She ducked down and cowered near the Halloween candy displays, frantically casting about for a plan. She could run—get up and sprint for the doors and the street, but that would give her away. Duncan wasn't sure where she was right now—couldn't even know she was in the store. If she ran, he'd have her. And worse, fleeing at full speed might bring the store detectives after her. If they grabbed her and held her, all Duncan would have to do was walk by, let loose an ultrasonic pulse, and she'd join Senator Vincent in the psych ward.

She glanced up and noticed one of the convex antishoplifter mirrors overhead. In it she saw a dapper-looking man in a blue blazer with a folded umbrella coming down the aisle on the other side of the counter. Duncan. No more than three feet away.

Head down, she ran in a crouch in the opposite direction and stopped at a break in the display counter. She checked the mirror again. Duncan was at the far end and turning into her aisle. She scurried around into the aisle he'd just left, moved along a dozen or so feet, and huddled, waiting, barely breathing as she pretended to compare the prices of the various widths and sizes of bandage gauze and adhesive tape.

She didn't dare peek at the mirror again. Not yet. If she'd

been able to see Duncan in it, he'd could just as easily use it to see her. Finally she reared up and cautiously peeked around a display of Ace bandages. It took her a moment before she spotted him. Near the front of the store now. Pushing through the door. Leaving.

But he wouldn't be leaving the area. He'd be wandering around, watching the Metro entrance, cruising the streets. He knew she was somewhere around here, and he wasn't going away. Trying to slip past him was too dangerous, especially in daylight. She needed a place to hide until it was dark.

Gina's fists knotted in frustration. She was so damn vulnerable with this . . . this *thing* in her leg. She wished she could be rid of it. Then she could walk up to Duncan and thumb her nose at him. If only . . .

She looked at the tape and bandages in her hands.

And came to a decision.

Where the hell is she?

Duncan opened the umbrella and looked up and down K Street as the rain increased its intensity, falling in sheets. The weather matched his mood.

This wasn't going well at all.

He tried to look on the bright side: If nothing else, the downpour was driving people indoors. That would make anyone still wandering about outside even more conspicuous. Gina would be easier to spot if she made a break for it. Obviously she'd ducked into one of the stores on this side of the street. She hadn't had time to cross to the other side or reach the far end of the block before he'd arrived.

She was here. This side. And she had to come out sometime.

But what if her fellow from the FBI was on his way to meet her here now?

That could be trouble. But not insurmountable. All he had to do was sidle up within range, press a button on the transducer, and TPD would begin seeping into her bloodstream.

But that scenario was risky. Far better to find her before the cavalry arrived . . . *if* it was even coming.

Duncan sighed. He'd have to search these stores one by one. Most of them were small. It wouldn't take long.

He noticed a Burger King down the block. A perfect place to hide. She could sit in the back and sip a cola and no one would make her move. He'd start there.

Gina clutched a white plastic bag filled with her purchases and checked the street and sidewalk outside as best she could from inside of the window. Duncan was nowhere to be seen. But that didn't mean he wasn't somewhere out there watching.

Her knees shook. Her hands nervously rolled and twisted the loops of the bag. She didn't want to go out there. She wanted to stay here where it was safe and dry, where Duncan had already searched and probably wouldn't search again. At least not for a while.

But she couldn't. Couldn't crawl into a hole and pull the earth over her. She'd made up her mind to *do* something about this, and dammit, that was it. She would not stay here and be a sitting duck any longer.

Across the street she could make out a bank, a copy shop, and a dingy marquee that read *The Tremont*. That little old hotel held one part of the key. The contents of the paper bag another. The rest was up to her.

She watched the traffic outside, waiting for a break . . .

Finally it came. Setting her teeth, she leaned against the door and burst from CVS into the downpour at a dead run, straight across the street and into the lobby of the Tremont.

Inside the revolving door she stopped and looked back on K Street. No sign of a blue-blazered man with an umbrella dashing across to intercept her. But that didn't mean he wouldn't be along soon.

As she hurried to the reservation desk she scanned the faded glory of the lobby. The brass needed polishing, the mirrors were smudged, and the carpet was showing its age. But there was still dignity here in the carved wood and dark green wallpaper. An old, independent dowager refusing to yield to the age of international hotel chains.

"I'd like a single please," she told the beige-suited young black woman behind the counter. "Just for the night."

The woman said, "Of course," and placed a card on the counter. "Please fill this out."

Gina paused with the pen poised over the NAME line. She didn't want to put her own name, but how much cash did she have? Thirty bucks? Maybe forty? Nowhere near enough to cover a room in the heart of D.C. And if she was going to use cash instead of a credit card, the hotel would be looking for at least one night in advance.

Reluctantly, she wrote in "Gina Panzella" and handed over her Visa with the registration card.

"Any luggage?"

"I'm having that sent over later."

She was tempted to make up a place from which her bags would be arriving and a story as to why she didn't have them with her, but decided to clam up. This woman didn't care and too much talk might make her sound as if she was hiding something. She was inexperienced at the art but guessed that lies, like medical reports and research papers, worked best when one observed the KISS rule: Keep It Simple, Stupid.

Five minutes later she was in a narrow room on the top floor with one double bed and an alley view.

Perfect.

She put on the chain lock, dropped into the single chair by the writing table, and closed her eyes. So good to feel safe. Temporarily safe. At least she didn't have to worry about running into Duncan here.

Gina looked at the phone and thought about calling Gerry, to tell him that she was going to be delayed. Maybe she should tell him why: because of his insistence on objective proof.

Well, she was going to give him his damn objective proof.

Forget calling Gerry. He'd only try to stop her.

She closed her eyes again. Why couldn't she simply stay here? Hibernate for a week or a month. Order room service and watch the movies on cable all day. Anything but go outside again and dodge Duncan so she could prove to Gerry that she wasn't nuts.

Her life seemed to be a lose-lose proposition right now. Why not just—

She bounded from the chair. No. She had to do this. And *now*. Had to go on autopilot. Couldn't think about what she was asking of herself. Had to fight the nausea and the revulsion and fear. Had to keep up the momentum. If she stopped or even slowed she might not be able to go through with this.

And the longer she waited, the greater the chance of Duncan tracking her here.

She grabbed the ice bucket and scurried down the hall to the service nook where she quickly filled it with cubes. Once back in her room, she replaced the chain lock, drew the curtains, and turned on the TV. She punched the remote until she found a noisy game show, then turned up the volume. Not too loud, but enough to mask any incidental noise. She checked the thermostat and pushed it up to 75.

She turned on the light in the bathroom. Bright, clean, white tile and tub, a marble vanity. She made sure the drain was open, then started the water running in the tub. As she waited for the temperature to reach a comfortable warm, she emptied the contents of the bag from CVS on the vanity counter. She set aside the smaller separate bag within, then opened the bottle of Tylenol Extra Strength and washed down four of them with a glass of water. Next she opened the bottle of Coricidin tablets. She would have preferred a test tube, but this glass cylinder full of cold tablets would have to do. She emptied the pills into the toilet. Then she began arranging the rest of her purchases.

The bacitracin ointment, gauze pads, Ace bandage, adhesive tape, and the hydrogen peroxide went to the rear of the counter; in front of them she placed the empty Coricidin bottle and the small traveler's sewing kit; along the edge she lined up the bag of cotton balls, the tweezers, the bottle of isopropyl alcohol, the Cricket lighter, and the package of single-edge razor blades.

The last item was an ice pack. She filled that with ice cubes and set it on the edge of the tub. She unbuttoned her jeans, slipped them off, and hung them on the towel rack. Gooseflesh ran up her thighs to the edges of her panties.

She soaked one of the cotton balls with the alcohol and then began rubbing it on her thigh, firmly but not too vigorously, in the area of the bruise. Didn't want to break anything under the skin. She then poured alcohol over the contact surface of the ice pack and pressed it over the bruise. This was welcomed by another rush of gooseflesh.

She glanced at the ceiling. No heat lamp. Too bad. Would have been nice.

Wedging the ice pack between her thigh and the vanity, she picked up the black and yellow box of razor blades. "SMITH single edge—Made in U.S.A." said the top. On the side: "Fits all single edge scrapers. For industrial use."

She had to smile at that. Industrial use? Not today.

She slipped one of the blades from the box, gripped it with the tweezers, then applied the Cricket flame to the cutting edge until it glowed red. As she let that cool on the edge of the marble vanity top, she pulled off her sweatshirt and tossed it toward her jeans.

Now she really could have used a heat lamp.

Still holding the ice pack to her thigh, she seated herself on the edge of the tub with her feet in the lukewarm water running from the spout. Another ten minutes and the iced-down area of her thigh was good and numb. She swabbed the area again with alcohol, then poured some over her hands. She picked up the razor blade.

And began to shake.

I can't do this.

But another part of her said she could. Told her she had to. Had to do it *now*, before the numbing effect of the ice wore off.

But the first part of her brain screamed, *Wait!*

What if this whole situation was another elaborate scam by Duncan? He'd already undermined her credibility—and made Gerry look like a fool. What if he'd pulled the same on her? A double reverse? Slip her a Mickey, steal her key, sneak into her apartment, and jab an empty trocar into her leg while she was unconscious? Who'd expect him to pull the same stunt twice?

But he might be counting on that sort of thinking, counting on her to go running to Gerry, crying about bad old Duncan sticking a drug-filled implant in her leg. And if and when she finally convinced Gerry to check out her leg, they'd come up with another negative MRI.

And anything she said after that would be dismissed as the ravings of a lunatic.

So she couldn't go to Gerry empty-handed—or, in this case, empty-legged. Either way, she had to *know*.

If only she had a syringe and some anesthetic.

Lidocaine! Lidocaine! My kingdom for some lidocaine!

But there'd be no lidocaine. Only ice.

Gina grabbed a washcloth from the counter and wadded it into her mouth. Then she used her left hand to stretch the skin over the bruise while she tightened her grip on the razor blade in her right.

Not too deep, now, she told herself. Don't want to slice the implant.

She took a deep breath and held it. With one quick move, she drove the corner of the blade's cutting edge into the skin half an inch distal to the bruise, then yanked it toward her.

She doubled over and screamed into the washcloth. Shuddering with the pain, she clung to the safety bar with her free hand and pressed her face against her knees as her eyes filled with tears and a cold sweat erupted from every pore.

And then, after a small eternity, the pain passed its crescendo. Her bunched muscles relaxed—slightly. She straightened, spit out the washcloth, and gasped for air. When she'd caught her breath, she leaned over and took a look.

Blood poured from the two-inch gash in her thigh. Thick crimson drops, startlingly red against the white ceramic finish, splashed along the inside of the tub and oozed down to the water swirling toward the drain. She felt faint and swayed back. For an instant she thought she was going to topple backward, but she hung on until the room stopped wobbling around her.

Gina allowed herself a tight, wry smile. She thought she was used to seeing blood. Other people's blood. Not quite the same as seeing her own.

She touched the wound edge and jerked her hand back. Exquisitely tender. Those severed nerve ends were screaming. This was when she really could have used some anesthetic.

Replacing the washcloth between her teeth, she clamped

down on it and groaned as she separated the wound edges. The subcutaneous fat was blood-red instead of its natural yellow. Gingerly she probed the fat with her pinky. A strange, curious, slightly sickening sensation, this groping among her own fat cells. Painful, but it wasn't the pain that was making her queasy. She'd never touched human fat with her bare hands before. Like playing with greasy tapioca.

The pain increased as she pressed deeper, searching for an opening, a depression, a channel, any clue that would tell her what course the trocar had followed.

And then her fingertip slipped a little deeper into one area of the fat. She stiffened. Could that be it? She probed further, but gently, feeling the fat give way easily before her. Yes. Something had been this way before. And recently.

And then her fingertip came to rest against something soft but firmer and smoother than fat.

Gina didn't know whether to be relieved or terrified. At least she hadn't imagined all this. There *was* an implant in her leg and only one man could have put it there.

And it had to come out. Now. And she had to remove it without breaking it. If she ruptured it, or even caused a tiny leak, she'd have done Duncan's job for him.

Biting down harder on the washcloth, Gina dug her finger deeper into the fat. Propelled by pain, air hissed in and out of her nostrils as she worked to get around the implant. Had to get behind it. Gently . . .

. . . gently . . .

Gerry slammed the phone down in the middle of Gina's instructions to leave a message after the beep. He'd already left two on her machine.

Where is she?

He glanced at his watch again. What for, he didn't know.

Only half a minute had passed since the last time he'd looked.

He stretched his neck to relieve the growing lump of tension between his shoulder blades. She should have been here by now. Visions of Gina wandering around the District, dazed and confused, replayed in his mind. Or worse yet, huddled behind a Dumpster in some alley, hiding from imaginary enemies.

Damn it. He couldn't concentrate on anything. All he could think about was Gina. The way she'd sounded . . . like her world was coming to an end.

Only one thing to do. Go out and look for her.

He picked up his car keys and called the switchboard. He left instructions that if a Gina Panzella or a Dr. Panzella called, or anyone called about her, or if she showed up in person, to put her through to his car phone.

On the chance that she might be hiding in her apartment, afraid to pick up the phone, refusing to answer the door, he grabbed the Electropick on his way out. Just in case.

He got his car out of the Bureau's underground lot and drove up Pennsylvania toward the White House, trying to backtrack along the most logical route for her to follow from Adams Morgan. She'd have to come down Connecticut, but after that it was anybody's guess.

He worked his way up to K Street where he saw a couple of cops standing outside their unit at the top of Farragut Square watching a sanit man sweep up some broken glass. He flashed his ID and asked what had happened. The older of the pair, heavyset with a mustache, leaned in the window. His breath reeked of old coffee.

"A one-car MVA. Nobody hurt. Driver hopped out and took off. You can bet what that means."

Gerry nodded. "Hot."

"You got it."

Just so no stone was left unturned, Gerry said, "You remember what make it was?"

The cop shrugged. "Nah. It was already towed when we got here. They're running the plates, though. Somebody you looking for?"

"Not likely. Just thought I'd ask."

As he drove away, he made a mental note of the location. If he couldn't find Gina, he'd check with the locals later on the registration of that car.

He turned back and headed up Connecticut. Maybe the best place to start was Gina's apartment.

Gina leaned, gasping, trembling, against the side wall of the tub alcove. When the pain receded from excruciating to merely brutal, she opened her hand and looked at the bloody little lump lying in her palm.

Gotcha.

She was safe. Even if Duncan bathed the entire hotel with ultrasound, he couldn't harm her. But she wasn't out of the woods yet. She had a deep, wide gash in her leg that had to be closed.

But first: Save the evidence.

She reached over to the counter and grabbed the Coricidin bottle. Carefully she scraped the sticky implant off her palm with the lip of the bottle. She'd already learned the hard way how much more fragile these things became once they'd been implanted. The implant slid down the inside of the bottle, slowly, like some sort of scarlet slug, and came to rest on the bottom. She capped the bottle and returned her attention to the incision in her leg.

Bleeding had slowed considerably. The blood oozing around the growing clot was thick, almost syrupy. She reached for the sewing kit and began threading a needle. The adrenaline tremor from the pain and stress caused her to miss on the first few tries. She was beginning to fear that she'd never get it threaded, but finally the tip slipped through the eye.

She considered sterilizing the needle with the Cricket but discarded the idea. She couldn't sterilize the thread that way, and the wound was already grossly contaminated. She was covered for tetanus, but she had to get herself some antibiotic—a broad-spectrum cephalosporin preferably—to fend off the inevitable infection that would follow this egregiously unsterile little surgical procedure.

By way of compromise, she doused the needle and soaked the thread with hydrogen peroxide. She laid that aside and replaced the washcloth in her mouth. Then she expressed the clot from the wound and poured the peroxide directly into it. She groaned into the cloth as pink foam erupted from the opening. She writhed from the sharp, stinging agony of the nest of enraged hornets trapped inside her thigh.

When that passed, she wiped the sweat and tears from her eyes, pressed the wound edges together, and began suturing. She started at the distal end, figuring it would be easier to work her way up.

Gina winced as she forced the needle through her skin. Painful, but nothing compared to what she'd already put herself through. The needle was sharp enough, but it was designed for fabric, not the toughness of human skin. And it was straight, which made the job all the more difficult.

Forget the lidocaine, she thought. I'll settle for a hemostat and a curved needle now.

A few subcutaneous sutures and a vertical mattress repair would have been ideal, but out of the question without gut and a curved needle. She had to settle for a simple, single loop.

She tied the first suture carefully, afraid to pull too hard and break the thread. She'd bought the heaviest she could find, but still this wasn't silk or nylon, this was plain old thread. If this repair was going to hold, she'd have to place the sutures close together, no more than an eighth of an inch apart.

She finished the first knot and cut the free ends with the little scissors from the kit. There. One done. Only fourteen or fifteen more to go.

Half an hour later, she was done. She foamed the blood off her skin with peroxide and examined her handiwork. Sixteen puckered sutures in a neat row. She blotted it dry, smeared some bacitracin ointment over it, then covered it with gauze. She held that in place with a few strips of adhesive tape, then wound the six-inch Ace bandage around her thigh to make a pressure dressing. Then she swung her legs out of the tub and stood up.

And almost fell as black spots exploded in her vision and a diesel-engine roar filled her head. She went down on one knee and clung to the vanity until the room stopped swaying and spinning.

She pressed her forehead against the cool marble and gathered her strength.

Weak. She'd figured she'd be weak afterward, but not this bad. She reached for the other little bag she'd picked up in CVS and pulled out a package of Snickers bars. Good old Pasta had always suffered chocolate attacks in times of stress and hadn't been able to resist all that Halloween candy. Gina was glad she'd given in to her. She'd need some extra calories for healing, some glucose for energy. Another thing she knew she needed was fluids. After wolfing down three of the Snickers, she filled the glass by the sink with cold water and gulped it down. She washed down four more Tylenols with a second glassful.

She felt a little better, but no way ready for the road. She pushed herself to her feet and, keeping a hand on the wall for support, made her way to the bed. She turned off the TV as she passed. She yanked down the covers and gingerly, gently, eased herself between the cool sheets. She shivered. Had to get some rest. She was safe now. Just a nap for an hour or so, then she'd call Gerry. She had the implant. She could show him hard evidence now. He'd have to believe. Everyone would believe.

After she had some sleep . . .

34
THURSDAY AFTERNOON

GERRY WAS BEGINNING TO FEEL A LITTLE FRANTIC.

He couldn't help it. He'd been to Gina's apartment earlier. He hadn't been able to find her car on the street. He got no response to his repeated knocks on the door, so he'd used the Electropick to let himself in and found the place deserted. No sign of a struggle, no note left, no indication that Gina hadn't made a routine departure this morning fully expecting to return at her usual time tonight.

He'd even called Lathram's surgicenter. The receptionist had said Gina wasn't there and wasn't expected in today. He thought he'd heard something in her voice, as if she wanted to say more, but that could have been wishful thinking.

He'd checked all eleven of the District's emergency rooms and even a few in northern Virginia and southern Maryland. No Gina Panzella or Jane Doe fitting her description had come through. Same with all the local police departments. No one named Panzella or anyone like her on the arrest records.

And then he'd remembered the accident over by Farragut

Square. He'd placed a call to the D.C. Police and was hanging around his desk waiting for a call-back now. He didn't have much hope of help from them, but he wasn't ignoring any possibility.

The phone rang.

"Agent Canney?" said a nasal voice. "We have the ID on the vehicle in that one-car MVA you inquired about. Belongs to a Regina Panzella of Kalorama Road here in the District."

"Damn!" Gerry said. He should have checked this out hours ago. "And the report says she left the scene of the accident?"

" 'Driver abandoned vehicle,' according to the report."

"Nothing else?"

"Witnesses said she was female, dark hair, and was the sole occupant."

That fit Gina.

"Okay. Thanks a lot."

"Any time."

So where was she? She'd cracked up her car and run away. Where to? It had rained most of the morning. How far could she go on foot in the rain?

Gerry reached for his coat. Better go and inspect the scene. But another thought occurred to him as he was leaving. He called down to the data center and told them to research the credit sources for Regina Panzella. Find out what credit cards she carried and see if she made any charges today—and where.

Who knew? Maybe she rented a car. Or bought a motorcycle. Who could tell what she was going to do next?

Gerry left for Farragut Square. Without knowing Gina's credit card number or even her card company, it would take a while. The information would be waiting when he got back.

He hoped he wouldn't need it.

*   *   *

Duncan was exhausted, frustrated, angry, and not a little afraid.

But at least the rain had stopped.

That was about the only good thing Duncan could say about the afternoon. He stood on Seventeenth Street, on the edge of Farragut Square, and eyed the pedestrians. So many more now that it was getting late. Workers, released from their offices, were beginning to crowd the sidewalks. He lifted his gaze to the square's eponymous statue. Appropriately enough, a seagull was squatting on its hat.

About time to give it up. He'd patrolled the area for hours on foot and in his car, ranging as far north as Scott Circle and as far south as the White House itself, and had found not a single trace of Gina.

It was fear that kept him from packing up and heading for home. Or for the hills.

What if Gina had managed to convince her FBI boyfriend that she carried an implant in her leg? And what if he'd been able to arrange its removal? The tables might have been turned on him this afternoon while he was wandering around. His role might already have changed from hunter to hunted.

He'd better find out.

Duncan glanced at his watch. Barbara still would be in the office. He pulled out his cellular phone and called in.

"Did you find her?" were the first words out of Barbara's mouth.

"No luck yet," he said. "Just checking in. No word from Gina, I take it."

"Nothing," Barbara said. "Someone called for her, but—"

"Who?"

"That guy she's been seeing. Gerry Canney."

Duncan stiffened. The FBI man? That didn't bode well.

"When did he call?"

"Late this morning. He was looking for her."

"You remembered what I told you, didn't you?"

"Yes. I just said she wasn't here and wasn't expected in."

"Excellent. We need to protect Gina until we can find out what's wrong with her and get her some help."

"I know. It's just that he sounded worried."

"We're all worried, Barbara." *Especially me.* "Any calls for me?"

"A couple of people looking for appointments. Mr. Covington called to complain about your canceling all surgery this morning. He said his wife was hysterical."

"She's had that nose for almost fifty years; she'll survive another week with it. No others? No visitors?"

"No. It's been pretty quiet."

That was a relief. No calls or visits from any law-enforcement agencies looking for Dr. Lathram. A good indication that Gina had yet to convince anyone.

Maybe there was still time.

Time for what? He couldn't see much use in patrolling this area any longer. He had to face it: Gina was gone. She'd hopped a cab, or sneaked into the Metro, or simply walked away. She could be in Virginia or Maryland by now. Or down at the FBI Building. If she was still around here he would have seen her.

He reached into his pocket for the car keys and found the pager-transducer. Conflicting emotions swirled within him. If Gina walked past right now he'd use it on her, without hesitation, not out of malice but out of the most basic drive of all—self-preservation. And yet . . . some small part of him was almost glad that she had eluded him.

He found his keys. Time to go. But where? Home to sit and wait for the ax to fall? Even if no one came to put the cuffs on him, his plans for the president tomorrow would have to be changed. He would simply do the surgery and forget about the implant. He would destroy the TPD, and then it would be Gina's word against his.

Except for that implant in her leg.

Damn, damn, *damn!* His options were becoming narrower with each passing hour.

As Duncan turned to head for his car, he saw a monotone sedan pass and pull into the curb a few dozen feet from him, stopping directly under a no-parking sign. A warning alarm rang in his brain, so he turned and crossed Seventeenth, keeping his face averted until he reached the other side. As he mingled with the thickening rush-hour crowd there, he glanced over his shoulder and saw a young, fair-haired man standing on the sidewalk, surveying the square. He seemed to be looking for someone.

Terror slammed Duncan from behind but he resisted the urge to run. He had seen him before—with Gina at the Guidelines committee hearing. Canney the FBI agent.

Is he looking for me?

Keep calm, Duncan told himself. How could he be? He drove right past me. And besides, why, of all the possible places in the District, would he look for me here?

He had to be looking for someone else.

For Gina.

Excitement surged through Duncan as he stepped back into a doorway and continued to watch Agent Canney.

I'm still safe, he thought. If the FBI doesn't know Gina's whereabouts, then no one does—at least no one who matters.

He watched Canney walk across the grass and among the shrubs and benches of Farragut Square, watched him search the entire perimeter, pausing where Gina's car had hit the curb. His movements were quick, efficient, but Duncan detected an underlying anxiety and uncertainty.

Duncan could have told him: You're wasting your time.

He watched Canney canvas the area, then get into his car and leave. And with the agent's departure Duncan suddenly found himself refreshed, invigorated. He wasn't going home. Not just yet.

He'd hang around a little longer. At least until dark.

Gina awoke in pain and confusion. She'd rolled over onto her right side and felt as if something were taking a bite out of her thigh.

She was hot, wet, bathed in sweat. Her bra and panties were glued to her skin. She threw off the covers. Dark . . . where—?

A few blinks and she recognized the hotel room. It all came back to her. Sitting on the tub, cutting into herself . . .

She sat up and experienced only an instant of light-headedness. No question, the rest had done her good, but how long had she been out? She turned the clock radio toward her. 5:05.

My God, I slept away the whole afternoon!

She eased herself to her feet and wobbled only slightly on her way to the bathroom. She had to see it, had to make sure it was still there.

It was. The Coricidin bottle sat where she had left it on the marble counter. She ran the sink water and drank three glasses without taking her eyes off the implant resting within, turning brown now as its blood-streaked surface dried.

She brought it with her when she returned to the bed. Still weak, but feeling lots better, she carefully lowered herself to sit on the edge. Time to call Gerry. Time to meet with him and show him what Duncan had placed inside her.

She got an outside line and punched in his office number. The FBI operator said he wasn't in at the moment. Would she like to leave a message?

"When will he be back?"

"Agent Canney did not say. May I ask who's calling, please?"

"That's okay," Gina said. "I'll call back."

Maybe he got tired of waiting for her and went home. She called his house but got only his answering machine.

Maybe he was in transit. She'd have to wait till he picked up Martha and got home . . . if home was where he was headed. She wondered if he was worried about her, or even thinking about her. It would be comforting to know that someone besides Duncan was wondering where she was.

She unwrapped the Ace bandage from her leg to expose the gauze beneath. She noticed that blood was beginning to seep through the dressing. Gingerly, she peeled it away. The antibiotic ointment kept the gauze from sticking. The incision looked good; the thread seemed to be holding. But as she stared at the wound, and then at the little bottle containing the bloody implant, she was filled with an overwhelming despair.

Gerry's not going to believe me.

The realization made her sick. What would he think when he saw that bloody thing in the bottle? No one had seen her cut it out. No witness to the procedure. Who was to say she hadn't cut herself and smeared the implant with blood to convince others of her delusions? Self-mutilation was common in certain forms of psychosis. Or maybe she'd be diagnosed as some sort of variant of Munchausen syndrome.

She'd done something extreme, something radical, something that would appear bizarre and, well, deranged to anyone who didn't fully understand the threat the implant posed to her.

In short, showing Gerry that bloody implant and telling him she'd cut it out of her own leg might only confirm his worst fears about her sanity. Her paranoid delusions had now escalated to self-mutilation.

Gina pressed her hands to her face. Couched in a sob, her voice rang through the tiny room.

"What am I going to do?"

She had to find someone who'd believe her, someone who wouldn't think she'd watched too many episodes of *Twilight Zone*. . . .

Oliver.

Of course. Oliver would believe her. He was the only other person in the world who knew about both TPD and the implants. He'd understand why she'd had to cut herself open to remove the TPD.

But how would he react when she told him Duncan was behind it all? Oliver was so devoted to his older brother. Damn near worshiped him. Would he be able to accept the idea that Duncan was hurting people?

Another thought, a shattering one: What if Oliver was involved?

No. She couldn't buy that. Oliver was the straightest of straight arrows. He'd be crushed at the thought of his implants being used to harm instead of heal. And if he were involved in any way, he'd *never* have given her Dr. VanDuyne's name.

That was it. She'd present her case to Oliver, and once he was convinced, the two of them would go to Gerry or the Secret Service, or anyone who could stop Duncan.

She stood up quickly, then sat down again, suddenly weak. Maybe she should eat something first. No breakfast, no lunch . . . just a few Snickers bars. She was asking for trouble if she didn't pack in a few calories pretty soon.

She pulled out the room service menu and ordered a hamburger, fries, and a Coke—protein, complex carbs, and caffeine. That ought to keep her going for a while.

She stood up again, a little more deliberately this time, and made her way back to the bathroom. She redressed the incision with clean gauze and secured it again with the Ace wrap. Then she pulled on her sweatshirt and carefully slipped back into her jeans. She was looking pretty normal by the time room service knocked.

She glanced out the window as the waiter positioned the rolling cart and uncovered the food. The aroma set her mouth to watering. She hadn't realized how hungry she was. Dusk outside. She'd gobble down her food and wait until it was fully dark, then she'd hustle out to the curb, jump into the first waiting cab, and make a beeline for Oliver's house. Oliver lived in the northwest extreme of the District. She'd been there once for a dinner party. A nice little ranch in a nice neighborhood, but not even close to the same class as Duncan's.

Probably didn't even have to wait until dark. Duncan was surely long gone by now.

Tracking down Gina's credit trail took a little longer than Gerry had expected. He'd had to call Mrs. Snedecker and ask her if she'd keep Martha a few hours longer and feed her dinner. He'd spoken to Martha to tell her that he'd be late and had been warmed by her cheery "Okay." Good thing she liked Mrs. S.

The credit trace came through a few minutes later showing a charge to her Visa from the Tremont Hotel on K Street.

K Street! Christ, he'd just been there! What was she doing in the Tremont? Hiding?

More baffled than ever, he got the number from information and asked the desk to connect him to Ms. Panzella. He let the phone ring a dozen times, almost hung up, then listened to at least half a dozen more rings.

Where the hell was she? If she'd already checked out, the desk wouldn't have connected him. Was she afraid to answer the phone?

Gerry grabbed his coat and headed out.

* * *

As night shrouded the District in umbral gloom and the streetlights flared to life, setting the misty air aglow, Duncan decided to call it quits. Obviously she was nowhere about, most likely gone for hours. Futile to dally here any longer.

But what next? Where next? He couldn't quit now. Too much hung in the balance. As he headed for his car, he made a last-ditch effort by experimenting with a little mental exercise.

If I were Gina, and I were still in the vicinity, where could I possibly be? Where could I have hidden this long?

He rolled the question through his mind as he walked along the north end of the square. He was turning down K Street when the marquee of the Tremont Hotel caught his eye.

He paused, shook his head, took a few more steps, then stopped at the curb and stared. He'd noticed it before, but . . .

Could she have rented a hotel room? Not likely. He could see the possibility of her running in there, renting a room, and using it as a safe place to meet with her FBI man. But obviously she hadn't done that, or else Agent Canney wouldn't have been wandering around Farragut Square like a lost soul a little while ago. And Duncan couldn't see Gina holing up there by herself all afternoon watching television.

But still . . . it was one place he hadn't checked out. It wouldn't take him long. What were a few more minutes added to all the time he'd already wasted?

He entered the lobby and strolled toward the registration desk. The young man behind the counter looked at him expectantly. Duncan debated how he should pose his questions about her, then realized that no decent hotel gave out guest room numbers.

He smiled at the desk man whose badge said *Roy*. "House phones?"

Roy pointed to the far corner of the lobby. "Right over there, by the big fern, just past the elevators."

Duncan nodded his thanks. He found the row of phones and dialed "O" on the nearest.

When the operator answered, he said, "Panzella room please," and was startled when she thanked him and connected him.

Stunned, he listened to the phone ring, wondering what he was going to say. He realized he could say nothing. He couldn't let her know he'd found her.

He hung up and leaned against the wall.

She's here.

She'd probably been here all day. But what had she been doing all this time? And why had she registered under her own name? Such a dumb thing to do, and Gina was anything but dumb.

It didn't matter. None of it mattered except the fact that he'd found her. All he needed now was her room number. He glanced over at the registration desk. Roy was alone there. Would a hundred-dollar bill—?

And then the revolving doors began to move and Special Agent Canney strode into the lobby. Startled, Duncan froze, his heart pounding.

No! Not when I'm so close!

He ducked behind the large fern and peered through the branches. Canney was showing his ID to the desk man and talking fast. He looked agitated. Apparently Gina had finally got in touch with him. But if so, why was he showing his ID?

What did it matter? Duncan realized that a solution had just presented itself. The elevators were only a few feet away. Canney would go up to Gina's room and bring her down, or perhaps call her to come down and meet him. Either way, she'd have to pass close to Duncan's position.

He removed the transducer from his pocket. She'd be in range. She'd feel a twinge in her thigh, but that would be it.

She'd probably get all the way to the FBI Building before the TPD kicked in.

All he had to do was wait. He'd been waiting all day. He could wait a little longer.

"I want her room number, and I want the key, and I want them *now!*" Gerry said.

The desk man had called out the manager—Joel Heinrich, according to his name tag. A fussy little man with a thin mustache.

"I'm sure you need a warrant for that kind of search. I'm certainly not authorized to barge into a guest's room—"

"Dr. Panzella has not been well lately," Gerry said, improvising. "She's not answering her phone. She may be unconscious."

That got him.

"Sick?" The fussy manager evaporated. "You mean with something contagious?"

Gerry lowered his voice and moved in for the kill. "We don't know. We hope not. Something went wrong at the lab. We want to find her and quarantine her with as little fuss as possible, if you know what I mean."

Heinrich knew exactly what Gerry meant. He nodded curtly and reached for his phone. "Very well. Just let me check her room once."

He punched in four numbers, listened for a moment, then hung up.

"She might simply have gone out to eat."

"Let's hope so," Gerry said, but didn't mean it. He wanted to find Gina and settle this mess. "If that's the case, I'll wait down here for her return."

Heinrich searched the key rack, selected one, then pointed across the lobby.

"I'll meet you by the elevators."

A few minutes later they were on the fifth floor and Heinrich was knocking on the door to 532. Gerry hovered impatiently behind him, anxious to get in there, yet dreading what he might find.

"Dr. Panzella? Dr. Panzella, this is the manager."

No reply.

Please, God, nothing nasty, Gerry thought as Heinrich fitted the key into the lock. Please.

As soon as he heard the latch click, Gerry pushed past him and barged inside.

"Wait here."

The lights were on. A half-eaten burger and fries swam in spilled cola on a rolling cart by the rumpled, empty bed.

"Gina?"

He stepped into the bathroom. An iron fist slammed into his chest at the sight of the bloody razor blade by the sink. He stepped closer and the red in the tub caught his eye. He groaned. The porcelain was splattered up and down with blood.

Christ, what happened *here?*

He put a hand out and leaned against the wall for support as he dragged his gaze from the tub back to the sink counter. The bloody razor, and bottles of alcohol and peroxide as well, and a needle and thread . . . a bloody needle.

First some fantasy about the president having surgery, now . . . this. Whatever it was.

"Aw, Gina," he whispered. "Gina, Gina, what have you *done?*"

He stepped back into the other room and found Heinrich standing there, looking bewildered.

"Is something wrong? Is she here?"

Gerry brushed past him and checked the closet. Empty. A glance at the bed told him there wasn't room to hide under the box spring.

"She's gone." He propelled Heinrich out into the hall.

"Look. I want this room sealed. No one—*no one*—is to go in there. Not housekeeping, not room service, not you, not anybody. Is that clear?"

"But why?"

"For the moment I'm treating it as a crime scene. So if that room is disturbed in the least, I'll have you up on charges of obstruction of justice and accessory after the fact. Do we understand each other?"

"Yes. Yes, certainly."

Heinrich pulled the DO NOT DISTURB sign from inside the door and hung it on the outside knob. Then he closed the door and rattled it to make sure it was locked.

"I'll leave word that 532 is off-limits until further notice."

"Good."

Yeah, good. Fine. Heinrich knew what he had to do. But what was Gerry's next move? He was worried sick. What had she done to herself in that bathroom? And where was she now?

He had to find her. And soon. If it wasn't already too late.

Something's wrong.

Duncan was baffled and disappointed when Canney returned to the lobby without Gina, but then he noticed his grave expression and agitated manner and knew he hadn't found what he'd expected in Gina's room. Or had he found *more* than he'd expected?

Duncan wished he had a key to that room. What had Canney seen up there? Just one look was all he asked.

"Any questions?" he heard Canney say to the manager. "You've got her description and you've got my card. Anyone sees her, you call me right away. Clear?"

The manager nodded and mumbled something that Duncan missed. It wasn't important. What mattered was that Gina wasn't here. She'd left without checking out. And

Canney didn't expect her back soon, otherwise he'd be hanging around.

He watched Canney's departure, but stayed behind the fern a while longer, giving the agent plenty of time to reach his car. And giving himself time to plan his next move.

Gina was proving damnably unpredictable. He felt his nerves fraying with every passing hour that she remained out of reach. He wondered how much more of this he could take.

When had she rented the room? How long had she been there? And where the hell was she *now?* Back in her apartment?

Duncan sighed. Where else could he look? He'd go back to Adams Morgan and check it out. If she wasn't there, he could see nothing else to do but go home and wait.

If he didn't find her soon, he'd have to change his plans for tomorrow. And he did *not* want to do that.

35
THURSDAY NIGHT

GINA STUCK HER HEAD OUT THE WINDOW OF THE CAB
and glanced nervously up and down Connecticut Avenue.

"Shouldn't it be here by now?"

The cabby leaned against the fender by the open hood of
his vehicle and puffed on a little cigar.

"I call in. He be along any minute. Any minute. You
wait."

She withdrew into the interior. She didn't want to
stand out on the street in plain view. That was why she'd
asked the driver to call her another cab. But maybe she
should have risked hailing one. Dozens of cabs had passed.
She'd be well on her way to Oliver's by now if she'd grabbed
one.

But that call back at the hotel . . . her heart was still
racing from the fright it had given her. She'd knocked over
her Coke and nearly choked on a french fry when the phone
had started ringing.

Maybe it had been an accident—a misdial, someone
calling 533 or 432—and maybe it hadn't. Maybe it had been

Duncan—God, she didn't want to think that. Or maybe it had been Gerry. Maybe she'd never know.

Whatever its origin, the sudden jangle of the phone had completely unnerved her. She'd stared at it in horror for a few pounding heartbeats, thinking someone had found her, someone knew she was there, and then she'd bolted. No precautions, no stealth. She hadn't even waited for an elevator, taking the stairs instead and limping through the lobby for the street.

In retrospect, now, she realized how foolish that had been. But she'd had to get out, right then, not a second later. The hotel that had been her refuge all afternoon suddenly had become a trap.

Fortunately the lobby had been empty. That had been her good luck. Her bad luck had been picking a taxi that would gasp and die a couple of blocks from the hotel.

"He comes now," said her driver.

Gina craned her neck and saw another Diamond cab pull up behind hers. She jumped out, waved her thanks to her driver, and hopped into the newcomer. She gave the driver Oliver's address and was jounced back into her seat as the cab lurched ahead. She winced with the stab of pain from her left leg.

Okay. She was on her way again. No more mishaps. Really, what were the odds of having two cabs in a row break down? Astronomical. She allowed herself to relax and began rehearsing how she'd break the news to Oliver.

As the cab pulled to a stop at Dupont Circle, Gina glanced out the window to her right. A cold tingle spread across her shoulders as a black hood with a familiar three-armed ornament slid into view. She caught her breath and froze, keeping the cab's rear post between herself and the other car.

Just a black Mercedes, she told herself. Thousands of them in the District.

The Mercedes inched ahead, anxious for the green. The

windshield came into view, then the steering wheel and the hands gripping it. A man's hands. And then the driver himself.

Gina gasped and pressed herself back into the seat.

Duncan.

Keep calm, keep calm, he can't see you.

But he was *here,* not half a dozen feet away. Had he been downtown all this while? My God, she could have run into him outside the hotel. That must have been him on the phone. But he hadn't been in the lobby. Maybe he'd been calling all the hotels downtown asking for Gina Panzella's room. But then why was he heading away from the Tremont instead of toward it? This made no sense, no sense at all—

She huddled there, begging the light to turn green. When it finally did, the cab and the Mercedes entered the circle together. But halfway around, Duncan's car turned off onto Connecticut while her cab stayed on until P Street.

Gina slumped in the seat. Safe. But where was he going? Connecticut wouldn't take him home. That was the way to . . .

. . . *my place.*

As the cab turned off P and took Wisconsin uphill toward Bethesda, Gina considered her options. Her original plan had been to call Oliver from her room before heading uptown. But she'd fled before making that call. Maybe that would work to her advantage. Maybe it was better to drop in on him cold. What if he spoke to Duncan between her call and her arrival?

She shuddered. Better—safer—to knock on Oliver's door and wing it from there.

She spotted the Naval Observatory on her right and knew she was getting close.

The cab turned left off Wisconsin and soon she was leaning forward, scanning the street for any sign of a black Mercedes. She couldn't imagine how Duncan could have beaten them here after turning off on Connecticut, but she'd learned the hard way never to take anything for granted where that man was concerned.

No Mercedes in sight. She paid the cabby and hurried up the walk. She rang the bell, dreading to see who'd answer. Her life seemed to have turned into a Hitchcock movie. She'd be only mildly surprised if it turned out to be Duncan.

"Gina?" Oliver said as he opened the door. "What on earth are you doing here?" He pushed open the screen door for her. "Come in, come in."

"I hope I'm not interrupting anything," Gina said, her eyes quickly searching the cluttered living room and what she could see of the dining room beyond. "You don't have company, do you?"

He smiled and shut the door behind her. He wore a V-necked sweater over his usual white shirt, and ankle-high slippers on his feet.

"No. Although I probably should have. I'm too excited about tomorrow to sleep. I'm glad you came."

"You may not be when I'm finished."

His smile faded. "Is something wrong?"

"Yes," she said, pulling the vial from her pocket and pressing it into his hand. "This."

He stared at it. "An implant?"

"Yes. I dug it out of my leg this morning."

Oliver stared at her uncomprehendingly. "What? How . . . ?"

Gina decided to hit him with everything at once. She watched his expression carefully. If for even an instant he looked as if he weren't shocked, or was faking surprise, she'd be running for the door.

"Duncan jammed it into my leg last night while I was out cold. He's been after me all day trying to dissolve it with ultrasound."

A tentative smile flickered across his lips. "This is a joke, right? You and Duncan—"

"It's no joke, Oliver. That thing's filled with TPD."

"TPD?" he said, still smiling. "What's—?" And then the smile faded. "TPD? How could you know about TPD?"

"Triptolinic diethylamide. Duncan keeps a vial of it in his office."

"Impossible. That's a defunct compound."

"I know. Tested and discarded by GEM Pharma, your old company."

"Right. I have the last sample."

"Really? Where?"

"In my basement. I'll show you."

He led her through the dining room to the kitchen, and from there down a flight of steps.

"This is my private little lab," he said as he turned on the overhead fluorescents. "For years I spent every night of the week and every spare moment on weekends here."

Gina looked around the largely unfinished basement at the benches, retorts, ovens, centrifuges, and rows of other equipment she didn't recognize, all dusty with disuse.

"Is this where . . . ?"

"Uh-huh. I developed the implant membrane here. And over there . . . " He flicked on another set of lights. "I call it my rogues' gallery. All the useless or discontinued compounds I worked on during my years with GEM. I kept a sample of each one."

Gina was startled by the array of bottles lining an entire wall. There had to be hundreds there, perhaps even a thousand.

"So many. How would you ever find a particular one?"

"Easy. They're in alphabetical order." He gave her a sheepish look. "I can't help it. That's the way I am."

He stooped and ran a finger along one of the rows. "R . . .

S . . . T . . ." He squinted at a few bottles, grunted a few times, then straightened and turned to Gina. "The, um, TPD . . . it's missing."

"I know," she said. She pointed to the pill bottle he still clutched in his left hand. "Some of it's in there. Duncan has the rest."

He stared down at the bottle, then at her. "You've got to be mistaken. Duncan wouldn't do something like that. What reason would he have?"

"Because I know about the others."

"Others?"

"Let's go upstairs and I'll explain everything."

They sat in the kitchen, Gina sipping a can of Pepsi, the bottle containing the implant sitting between them in the center of the table, and Oliver leaning forward, listening intently, a look of growing horror on his face as Gina explained what she suspected about the deaths and mishaps involving Senators Vincent and Schulz and Congressmen Allard and Lane.

She shivered with a sudden chill. Was it the Pepsi or was she starting a fever? Her strength seemed to be fading.

"Are you okay?" Oliver said.

"My incision might be getting infected."

"What incision?"

Since showing was better than telling, she stood, unzipped her jeans, and turned sideways as she slid them down to her knees.

"Gina!" Oliver said, averting his face at first, then staring as the Ace bandage was revealed.

Gina unwrapped the Ace, then peeled the gauze halfway back to reveal the incision. An angry red had invaded the edges.

Oliver sucked in a breath. "Oh, dear Lord. You did that? To your*self?*"

Gina let him get a good look, then she smoothed the gauze back into place and began rewrapping the Ace.

"How else was I going to get it out, Oliver?"

He said nothing, simply sat and stared at her, wonder in his eyes.

"Do you have any antibiotics in the house?" she said as she pulled her jeans up.

"I've got some amoxicillin."

Not her first choice but it would do for now. "Can I have a few?"

"Of course."

He hurried away and returned a minute later with an amber plastic bottle. Gina washed down four of the 500-milligram capsules with water and pocketed four more for later.

Oliver was staring at the vial with the implant, shaking his head and speaking to himself as much as to Gina.

"I . . . I can't believe Duncan would do such a thing. Well, maybe to the committee members . . . I could see that . . . I mean, after Lisa died he went a little crazy, made all sorts of threats . . . but you . . . he thinks the world of you . . . he'd never . . ."

Poor Oliver, she thought. His heroic image of his older brother is coming undone.

"He knows I'm on to him," Gina said softly. "And he knows I'll be in the way tomorrow."

Oliver's head snapped up. "Tomorrow? Oh, no! You don't think—he *wouldn't!*"

"Yes, he would. That's why he did this to me. To give him a clear shot at the president."

Oliver shot to his feet. "I've got to go see him. I've got to stop him. I can talk to him. He'll listen to me."

"Will he? I wouldn't count on it."

"He'll have to. Now two people know. And soon more will." He grabbed a jacket that had been hanging over the

back of a chair. "He's beaten. But still I've got to see him."
Anger flashed in his eyes. "Using my implants for something
like this! I've a good mind to . . ."

He didn't finish the thought. Instead, he pointed to the
bottle on the table.

"Can I take that with me?"

Gina grabbed it and held it tight in her fist.

"No. Sorry. This is the only proof I've got that I didn't
make all this up. I'm not letting it out of my sight. And you
realize, don't you, that as soon as you confront him he'll
know how you found out and he'll know where I am. And
since I have the only hard proof against him, I think maybe
I'll disappear for a while."

"Good idea. Don't even tell me where you're going, just in
case—" He shook his head to clear it. "Who'd ever believe
I'd be thinking this way about my brother?"

"I know how you feel. Can you call me a cab?"

Another shiver rattled her teeth as Oliver was phoning the
cab company. She was definitely getting a fever. She hoped
whatever was infecting her wasn't penicillin resistant.

"They'll have one here in about ten minutes," Oliver said.
"I'm going to call Duncan."

"No!"

"Just to see if he's home. No sense in going over there if
he's not in."

He dialed, waited, then said, "Duncan. It's me. We need
to talk. No, in person. I'll explain when I get there. See you
in a few minutes."

He hung up and bustled toward the door. "Wish me
luck," he said. "And lock the door as you leave."

Gina shivered again as the front door closed behind
Oliver. It was almost over. Duncan was at his place; Oliver
was on his way there; a cab was on its way here. But where
was she going?

Not another hotel. She couldn't stand the thought of another strange little box with a bed and a TV that passed for a room.

Her folks' place? The old homestead. The thought comforted her. She'd make a quick stop at her apartment for a change of clothes, then head over to Arlington. She'd be safe there. Another chill wracked her. And warm.

Where was that cab? She took a look out the window but the driveway was empty.

She went down the hall and found Oliver's bathroom. On the top shelf of the medicine cabinet she found a thermometer. She rinsed it off, shook it down, and stuck it in her mouth. After a couple of minutes she checked it: 102.4 degrees.

No wonder I'm shivering, she thought. I'm sick.

Well, she had two grams of amoxicillin perking through her bloodstream. It had to kick in soon. She'd left her Tylenol at the hotel, so she took a few of Oliver's.

A car horn honked outside. She hurried back to the living room and peeked out a corner of the front window. Her heart was pounding, from fever as much as fear.

If I've fallen into a B movie, she thought, there'll be a black Mercedes idling out there.

But no. It was a Diamond cab. She hurried outside, thinking that if she were in a real schlock movie, Duncan would be behind the wheel, disguised as the driver. But a black face peered out the driver window as she approached and pushed open the rear door from inside.

"Where we going?"

She gave him her address and they were off. She huddled in the back seat, shivering.

"Would you mind turning up the heat?" she said.

She was so cold her teeth were chattering.

* * *

Duncan sat mute, shaken. Oliver's arrival had taken him completely by surprise. He'd never seen his brother like this. He'd burst in and immediately launched into a blistering verbal attack. Duncan didn't know which shocked him more—Oliver's naked, self-righteous anger, or the fact that Gina had reached Oliver and told him everything.

The words poured out of Oliver in a steady, rapid-fire fusillade. Not just his anger, but the story of Gina slicing open her own leg in that hotel room and removing an implant with drugstore equipment.

Despite his ongoing shock, Duncan had to admire the unwavering determination and pure guts Gina had shown. He doubted he'd have been able to do the same had situations been reversed. But he was glad he hadn't underestimated Gina. He'd half anticipated this. That young woman did not know the meaning of the word quit. And she was as intent as ever on stopping him.

And she just might. His whole world seemed about to crumble around him. Visions of headlines and courtrooms and, Lord, prison swirled around him. Everything was falling apart—

He shook off the visions. He had to settle down and deal with Oliver. The situation was still salvageable—barely. He'd have to move fast. But before he could do anything, he'd have to neutralize Oliver.

"What did she tell you—what *exactly* did she say she removed from her leg?" Duncan said.

"An implant—one of *my* implants—filled with TPD, of all things."

Duncan shot from his seat and adopted a fiercely indignant pose. "And you *believe* this fantastic story?"

But Oliver wasn't backing down. He leaned into Duncan's face.

"She's got the bloody implant in a bottle. She showed me. She's got a fresh incision on her leg. She showed me that too.

She knows about TPD, Duncan. How could she know about TPD if she didn't find it in your office as she says? And on the way over here, I remembered our discussion about my rogues' gallery earlier this year and telling you about TPD. You were very interested, wanted to know all about it. And tonight I couldn't find my sample bottle in the gallery. Where's my TPD, Duncan?"

Damn it. He was caught. No way to deny this. But worse was the look in Oliver's eyes. The almost worshipful regard was gone, replaced by anger and . . . fear.

My brother fears me.

That hurt. But no less than he deserved.

Don't fear me, Oliver. Even if I can't explain the TPD.

TPD. That was the rock-steady anchor of Gina's story. He could ascribe everything else she'd said or done to mental illness of one form or another. But that damn TPD . . . that was real. Oliver knew it better than anyone. And he'd already guessed that on one of his visits to his home, Duncan had crept down to the basement and removed the world's last remaining sample.

"Answer me, Duncan," Oliver said. "Where is it and what have you been doing with it?"

No sense in denying he'd taken it. He slumped his shoulders and sighed. "It's downstairs." He turned and began walking away. "I'll show you."

Duncan's admission worked a dramatic change in Oliver's demeanor. Suddenly he was solicitous.

"You've been working too hard, Duncan," he said as he followed him to the cellar. "I've warned you about that. You need a long rest and . . . and maybe some . . . maybe you could talk to someone."

"You mean psychotherapy?"

"Well, yes." Oliver was obviously uncomfortable telling his brother the doctor that he needed to see another doctor. "I think that might be a good idea. I've been under terrible stress lately. And I never did get over Lisa's death . . . finding her like that."

"I know, Duncan. You've been through a lot."

Duncan turned on the lights. The basement was finished but dusty and musty. The previous owners had set it up as a game room but Duncan rarely set foot down here. He led Oliver to the center of the room, then stopped and looked around, feigning puzzlement.

"Now where did I put that?" He turned in a slow circle, then snapped his fingers. "I know. Wait here."

He hurried for the stairs and bounded back up to the main floor where he shut the basement door and locked it. He heard Oliver rush up the steps, try the knob, then start pounding on the other side.

"Duncan! Duncan, don't do this! This is insane!"

"Just one more thing left to do, Oliver," Duncan said as he wedged one of the heavy kitchen chairs under the doorknob as a precaution. He braced the kitchen table behind that for extra insurance. "Make yourself comfortable down there. I'll let you out later when I'm through."

No windows down there, no phone. Oliver would be neutralized until Duncan had finished what he had to do.

"She's not at my house, if that's what you're thinking. I told her to disappear to someplace safe and I don't even know where. So if you're thinking of finding her and destroying the evidence, forget it. You'll never find her."

"We'll see about that," Duncan said.

A good chance Gina wouldn't go into hiding without stopping at her own place first. Especially if she felt safe.

He checked his coat pocket to make sure he still had his minitransducer with him, then he hurried to the garage.

Yes, as Oliver had guessed, he was certainly interested in retrieving the implant Gina had excised from her leg. That was hard evidence against him. But that wasn't the only implant involved here.

Good thing he'd had the foresight last night to place two in her thigh.

Gina felt as if her apartment were filled with water. Every move was an effort. The very air around her weighed her down. It was an ongoing test of her will to resist crawling into her bed, still unmade from this morning, and pulling the covers over her head.

At least she'd managed to change her sweaty clothes and underwear. A shower would have been wonderful but she couldn't risk the time. She'd take one in Arlington, and give her folks some excuse about having the flu or something to explain her sickly looks.

She was feeling weaker than ever as she finished packing a small gym bag with another change of clothes. But at least the chills had stopped. As a matter of fact, she was beginning to feel warm. Hot even. Maybe the amoxicillin was kicking in. Or maybe the Tylenol was breaking the fever. She was actually a little clammy now.

And then a cool draft wrapped around her feet and she thought she heard a click from the front room.

The front door?

Oh, no. It couldn't be.

Trembling, feeling weaker with each thudding heartbeat, she stepped to her bedroom door and peered into the front room. It looked empty. But it was dark, full of long shadows cast by the light from her bedroom. She'd left it dark so that anyone passing by wouldn't see the lights and know she was home.

Her gaze darted to the mantle where she'd left the bottle with the implant. Still there. She shuffled over and grabbed it. Yes. Same bottle. And there was the implant, safe inside.

Suddenly the glass tingled against her skin. Gina watched in horror as the implant shriveled and dissolved into a puddle of liquid. The membrane was gone, leaving only the TPD and a few floating streaks of dried blood.

She heard a rustle behind her and Duncan was there, stepping out of the shadows, the pager in his hand. Tears streaked his cheeks; his expression was tortured, his voice husky, hovering on the edge of a sob. She turned to run, to scream for help, but she could not. Her mouth was dry, and she was so weak. Without taking her eyes off him, she reached out a shaky hand and found the edge of the couch. Two steps were all she could manage before she slumped onto the cushions.

"I'm sorry, Gina. You've left me no alternative. This is something I must do. Not just for me. For all of us."

Gina opened her mouth but could not speak. Her body was bathed in sweat. She could feel it running down her skin in rivulets. An angry buzz was growing in her head.

Duncan stepped forward and took the bottle from her slick, nerveless fingers.

"I know you'll never forgive me, Gina. But I hope someday you'll understand why I had to do this."

The buzzing grew louder as Gina tried to lift herself from the couch, to reach for Duncan, claw at him, but then the already darkened room went completely black, and the buzz exploded into a deafening roar, and she felt herself falling back . . .

But she never landed.

36
FRIDAY

DUNCAN HAD LOST ALL HEART FOR THIS SCHEME.

Feeling utterly miserable, he drove through Chevy Chase in the predawn grayness and thought about Gina. He'd thought of little else since last night. He wondered how she was. He'd called 911 from the first public phone he found after leaving her and gave the operator Gina's address, saying there was an unconscious woman in the apartment. The EMTs would come and take her away. He hadn't stayed around. The police would be noting any onlookers, wondering which one had made the call. Duncan couldn't afford to be seen.

Placing a second implant in the trocar after he'd pierced Gina's thigh had been a last-second decision. A subliminal voice, more aware of her tenacity and relentless determination than his conscious mind, must have whispered to him, urging him to buy himself some insurance where Gina was concerned. Whatever it was, it had been right on the money. Gina had cut her own leg open and dug out one of the implants.

But only one. Duncan had dissolved both—the one in the bottle and the one still in her thigh. The evidence was gone, and so was a brilliant mind. It would be years before the effects of the TPD wore off. Gina would find it almost impossible to get licensed when she recovered. All her years of training, worthless. All her hopes for a career in medicine, dashed.

Duncan had sobbed like a child all the way home. He'd had to sneak into his own house so he wouldn't have to speak to Oliver. He knew his brother was comfortable down in the basement. It was heated and had its own bathroom; the extra fridge was down there, filled with juices and soft drinks. Every convenience but a phone.

Oliver probably spent a more comfortable night than I did, Duncan thought.

Duncan had lain awake the entire night on the couch, hearing Oliver occasionally shout his name, and watching over and over against the backs of his eyelids the replay of Gina's wounded, terrified expression before she passed out.

For a while he considered dropping all his plans. He could call that Secret Service agent who'd given him his card, Decker was his name, and tell him the surgery was off. Or call Dr. VanDuyne and tell him to tell his patient, the president, to go to hell and find another surgeon to fix his goddamn eyelids.

But after all he'd gone through, he couldn't allow himself such a luxury. Not after what he'd done to Gina. Unconscionable, but he'd done it for a cause. To fail to follow through would mean he'd made her suffer for nothing. And that would be monstrous.

That was why he was driving to the surgicenter at 4:30 A.M., half an hour earlier than planned. Oliver was still locked in the basement at home. As soon as the president left for Camp David, hopefully carrying an implant in his thigh,

Duncan would return and release Oliver. What happened after that would be up to his younger brother.

Possibly he could convince Oliver to keep quiet. He'd return the remaining TPD and swear he'd done nothing to the president. He'd say he'd suffered through a period of aberrant behavior but he was better now, and he was going into therapy. He'd profess to know nothing of Gina's condition, and swear again that he'd gone looking for her last night but had been unable to find her.

Oliver would suspect, but he couldn't know. After all, Gina had removed the implant—Oliver had seen it himself. And if Duncan could convince him that he was on the straight and narrow from now on, that they should put all this behind them, Oliver might go along. Probably. Hopefully.

After all, if the affair were made public, Duncan's opprobrium would attach to Oliver, and to Oliver's implants. His invention would be forever tainted by its misuse with harmful intent. The FDA might even hold up its approval.

Oliver will keep his peace, Duncan told himself. What harms me harms his implants. And he knows the good they can do will far outweigh the harm I've done.

He unlocked the private entrance and walked inside. He went to the keypad to disable the alarm and found it already off. Damn it. Barbara had forgotten again to set it before she left. If she weren't such a good secretary . . .

He'd deal with her next week. Right now he had other concerns. The advance team from the Secret Service would be arriving in about half an hour to secure the building.

Plenty of time to fill an implant with TPD.

He turned on the inside hall lights and outside spots, then went to his office. He froze when he turned on his office lights and saw the books, journals, and papers scattered across the floor. The office was a shambles. Someone had broken in and torn it apart. Why? What could they be looking for?

·The TPD?

He leapt to his desk. He groaned when he saw the splintered drawer. It looked as if someone had taken a hammer to it and smashed it open. He rifled through the contents. The TPD vial was gone. So was the trocar.

No!

His heart tore into overdrive. He hurried back into the hall and stood looking up and down its length.

Somebody had found the TPD and stolen it.

But who? Oliver was locked up and Gina was in an emergency room somewhere. Who else knew about—?

Duncan whirled as he heard a faint noise, like a chair being moved. It had come from down the hall. He saw that the door to the lower level was open.

From downstairs? Who would be down in the records room or—

Oliver's lab!

Moving as quietly as possible, Duncan hurried along the hall and tiptoed down the stairs. At the bottom he saw light flooding out from the open door to Oliver's lab. And noises from within. Oliver must have escaped from the basement. Gina had told him where the TPD was hidden and now he was here disposing of it.

Discarding all caution, Duncan raced forward to the door.

"Oli—!" The word clogged in his throat, shutting off his air. He couldn't breathe.

A pale, disheveled woman in a sweater and sweatpants, with wild-looking dark hair, stood at the counter, the vial of TPD in her hand. She looked up. Her wide, shocked eyes spit dark fire at him.

He found his voice. "Gina!"

As she raised her arm to hurl the vial at him, Duncan lunged for her, catching her arm before she completed the motion. She screamed, scratching his face with her nails and beating at him with her free hand as he tried to pry the vial from her fingers. Lord, she was strong, like an angry tigress, but he fended her off and finally managed to get the vial away from her. And then she attacked him with both hands, screeching incoherently through her clenched teeth. She was a banshee, a female berserker. Was this what the TPD had done to her?

And then she broke away from him and darted toward the door. He caught her arm and swung her around against the counter, then slammed the door closed and leaned his back against it.

He faced her, staring at her as she stared at him, both panting.

"You bastard!" she screamed, as tears started in her eyes. "You rotten filthy son of a bitch! How could you do that to me?"

With that, she folded her arms on the counter, lowered her head onto them, and began to sob.

Duncan was dumbfounded. She seemed sane now. Upset, yes, but completely rational. But the implant . . . the TPD. Could the transducer have failed to dissolve it?

That had to be it. Low power, interference, whatever the reason, the ultrasound had failed.

Good Lord. What did he do now?

One thing was certain: He needed time to think. He turned to the door, found the lock, and twisted it. If nothing else that would slow her up if she tried to—

He cried out as a cold, sharp stab of pain pierced the back of his thigh. He clutched at the spot and turned.

Gina stood directly behind him, facing him, the trocar clutched in her hand like a dagger.

Duncan's blood froze. He snatched the trocar from her.

"No! You didn't! Gina, you *didn't!*"

She nodded slowly, her eyes wild, a slow smile spreading across her face.

Over her shoulder Duncan spotted a tray on the counter

with three implants and a syringe. He touched the back of his leg again and checked his fingers.

Blood.

His sick fear was overcome by a flash of anger. But as he stepped toward Gina she raised her other hand. Her fingers were wrapped around the transducer handle of the tabletop ultrasound Oliver used in his experiments on the membranes.

Duncan slammed himself back against the door.

"No, Gina!" He'd wanted to shout the words but they came out in a hoarse whisper. "Please . . . *don't!*"

"Why not?" she said, still smiling crazily.

The wild look in her eyes terrified him to the very core of his being. She was teetering on the edge. One wrong word, one wrong move, and she'd slip completely out of control.

"Why *not?*" she repeated. "You wanted to do it to me."

"No, Gina. That was the last thing I wanted. I had no choice. I—"

"*Spare* me the lies!" she said, jabbing the transducer at him. "I passed out last night because I was sick and scared and weak. But you thought it was the TPD hitting my system. You tried to fry my brain last night, Duncan. And you came damn close. If my fingertip hadn't happened to brush against that second implant while I was digging out the first, I'd be in the lockup ward at D.C. General right now. As it was, I came to and got out of my apartment just before the ambulance arrived."

"That should be proof that I didn't want to harm you. *I* called that ambulance."

"Right. *After* you gave me an ultrasonic zap."

She moved closer and Duncan edged away to his right. He didn't dare make a grab for the handle. Her thumb was on the power button. A little pressure on that and the implant in his leg would dissolve, after which his mind would quickly follow suit. He had to keep her talking.

"You don't understand," he said, continuing to edge away. "Oliver told me you'd removed both. I only came—"

"Oliver didn't know that! He only saw the one in the bottle—the second one. The first one fell into the tub and broke and washed down the drain."

He kept moving, inches at a time. He would have loved to put the counter between them, but she was following his every move, waving that transducer at him.

"Gina . . ."

"How could you do that to me, Duncan? How could you try to ruin my life like that? You might as well have put a gun to my head. I *trusted* you, Duncan!"

His heart started hammering as he saw the fury begin to mount in her eyes. He looked around for a weapon, a way out, anything, but he was trapped. He'd have to stop backing away and go after her, have to risk grappling with her.

And then he spotted his salvation, not two feet away. He averted his eyes. Couldn't let her see him looking at it. If he could reach it before she blew . . .

"And I trusted *you*, Gina," he said, hoping to buy some time if he could put her on the defensive. "I gave you a job, gave you the keys to my building, and what did you do? You picked the lock on my desk drawer and invaded my privacy."

The anger in her eyes receded, but only a short way.

"How did you find that out?"

He was close now, almost within easy reach. If he could get his hand up . . .

"You left a piece of your lock pick behind." He raised his right hand with the thumb and index finger an eighth of an inch apart. "Just a tiny—"

He darted his hand to the right, grabbed the power cord to the ultrasound unit, and yanked it from the wall, leaving Gina holding an inert piece of metal.

Duncan slumped against the counter. Lord, that had been close.

He held out his hand. "Give it to me, Gina. It's useless now."

"Don't count on it!"

She reared back and threw it at his face. Duncan twisted away and ducked, but not in time to avoid it completely. The transducer handle thudded painfully against his skull. By the time he straightened, shook off the pain, and looked around, Gina had unlocked the door and was pulling it open. She was out and gone before he could grab her.

Ignoring the pain in his leg, Duncan gave chase, limping after her as she headed for the stairs.

Gina gasped for breath as she pounded up the steps. She'd taken the rest of the antibiotic she got from Oliver, but she was still sick, still weak. She wasn't going to outdistance Duncan for long.

She reached the first floor and broke into a run down the hall—

Right into the arms of three men in suits.

"What the hell's going on here?" said the tall, dark one in the middle, as the one to his right, the one she'd bumped into, grabbed her upper arm and held it. His fingers felt like steel. She might as well have been manacled to him.

"Agent Decker!" said Duncan's voice behind her. "Thank God you came early! I found this young woman here when I arrived. Apparently she broke in sometime during the night." He held up the trocar. "She just stabbed me with this."

She twisted around and saw Duncan standing in the doorway to the basement, panting.

"I just did to him what he was going to do to the president today."

"Whoa," said the tall, dark one Duncan had called Agent Decker. "Hang on there, ma'am—"

"She's deranged," Duncan said, moving closer. "She's had a complete break with reality."

"That's not true!" Gina cried. "I work here! I'm a doctor. And he's planning to kill the president today."

That was an overstatement, but she needed to get their attention. And now she had it.

"Yes, she used to work here, Agent Decker," Duncan said quickly. "We've noticed erratic behavior lately and we've been trying to arrange psychiatric help. Unfortunately, she decompensated before we were able to finalize those arrangements."

"What's your name, ma'am?" said Decker.

"Dr. Gina Panzella. I'm a board-eligible internist, and I'm as sane as you are." She launched into an account of the mishaps that had befallen former members of the Guidelines committee who happened to be Duncan's patients, but Duncan interrupted her after a few sentences.

"Agent Decker, do we have to listen to these ravings? Check with the FBI. Just last week she led them on a wild-goose chase with some story of my implanting some poison in Senator Marsden."

"Wait," Gina said. "Don't listen to him. He pulled a reverse on that one."

Duncan shook his head sadly as he stared at her. God, the bastard was a good actor. A regular Jack Nicholson. You'd almost think he truly felt sorry for a former colleague's deteriorating mental condition.

"After a full medical exam on the senator," Duncan said, "including an MR scan, they found nothing and ended up looking like fools. You can check it out."

"Trust me," Decker said. "We will check it out. We check *everything* out."

"Good. The name of the agent in charge of that particular boondoggle was Canney. I'm sure he rues the day he was conned into believing Dr. Panzella."

"Canney?" Decker said. "Yeah. I'll give him a call."

"Come *on!*" Gina said. "You've got to listen to me!"

"We listen to everybody," Decker said. He turned to the man who was holding her. "You and Briggs take her downtown and get her statement. I'm going to get in touch with Mallard and see if we can put this deal off for a while. I don't like the smell of this. Don't like it at all."

"Thank you, *God!*" Gina said as they started leading her toward the rear of the building. "I don't care if you believe me or not, just don't let the president come here today."

Decker looked at her with new interest as he opened the door to the parking lot. "That's not always our decision, ma'am. So, you know Gerry Canney, do you?"

He knew Gerry's first name! "Yes! Since high school. Do you?"

"We've-met. Are you the one who told him about the president's surgery?"

"That's me! You're the one he called?"

Decker didn't answer that. He was staring at the car that had just pulled into the rear lot.

A long night. A bad night. Gerry hadn't had a wink of sleep since 6 A.M. yesterday morning. He was tired, his stomach lining was on fire, and he was generally pissed.

After leaving the Tremont Hotel last night he'd been unable to find a trace of Gina. The only action he'd had was the 911 call to her apartment that turned out to be a false alarm. Nobody home when the ambulance got there, but the door had been wide open.

Something strange and ominous about that call. Something going on that he couldn't quite grasp. Something just out of reach. And it was that tantalizing closeness that had kept him running all night.

He hadn't been able to stop, hadn't been able to drop it. He'd called Mrs. Snedecker and asked if Martha could stay overnight. Martha didn't mind. She liked sleeping over anywhere. Sometimes that worried him. He'd talked to her on the car phone, then kept driving, periodically stopping back at the Bureau building. He'd even spoken to Gina's parents. No, they hadn't heard from her. He hoped they were telling him the truth and he hadn't been patrolling the whole damn northwest all night for nothing.

He'd just made another stop at Gina's apartment. Still empty. And now, for the third time tonight—or this morning, rather, since the sun was threatening to rise—he was checking out Lathram's building.

He pulled into the rear lot and was startled to find three cars there—two of them Federal, according to their plates. As he parked and got out of his car, he saw a very grim-looking Gina being escorted from the building by three guys in suits.

Weak with relief, he leaned back against the car. Thank God!

At least she was alive, though not looking too well. And the three with her—had to be Secret Service. Bob Decker was one of them.

Secret Service . . . the president's surgery. Shit. If she'd been right about that, what else had she been right about?

He slammed the car door behind him. God *damn* it!

Gina's face broke into a smile. "Gerry!"

"Speak of the devil," Decker said, "we were just—"

"You son of a bitch!" Gerry shouted as he strode toward them. "Son of a *bitch!*"

The two other agents with Decker pulled back and their hands started drifting toward their jackets.

"It's okay," Decker said. "I know him. A Fibby."

"Gina," Gerry said, "are you okay?"

She beamed at him. "I am now."

She looked so small and fragile between them. Gerry wanted to take her in his arms and tell her she'd be all right, but now wasn't the time, not in this place, not in this company.

He turned to Decker. "You told me you knew nothing about any surgery on the president, yet here you are at Lathram's surgicenter at five in the morning. You want to explain that, pal?"

Decker shrugged. "The Man says he doesn't want anyone told, no one gets told."

"This could have ended up a disaster, you know."

"You mean if we'd let this young lady run loose in there?"

"No, I mean if she hadn't found her way here."

"Gerry!" Gina said, her eyes wide. "You mean you believe me?"

"I don't know exactly what I believe, but I know there's enough fishy stuff connected with Dr. Lathram that you shouldn't let him come within a couple of miles of the president."

Decker's bantering manner was gone. "He told us this little lady led you and the Bureau on a wild-goose chase last week."

"It was a wild-goose chase, all right, but I'm not so sure anymore who was leading us."

"And the doc inside says she stabbed him."

"With the trocar," Gina said. "The same one he used on me. The one he was going to use on the president."

Gerry winced at the way that sounded. So far out. Who on earth would believe her?

Which worked perfectly to Lathram's advantage.

But what if he'd intended that all along?

"My agents'll take her downtown and get a statement—"

"No, wait!" Gina cried. "We can settle this all now. I know how."

"Come on, miss," said the red-haired agent holding her, and began guiding her toward the car.

Gerry put a hand on his chest. "Give her a minute. Let's hear her out. Maybe if I'd done that a while back, the five of us might be home in bed instead of standing here at this ungodly hour."

She'd been right about the president's surgery. What else had she been right about?

The grateful look Gina gave him more than made up for all these sleepless hours.

"All right," Decker said. "Five minutes, then she's on her way."

Duncan couldn't imagine how things could get much worse, but assumed they probably would.

As he watched the Secret Service agents escort Gina to the parking lot, he discarded all plans of making further use of the TPD. Damage control was the immediate and most pressing concern.

And the first, all-important task was to dispose of the TPD.

Duncan pulled the vial from his pocket and hurried back downstairs to Oliver's lab. He placed it in the utility sink, covered it with a paper towel, and smashed it into tiny fragments. He ran water into the sink for a while, then dumped the remaining glass shards from the strainer into the soggy paper towel. He rinsed the syringe Gina had used, running acetone through the barrel and the needle to destroy any trace of TPD. Then he simply dropped it in the sharps receptacle with all the other used syringes.

He left the water running while he went back upstairs to the men's room and flushed the remnants of the vial, its label, and the paper towel into the Chevy Chase sewer system.

And that was that. TPD? I don't know what she's talking about. Search the place. Be my guest.

The last remaining sample of the compound was nestled in his thigh.

That was a truly horrifying thought. Imagining what would happen to him if it ruptured before he could have it removed broke him out in a sweat. He'd have to be *very* careful for the next few hours. And by this afternoon, when everything settled down, he'd have the implant removed. Any one of his many friends among the surgeons of the area would take care of that on a moment's notice.

He rinsed his hands. As he dried them he stared at himself in the mirror.

It's over, he thought. Maybe you accomplished something by disrupting the Guidelines committee, maybe you didn't. At least Lisa is avenged.

Any regrets?

Only having to act against Gina. And having to pass up a once-in-a-lifetime opportunity to strike against that wampus in the White House.

He sighed. But a man had to know when to quit. And that time was now.

He dried his hands and stepped back into the hall.

"Dr. Lathram." It was Agent Decker's voice.

He turned and saw a small crowd approaching him. Gina, the three Secret Service men, and a fourth man. Canney, the FBI man. What was he doing here?

"Can we go downstairs?" Decker said. "We're trying to clear up a few things here and I wonder if you could help us."

Duncan didn't like the sound of that, and he didn't like the predatory look in Gina's eyes. For an instant he considered calling a lawyer, but decided against it. That would look suspicious and only draw things out.

He could handle these people.

*　*　*

Gina listened as Agent Decker began talking. He was a cool character, seemed almost imperturbable. But his blue eyes never stopped moving. This guy didn't miss a trick.

"Now Dr. Lathram, you stated earlier that Dr. Panzella stabbed you. Are you willing to file assault charges?"

Gina saw a look of relief flicker across Duncan's features.

"No. Absolutely not. She's not herself. I don't want her jailed, I simply want her to receive the proper therapy."

Gina clamped her jaws to keep from shouting. As planned, the red-haired agent—his name was Reilley, she'd learned—had positioned her on the far side of the lab bench. Gerry stood on the near side, partially blocking her from Duncan's view.

Dear Gerry. She'd never been so glad to see anyone in her life as when he'd cruised into the parking lot this morning. He hadn't given up on her, hadn't written her off. He'd been up all night searching for her. She'd wanted to throw her arms around him.

"That's very generous of you," Decker was saying, "but we're concerned about your safety. Dr. Panzella said she left some sort of poison pellet under your skin when she stabbed you."

"Ridiculous," Duncan said. "It's part of her delusional system. She imagines I've been doing that to other people, including herself, so now she thinks she's done it to me. She needs therapy, gentlemen. And the sooner you get her to a facility that can care for her, the better."

So damn glib, Gina thought as she quietly reinserted the plug of the ultrasound's power cord into the wall socket. The "silver-tongued devil" made flesh.

She pressed the ultrasound's power switch to ON. The red light began to glow.

"Ready," she whispered.

Gerry turned and winked at her as he picked up the

transducer handle. He turned back to Duncan and held it up where he could see it.

"If that's true, Dr. Lathram, then I don't suppose you'd mind if I ran this over your leg."

Gina saw Duncan's eyes widen, saw his gaze dart to the glowing power indicator on the machine. He spun and tried to flee, but Briggs was at the door, and Duncan wasn't getting past him.

"Keep that away from me!" he cried. "For God's sake, turn that thing off!"

Decker glanced Gina's way and gave her a little nod of acknowledgment.

Triumph burned through the haze of her fatigue. Yes! Add one more to the believer list.

Decker's features hardened as he turned back to Duncan, but he didn't get a chance to speak. Gerry had taken over.

"Sit down, Dr. Lathram," Gerry said, gesturing carelessly to a chair near the counter with the transducer.

"Please," Duncan said. "Be careful with—"

"Sit *down!*"

Duncan sat.

Gina watched admiringly as Gerry commanded the room.

"Is there an implant filled with something called TPD in your leg?"

"No."

Gerry examined the transducer handle. "Then I guess there'd be no harm in my turning this thing on and—"

"All *right!*" Duncan cried. "Yes! Yes, there is! There's an implant in my leg!" He was visibly trembling now. "Please put that thing away!"

"Just a couple more questions. Did you stick a similar implant in Senator Vincent's leg after you did plastic surgery on him?"

"I don't have to answer that," Duncan said.

"Of course you don't," Gerry said. He half turned to Gina

and pointed to the ON button on the handle. "Is this the one that makes it work?"

"Yes!" Duncan shouted. "Yes, I did!"

He said it! Thank God!

"And how about Lane and Allard and Schulz?"

"Yes, yes, yes!" He was on his feet, backing away, his voice rising toward a scream. "Are you satisfied? *Yes,* goddammit! Now turn that thing off!"

"I've heard enough," Decker said.

"So have I," said Gerry. He placed the handle in its cradle on the ultrasound machine.

It's over, Gina thought, sagging against the counter. Over at last.

Decker turned to the agent next to Gina and pointed to Duncan. "Reilley, why don't you keep Dr. Lathram company. Everybody else stay right where they are for the moment. I'm going upstairs to make some calls."

Gerry stretched his hand across the counter to her. Weak with relief, she clutched it.

"How's it going?" he said.

"Much better, now that you're here."

He stared into her eyes. "Tell me . . . back at the Tremont . . . the blood in the bathroom . . . did you . . . ?"

She nodded and he squeezed his eyes shut for a moment. When he opened them he was looking away.

"You are incredible. And I'm sorry I doubted you."

Those words were music. She took his hand in both of hers. "We were both being manipulated by a master. The important thing is you cared enough not to give up on me. That means the whole world to me."

Gerry glanced over his shoulder at Duncan. "He doesn't look like a guy who's going down for two counts of second-degree murder and a host of federal crimes."

Gina saw what he meant. Duncan looked cool and calm in his chair now that the ultrasound transducer had been put away. She began to move around the counter to get closer to him.

"Where're you going?" Gerry said.

"I want a few words with my former boss." *My former idol.* She had to be careful here. She had something to say but she didn't want her feelings to get in the way. Just looking at him now made her want to burst into tears.

"Do you realize what you've become, Duncan?"

He gazed up at her blandly. "I have a feeling you're going to tell me."

"Ever since I came to Washington you've been talking to me about ethics and honesty and probity and how nobody in the government adheres to any moral and ethical standards. And you weren't far off the mark, unfortunately. But I always assumed you were speaking from higher ground. You weren't. During all that talk you were desecrating your oath as a physician. I know those men hurt you, and they may well have been the crooks, cheats, venal, low-rent, bloodsucking leeches on the public trust you said they were, but that doesn't matter. They came to you as a doctor and you accepted them as patients. They were counting on you being better than they were. That's a sacred trust—*primum non nocere*—and you defiled it."

She noticed Decker slipping back into the room, but he didn't interrupt her. Good. She wasn't finished yet.

"I know what you used to be, Duncan—*who* you used to be—and I admired that person like no one else in the world. But you became exactly like the people you detest so much: the end justifies the means, anything goes. Look what you tried to do to me." She realized how angry she was becoming. She had to shut up before she exploded. "You *became* the enemy, Duncan. And you're going to pay for it."

"Maybe," he said softly. "And maybe not."

"Don't kid yourself," she said, feeling her fury escalating. "You just confessed in front of a roomful of people."

He smiled at her. "Whatever statements I made were coerced from me, elicited under threats of damage." He looked around at the four government agents. "Ask any of these gentlemen if they think one word of what I said here will ever be admissible in court."

Gina looked around. No one had to say anything. Gerry's eyes spoke volumes.

Something snapped inside her. "You mean he's going *free?*"

Gerry started to say something but Gina didn't hear it. All the pain, all the anguish, the terror, the self-doubt, the betrayal, and Duncan was going to *walk!*

She turned, grabbed the ultrasound handle, thumbed the power button, and slammed it against Duncan's leg.

"Walk away from *that!*"

Duncan screamed "NO!" and clutched at his thigh. "Oh, God, *NO!*"

The lab was suddenly bedlam, Reilley pushed her away from Duncan, Gerry pulled the handle from her hand, while Decker was saying, "Jesus H. Christ! Gerry, get her the hell out of here!"

Gerry grasped both her upper arms from behind and gently but firmly propelled her toward the door, guiding her past Duncan, who was now bent double as he clawed at his thigh, whimpering and moaning, "Oh-no-oh-no-oh-no, please, God, no-oh-no-oh-no!"

And then they were in the narrow passageway outside the lab. Gerry shut the door behind them and turned her around to face him.

"My God, Gina! I can't believe you did that."

"I want him to be as frightened as I was. I want him to know what it feels like to be utterly terrified."

"I can appreciate that. Look, I know what he tried to do to you, but after all you just said, I never thought . . ." He ran out of words and stared at her. "Why are you smiling?"

She truly loved this man's sense of decency.

"I guess I forgot to mention that Duncan's implant was empty."

"Empty?"

She nodded. "Right. He burst in on me before I had a chance to fill it, so I stuck him with an empty one."

She watched Gerry's expression slacken, then saw his lips turn up at the corners. A second later he was shaking his head and grinning.

"I love it. Give him a taste of his own medicine—or let him think that's what he's getting." He slipped his arms around her and pulled her close. "I was so worried about you. Why didn't you call?"

"I didn't think you'd believe me." Suddenly she felt weak and shaky. "Can we sit down?"

He guided her to one of the chairs in the lounge area and pulled another up close beside her. He slipped a protective arm over her shoulders.

"That will never happen again, Gina. I'll always believe you. I swear."

"Good. Hopefully I'll never again be in a situation like this."

"That makes two of us. Three of us, counting Martha. She's missed you." He leaned closer. "I think this morning will square me with the Bureau. Which means I'll probably be moving up. I'm thinking of moving Martha away from the District. How about you? Still itching to work on the Hill?"

Gina shook her head. "I've had it with this place. I think I'm going to look for a practice in a nice little town where only things are for sale, not people."

"Great." His eyes held hers. "Maybe you could pick one with an FBI office nearby. How's that sound?"

"That sounds nice," she said softly.

The lab door opened behind them. Briggs stepped out and

walked past, heading for the stairs. He gave Gina a wary look. As the door swung closed again, Gina heard Duncan's voice.

"You've got to get me to a hospital! *Now!* Not later! This is an emergency!"

And then the door clicked shut.

"How long before we tell him?" Gerry said.

"Tell him?" Gina said. "I'm not going to tell him. He'll figure it out sooner or later. Let the bastard stew till then."

Gerry laughed. "Remind me never to get on the wrong side of you."

She grabbed his tie and pulled him closer. "Believe that, buster. Don't ever forget it."

They kissed.